THE ADVENTURES OF GRACE PENDERGAST, GALACTIC REPORTER

ALSO BY ALYCE CASWELL

Standalone Titles

Love and Lockdown

The Eyes of Charon

The Galactic Pantheon Series

The Tortured Wind

The Twisted Vine

*The Flickering Flame**

*The Shifting Ice**

*The Whispering Grass**

*The Creeping Moss**

*The Galactic Pantheon Novellas***

*The Adventures of Grace Pendergast, Galactic Reporter***

*novella
**collection

THE ADVENTURES OF GRACE PENDERGAST, GALACTIC REPORTER

Alyce Caswell

ISBN: 978 0 6485444 4 9 (EPUB)

ISBN: 978 0 6485444 5 6 (Print)

Cover design by Hampton Lamoureux, TS95 Studios © 2021

THE EXONERATION OF GERNS, BOTANIST

1

THE DISAPPEARANCE OF RUDBECKIA, PRINCESS

25

THE CLONING OF DIANA NUMENI, PRESIDENT

87

THE TRANSGRESSIONS OF EMAN PROST, CEO

149

THE AWAKENING OF IGNEAS, SUB-LEVEL GOD

213

The Contracting of Brez and Alex, Warlords

241

The Education of Selben, Teenager

283

The Family of Finara, Fire Goddess

309

The Discovery of Dom Zhang, Graphic Artist

323

The Framing of Sean Akiyama, Husband

361

Sean Akiyama's Greatest Adventure

407

THE
EXONERATION OF
GERNS, BOTANIST

CHAPTER ONE

Grace Pendergast, first e-paper reporter of the 66th century, was destined to revitalise an ancient profession that dated back to Old Earth. Among a sea of shouting, brightly adorned mediaists, she would be an island of calm, an authoritative voice that had to be believed, despite the fact that she never included a single image in her reports.

But this achievement was still ahead of her, in a future where she wasn't fresh from meeting a member of the Galactic Pantheon and burying what could have been the greatest scoop in the history of species-kind.

Right now, barely a month into her first serious relationship, she was sitting in a bar, idly sliding her finger along the rim of her glass. The run-down settlement she'd hitched a ride to wasn't all that unique — in fact, it resembled every other dive she'd fallen into during her former career. As had happened with many inconsequential settlements, the Galactic Law Enforcement Agency had withdrawn a permanent presence from the moon years ago. And it showed.

Tourists and traders rarely visited a place where they weren't protected by GLEA's agents and their tech-sourced powers. So the streets here remained unpaved and the Web signal was sluggish and barely serviceable. At least there wasn't any paint to be peeling — all the buildings in the settlement were made out of the barest steel, both inside and out.

Saren, the unfortunate name for this unfortunate moon, had almost been entirely overrun by a virus that had left only a small patch of land habitable. Grace, sitting amidst colonists who favoured battered and padded tunics, stood out in her sharply pressed pantsuit. The silver prosthesis that began where her right leg ended was for the most part concealed, but she had seen a few eyes travel to where a pale brown ankle should have been.

I really hope this isn't a waste of time, Grace brooded.

A sultry voice entered her mind. *You know what's not a waste of time? Visiting your girlfriend. Not that said girlfriend is angling for your company or anything...*

Grace closed her eyes, trying to stifle her outward reaction. Apart from her fingers gripping the metallic slab that formed the bar's counter, she thought she didn't do too badly. Then she remembered her eyelids and growled softly as she peeled them apart. Another oversight.

'You alright?' the bartender asked in a low voice, leaning over as if to encourage a private confidence. The cleaning cloth in her hand was noticeably slack on the counter.

'I can't even have a drink without some god intruding on my thoughts,' Grace muttered.

Hey now, you said I could. Finara's pout, though Grace couldn't see it, was vivid in her mind.

Grace fought the desire to reply. And lost. *We discussed an appropriate level of intrusion, Ms Fire Goddess. Should we have that discussion again?*

If one of us gets to be tied up for it.

Grace could not bring herself to be annoyed. She clenched her thighs together, smiling at the memories Finara's words had evoked, then realised that the bartender was staring at her. Self-conscious, Grace smoothed her hands over her pants and winced when she saw that there was a splotch of dirt caked onto the fabric.

'Which one?' the bartender asked.

'What?' It was Grace's turn to stare.

'There's gotta be a hundred of them starking gods floating about the galaxy,' her companion said, waving a hand towards the grimy ceiling. 'The Creator God made up a whole pantheon of sub-level gods to look after us, didn't he? So lay it on me. I might be able to help you out. I *am* a bartender, you know.'

Grace shook her head, causing her brown coils of hair to bounce. 'This is beyond even your capabilities. And the gods aren't even the real issue here.'

'Alright, let's go with the real issue then.' The bartender's eyes sparkled. 'It has to be a lot more manageable than dealing with a sub-level god in your head.'

'Manageable!' Grace laughed harshly.

'No need to snap. It's not my fault if your life's a mess.'

'I'm not sure you deserve an apology,' Grace said, then knocked back her drink in one smooth motion. She licked her bottom lip. 'Here goes. My career: dead in the atmosphere. Flushed out the airlock. Now, it might not matter to my girlfriend — she's got the family business, after all — but it does to me. I need something of my own. Something to define my life. Something that isn't a relationship.'

'Ah, stark,' the bartender sighed. 'Should have figured that someone as gorgeous as you would be attached to someone.'

Grace lifted her eyebrows. The compliment hadn't made her uneasy — she was getting better at accepting them ever since Finara had come into her life and found every micrometre of her to be beautiful, always taking time to whisper those full lips along the half-moon scar that ran through Grace's left eyebrow.

But this wasn't the moment that Grace would have chosen to hear it.

'Sorry,' the bartender said, not sounding very sorry at all. At least she was Grace's type, unlike the men who frequently tried to sweet-talk her. 'So how are you going to define your life?'

'I was a mediaist once,' Grace said, waiting for that wistful note in her voice and for once not hearing it. She realised she was relieved that it was behind her, that no more deaths could be laid at her feet. Over a year ago, one of her Webcasts had revealed a rebel faction's secret base, which had then led to their enemy bombing the area, killing hundreds and maiming Grace. Most people would have given up after that — and she had, for a while. But there were still so many wrongs to right, so many victims crying out for justice because the authorities couldn't or wouldn't do anything.

Grace swallowed. There was still one victim she had never found justice for.

'Now I want to write instead,' she told her audience, refusing to let the lingering darkness in her memories swallow her. 'I need to continue to expose the truth, but now I'll do it with words. No images. No footage. Nothing that could endanger anyone.'

'That sounds boring,' the bartender noted. 'And to be honest, no one *reads* anymore.'

'I do,' Grace said testily.

The other woman's smile seemed more performed than it was genuine. 'Alright. But you'll need a big scoop.'

'I had one.'

'Did you.'

'I couldn't release that report because people would have died,' Grace explained in as even a tone as she could muster. She couldn't very well say that the god of water had become incensed that Finara, his sister, was speaking to a mediaist and revealing the Galactic Pantheon's secrets. He had only ceased attacking mortals after Grace had buried the story.

Grace sighed and gestured at the dusty brown bottles lined up on the wall behind the bartender. 'Stop judging me and get me another drink.'

'Not going to change your situation, is it.'

'It might help me to forget.'

'A moment's oblivion is all I can promise,' the bartender warned Grace. 'The brew's watered down.'

'Just keep pouring until I tell you to stop.'

CHAPTER TWO

Shrill alarms punched through the flimsy walls, filling the room with noise and chaos.

Grace sat up immediately and cried out when her head collided with the bunk above her. Cursing, but glad that she hadn't changed her clothes to sleep, she hurried out of the empty shared accommodation behind the bar (it seemed no one else had paid for the privilege or come to the moon seeking a bed in the first place) and onto what passed for a street. Soft solar-powered lamps clung to nearby buildings, revealing a squirming, panicked throng of arms, legs and tentacles.

'What's going on?' Grace demanded of the crowd.

The nearest human raised his trembling finger. 'The orbital sensor net. It's seen something.'

Vivid red splotches darted their way across the darkened sky. Grace winced, knowing that Saren could not afford to replace the sensor net. Not that it had been much use; all it had done was let them know that danger was coming.

A pregnant pause filled the air as the lightshow dimmed. Grace held her breath — and then the pirate ship burst through the veil of clouds, its multiple lascannons glowing with murderous intent. Wicked spikes, also alight to ensure that no one below missed them, dotted the vessel from prow to stern, making it look like some sort of reptilian predator.

Grace had to give the Sarenite settlers some credit. They didn't run or scream.

But they did fall to their knees and start begging their sub-level god to come save them.

'I thought there was a Chipper starship stationed nearby!' Grace snapped at no one in particular, using the slang term for a member of the Galactic Law Enforcement Agency. But she knew that to the understaffed GLEA, 'nearby' could mean behind a neighbouring moon or even two whole systems away.

Fear didn't make its presence known. Only anger burned through Grace's veins.

She hadn't survived the darkest moments of her life to have it end like *this*, at the hands of pirates who wouldn't even know the name to give her smouldering corpse.

Finara, she remembered. *Finara can save me. All I have to do is ask.*

It was tempting. Too tempting.

Perturbed, Grace forced herself to look around at the other beings, at those who couldn't ask their immortal girlfriends to spirit them away to safety. She couldn't leave them.

Finara! she called inside her mind, well aware that the goddess had left a fragment of her invisible presence behind. *I need your help. There's a pirate ship coming in hot and I can't...I can't go through this again! I can't watch everyone die!*

Grace, relax. My bro is handling it.

Whatever Grace had been expecting to hear, it certainly wasn't *that*.

She prepared a furious retort, but never got to unleash it. Instead of ploughing towards the town and strafing it, the ship swiftly levelled out and its lascannons drooped. Even the manic lighting that had heralded its presence died. Somewhere out there a vessel of violence remained, lost in the darkness. If not for the roar of its engines, still uncomfortably close, Grace would have thought that it had disappeared entirely.

'Thanks to Bagara! Thanks to Bagara!' chanted the writhing mass of flesh on the ground. The settlers were praising the rainforest god; they did not know that he wore the less glorious name of 'Kuja', or that his given title in the Galactic Pantheon was 'the Rforine'.

Grace crossed her arms and sighed in disgust.

Were all gods this obsessed with adulation? Finara's attitude was slowly improving, but she had many brothers and sisters.

Kuja's not like that, Finara defended. *It's just a side effect of his insistence on being known as the god of lost causes and casualties. You can see for yourself. He wants to meet you.*

Grace took an involuntary step backwards and hit the exterior wall of the bar. Her eyes darted around, looking for anything from an out-of-place flower to a man with bark for skin.

A gentle laugh brushed her mind. *I'll tell him not to hang around. Totally unrelated, but what would you do with a big honking starship that now belongs to no one?*

'What...' Grace cleared her throat and forced herself to use her thoughts instead. *What did your brother do with the crew?*

Oh, they're fine, Finara assured her. *The Chippers took them into one of their prisons. They're always happy to leave the catching of criminals to us if they can. Saves money.*

'Celebrate with us! Rejoice!' the man who'd pointed at the sky earlier said, clapping a hand to Grace's shoulder. 'Bagara has come to our aid once again! He always will!'

Grace pinched his hand with two fingers and removed it

from her person. 'I will keep my admiration to those I know personally, thank you.'

She expected the man to get angry. But he simply shrugged. 'Suit yourself. Bagara doesn't care who you worship. So I won't either.'

'How magnanimous of you,' Grace said dryly. It then occurred to her that she should make use of this opportunity. 'I've heard that Bagara speaks directly to some of his followers. Has he ever said anything to you?'

The man shook his head. 'No. I've never asked him to. He looks after us so well already. But it's nice to know he'll listen if I do need him.'

'Do you know anyone who *has* heard from him?' Grace asked.

'Of course!' As if it was obvious. 'Gerns! Everyone knows he talks to Gerns.'

'Gerns?' Grace repeated, as though she had never heard that name before, as though she hadn't spent the past day on Saren trying to find hide or hair of this particular being.

The settlers in the bar had not been interested in speaking to a stranger when they could instead get drunk in the reliable company of their friends.

Clearly, Grace should have considered the more sober locals.

'Yeah, Gerns, she's a botanist who works for Yalsa Industries,' the man said, nodding.

'Do you think I could speak to this Gerns?'

His finger sought a boulder embedded in the tree line. 'Her place is a klick behind there.'

Ah, finally, Grace thought. *Finally what I came here for.*

What are you up to, Ms Gorgeous Mortal? Finara demanded. *And why the stark did I show you how to hide your surface thoughts?*

Grace merely smiled.

CHAPTER THREE

'I didn't see you in town last night,' Grace said, picking her way through the dim laboratory, trying not to bump into any of the long tables laden with trays full of plants and soil. 'Are you that confident in your god? Or did you sleep through the excitement?'

No answer. Grace halted her steps and let her gaze rove around the building once more. The walls looked as though they had been grown instead of built, trees twisting this way and that until they enclosed the space entirely, even forming a roof. It unsettled her. But not enough to make her assume it was the work of a god and not an intelligent mortal.

Grace crossed her arms and waited. Silence was a good tool.

Someone was always tempted to fill it.

'Now, I said to myself,' a disembodied voice began, soft but full of danger, '"Gerns, no one's gonna come up here and intrude on your personal space, they're not that stupid". Now me, I didn't want to deal with people for another few months, when I have to resupply, but here you are. Intruding.'

Grace's lips curved, but she quickly tempered the smile. 'I *am* intruding. I do apologise, Gerns, but my curiosity outweighs any politeness right now.'

A wet sound, possibly a cluck. Gerns was a Jezlo; for her, it was a sign of amusement. 'I can't give you an introduction to Bagara, if that's what you want.' There was a long pause. 'Now me, I'm not *supposed* to know what he looks like...but he's not as smart as he thinks he is. I've seen him. And somehow you've got me talking and talking when you could be a criminal. An assassin. Or worse — a mediaist.'

'I understand you don't give interviews on screen,' Grace said, now keeping her eyes straight ahead, avoiding the urge to scrutinise the shadows in the corners of the vast room. 'As you can see, I don't have a vidcam.'

'No cam, sure, I can see that, but you speak like a mediaist. Get gone before I feed you to my flesh-craving jundabee flower!'

Grace rapped one of her heels on the floor in frustration. Since there was dirt beneath her instead of concrete, the sound that followed was hardly satisfying. 'A lot of mediaists like the sound of their own voices. They don't listen. They'll edit footage together, make it look like you agree with them, and then throw you to the wyverns for as little as a coin-chip.'

Grace was painfully aware that she hadn't won yet. 'I know what it's like for the galaxy to see you in an unsavoury light.'

'What's this got to do with me?'

'Bagara's Puppet, that's what they called you,' Grace charged on, then belatedly softened her tone. 'Because when a god asked for your help, you gave it. All of those mediaists discarded your scientific experience and ignored your astounding achievement in saving Saren's crops from a terrible virus, a virus you have since eradicated completely on other worlds.

'They assumed you were just a mouthpiece. But I think we both know better.'

Grace didn't bother holding her breath while she waited for a response. She made sure her trembling hands were in front of her instead of shoved into her pockets. Her anxiety and hope were genuine. She wanted the Jezlo to see that.

'You seem to be in love with your *own* voice, mediaist,' Gerns said finally.

'Perhaps I am,' Grace conceded. 'But if I can use my voice to give you one, then I don't care.'

Gerns surprised her then by stepping into the light, her tentacles held loosely beside her, one of the least threatening stances a Jezlo possessed. 'Now, are you a tea or a coffein woman?'

'I'm a whisky woman, actually.'

'I think I've got something to your taste.'

***

One of the easiest ways to describe a Jezlo was this: 'a gelatinous mass with six wobbling tentacles'. But that would reveal nothing about how cheerful and laid-back they were as a species. They were a delight to speak to, once they got going. Even though Gerns had been burned by her past interactions with mediaists, she was in danger of talking the entire day away.

But then Gerns set down her carbon-fibre tumbler and fixed her tiny black eyes on Grace. 'Now me, I'm not stupid enough to think you came all this way to Saren just to tell my sob story in...*text form*, of all things.'

Grace leaned back in her chair and rested one leg over the other, pleased. She had forgotten how much she preferred sources who didn't blindly give up everything. She relished the challenge. 'I'll have to tell you my own sob story to explain it.'

'Will I need another drink for this?' Gerns asked.

'I'm not sure about you, but I'll need a fresh one.'

When they were once again slaking their thirst, Grace told her companion everything — well, almost everything. She didn't mention that a goddess had saved her and made her want to live again, or that she was dating the aforementioned goddess. How could she ever discuss such a thing with anyone? No, it was already difficult enough to recount the deaths of those who had trusted her. As for the much older blood on her hands...not even Finara knew about that.

'So I decided I wanted to tell the truth and reach the galaxy in a way that can't hurt people,' Grace declared and upended her tumbler, finishing her drink in one long draw.

'You're dangerously naive if you think no one'll get hurt,' Gerns said, weaving a tentacle in front of Grace like a warning. 'There's always a casualty. Someone's reputation. Someone's safety. A source who speaks will have to go on the run.'

'I won't name them if that's the case.'

'No named sources? You're doomed to the life of a novelist, Ms Pendergast.'

'I don't see it as a problem, if no one believes what I write,' Grace fired back with a cocky grin. 'I imagine most people will think as you do and tell me anything I want them to.'

Gerns watched her for a moment, then shook so violently with amused clucks that her tumbler hit the ground and rolled away. After retrieving it with a tentacle, she told Grace, 'You just might have a chance, you just might. Look now, I shouldn't say this, but I've got a hacker friend who can make the right story go viral.'

'The right story,' Grace repeated.

'We both know that a botanist trying to snatch back credit for saving a town isn't all that interesting.'

Grace pursed her lips. 'But one day, if I break a big story and have other articles in my archive for people to read...'

'...then they'll be less likely to label you a one-cast wonder,' Gerns remarked. Her tentacles quivered with curiosity. 'Do you have a name for what you're planning on doing?'

'On Old Earth, reporters published their stories in text form, usually printed on flimsy pieces of paper,' Grace explained, holding up her techpad and hoping that the gesture indicated she'd done a bit of research on the Web. 'When they were transitioning from print to digital, they made a distinction between *books* and *ebooks*. So I'm thinking "e-paper". Something new.'

'Like a buzzword, I see,' Gerns said, nodding her large head.

'Exactly like,' Grace confirmed.

They drank some more. An easy silence united them now, one that had no purpose behind it and did not need to be filled by either party. After a while, Gerns said, 'Now me, I said to myself, "Gerns, this human's asking too many questions about the god stuff. Weird questions." So tell me, Ms Pendergast, what's your interest in the gods?'

'It's only a hobby, nothing I'd ever write about,' Grace said, holding her tumbler out for another refill. Her whole body was infused with heat, but she was too used to operating under the influence of alcohol to let it impinge on her discretion. Still, she found she trusted Gerns, because the Jezlo had inferred several times in their conversation that she had met the human form of the rainforest god — and she still refused to name Kuja or describe him.

'What I've seen...' Grace allowed herself two small sips of whisky. 'I've seen beyond the veil of mortal ignorance. It's a lure to me. It's information no one else has. And I want more.'

'Get too close to the flames and you'll get burned,' Gerns warned her.

'The flames and I have an understanding,' Grace said, lifting one sly eyebrow.

Gerns crossed her tentacles across her torso and moved her head from side to side. 'Arrogant. You'll get yourself smote. Not all the gods are friendly.'

Grace frowned, overcome with a sudden sense of premonition that she couldn't explain, even to herself. 'Someone...someone might need to hear what I've learned one day.'

'I think I gave you too much drink.'

'Got any more?' Grace asked, grasping at the distraction.

'Now me, I surely do, but who says I'm sharin'?'

'We could toast to the future success of my e-paper.'

Gerns clucked repeatedly. 'Any excuse, mediaist. Any excuse.'

CHAPTER FOUR

I wonder what happened to that starship in the end, Grace mused. She was sprawled facedown on the bed and completely at the mercy of the goddess who was kneading her naked flesh.

A finger skipped down her spine. 'How can you possibly still be thinking about that? I clearly haven't been distracting you enough.'

Grace stretched luxuriously and turned to look up at the woman who had saved her in more ways than one. 'The Firine' was Finara's official title among the countless siblings who formed the Galactic Pantheon, but the mortals in Finara's domain had yet to give her a name, something that grated on the goddess.

'Sex is like meditation,' Grace replied, smothering a yawn. 'It clears your thoughts. So obviously my head needs to be filled up again.'

'I think I need to fill it with something else,' Finara said, leaning in to kiss her.

But what about the pirates' starship? Grace asked mentally, then laughed when Finara groaned and pulled away from her.

'You won't let this go, will you?' the Firine demanded, hands on her hips.

'Your girlfriend *is* a mediaist, Finara. We're not known for letting things go.'

'I thought you were an e-paper reporter now.'

'I'm the only e-paper reporter in the galaxy. I can define what we're like, can't I?'

'Stark you, that grin of yours is far too sexy,' Finara muttered and kissed her again, this time deeper, slower, more tender. Unable to resist, Grace gave in to her magical touch once more.

Several minutes later, when they were facing each other and hidden beneath the streaky shadows of the hotel room that Finara had booked for the next two nights, a distracting warmth began to fill Grace's chest. She bit down hard on the inside of her cheek, trying to ignore the sensation. She failed.

'So about that starship,' she said abruptly.

'Kuja was thinking of giving it to the Chippers,' Finara replied, her lips curling in disdain. She tolerated GLEA and shared with them the burden of looking after the galaxy's mortals, but she wasn't particularly fond of the Agency. 'I think they already get enough money and other things donated to them.'

'They don't have enough agents to protect everyone,' Grace said, trailing her fingers through Finara's hair. The midnight-black locks did not match the fine brunette eyebrows that were arched over the goddess' flame-filled eyes. 'The settlers on Saren had an early warning system, could probably get another one if they saved up long enough, but it's not going to help them if the Chippers are too far away. And your brother surely has enough people to run around after...'

'Kuja's wife would appreciate him stretching himself a bit less,' Finara agreed with a nod. 'A good idea. I like it. I'll tell Kuja to hand the ship over to the settlers so they can protect themselves. I'll even get him to send someone to teach them how to operate it.'

'You should let me finish saying my thoughts out loud,' Grace remonstrated her, but she was unable to curtail the smile.

'There are other things in your mind I could mention.'

Grace shivered. 'Please don't. I'm not...I don't even know if those feelings are real, or if I feel them because of what you did for me, or because I'm fascinated by your family...'

'I can wait until you figure it out,' Finara said, her lips whispering over Grace's collarbone. 'In the meantime, never doubt that I love you.'

'But what if I never figure it out?' Grace asked, embarrassed by the obvious hitch in her voice.

'I don't really care, Grace. So long as you're happy.'

'I am. I am happy.'

'Then that's all that matters.'

Later, sitting in the chair by the desk, Grace could hardly believe that the gorgeous fire goddess was dozing on the bed, exposed and vulnerable in her human form. That a deity would do such a thing in front of a mortal — in front of *her* — was undeniably thrilling.

Grace turned back to her techpad. Her story on Gerns had only been viewed three times in the past day. But she couldn't bring herself to feel bothered by this. There was something oddly relaxing about having a lover, someone who was there for you without question or pause. It made everything else seem insignificant and much more bearable.

For now, Grace would keep using the coin-chips Finara gave her to travel the galaxy. Hopefully soon she would be able to support herself instead.

And then...then she would know if she truly needed the goddess in her life.

Grace feared that day.

But there was no use worrying about it when she had work to do.

THE DISAPPEARANCE OF RUDBECKIA, PRINCESS

CHAPTER ONE

When a wealthy planet finds itself in trouble, it attracts mediaists like space wyverns to a corpse freshly ejected into vacuum. If the drama includes a teen princess who has gone missing hours before her wedding to the prince of a nearby world, one with which her parents had warred for decades...you're going to have to wade through a lot of junk just to get anything close to a fact.

Not that this deterred any mediaist. They were good at shouting their own facts into their vidcams. Discerning viewers knew better than to *fully* believe them — well, that was the excuse they used whenever someone uncovered a lie in their reports. A Webcast was a show, a good time, and it was never up for serious debate. Everyone knew that, of course they did.

'Clusterfuck,' the man beside Grace said, jerking his head at the ornate stage where a spokesperson had yet to appear. The spherical vidcam hovering beside him burred impatiently. 'Giant clusterfuck.'

'Pendergast,' Grace returned. 'Grace Pendergast.'

In front of them writhed a pit filled with thousands of maniacally grinning beings, all of them addressing their vidcams, all of them here alone, all of them avoiding any contact with the person beside them.

But this man looked right at her when he made his own introduction. 'Sean Akiyama.'

He then tilted his head down so that his eyes, a darker brown than hers, bore more deeply into her. Grace almost laughed. Her companion was attempting to be charming and seemed to think he had the good looks to pull it off. Clearly his scruffy charcoal hair and casual attire of jeans and a loose shirt didn't dampen his style — that or he didn't let them. His most interesting feature, however, was the scarring on his temple which indicated that he'd worn one of GLEA's chips at some point. There were many reasons why someone chose to leave the Galactic Law Enforcement Agency. No doubt he had been asked about it many times.

Grace lifted both eyebrows and kept them high on her forehead for several seconds, letting her silence speak for her.

'Guess I'm not everyone's spaceport of choice,' Sean Akiyama said with a dramatic sigh. His broad grin morphed into a more genuine smile. 'So what d'you think? Princess Rudbeckia didn't want to marry the guy? Because he's not her true love? Kind of weird, though. I mean, royals on Utalia are only allowed to marry one person, but they can bang like a hundred others, no questions asked. She could have always kept that true love stashed somewhere.'

Grace considered interrupting him but found she didn't want to. It had been a while since anyone who wasn't a source or a goddess had spoken to her.

'*Unless...*' Sean's tone grew thoughtful. 'Unless her true love isn't happy about being relegated to second best — not that there's anything wrong with being someone's side piece, you just can't get ideas above your station. Sooo, if you manage to convince the princess to run away with you...there are ways to do that. And I should know. I'm all about the clandestine shadowy stuff.'

'Clandestine shadowy stuff,' Grace repeated.

'There's a slimy underworld on every planet. You just have to look for the people no one's paying attention to. It's a good place to start, if you want to disappear yourself.'

Once his animated gestures had ceased, Grace said, 'I think you're getting ahead of yourself, Mr Akiyama. Princess Rudbeckia fell in love with Prince Julian while they were both at university. By all accounts, *he* is her true love. Why would she run from him now? She could have done it back on Enoc, with the full support of her mother and father.'

Enoc was the planet of choice for young royals who wanted a tertiary education. While there was always a chance that friendship (or more) could be formed with the beautiful Enocian heir, Princess Jewel (applications for medical degrees had exploded the moment she'd chosen that field of study), Enoc was favoured because its queen had instituted a decree that protected any royalty from arrest by the Galactic Law Enforcement Agency, no matter the indiscretion. That included murder. Even second-born sons like Prince Julian enjoyed such benefits.

'The young lovers went to great lengths to convince both royal houses to aim their orbital lascannons away from each other,' Grace continued, making sure she kept to what was regarded as public knowledge. 'So Princess Rudbeckia is unlikely to have a side piece, especially after the amount of effort her parents and the prince's fathers put into the negotiations.'

Sean winked. 'Yeah, well, some of us know more than others.'

Rather than dignify his cocky statement with a response, Grace let her eyes rove back to the stage at the front of the immense hall. She and her companion had managed to find standing room at the fringes of the mediaist frenzy, though this meant sharing a tiny walkway that reminded Grace uncomfortably of the edge of a cliff. The chrome railing was a small mercy, but it moved constantly as people jostled against it, trying to get the best angle for their viewers. Most of them ended up balancing themselves precariously over empty space.

You were meant to keep your vidcam within a certain distance of your body. But this was an unwritten rule, much like the one about not talking to the person next to you in case they stole your scoop. Grace had already forgiven Sean for his attempt to charm information out of her — at least he'd tried it on someone who was around the same age as him.

Flirting was just one of many tools a mediaist kept in their arsenal for extracting information. Grace wasn't innocent on that score, but she rarely got the lasball through the hoop on those occasions so it wasn't the first method she used.

And it wasn't as though she carried around a sign declaring that her girlfriend of two Old Earth years was Finara, the goddess of fire, known by her siblings as the Firine — and now known across the galaxy as She of the Fire. Finara wasn't so keen on that name, but since some mortals she had recently rescued had come up with the title and started worshipping her with fervour, she could hardly scoff at it.

'I won't be writing any assumptions about Princess Rudbeckia just yet,' Grace finally said. She hoped she wouldn't regret indulging Sean's apparent need for conversation.

He was staring at her, she realised.

'Writing,' he said slowly, as though unsure that he had heard her correctly.

'Yes. Writing. I'm an e-paper reporter.'

'E-paper? What the stark is that?'

Grace sighed. She knew it was highly unlikely that any of the thousands of mediaists crowded into the hall beneath her had stumbled across her work. She had forty-eight articles behind her now, including one that exonerated 'Bagara's Puppet'. Her volume of work wasn't the problem. No, if she wasn't pursuing stories no one was interested in, then she was competing with well-established mediaists and their dazzling Webcasts.

But she was now up to two hundred views per story.

Those few sets of eyeballs in a galaxy populated by billions weren't likely to attract a paying sponsor yet, but she figured she had time. She was only thirty-four, she had decades ahead of her. Or eternity if she married She of the Fire...

Grace violently shoved away that thought, disgusted with herself. Sean was now giving her a searching look, one that caused the skin around his eyes to crease, so she forced a lopsided smile. 'I cover events by writing about them and posting those reports on the Web. I expose the truth without using a single image or naming my sources. This way I don't endanger anyone.'

'You can't be making much money,' Sean noted. 'Not a single image, hey? Not naming your sources?' He shook his head. 'You're braver than me, Ms Pendergast.'

'Bravery and stupidity are often seen in each other's company,' Grace told him.

'Oh, that's fine, I'll be stupidity and you can be bravery,' Sean said, flashing that winsome smile of his.

Time to crash this system before it got going again. 'I have a girlfriend.'

Sean's grimace was no surprise. What he said, however, was. 'Sorry. Sometimes I have trouble switching off the charm. It's kind of annoying because people tend to think I like them, even the males of other species, and much as I'd like to seduce as many sources as possible...yeah, I'm only into bipedal women.'

'Not a useless affliction, having people think you like them without even trying.'

'No, not useless,' Sean allowed. 'But it's a not-so-great reminder of my childhood in GLEA's Orphanage Division. I was thirteen when they kicked me out for asking too many questions about the sub-level gods. Since they're big on only worshipping the Creator God, that wasn't exactly the best decision I've ever made. Anyway, the experience kind of forced me to make sure I never got treated that way again. People-pleasing is now my default mode. Wow, that got personal fast.'

'I'm good at making people talk,' Grace said.

'That's not even an affliction, that's just awesome.'

Curious despite herself, Grace was about to probe further into his past when a sudden silence extended in all directions, making her wonder if she'd done something to mute every mediaist in attendance. But the massive floor-to-ceiling vidscreens at the front of the hall had just switched on, showing the centre of the stage.

A Utalian spokesman stood alone before the mediaists, his bald head bowed.

'Something's wrong,' Grace murmured.

'More wrong than a missing princess, you mean?' Sean asked out of the corner of his mouth.

Grace didn't respond, instead keeping her focus on the unmoving Utalian. Bipedal and average in height, they seemed to share much in common with humans. But they grew no hair except for eyebrows, had red skin and could withstand temperatures that would easily boil other species alive.

This Utalian wore the robes of the royal household and was thus subject to the rule that forbade palace workers from showing any emotion. But his violently shaking shoulders were bombing that protocol to pieces from high orbit.

'Zoom in,' Sean murmured aside to his vidcam. 'Gods, you're right. He looks destroyed.'

Finally, the spokesperson lifted his head, vivid sapphire tears staining his ruby cheeks.

'The princess...' He drew a deep breath that swiftly descended into sobs.

'What about the princess? Go on, what about her!' shouted a mediaist down near the stage, an amplifying device attached to their vocal cords.

'Show some respect in this difficult time!' boomed a new voice.

The curtain on the side of the stage sprang away from the wall to reveal Ton Tinel, the galaxy's most famous, most sponsored — and therefore richest — mediaist. Without the colour-altering filter he had apparently been using on his vidcam, and standing beside a man who shared his complexion, it suddenly became very obvious that Ton Tinel wasn't human. No, he was Utalian, through and through. Grace suspected he'd hidden this to appeal to his predominantly human viewership.

Murmurs swept through the hall as Ton Tinel came forward to lay a bracing hand on the spokesman's shoulder. Tinel's expression, sharp enough to cut steel, threatened to behead anyone who dared to make the moment about his own personal reveal.

'No, no, no,' Sean said in a low moan, his techpad clenched in his hand. On the device's vidscreen a miniature version of the famed mediaist was speaking. 'Ton Tinel *just* posted a Webcast he recorded earlier. Oh shit, I'm in trouble...'

'It is my sad duty to inform you,' Tinel declared in his usual even voice, though it had been given volume by his own amplifying tech, 'that Princess Rudbeckia has been kidnapped.'

Ton Tinel then did something Grace had never seen him do — he faltered and let his gaze drop to the floor for so long that his audience grew impatient. This wasn't like him at all; he was a seasoned performer who knew exactly how to time his delivery. And Grace was certain about this, because she'd watched thousands of his Webcasts when she had been training to become a mediaist. It was probably a good thing a big shot like him had never heard of Grace Pendergast. She'd feel beyond ashamed if he'd seen her fateful Webcast that had led to the deaths of hundreds of people.

'Kidnapped? Kidnapped?' The words echoed among the assembled mediaists. 'Who? Who?'

Tinel closed his eyes briefly. 'An anonymous message was received this morning. The message...the message coincided with the delivery of a severed hand. It matches the princess' DNA and markings.'

Gasps, combined until they were almost theatrical in nature, filled the hall.

'No demands have been made as yet,' Tinel went on, 'but we were told to expect them. In the meantime, we will be investigating anyone who might hold ill will against the royal couple.'

'Oh gods, *no*!' Sean wailed loudly, earning himself several reproving looks.

'Keep it together, man!' someone belted back at him.

Ton Tinel, his duty done, began to turn away from the mediaists. But then he shook his head, swung back towards them and rushed out, 'On the request of Princess Rudbeckia's father, the Unandan delegation has been grounded indefinitely. They have responded by giving us two Old Earth days to find the prince's bride, or they will — '

A pair of Utalian royal guards burst onto the stage and roughly grabbed Tinel's arms. The mediaist who had earned a reputation for never backing down, for never being intimidated, merely bowed his head and allowed himself to be led off the stage before the storm of questions could begin.

Would war be declared in two days, is that what the Unandans had threatened? Was Prince Julian behind this? Or was it his fathers, both famously against the match?

They only found a hand, Grace thought distantly. *But where is the rest of her? And what can Princess Rudbeckia's kidnappers hope to gain from this? They can't be from Unanda, the prince's homeworld. They wouldn't risk another costly war so soon after the last one. They'd want to build up their coin-chips first before doing something like this.*

And why does the Utalian royal family have such a firm grip on Ton Tinel? He told us about the Unandan delegation being grounded, but he clearly wasn't meant to...

Grace glanced over at Sean who was pale, his lips shivering. He didn't seem to notice the hordes shoving him alarmingly close to the railing. She thought back to his words and replayed them in her mind. At the time, she'd thought he was disappointed that Ton Tinel had scooped everyone (something he did quite often), but now she wondered. A mediaist in the same position as everyone else in the hall wouldn't say 'I'm in trouble' and sound *that* worried.

'Let me shout you a drink,' Grace suggested.

Sean turned blank eyes onto her. 'What good can a drink do me? My life is over.'

Grace still wasn't sure if he deserved her help, but she knew she wouldn't be able to turn back now. 'Relax, Mr Side Piece. Your princess isn't dead yet.'

'She's not my...I'm not her...' Sean cleared his throat. 'What do you mean, not dead *yet?*'

Grace said nothing, just let the silence mount.

It didn't take him long to snap. 'Fine, since you seem to want the scoop that badly! I only slept with her a couple of times in the past week and that's gonna make me look guilty as stark — but it's not like I told her we should run away together or anything!'

'You'd better let me shout you that drink,' Grace said mildly.

CHAPTER TWO

Most bars within spitting distance of the palace were filled to the brim. Grace's choice of both watering hole and accommodation took half an hour to reach on foot. The inn's other drawback was its most famous neighbour, a vibrant yellow lake that was supposed to be Utalia's greatest feature. Tourists flocked to it in droves during the day, though Grace wasn't sure if that was because they actually found the lake beautiful, or because mediaists paid by the Utalians had told them it was. The lake's ammonia-tainted reek didn't seem to make it into anyone's reviews of their visit — that or they didn't want to admit they'd made a mistake in seeking it out.

The inn was also squashed between a greasy eating establishment and a piecemeal robotics brothel with a sign out the front that boasted: *No full bots! We promise the only uprising will be in your pants!* Presumably, this was meant to reassure potential clients who were uneasy about the thought of a bot uprising in this millennia.

So it wasn't in the greatest district on Utalia, but it was out of the way and it had the cheapest overnight rate, which meant that Grace didn't need to burn through quite so many of Finara's coin-chips. The goddess didn't steal her money — she worked hard for it, as a fire dancer of all things. Not that Grace had any problem with watching her girlfriend's skin glisten with sweat while she performed.

Sean Akiyama was slumped over the bar, his shirt firmly fastened to the stickiest patches on the counter. Perhaps he didn't notice his dank surroundings or perhaps he was used to far worse. He did, however, notice when Grace dropped a drink in front of him and made quick work of drowning himself in the tall glass.

Grace carefully outlined everything she'd ever heard about Ton Tinel. This seemed to rouse Sean somewhat.

'You know Ton Tinel?' he asked, blinking slowly.

Grace winced. 'Not...personally. But I know something of his character.'

'Yeah, the big shot with deep pockets who somehow manages to keep out of trouble, no matter who he upsets,' Sean bit out. 'So you think he wasn't supposed to mention the Unandans? Why?'

'He must have his reasons for not leading with that piece of information on the stage,' Grace said. 'Most likely the Utalian royal family told him to keep it quiet. But he would never agree to repress the truth...at least, before his own rulers asked it of him. Obviously, his character is now in question.' She allowed the sigh. 'You should never meet your idols, so they caution.'

Sean snickered, wiping his hand over his mouth. 'You haven't met him yet, Ms Pendergast.'

'Alcohol robs you of that charm you were bemoaning earlier,' she fired back.

His whole face drooped and he peered into his glass. Its empty state did little to placate him.

'I hope the princess didn't run away because of me,' Sean brooded. 'I was just gonna ditch her after I got some tidbits about the wedding that no one else had, you know? But if she did this...she must really love me!' He perked up considerably.

Grace fought the urge to roll her eyes up towards the grimy ceiling. 'You're suggesting she cut off her own hand and sent it to her parents, just so she could run off with a two-bit mediaist.'

'Three bits, at the very least!' Sean protested. 'Do you think she'll get to keep any of the money in her accounts? Oh, I get it! She's probably asking for a ransom so she has money when she fakes her own death...she'd have to, right? Fake it, I mean. Otherwise people would keep searching for her.'

One of his wild gestures knocked his glass onto the floor and caused it to shatter. Sweeping the shards aside with one of her heels, Grace didn't bother to hide the anger thrumming through her voice. 'Ill-gotten wealth is no reason for you to marry the princess. You would be plunging this entire system into war, because undoubtedly that is what Unanda has threatened if the princess doesn't appear. War. And never mind that such vows should be heartfelt and eternal.'

Sean waved a flippant hand. 'Love transcends war. It always does in the vids. And whoa, why does it have to be "eternal"? No, thanks.'

'Vids,' Grace repeated, her lip twisting. 'Obviously you have never seen the vid about the star-crossed lovers on Old Earth. And they say that one is a true story.'

'History vids are boring.' Sean frowned, his gaze growing distant. 'Look, I can't just sit here and get drunk. I need to find Rudbeckia. If she did this for me, then she must be waiting somewhere, somewhere we've been together or spoken about...'

'Did she tell you she was going to maim herself for you?' Grace demanded.

'No, but she's got to be near medical facilities! Think, Sean, think,' he told himself seriously. 'She'd have gone to a hospital.

Or a clinic. Maybe she dropped a hint for me? Shit, I wasn't really paying attention — I was getting laid, you know?'

'I do know,' Grace said dryly. It had been a long month since she'd last seen her girlfriend. She had worked on back-to-back stories for weeks, running herself ragged and trying to force her way out of obscurity. All this had done was make her irritable and lonely.

I really need a holiday, Grace thought wistfully.

Yeah, no disagreement here, Finara's voice told her. *And hey, you're not the only one who's lonely. If by 'lonely' you mean incredibly horny...*

Grace was now far too used to this method of communication to allow her outward expression to crack. *Finara, you are well aware that I did not ask for your interference. I am busy.*

Too busy to go into the alleyway across the street so I can finger you?

Heat spread through Grace's cheeks and she was grateful that her complexion never allowed a blush or Sean might have started asking awkward questions.

'Alright, I will make a list of places where the princess could have had her hand removed,' Grace said out loud, drawing Sean's wandering attention back to her. 'You'll need my help, though I should warn you that I will try to scoop you. But your options are badly limited at this point.'

Sean absently tapped his fingers on the counter. 'You said you don't use images or names in your e-paper, anything that can identify perpetrators. And since no one reads your stuff anyway...'

Grace swallowed the words she wanted to hurl at him. She was usually more patient than this, she was sure of it — that holiday couldn't come soon enough if being overworked was eroding her ability to operate effectively.

Seeing sense, Ms Stubborn Reporter? Finara teased.

A discussion for another time, Grace replied. *After this story. I promise.*

'It wouldn't be safe if people knew my name or what I looked like,' Sean decided, breaking the carefully crafted silence, just as Grace had known he would. 'And I'm too close to this thing. I'm the source. I'd be too biased if I Webcast it myself. See, I paid attention in my mediaist classes. I mean, I didn't go to a university, I just stole the lecture files, but...'

'Ethics are only halfway out the airlock then,' Grace commented. 'Our species is saved. Of course, I'm curious as to why you'd want to erase all the hard work the princess has done to be with you. And why you'd do it in one of *my* reports. I think you'll exploit my help and run a story about this yourself.'

'I just said I didn't want my name or image getting out!'

Grace speared him with a stern look, wholly unconvinced. 'Easy enough to get a new name and start writing under it, isn't that right, Mr Akiyama? You like my e-paper idea so much you want to steal it? You're probably used to stealing stories and ideas. Not to mention you're awfully bad at lying. You really are only bit-rate.'

Sean scowled. 'Have you always been this suspicious of people?'

'No, and I wasn't always this sure of myself either,' Grace answered honestly.

'So...are you...?' Sean trailed off, his eyes wide with what could have been genuine hope.

Grace reached for her own drink. She slowly lifted the glass to her mouth and let it linger there, as though she was still debating whether or not she should help him. It would do him some good to stew, she thought.

'I'll do what I can for you, Mr Akiyama,' Grace told him. 'I need to increase my readership anyway. Covering a story of this magnitude will do that, even if I do have to share the story with a source who should know better.'

'Thank you, thank you!' Sean said, grinning broadly and waving at the bartender who brought him another drink on Grace's tab.

She let him. Mostly because she was planning to tell the princess everything about his true character — it was likely the last free drink he was ever going to get.

My, you have a vindictive streak, Finara mused.

Grace's jaw tightened. *No one deserves to be deceived in that manner.*

He was a fool to try to deceive you, the goddess said. *I'll go and give you some privacy now. But if you call my name, I'll come straight back to you. Okay?*

Grace swiftly snapped her eyelids together, halting the build-up of heated tears. She never allowed Finara to hear it, but there was one thought that continued to haunt her. *And will you still protect me when we are no longer together? When you finally tire of waiting for me to love you?*

Grace knocked back her drink and ordered another.

She figured she didn't deserve any better company right now and made herself stay with Sean until the planet rotated into deep night.

CHAPTER THREE

Grace, my love. Wake up. Someone's coming.

Grace peeled open eyelids that rasped like sandpaper on the sensitive balls beneath them. The night was darker than the stains on the ceiling above her and the ancient generator providing power to the bot brothel next door was still whirring away uninterrupted. But she didn't question Finara's words. The Firine always left a fraction of her presence behind with Grace, one that did not pry into any intimate thoughts — and when Finara said she was giving Grace privacy, she meant it. Only imminent danger to Grace's life would cause her to renege on that promise.

Grace shot out of bed, fully dressed as always, and slid her palms down the sides of her pants, straightening them as best she could. She wondered, not for the first time, if she should have bought a lasgun for protection. But it was hard enough getting someone to trust you without carrying a weapon on your hip as well.

Grace slapped the panel beside the door — it dutifully *snicked* open — and moved across the corridor. She wasn't sure how much time she had to escape. There could be any number of reasons that people were after her, but Grace had a pretty good idea it had something to do with a certain not-so-lovelorn mediaist. The door to his quarters yielded to her palm print; she was the one who had laid down the coin-chips for it, after all.

Sean groggily raised his head. 'Wha...thought you had a girlfriend...'

'Get dressed,' Grace hissed. 'Someone's coming. Someone found us.'

'How?' he demanded, grabbing the jeans he'd discarded on the floor. 'Who did you tell? Stark it, I thought I could trust you!'

Grace turned her back to him, eyes casing out the shadows filling the corridor. 'You can trust me. So shut up and let's get going.'

They made it to the stairs at the end of the floor in about a minute, far too slow, but Grace didn't waste any time berating her companion. He'd frequently bemoaned the lack of hoverlift and that had already cost them precious seconds.

'What about the windows?' Sean asked around the hand he was using to smother his yawn.

Grace seized his arm and tugged it down the next section of stairs. Sean followed his limb, cursing and dragging his feet.

'The lake, the one that looks and smells like urine,' Grace explained tightly. 'It surrounds the back of this establishment. You really don't want to fall into it. The liquid is toxic to humans.'

'Right. Gotcha.'

Relieved that they had finally left the stairs behind them, Grace gave his arm one last, hard yank — and stopped dead, her breath and every rational thought deserting her.

There was a man in a white suit sitting at the bar. And she knew exactly who he was.

'What gives?' Sean yelped as he collided with her back.

'Ton Tinel,' Grace breathed.

'What's Ton Tinel got to do with us sneaking out of the building?'

'Quite a lot actually,' the most famous mediaist in the galaxy responded, then set down his glass of violet wine.

Of course he drank wine, Grace mused. He was too sophisticated for anything else. Confusion quickly morphed into annoyance. *Someone's coming, you said? He's already here — some warning, Finara!*

He's not carrying a lasgun like the ones outside though? Finara said, sounding defensive.

Grace swallowed, but her mouth remained dry and useless. *Ton Tinel, of all people! Gods, why is he here?*

Search me, love. You know you want to. Grace could vividly picture the wink that Finara would have performed to cap off that sentence.

You have mind-reading abilities — use them! Grace all but roared at her.

'Ton Tinel! What the fuck!?' Sean exclaimed.

The mediaist is here for your new friend, Finara supplied mere seconds later. *You won't be hurt. Ton Tinel specifically asked for that from the Utalian royal guards who escorted him here.*

Grace blinked. *Really? Me, specifically? I'm sure he just meant any innocent bystanders.*

'Sean Akiyama, you are under arrest,' Ton Tinel announced, the golden whirls in his orange eyes doing nothing to soften his stern gaze. 'Kidnapping and demanding ransom are both illegal acts here on Utalia. As such, no Chipper can help you out of this situation, since GLEA is restricted to upholding a planet's laws. So it would be best if you simply complied, instead of leading us on one of those climatic chases to a Chipper outpost that they are so keen on showing in the vids.'

'What do I do?' Sean cried, his desperate gaze fixing on Grace.

'Ms Pendergast.' Tinel acknowledged her with a nod. 'I will allow you to accompany us back to the palace. No doubt you consider Mr Akiyama your responsibility. It is your fault he was discovered, after all.'

He knows my name, Grace realised with an unwanted and totally inconvenient thrill.

Thankfully, her voice returned just in time.

'So much for being the galaxy's most impartial mediaist,' Grace said. 'What happened to your lauded objectivity? Are the king and queen paying you for your interference?'

Tinel's scarlet forehead creased. 'Much as I love my homeworld, no amount of remuneration could make me stay when I have work to do elsewhere. I am currently unable to leave until Their Majesties are satisfied with my participation in this matter.'

'You said it was my fault Mr Akiyama was found — why is that?' Grace demanded, laying a hand on Sean's shoulder and making it very clear that he was under her protection.

Tinel sighed, something akin to a grimace settling across his wide lips. 'His name and image are well known to Utalian security — he was captured by vidcams inside the princess' chambers. Princess Rudbeckia was fond of recording her...indiscretions.'

Sean swore and slumped against Grace, the fight leeching out of him.

'Mr Akiyama was not found at the lodgings he had rented under his name,' Ton Tinel went on. 'But our vidcams saw you with him earlier. So we used your name instead and naturally that led us right here. I know who you are, Grace Pendergast.'

'You know...' Grace drew a breath. 'How? I'm no one.'

Ton Tinel straightened, his eyes never leaving hers. 'I make it a point to keep tabs on all upcoming mediaists. Not many of them prove to be viable threats to my career, but there was a very capable young woman who had the potential to become one. She made a mistake and, grave though it was, I expected her to rise above it, not disappear and rob me of any decent competition.' He smiled. The effect was startling, turning him from firm adversary into pleasant companion. 'Imagine my delight when my search program found her name again. In an e-paper. I've been reading your stories since the piece you did on Bagara's Puppet.'

Grace stared at him, painfully aware that her silence was giving more away than it ever had before. But the goddess of fire wasn't so dumbstruck. Her mind-voice returned, fierce and full of bite and fury. *He's using your admiration of him against you. Dick. I could incinerate him in an instant.*

I'd rather you didn't kill every mortal who happens to offend me, Grace said, but she didn't hide how grateful she felt. *Thank you. I needed some sense knocked back into me.*

You can thank me by taking time off after this mess is sorted.

Done.

'Your regard means nothing to me, Mr Tinel,' Grace said, shaking her head to express her disappointment in him. 'It once did, but you have tarnished your own reputation before my very eyes. I know there are Utalian royal guards waiting for us outside; they are here because of information *you* gave them about Mr Akiyama. You're working with them. What will people say when they know you can no longer be trusted to remain independent and impartial?'

Ton Tinel looked away. 'It was not a decision that was taken lightly, I promise you. But...this admission costs me...I am also in the princess' personal vids. I have to work with the royal guards. It goes a long way to convincing the king that I was not responsible for his daughter's disappearance.'

'You...' Sean took a step forward, his mouth gaping. 'I was competing with you this whole time? Ton Tinel? I never had a chance!'

Grace quickly shoved him as far away from the exterior wall — and the heavily armed guards behind it — as possible.

'And how is Sean Akiyama any more guilty than you?' she demanded of Tinel.

The famed mediaist curled his fingers around his wine glass but did not lift it, though he looked sorely tempted to. 'He's not. But there are a good deal of suspects to round up and question. I am hoping to help expedite the process so that the real investigation can begin. We have less than two days before the Unandans start a war over this and I do not believe that any of Princess Rudbeckia's lovers were responsible. We need to look elsewhere.'

'How many suspects are in the princess' personal vids?' was Grace's next question.

'One hundred and fifty-seven,' Tinel answered.

Sean tumbled onto his hands and knees and made a sound that Grace hadn't thought possible for a human to emit. She supposed his ego had just taken a battering.

Regret threw a shadow over Tinel's next words. 'And many of those beings fancied that the princess was in love with them.'

'All it takes is one violently-inclined lover finding out just how much competition they have...' Grace tipped her head to the side, regarding the mediaist with narrow eyes. 'But you don't believe that jealousy was the motivation here. Clearly the king and queen aren't in agreement with you or they wouldn't have forbidden you to mention the Unandans earlier. At least, I'm assuming that's why they pulled you off the stage so fast.'

Tinel nodded. 'I took a risk, saying what I did. But someone needed to look into the Unandans in my stead, free of the king and queen's interference. The real culprits must be found.'

'You expected someone else to uncover the information that would exonerate you,' Grace surmised.

'I was hoping it would be you,' Ton Tinel said, smiling.

Grace stared at him.

That dick, Finara seethed. *He wants you to risk your life and chase a lead that might land you in prison. The Utalians could fix this mess themselves by looking into their former enemies.*

The Utalian rulers are probably hoping to avoid insulting the Unandans, Grace told her.

Finara's words took on a thoughtful tone. *Yeah, they don't want another war. Some of my followers live here, so I've heard their prayers. They've already lost so many loved ones because of all the fighting. Grace, love, you don't have to do this.*

But this is my chance for a much bigger story. Grace almost laughed. *And he's always had more faith in my abilities than I ever did! Was he truthful about following my career?*

Yes. He's been watching and reading your stuff since you were at least twenty.

Grace blinked back tears. So. Ton Tinel wasn't lying. And at some point he had even considered her worthy enough to be a competitor.

It was a wonderful discovery, but...

'If you won't tell the truth about your connection to this

49

story, then I will,' Grace declared, ignoring the increasingly loud moans of distress coming from Sean's direction. 'The galaxy deserves to know that the great Ton Tinel isn't as objective and as untouchable as he claims to be.'

Ton Tinel's expression darkened. 'Very well. Your readership is so low it won't matter. No one will believe you. Don't expect me to help you with your career after this.'

Grace gave him a neutral nod, thinking of a certain promise from a certain source.

Gerns, a botanist Grace had befriended, claimed to know a hacker who could make one of Grace's stories go viral. Grace had resisted temptation for almost two years.

But this...this was the one.

The one to call in her marker for.

'I don't need your help,' she told Ton Tinel. 'I never did.'

'One day, Ms Pendergast, you will understand my position. It's one I've often found myself in. Doing what we do, seeing what we see — it forces us to take on a more active role. Sometimes we have to change the story. For the good of the galaxy.'

Grace's lip twisted. 'I will never let myself sink to your level.'

'You say that now,' Tinel remarked. 'But what happens when lives need saving? Will you stand by and write an objective report, or will you do something about it?'

They broke eye contact when Sean picked himself off the slimy tiles lining the floor and marched away from the bar. He paused when he noticed them watching him, then jerked his head at the door. 'I think I'm safer outside. But if you're not going to kill each other, will you at least come out and make sure the guards don't shoot me on sight? I'd appreciate it.'

Feeling suddenly foolish for forgetting the matter at hand, Grace hurried after him.

CHAPTER FOUR

Grace stepped forward, arms linked behind her back, and pointedly ignored the guards lined up around the perimeter of a concrete box that would eventually see one hundred and fifty-seven suspects. Most of the unfortunate souls that had been arrested were male, though some were of no specific gender and others weren't even bipedal (fifteen different species had been represented so far). What they all had in common was the indignant surprise they displayed when confronted with the knowledge that they weren't the only one who had been bestowed with Princess Rudbeckia's affections.

'Can you see that we will get nothing out of these interviews?' Ton Tinel asked, standing at Grace's left.

Representatives from the local GLEA garrison had offered to conduct the interrogations and their help had been gratefully accepted, since their neutrality would make any findings more believable. Clad in bright purple jumpsuits and carrying chips in their temples, the Chippers looked wholly out of place when they were surrounded by Utalian guards who wore muted grey uniforms. The current subject, held still by lascuffs while the agent in the opposite chair hurled questions at zir, was a scale-skinned Banis.

Grace kept her lips in a firm, straight line. 'I can't see into these people's minds, so I don't know if you're right. The gods

53

could tell us. But I wouldn't ask them for that kind of interference.'

'Why not, Ms Pendergast? I suspect it is not because they might kill you for daring to impose on them.'

'You suspect correctly, Mr Tinel,' Grace remarked. 'It would be too easy, to use the powers of the gods. And it wouldn't be right. We should not expect anything from them.'

Don't expect me to stop protecting you, Finara said flatly. Her presence had yet to fade into the background. *Because I won't, Grace. I love you too much for that.*

Grace swallowed once, then twice, mindful of Tinel's sharp eyes and intellect.

She remembered that she *had* asked Finara to interfere, to read Tinel's mind earlier, and failed to banish the hot shame that swooped through her.

'But I'm inclined to agree with you,' Grace said, when she was sure that her voice would remain steady. She waved a hand at the Banis, who was spewing yet another breathy story about sailing around a certain piss-yellow lake on the princess' private yacht. 'We won't find the perpetrator among the princess' lovers. There's too many of them.'

'It's certainly slowing down the investigation — we'll still be standing here when war is declared,' Tinel noted. A burgundy shadow passed over his scarlet features. 'I wonder...Rud — Princess Rudbeckia is one of the smartest women I have ever met. It's unlikely she would have forgotten to turn on her yacht's shield. She's also an accomplished shot with a lasgun.'

Grace pictured the kidnapping anew with this extra piece of information. The princess could still have been overwhelmed by a starship entering the atmosphere, but the yacht's shield would have been expensive and unique, maybe even strong enough to withstand an orbital bombardment...

'Perhaps the princess knew that her parents would be too busy investigating her lovers to stop her carrying out her own escape plan,' Grace mused. But she doubted the words before she'd even voiced them.

'It's...possible,' Tinel said slowly. 'But you're suggesting that she chose to leave. No. The princess spoke of her upcoming nuptials without a trace of discontent. She really likes Prince Julian. Of course, given her ability to make me believe I was her only extramarital suitor, I could be mistaken.'

That small, self-deprecating smile looked strange on him. To Grace, Ton Tinel had seemed almost god-like for decades. But now, compared to Finara and the other members of the Galactic Pantheon, he was unimposing and powerless. He was just like any other mortal.

Perturbed, Grace forced her gaze back to the Banis in front of them. 'Maybe Prince Julian didn't want the wedding to go ahead?'

'He is my main suspect,' Tinel said. 'The Unandan vessels were sealed at his order and he refuses any visitors, as per his diplomatic rights.'

'Were there any doctors or surgeons among the princess' lovers?' Grace asked, thinking of the severed hand which was now being kept in stasis. She had been allowed a brief glimpse and the cut was too precise to be the work of a careless blade.

'No. That is the first thing I ascertained. The princess does not know any such person.'

'Are you sure, or are you only assuming this because none of them were caught on vidcam?' Grace rubbed her forehead, but the lines in her skin kept deepening. She wasn't convinced that

Prince Julian was the culprit. 'If the princess is as smart as you say she is and she did all this to buy time to flee the planet...then she would make sure that nothing important showed up in those vids of hers.'

Tinel nodded, his eyes whirling with renewed interest. 'She may still be on Utalia. Her image has not been caught on any vidcams near the spaceport and the only ships that aren't docked there belong to the Unandans — they're parked in an old crater outside the city instead. This makes the prince look very suspicious.'

'It doesn't matter who's behind this,' Grace said. 'When Princess Rudbeckia fails to turn up before the deadline, the Unandans will start a war.'

'And many lives will be lost,' Tinel murmured.

Grace drew air deep into her lungs for several moments before releasing it, hopefully exhaling the temptation along with the carbon dioxide.

No such luck.

'Excuse me,' Grace said weakly, then turned and marched out of the room. Behind her the Banis was being replaced with Sean Akiyama, just another being in a long line of suspects.

After ensuring that she was alone in the corridor, which was lined with the ostentatious marble that royals on various planets seemed to favour, she gave a shout of frustration and kicked the wall. Pain flared inside her toes, alerting Grace to the fact that she had used her flesh-and-blood foot instead of the one provided by her prosthesis. She cursed and hopped around, only dropping her scuffed black heel to the floor when the corridor became seared with heat.

'Vidcam — twenty metres behind me,' Grace said quickly.

'Already fried,' the Firine informed her in a very real, very human voice. 'So're the other ones further down. What gives, Grace? I bought you those shoes barely a month ago! You've destroyed at least six pairs so far and I'm not sure how many you're going to need for the rest of the year, much less an eter...' Finara cleared her throat. 'What's wrong?'

'You already know,' Grace accused. 'I can't control my surface thoughts at the moment.'

'It's still polite to ask. Or so my girlfriend tells me.'

Grace wheeled around. Her glare eroded almost immediately at the sight of the fire goddess in a scarlet two-piece outfit that didn't cover much of her taut olive skin — but that wasn't her most alluring quality. No, it was the warmth that robbed her smirk of any arrogance, and the secret softness in her flaming eyes that only one mortal had ever been allowed to see.

Grace marched forward, pressed her girlfriend against the impossibly smooth wall and drew her into a deep kiss. This temptation was easier to allow. So Grace chased it further and further, a hand curving around Finara's back and sliding lower —

'Nope, you're not kissing away your problems, Ms E-Paper Reporter,' Finara said with a gentle *tsk*. She was suddenly several paces away.

Grace tried to follow the Firine, but the wall refused to release her. She looked down, bemused — her wrists and ankles were encased in cuffs made out of flickering fire. It didn't surprise her that they failed to burn her or scorch her clothes; it annoyed her that they existed at all. She sealed her lips tight, repressing the urge to say exactly what she was thinking right then.

Finara took the time to deliberately arrange her arms in front of her, crossing them the same way that Grace had done so many times. 'Just *talk* to me, Grace. Reading your mind — and trying not to when you're leaking shit all over the place — is exhausting.'

Silence was a shield that Grace badly wanted to use right now. But she couldn't.

Not against Finara.

'I can't find the princess but I know someone who can!' Grace cried.

'You're assuming that she's somewhere inside my domain,' Finara noted, not even bothering to pretend that she hadn't guessed who Grace had meant to approach about this. 'Or that she's in a domain of a sibling I'm friendly with.'

Grace sighed and let her chin drop to her chest. 'I hate myself right now. I hate that it even occurred to me. I'm so weak.'

'Hey, you can't help it if your girlfriend's this awesome,' Finara said in a playful tone. Grace lobbed a scowl at her, but it melted away when she saw the worry streaking over the goddess' face in a way that wrinkles never would.

'Don't do it,' Grace pleaded softly. 'Don't let me. Never let me use you this way.'

The flames in Finara's eyes dimmed, allowing her natural hazel irises to bleed through. 'Grace, love, I would do anything you asked of me, even this. That's why I can't be your gatekeeper. But I know you. I know you'll only come to me when you've exhausted all other avenues.'

Grace swallowed. Ton Tinel's words were still fresh in her mind. *What happens when lives need saving? Will you stand by and write an objective report, or will you do something about it?*

'I know you,' Finara repeated. 'And I trust you. Isn't it time you trusted yourself?'

Grace felt the cuffs fall away but stayed where she was,

capable of standing on her own, capable of solving this mystery without Finara's help. She was sure of that. She *had* to be sure.

Because if going to a goddess was an option, then it had to be her last one.

'The princess' lovers are a dead end,' Grace decided. 'It's a distraction. We should be looking into those with the tools and experience to remove a hand so expertly. Doctors, surgeons, anyone who studied medicine at university...'

'That's still way too many people to look into,' Finara reminded her.

'Another time-waster from the princess,' Grace agreed. 'I'm going about this the wrong way. How did the hand get to the palace? Every package in Utalia is scanned thoroughly before dispatch. It's hardly something a licenced courier would carry. It'd have to be someone who's used to moving sensitive goods, someone who has to mingle with other criminals in order to get their next job.'

Finara's lips twitched. 'Criminals, huh. Love, we both know you don't have contacts in any planet's underworld yet. Maybe you should work on that.'

'Most women wouldn't let their girlfriends get mixed up in this sort of thing,' Grace noted.

'Don't think I'm letting you do this shit alone.' A dangerous pause, then those hazel eyes flamed once more. 'And don't you dare ask me to leave.'

Grace was unable to kill the smile that spread over her features. 'I won't. Because I don't have time to argue with you right now. Later, however, that's a different matter. You should know that a certain fire goddess has versed me in the art of persuasion...'

Finara growled softly and a moment later Grace found that it was her turn to be pinned up against the wall, Finara's thigh angled between her legs just so. She closed her eyes, moaned, gave herself over to her lover — and sighed in exasperation when the pressure of Finara's body vanished, leaving her cold and aching. Grace scanned the corridor and could find no obvious sign that the goddess was still around, but Finara was most certainly there, watching over her.

Grace lifted her chin and strode back into the interrogation arena, her steps sure and steady. Ton Tinel looked up immediately.

'If you can be allowed out of confinement to help the authorities,' Grace began, crossing her arms, 'then so can Sean Akiyama. I need him to be released. Now.'

'You think he can help find the princess?' A desperate note there, most unlike him.

'Of course. But if this is her doing and I can't convince her to come back, I'm not turning her in. Unlike you, my future does not rely on the goodwill of the Utalian rulers.'

Tinel stared at her. 'The king and queen will kill you if you run such a story without telling them her whereabouts. And that's only if the Unandan kings don't find you first! They will do terrible things to get you to yield their son's promised bride.'

Grace rested a hand on the right knee of her pants, her fingers bunching up the material to reveal her silver prosthetic leg. 'I once gave up the whereabouts of more than four hundred people and the price I paid for their deaths was embarrassingly small. I'm ready to pay the full price to protect the whereabouts of one single person.'

'And what if giving up one person saves thousands who might die in a preventable war?'

Grace winced. 'I will never give up my sources. Never.'

'You don't need to keep atoning for what happened to those rebels on Eransia,' Tinel said gently.

'Yes, I do.' Grace kept her voice harsh, uncompromising. 'Release Sean Akiyama. Now.'

CHAPTER FIVE

'You gotta understand, it's not like I deliberately went looking for these sorts of people...' Sean gestured around at the surly faces watching them as he walked Grace through the claustrophobic warren known locally as The Shadow Market. '...they're the ones who found *me*, after the Chippers tossed me out. I would have starved to death without the help of some of the street's worst criminals. We're like one big happy family, with cousins on every planet. Anyway, it's nice to know that wherever I go in the galaxy, there's at least one place where everyone looks after their own. Home is where the crooks are.'

'Did you happen to tell the princess about your unsavoury connections?' Grace asked him.

Sean stopped dead, looking thunderstruck. 'You know what, she did ask if I knew much about the underworld here, said she wanted a better picture of the planet she'll rule over one day. I'll admit I was a little worried she wouldn't answer any of *my* questions. So I told her everything.'

'Everything,' Grace repeated. 'Including where to obtain the services of someone willing to remove a hand and send it to the palace?'

'She never asked that outright, okay?' Sean snapped. 'She was more interested in hearing about where these unsavoury types do business, how they get around the galaxy without any authorities finding them...' He smacked his forehead with the heel of his palm. 'Gods, I'm so stupid! I thought I was the one using her, but she was stitching me up the whole time.'

Grace decided not to point out that he probably deserved to be treated the same way he'd intended to treat someone else. 'How likely is it that your sources here will talk to us?'

'Not very,' Sean admitted.

Grace raised her eyebrows.

'Uh, I'm the reason some of them got arrested,' Sean said and flung his grimace around The Shadow Market, as though the beige walls were closing in on him. 'Their faces got tagged because of my old Webcasts and Chippers went after them. Word gets out fast in the underworld. My good looks and charm stopped being enough to coax my sources on screen. Totally killed my viewership.'

'Your poor viewership,' Grace said dryly.

'I get that I fucked up! Seriously! I'm lucky no one *died* because of me.'

She eyed him for a moment, trying to ascertain if he was comparing his experiences to hers in order to make some point (she had explained her past earlier, making sure he understood why she wouldn't let him buy another vidcam after his had been confiscated by the Utalian guards), but he seemed genuinely distressed. His hair stood on end even before he raked his jagged fingers through it and his brown eyes were hollow. Finally, he said, 'I can't change what happened, but I can change how I do things from now on. The way you did.'

He really needs a better role model than me, Grace thought.

Love, you're the only one he's got, Finara countered.

Grace cleared her throat; the lump forming inside it stuck briefly. 'Alright, Mr Akiyama, who do we speak to first?'

***

'No starking way am I talking to that lout!' the shopkeeper exclaimed, shaking his head furiously and retreating until his back hit the wall behind him. 'I've got no interest in a prison cell!'

'Jed, you know I can go next door and buy a lasgun, then come back in here and shoot you,' Sean said, tipping his head towards the exit of the tiny shop. The shelves were lined with twisted, useless pieces of metal but, unsurprisingly, Jeddiah Small's business also dealt with something far more lucrative: unregistered couriers who don't ask questions. For the right fee, of course.

Jeddiah slapped a hand behind the counter and jerked it back into view, a lasgun held fast in his grip. His crimson lips, the only indication that he had some Utalian blood, twisted into a snarl. 'Oh yeah, I got myself a piece because of that stunt you pulled on me. I didn't forget about it.'

Grace rubbed her temples. 'Sean. What happened to your ability to charm people?'

'I had to go to Plan B that time, okay?' Sean grumbled.

Jeddiah jerked the barrel of his weapon towards Sean, but his next words were aimed at Grace. 'How'd you get stuck with this shitball?'

'I'm with him entirely by choice, I'm afraid.'

'Suppose you got your reasons.'

'Yes, I do,' Grace replied. 'Some I'm rethinking, trust me.'

Jeddiah chuckled. 'Yeah, I bet you are.'

Grace forced her mouth to form what she hoped was a flattering smile. 'Mr Small, I'd very much like to hear what you can tell us, especially if Sean is right about you being the best and most discreet courier service on the planet.'

'I won't be goin' on cam,' Jeddiah warned as his lasgun dropped out of sight again. 'I seen what happens to those who talk to Mr Shitball here.'

'Does it look like we have a vidcam on us?' Grace asked, quirking an eyebrow.

Jeddiah's heavy frown rested on Sean. 'Sure, my sensors aren't picking up one of those floaters, but this shitball you're with has a knack for sneaking other cams in.'

'I'm an e-paper reporter,' Grace explained calmly. 'And so is our shitball friend here. That means we don't publish any images or footage. We only use the written word and keep the names of our sources out of our articles.'

'How the fuck does anyone believe you though?' Jeddiah demanded.

Grace rested a hand on the techpad case she kept clipped to her belt. 'I'm not sure any of our readers believe us. But they still read our work.' She chose not to mention the fact that her readers only numbered two hundred, or that Sean currently had a word count of zero.

'Usual payment, shitball?' Jeddiah directed at Sean.

Sean grinned. 'You'll have to ask my boss.'

He better not be trying to get on my good side, Grace thought with venom.

Grace, he's deferring to you because he respects you, Finara told her, a hint of teasing in her tone. *And it has absolutely nothing to do with your exquisite arse.*

Haven't you got some people to save?

Sure. But see, I have this ability where I can be in thousands of places at once...

Grace sighed. Both men were watching her expectantly.

'Usual payment,' she agreed. 'But add fifty coin-chips on top and buy something nice for yourself. Sean's paying.'

'What? No way, Grace!' Sean protested.

All Grace had to do was give him one of her trademark silences and he gave in.

***

Utalia's closest neighbour, Unanda, could be seen through the orange-smeared sky both day and night; it was a gleaming emerald-and-sapphire sphere, the perfect home for Old Earth settlers and their human descendants. The Unandans, given the climate they preferred, would not have been comfortable on Utalia's acidic terrain, but they had always coveted the precious minerals that the Utalians possessed. And so many centuries ago a war had begun — and it had lasted, despite multiple lulls in hostilities, until a prince and princess had fallen in love on neutral Enoc.

The Utalians preferred to create ships in the shape of large concrete boxes that didn't blend into any background, starry or otherwise. Their firepower and sheer numbers meant that they didn't need to hide. The Unandans had learned to counter force with smarts — their ships were sleek and small and were designed to hit space before anyone noticed they'd taken off.

The crater Jeddiah had directed them to was full of the latter.

'So the hand came from the *Unandans?*' The pitch in Sean's voice rose substantially.

'Don't ask me. Jeddiah's your source, not mine.'

'Well, he said someone in this crater commissioned a courier.' Sean frowned. 'And that courier spoke to a woman wearing royal Unandan robes, which is strange...'

'...because in Unanda only a man may claim to be a member of the royal house,' Grace finished. She pursed her lips. 'There isn't a doctor among the delegation, according to the information Mr Tinel gave us, though that could be wrong. But I wonder. The princess didn't study medicine while on Enoc, did she? No, I don't think so, and neither did the prince.'

Sean made a soft exclamation. 'They didn't. But I know who did — Princess Jewel of Enoc!'

'Princess Jewel?' Grace shook her head. 'I know she and Prince Julian had a brief fling before he met Princess Rudbeckia at university, but that's an awfully big leap in logic.'

'You got a better lead?'

'No,' Grace admitted. 'And it does make sense for Prince Julian to derail the wedding so he can marry a wealthier Enocian royal instead. Princess Jewel is also human, so she could be mistaken for a Unandan. But how would she get onto one of these ships? I doubt the Unandan kings would have allowed a foreigner amongst the delegation, especially one the prince has a history with.'

'There's not a lot of space between Utalia and Unanda, but enough for someone to board a ship.' Sean's gaze was lot to the sky for several moments. 'And it's said the prince insists on flying his own private vessel. I think he got it as a graduation present. No idea what it looks like.'

'It would be something small,' Grace said. 'Something fast enough to outrun his escort. Something that could sneak away and rendezvous with someone else's ship. But a lot of these vessels meet those requirements.'

Found the princess, a pleased voice announced inside Grace's head.

Grace ground her teeth together. *I can figure this out on my own, Finara.*

I know you can. The goddess exuded complete faith in Grace's abilities. Grace wasn't sure she had earned that faith yet.

'The Unandans burn the names of their vessels onto the hulls,' Grace said, her eyes gliding from ship to ship. 'The thinking is that if you get too close, you won't live to tell anyone what name you saw. So what would a lovesick young man name his ship after having to leave Princess Jewel behind?'

'Noooo, that's too cheesy,' Sean said, sounding appalled. 'Yuck.'

He was pointing directly at a ship bearing the words *Diamond Heart*. Diamonds were the galaxy's favourite jewel and had been for millennia.

'Seems like that's our destination,' Grace commented. 'All the other vessels are named after different types of swords.'

'So are we going to just waltz over and knock?' Sean asked.

'Why not?'

'We don't have any shielding devices or lasguns!'

Grace started walking. 'We have a much greater weapon.'

'Uh, what's that?' Sean called after her.

'Blackmail,' she said simply.

CHAPTER SIX

'My name is Grace Pendergast, e-paper reporter, and I would like to speak to Prince Julian, Princess Jewel and/or Princess Rudbeckia at your earliest convenience,' Grace said, curving her lips and hoping it would make her sound more pleasant. 'Preferably soon, if you don't want me or my companion to inform the king and queen about the contents of this vessel.'

She lifted her hand from the sensor pad beside the ramp, deactivating the external communicator. Above her and Sean, gleaming vidcams whirred, taking in their faces and judging if they were a threat. Grace took a step back. Alarmingly large lascannons might be fixed to the ship's belly, but far more manoeuvrable fist-sized lasguns were clustered around the entrance.

'You didn't mention my name,' Sean noted. 'That could have helped us. The princess might want to see a familiar face.'

'We don't yet know if she's calling the shots here,' Grace said. 'Or if she remembers you at all.'

Sean sighed. 'Yeah. I'd have trouble remembering one hundred and fifty-seven names and faces too.'

The door slid open.

Grace and Sean exchanged glances, nodded as one, then walked inside together. The corridors tightened around them like tiny silver veins, but mercifully distant lights soon guided them to the bridge, where they found the ship's occupants entwined on a couch and wearing identical smug expressions.

Grace darted a look around at the consoles. Mostly automated. The prince only had to speak a destination and the ship would take him there. He'd probably never used manual controls in his life.

'Uh, so,' Sean began, his voice uncertain, 'are the three of you...together?'

'How astute the cretin is!' Prince Julian exclaimed, rising from the couch in all his unclad glory. Behind him remained two similarly nude women: Princess Jewel of Enoc and Princess Rudbeckia. One of Princess Rudbeckia's hands didn't match her crimson skin; it appeared to be dark brown and much more human. Synthflesh, Grace noted. Of course the prince could afford to give her the very best, even if it was more suited to someone from his species and of his colouring.

'We should kill them,' Princess Rudbeckia said. Grace caught the flash of wounded disbelief on Sean's face. Clearly the Utalian princess hadn't recognised him.

'I wouldn't do that,' Grace said. Her forced smile was starting to hurt her cheeks.

'Why not?' Princess Jewel demanded.

It was Sean who answered. 'Because if you kill us, then we won't be able to stop a timed report going out, revealing where Princess Rudbeckia is hiding. The entire *galaxy* will know.'

'As I recall,' Grace said swiftly, trying to draw attention away from his lie, 'marriage on both Utalia and Unanda is restricted to two persons.'

Rudbeckia's ruby-red eyes alighted on her, dangerously thin. 'Enoc is a far more relaxed world, with far more favourable laws regarding marriage, and that is where I have chosen to live with my husband and wife.'

'Wait — ' Sean's finger jerked between all three of them, as though physically connecting the dots. 'You're — you're going to go live on Enoc? And not come back? Shit. The Utalians and Unandans will blame each other and have at it. That or band together and hit Enoc.'

Grace swallowed her fury. 'You would plunge two — possibly even *three* — worlds into war, with countless deaths on all sides...for love?'

'Wouldn't you?' Prince Julian asked, puffing up his scrawny chest.

'No, I wouldn't,' Grace said bluntly.

Stark, I love that about you, Finara murmured. *Your stubborn adherence to what you believe in. But, my love, this time you need to interfere and stop them.*

Finara, I can't!

An edge crept into Finara's mind-voice. *Don't you want to save millions of lives? Because people will die. Including people who worship me, people who expect me to keep them safe!*

Princess Jewel was watching Grace with dark, solemn eyes and Grace worried for a moment that she'd let something show on her face, such as the temptation mounting inside her. But then the princess crossed her arms and challenged, 'Are you going to try to stop us, peasant? You'll fail.'

Grace curled a fist against her hip, tightening her fingers until they ached. 'No. I won't stop you. We're e-paper reporters and as such we only record events and facts, not do anything to change them. But you can at least have your say through us, so people understand what is going on here.'

'Yeah,' Sean said, nodding vigorously. 'And since we're not Webcasting live, you can take some time to self-edit yourselves before we write anything down. It's always so confronting when you have a vidcam shoved into your face.'

Prince Julian's bravado sluiced into anguish. 'But you want us to go through with this sham wedding and that will hurt Jewel!'

'Of course they do, but they're not stupid!' Princess Rudbeckia snapped at him. 'They know we can give them a story that'll make them huge. Very well, Ms Pendergast. I want my overbearing parents to know what has caused their ruin. But I demand you publish nothing until we three are married on Enoc. That's one Old Earth month away.'

A month? Grace thought. *They'll let Utalia and Unanda fight each other for that long without telling anyone what's happened?*

'It takes time to prepare a royal wedding, even a rushed one,' Princess Jewel explained, her lip twisting. Grace knew she had failed to keep her feelings from her face on this occasion. And the Enocian royal had noticed.

'But how're you three getting off this planet?' Sean wondered. 'This ship's grounded, just like the others.'

'Only so long as we wish to avoid insulting the Utalians!' Prince Julian said, a hysterical laugh escaping him with the force of an out-of-control hovercar. 'But in a day war will be declared and insults will be the least of my fathers' concerns. The rest of the delegation's ships will return home, but I won't be going with them. I'll be heading for Enoc instead.'

'And the Chippers wouldn't dare arrest us!' Princess Rudbeckia exclaimed gleefully. 'Under the laws of Enoc, we will be free from the interference of foreigners on all matters.'

Grace pressed her forehead against the bridge of skin

between her thumb and index finger, hating herself for standing by and letting this happen. But she couldn't interfere. She couldn't. 'Alright. I can write this. I can hold it for a month. But you have to promise us an exclusive.'

'We're doing this?' Prince Julian gaped at both of his partners.

'Just imagine the amount of coin-chips the ensuing tourism will bring to Enoc,' Princess Jewel said, smiling widely. 'Everyone will want to visit and enjoy a romance of their own!'

Gods, they're all as terrible as each other, Grace mused. She was about to ask if they'd consent to an interview when she noticed Princess Rudbeckia frowning at Sean. He was doing his best to look everywhere else in the bridge.

'*You*,' the Utalian royal accused. 'You thought I would forget you. No. I know your type. Desperate, jealous, can't let go, can't share. You are a risk to our plans.'

'Hey, you're nothing special, Princess, I've had far more fun inside a Chipper outpost!' Sean burst out. He glanced aside at Grace, plainly stricken. 'Sorry.'

Grace sighed.

Prince Julian stomped his feet, pouting. 'They'll ruin everything!'

'Kill them both,' Princess Jewel ordered.

Princess Rudbeckia immediately rose from the couch and moved over to the wall, unclipping a weapon proudly displayed there and hefting it with both hands. It looked far too bulky and menacing to be a simple lasgun.

'Is that a — *flamethrower*?' Sean demanded, already retreating into the corridor ahead of Grace. 'In a starship? What the fuck were you thinking, bringing that in here?'

'We were thinking that you'd back into the fireproofed corridors!' Princess Jewel called.

'A Unandan vessel is never unprepared for intruders,' the prince added.

'Shit,' Grace and Sean articulated at the same time.

Princess Rudbeckia advanced, shaking with laughter, but the weapon in her grip never wavered.

Grace tried very hard not to think about a certain someone.

She failed. Utterly.

I don't want to die, she thought despairingly. *But I don't want to ask this of you either.*

Ignore your pride, Grace, just this once, Finara told her, not ungently.

Grace whirled around and gave Sean a shove. 'Get out of here! I'll slow them down.'

He might have at least had the decency to argue with her. But all he did was slap the wall and then he was off like a lasbolt, heading straight for the exit.

'A head start won't save him!' Princess Jewel taunted. 'And I can seal the access hatch!'

Grace glanced over her shoulder at the empty corridor, her lips forming her first real smile in hours. 'Neither of these things concern me. I just don't want him seeing this, especially if he's going to be hanging around me for a while.'

Princess Rudbeckia shrugged and fired a burst at the e-paper reporter.

I love you, Grace thought just before the flames hit.

The fire washed over her skin, a warm caress at first, but then it swiftly became an all-consuming cocoon of white-hot pleasure. Grace released a moan when the flames licked their way up her thighs, literally and metaphorically setting her on fire. The excitement of being encased in her lover's very essence, of being *invincible*, nearly drove her to climax — which would have been wholly inappropriate, given that the fire abruptly receded and the three royals were now staring at a very much alive (and very naked) Grace Pendergast.

Finara, you didn't need to destroy my clothes! Grace scolded. *Weren't you complaining about me ruining my shoes just last night?*

Laughter was apparently the only response she was going to get out of the goddess.

Shaking her head, Grace filled her voice with venom and disdain. 'I don't think I need to wait a month to publish my report anymore, do you? You have destroyed any skerrick of goodwill I had in the first place.'

'Please don't tell Daddy yet!' Princess Rudbeckia begged.

'Fuck you, I'll do what I want,' Grace snapped.

I'm a terrible influence on you but I can't say I regret it, Finara said, sounding amused.

Princess Jewel fell to her knees and began making her own pleas. The prince soon followed.

Grace rubbed her face, suddenly weary. 'Look. Your parents are abdicating in ten years when they turn seventy — isn't that right, Princess Rudbeckia? You can change the marriage laws then.'

Princess Rudbeckia sniffled. 'You're asking me to wait ten whole years?'

'That's exactly what I'm *commanding* you to do.' Grace lifted a hand and made a threatening gesture, as though she was about to summon flames. The princess flinched. 'And you'll do it. Or I will turn you to cinders, Princess. You're twenty years old. You're an adult. Act like it. Marry your husband first and avoid this senseless war. You can wait ten years to marry your wife — you'll live many more decades after that — and by then you all may have grown up somewhat. But I'm not holding my breath.'

Grace, the things I want to do to you right now, Finara purred. *This is a very hot look for you.*

You always think I'm hot when I'm naked.

That's not what I meant.

Grace grinned carelessly. *I know.*

'It's not fair!' Princess Rudbeckia wailed, smearing her palms over her wet cheeks. 'It's cruel to keep me from marrying the woman I love.'

'I know it's not fair,' Grace said, lowering her voice. She felt bad for the princess and wished she didn't, given that the woman had just tried to kill her. 'And I'm sorry. These laws shouldn't exist. But you endangered millions of lives when you ran away. And you've still got to think about what it means for three different planets to be joined together by marriage. I've never seen a situation like this. It's politically volatile.'

'I just started a new degree, a political science one,' Princess Jewel piped up. 'It could help.'

'Then you really should finish that degree before you get married,' Grace told her. 'In the meantime, I'll keep quiet and publish nothing about this whole mess. For ten whole years.'

'You'd have us believe that you'd bury a scoop?' Princess Rudbeckia demanded, suddenly no longer teary-eyed. Funny that.

'You don't really have any choice *but* to believe me at this point.' Grace crossed her arms over her bare chest. 'And if any of you mention what happened here, I can mention certain other things that happened. No royal on Utalia is immune to attempted murder charges. This isn't Enoc.'

'Does Ruddy have to go back?' Princess Jewel whined.

Grace sagged. 'Yes. Please. And she can tell Ton Tinel whatever story she wants to concoct. Leave me out of it. I want no part in disseminating lies.'

CHAPTER SEVEN

Within an hour, Grace was striding alongside Sean over dull grey floors and wearing a brilliant white jumpsuit that Princess Jewel had selected from her own extensive collection. Grace was of a similar build to the Enocian but not of a similar height, so she was well aware that her prosthesis was more visible than usual. However, the crowd in Utalia's major spaceport was far too fixated on the latest big Webcast to notice her, so no one stared or asked why she hadn't upgraded to synthflesh.

All around them, vidscreens filled with Ton Tinel's face were announcing that Prince Julian had bravely fought pirates for the return of his bride. It was a romantic story, easily digestible, and would probably spawn a hundred drama vids within a year.

All rumblings of war had ceased, but the crowd cared a lot less about that. Romance was far more exciting.

Grace was fighting a headache spawned by thinking about how long she'd have to wait for her work to pay off. Ten whole Old Earth years. Stark. She leaned heavily against the wall, not caring that grime was being caked onto her pristine clothes, and looked up at the nearby passenger vessels with longing. Her article count would stall whenever she took any time off, but that didn't mean her e-paper had to stall as well. And help didn't always have to come from an immortal goddess.

'Are you interested in a job?' Grace asked her companion.

A smug grin slapped across the grateful smile that Sean had

been wearing just moments beforehand. 'I thought you'd never ask. Being a free agent hasn't done me any favours. So where are we off to, Boss? Hopefully somewhere that we'll get a story we can actually tell.'

'Your boss is taking a badly needed holiday,' Grace said, rubbing her temples. 'But you can send her your reports and she'll consider publishing them in her e-paper.'

'Can my boss also consider giving her e-paper a name?' Sean asked. ''Coz people are going to start reading it. In ten years, anyway. It's not gonna impress my dates if I tell them about "that thingy I write with Grace Pendergast". Real classy.'

Grace pursed her lips, thinking back to the historical research she'd undertaken before starting her e-paper. Finally, she said, '*The Pendergast e-Post*. There, happy? Now go find me a story. I'll touch base in a month.'

He hooked his thumbs over the top of his jeans. 'So...am I getting paid?'

'Not yet. For now all I can cover are your expenses.'

'Guess I'm lucky to get that,' Sean said with a drawn-out sigh. 'I'll bill you when we next talk. See ya, Boss!' He threw her a jaunty wave and marched towards the nearest starship.

Grace watched him go, uncomfortable with the emotion she was feeling, not knowing what name to give it.

Worry, Finara supplied. *You don't like having to worry about someone. Love, I've done my fair share of worrying. About you. Yeah, it's definitely easier when you only have yourself to worry about.*

'Am I making a mistake, trusting him?' Grace asked, carefully retreating behind a starship and disappearing into its shadow.

Do you want me to keep an eye on him?

Grace allowed a grimace to escape. 'I wish I didn't have to rely on you so much. I feel so guilty.'

Finara's lips tickled her ear, heralding the arrival of the fire goddess in her human form. 'You don't need me, not for most things. Also, you're my girlfriend. I want you to succeed. I want you to be happy. So struggle on as much as you want — just know that when it comes to saving lives, especially your own, you can't stop me helping you. Don't ask me to stand by when you wouldn't.'

'Finara...' Grace drew a shuddering breath. 'About what I said...what I thought...'

The goddess pulled away and winked. 'Grace, I don't know what you're talking about. And even if I did, I know that's a thing you're definitely not ready to say to my face.'

'Ah, hmm,' Grace said vaguely, overwhelmed by relief. Finara wasn't going to bring up the fact that the L word had slipped from her mind in the (very literal) heat of the moment.

'Come with me,' Finara murmured, her fingers entwining with Grace's. 'And don't think so hard. You're on holiday.'

A vortex of fire roared into life, swirling up from their feet to their shoulders in moments.

Grace closed her eyes and succumbed to it without hesitation.

***

Sean Akiyama sat in his allocated cabin (a little more spacious than what he usually booked but hey, he wasn't paying for once) and smiled fondly at his tiny vidcam, an invisible patch that was quickly detachable and difficult to detect. He'd slapped it onto many surfaces before, including clothes, so the inside of a Utalian ship wasn't a big deal. Retrieving it had been just as easy; Grace had been too busy trying to explain her sudden nakedness to notice him feeling up the wall.

He connected the device to his techpad, humming as he accessed the footage and scrolled as fast as he dared towards the time frame he'd been absent for. Soon he'd know what had really happened back on the *Diamond Heart*.

Sure, Grace Pendergast had a self-sacrificing streak (anyone would know that about her after a day of her acquaintance), but her death would hardly have delayed his by more than a minute. When she'd turned to him and told him to run, she had worn a mildly annoyed expression. Fear had been entirely absent. If she'd stayed behind, it was because she'd been absolutely confident that she would survive. But the royals wouldn't have changed their minds about killing her without a starking good reason. What was she hiding?

So he waited. And he watched.

'Shit,' he said softly as a woman who had just been encased in flames started giving the royal trio a telling-off. 'So you didn't want me to see that, huh. I totally get it. I'd do more with this information than those kids would. I don't *think* you're a sub-level god, but the fire goddess doesn't let anyone use her powers, not even her own followers...'

Sean disconnected the patch and held it aloft in the palm of his hand, considering his options.

I can't be this much of a shitball, can I? he wondered.

The footage was worth so much it was practically priceless. This vidcam had never been directly connected to the Web either, in case of a remote hack, and so here he was, the sole owner of something pretty amazing. Exactly *what* it was remained unclear. But if a down-on-her-luck e-paper reporter hadn't used it to further her career, then it had to be a huge, juicy secret.

A secret that could make him wealthier than most of the galaxy's denizens.

With a sigh, Sean pulled out his lasgun, an outdated model he'd bought from the ship's captain (another expense, thank you very much), and rendered the miniature vidcam useless with a single low-powered shot. He experienced only a brief pang of regret.

'Yeah, can't really use vids as an e-paper reporter,' he told himself, trying to justify it to the man he had been a mere day ago. But he couldn't hide his thoughts from Finara.

I can't hurt Grace, not after what she's done for me, he'd decided.

Sean Akiyama lay back in his bunk and closed his eyes, blissfully unaware of just how close he had come to being killed by the goddess of fire.

THE CLONING OF DIANA NUMENI, PRESIDENT

CHAPTER ONE

Sean Akiyama, second e-paper reporter of the 66th century, looked out over the barren sands that covered the entirety of the small planet and drawled, 'So this is Dustball.'

'Exactly as advertised,' Grace Pendergast agreed and held up a hand against the star burning in the sky. A small shadow fell across her eyes, but it did nothing to dispel the glare bouncing off the cobalt dunes.

Sean shed his suit jacket and hung it over his arm. He had explained, far too often, that his abandonment of casual attire had less to do with Grace's preferences and a lot more to do with the fact that women tended to be easier to charm by a man in a suit. Adjusting the jacket to make sure it didn't wrinkle, Sean said, 'I thought Ilbb was bad, but this takes the platinum mine. No wonder mediaists have never touched down here.'

'It's a good thing we don't need any exciting images for our reports,' Grace said, glancing down when her communicator beeped. 'Our source, Janiche Jones, has informed me that she is on her way. Look interested if you can't look sympathetic.'

'Didn't get my contacts in the underworld by feeling sorry for them, did I?'

'Those contacts felt sorry enough to take you in when GLEA evicted you as a teenager,' Grace reminded him.

'There's a lot of paths that lead to crime,' Sean conceded. 'But our source picked Dustball to hide out on. It doesn't have a governing body or any laws enforceable by Chippers. Innocent people don't do that.'

Grace cleared her throat. 'Sean. There are many reasons our source might have sought sanctuary here. It is our duty to listen, to report, to inform — not to judge.'

'We're not supposed to interfere either,' Sean said. 'But for some reason Utalia and Unanda aren't at war.' He quickly danced ahead to avoid the glare she shot in his direction.

Finara, ignore me if I ask you to smite that man, Grace thought privately.

Come on, love, he's not that bad, Finara defended.

Since when did Sean earn your protection?

Since he proved himself and that's all I'll say on the matter. I have to go now, but I'll leave a small part of my presence behind. There was a tense pause. *I love you, Grace.*

Even in the heat, Grace shivered. She had thought those three magical words in a frantic moment some months ago and ever since then she'd been hyperaware of her girlfriend waiting for the sentiment to fall from her lips. Finara might make a show of being eternally patient, but she had a very short tether. She'd burn through it in no time.

'You alright, Boss?' Sean's voice cut through her reverie.

'Yes, of course,' Grace answered, moving forward to stand beside him, grateful that she had swapped her usual heels for more practical flats. Desert terrain wasn't particularly forgiving. 'Just deciding which angle I'll be taking with the interview.'

'Sure you were.'

Grace eyed him for a moment. 'I thought you wanted to shadow me so you could learn from the best. You do want me to stop correcting your work and let you publish more often, don't you?'

'If you didn't clam up so much, then maybe I would learn something,' he fired back and dropped onto the ground, legs crossed. He lasted a handful of seconds before leaping up with a yelp. 'Youch! Don't sit down, it's hot.'

'What would I do without you, Sean,' she said, completely straight-faced.

'Live in denial about your girlfriend problems?'

Grace opened her mouth, then closed it. Firmly.

'Stark,' Sean sighed.

'What?'

'I really thought I'd got you to crack this time.'

Grace lapsed into silence, annoyed that he had nearly pried something out of her. Sean shifted his weight between his feet a few times but didn't move more than a pace away. Their source remained markedly absent. To pass the time, Grace slid her techpad out of the case attached to her belt and pulled up the footage that most of the galaxy had already seen.

'So that's our source, the fearsome human who broke into Numeni Corp and stole their property?' Sean mused, peering over. 'I don't think she's even got a weapon on her.'

'Sometimes a techpad can do the work of a hundred lasguns,' Grace told him. 'All it takes is a bit of code to break open a door.'

'True, but it *does* take a lasgun to mow down the security grunts standing across the exit. How did she escape if not through them, huh?'

Grace did not have an answer for that. He had a point.

The woman they were about to meet claimed to be the one in the footage that Numeni Corp had released, but it was impossible to confirm this. The company had blurred the assailant's face, saying they would not reveal her identity while their paid security force was hunting her down. They'd specifically stated that they didn't want any mediaists finding the woman themselves and giving her and her 'destructionist' views a platform.

It always made Grace suspicious when corporations tried to ensure that theirs was the only side with a voice. Even more concerning, Numeni Corp had refused the help of the Galactic Law Enforcement Agency. The Chippers could be overbearing, but their services were free and covered the entire galaxy.

No, Grace wasn't going to give up on the idea that there was more to Janiche Jones' so-called 'rampage' than wanton destruction. Not until she'd spoken to Ms Jones, in any case. Most mediaists were already announcing in their Webcasts that the woman was a criminal. Some were even gleefully reporting that she had fled to another world to start indiscriminately killing whoever she came across.

Grace had kept her report centred on the facts (there weren't many) and had cast doubts on Numeni Corp's motives, citing previous investigations she had carried out against other corporations. This was probably why Janiche Jones (almost certainly an alias; it was the most common name in the galaxy) had reached out to *The Pendergast e-Post*. Grace wasn't exactly famous, but her body of work, however Ms Jones had stumbled across it, would have shown that there were times when the names of her sources were very deliberately left out.

'Boss, I know the real reason why you let me join you on this one,' Sean declared.

Grace glanced sideways at him.

'My superb connections!' he said and spread his arms, as if

inviting praise. 'You want me to see if I can't ask some *friends* of mine to help Ms Jones settle on some non-shitty world. New ID, clean bank account, the works. Too bad she hasn't got your connections.'

'What do you mean?' Grace asked.

Sean snorted and waved a hand towards the cloud-streaked atmosphere. 'I'm obviously talking about the program out there that's scouring the Web for any image of you and destroying it the moment it surfaces. A real expensive piece of work, I'm impressed, but you could also use it to help out, say, our most endangered sources — or maybe even your own employee. The one who may or may not be building up a reputation of his own.'

Grace loosened her jaw to keep herself from grinding her teeth together and shunted the fury out of her mind. She didn't want to distract Finara from her duties, especially since the goddess was discreetly working with the Chippers to evacuate a city lying in the shadow of an active volcano. Grace had had enough trouble convincing her girlfriend to assist the Agency after they'd sent through a message for 'She of the Fire's mortal representative'. Finara would use any excuse to get out of helping GLEA.

She's so sure I'm going to accept immortality, Grace thought. *That program would mask my unageing face from the galaxy. I haven't agreed to anything yet! Gods, the arrogance...*

'A program like that would have its uses,' Grace said at length.

'Call me crazy, Boss, but you don't exactly sound happy about it.'

Grace smiled briefly. 'I'm not calling you crazy.'

'What gives, Boss? If I was you, I'd love to have that program running for me!' Sean exclaimed. Grace wasn't sure what gave her away, but the next moment he was nodding sagely. 'Girlfriend's responsible for that, huh? You need it. No, listen! One day there will be thousands of e-paper reporters and no one'll care, but you're the first. People are gonna be curious about your identity. You'll become a target to those you've pissed off. So what's the harm in it?'

'She didn't ask me if I wanted this.'

Sean's eyebrows knitted together. 'Sounds like you two need to have a good, long chat. Don't worry, she'll make time for it if she wants to keep you around.'

There was no point responding to that so Grace didn't even try.

Eventually, as the star began taking its ten-hourly dive towards the horizon, their source came upon them, wearing a cloak and carrying nothing except for a small flask of water. She was a woman of average height and had three moles on one cheek, hardly a distinguishing feature among billions of humans. But she did look identical to one of the most famous women in the galaxy. Namely, the president of Numeni Corp.

'Warm greetings,' the fugitive said hoarsely, then swallowed. Her voice smoothed out but lost none of its tremors. 'Thank you for agreeing to meet with me, even though I'm sure you guessed I was using an alias and a poor one at that. I'm Diana Numeni. Something awful is happening at my company. And you're the only ones who can do anything about it.'

CHAPTER TWO

Night fell fast. Too fast.

Despite being aware of the planet's abrupt sunsets, Grace still found herself startled by the shadows racing past her and fumbled with the climate-controlled blankets that Sean had unpacked. She reached for a solar-charged heater next, pausing when she saw that it was a Numeni Corp product, and looked around for an ideal location for it. But she was too slow.

Diana Numeni withdrew combustible sticks from inside her cloak, then tossed them onto the ground and tapped them with a metallic rod. The ensuing explosion of light transformed the darkened sand back into vivid blue.

Grace didn't miss the fact that the flames curled towards her, like a meek child seeking the approval of a parent. A sudden ache of loneliness displaced the anger she had been feeling towards Finara only a few minutes earlier. When they were together, it was easier to use flesh instead of words to express her feelings. She couldn't tell Finara about her innermost thoughts, or about the dreams she'd been having lately, the ones in which her body was engulfed with fire, leaving Grace at the mercy of a goddess in her true form —

Grace forced her attention back to her techpad, which was showing a live feed being Webcast by a mediaist on the steps outside Numeni Corp's headquarters. A spokesperson for the company was overdue in delivering the latest update on the hunt for the intruder.

It was safer for Grace to keep watching the feed than to explore her own mind just now.

'What I want to know,' Sean drawled, 'is why you would attack and badmouth your own company.'

Numeni's eyes glinted like the surface of an obsidian blade. 'Because one of the greatest crimes in the galaxy is being committed by Numeni Corp. And I cannot allow it to continue.'

Grace was about to chase that lead when Numeni Corp's spokesperson appeared on screen, descending the stairs to take the podium. It was unmistakably President Numeni. According to the subtitles, she was harshly condemning the intruder, who still had yet to be named or given a face.

Wordlessly, Grace held up her techpad. Sean jerked a full pace away from Numeni.

'That's not me!' Numeni insisted, then deflated with a sigh. 'Well, it is, but it's not.'

Grace pressed her palm against the techpad, hiding the footage. 'Now, there are only two crimes that this galaxy can agree on — most planets do things their own way and have their own laws, but these ones are universal. What are they, Sean?'

'All cloning of sentient beings is banned,' Sean supplied, leaning onto his elbow and regarding Numeni with suspicion. 'And so is the construction of anything with artificial intelligence. 'Coz no one wants another galaxywide uprising on their hands.'

Grace hesitated, knowing her next question would be confronting. 'I am sorry to ask you this, Ms Numeni. Are you a clone or a bot?'

'Neither!' Numeni said hotly. 'I'm the original Diana Numeni. I'll prove it.'

She thrust her hand forward, without any urging, and kept it there while Grace detached the DNA scanner from her techpad and took the required readings. Grace lowered her eyes while she waited for the analysis, wanting to give Numeni a few moments to compose herself.

When the practice had still been legal, clones had been made with certain markers in their blood — markers that ensured they couldn't access the coin-chips in the bank accounts belonging to their source material. Clones who escaped the facilities that had birthed them had become understandably angry about their lack of rights and had banded together. Their attempt to take over the galaxy two centuries ago hadn't been quite as successful as the ancient bot uprisings, since clones were designed to have a short shelf life — usually a few months.

'If you're the original, why would they replace you?' Sean demanded.

'Because I found out they were using clones!' Numeni retreated into her cloak, her face downcast. 'I'm telling the truth — why won't you believe me?'

'Would *you* believe someone who looks like a clone?' Sean asked.

Numeni lowered her hood and fixed her frown on him.

Sean managed to look abashed.

'She's telling the truth,' Grace said, slipping her techpad into its pouch. The results were clear. 'I'm inclined to believe her story, whatever it is.'

Grace said nothing more and let the silence build, let Numeni remind herself that she had no one else to talk to. She wasn't going to find another reporter on Dustball, not for centuries.

'I think,' Sean said, well before enough time had elapsed, 'that we *need* to hear what you have to say, Ms Numeni. It's important on a galactic scale, if clones and bots are involved.'

'Just clones,' Numeni replied, seemingly mollified. 'And you are correct. You need to hear this. Everyone does. Too many corporations are placing profit before the safety of the galaxy. They *must* be held accountable.'

Sean winked at Grace. Reluctantly, she gave him a nod in return; his methods were different than hers, but they weren't entirely without merit.

Grace cleared her throat. 'Why don't you tell us what happened, Ms Numeni? Take your time. Any small background detail could be useful.'

Grace and Sean had several hours until the ship that had deposited them on Dustball came back to collect them — along with the second half of the fee promised to the captain — and Grace intended to make the most of the time they had. If this story was as huge as it promised to be, then she wanted every what, every when and every *how*. This wasn't just a report; it was history in the making.

'I'm sure you know what we make at Numeni Corp,' Numeni said. Pride softened her features as she paused to stroke the edge of the reflective blanket that Sean was using for warmth. 'Survival gear. For extreme conditions. But more than that, each piece is a work of art. Individually built, inspected and tested. We were the only company in the galaxy that used a living being's eyes and hands to ensure the quality of our products. Everyone else was using machines at the time.'

'An expensive feature to set your company apart,' Grace noted. 'Especially when you have to employ so many people.'

Diana's hand slid back into her lap. 'Yes. We had to pass on that cost to our customers. Our first clients didn't seem to mind, especially since they had the coin-chips to burn, and it was a novelty. But then other companies started doing the same thing — and they paid their people significantly lower wages. Which meant that their products were *much* cheaper.'

'So you had to pay your people less,' Sean spoke up.

'Most, if not all of them, resigned,' Diana said softly. 'But it was fine. Cheaper workers appeared almost overnight. I didn't meet any of them; all I cared about was how many we had.'

Grace pursed her lips. 'My research tells me you built your company from the ground up fifteen years ago. Numeni Corp's advertising makes a point of mentioning how you've worked every single job within the corporation. Let me hazard a guess. The cheaper workers that were provided were cloned off you, most likely given duplicates of your memories as well...'

'I didn't even realise.' Numeni's gaze was lost to the fire. 'I'm not involved in the day-to-day minutiae anymore. I just assumed my accountants were keeping everything aboveboard...' She laughed darkly. 'I must seem extremely stupid to you. Thinking that our newest workers had agreed to such low wages! Thinking nothing of it when my own techs asked for a detailed brain scan!'

'But you noticed that something strange was going on,' Grace told her. 'And when you found out what it was, you risked everything to try to put a stop to it. That's commendable.'

Numeni's smile looked like it was concealing the abrupt and painful removal of many teeth. 'It was the least I could do, considering that the safety of the galaxy was being so recklessly discarded in my name, and in my image.'

'So you went in and dug out the proof you needed,' Sean guessed, two knuckles pressed against his lips. 'Then they realised what you'd done, knew they couldn't say it was you without looking suspicious...and instead told everyone there was an anonymous criminal on the loose, in order to justify the mercs they're throwing onto the streets. But there's not much they can do when you're free and clear with the goods.'

'About that...' Numeni trailed off, her brow creasing.

Grace held in the sigh. 'You didn't get any solid proof. And you know that we run stories without naming our sources or showing the raw evidence.'

'Boss, this is important!' Sean exclaimed.

'We need more proof, otherwise this becomes a bedtime story,' Grace said evenly. 'It would make my e-paper little better than an adventure zine. This is not something we can blindly rush into.'

'But the *galaxy's safety* is at stake!'

Numeni kept out of the argument, but her eyes continued to burn into Grace's. She'd guessed correctly that Grace was the deciding vote here. Sean didn't call her 'Boss' for nothing.

'Why couldn't you get the evidence you needed?' Grace asked. Cloning was serious. It could mean another uprising, another deadly war with a foe desperate enough to do anything to survive. The galaxy was so divided, with its thousands of planets and respective governments, that it was impossible for any of them to agree on anything long enough to band together, even against a common threat.

Sean crossed his arms and gave Grace a look of savage triumph.

He knew she was hooked.

'As you may be aware,' Numeni began, her lip twisting, 'my company does not keep our server connected to the Web. Perhaps if we did, and gave our information freely to the public as TerraCorp does, this would never have happened. But what's done is done.'

'So you had to go after the server yourself,' Sean commented. 'Brave.'

'Did you make it to the server?' Grace prompted when Numeni's gaze grew distant. No doubt the woman was still blaming herself for what had happened at her company.

'Yes. Just.' A frustrated sigh hissed out of Numeni. 'I'm no beginner when it comes to accessing systems, but the server was too well protected. I needed a hacker. I'm lucky I escaped with my life. Given the choice, however, I'd have traded it away to get that information out there.'

Sean nodded fervently along with this. Grace didn't miss the sparkle in his eyes when he looked at Numeni, nor the shy smile he received in response. She swallowed the lecture she had for Sean about his inability to avoid intimacies with his sources.

'Why Dustball?' she asked instead.

'It's where I came from,' Numeni explained, staring straight through the darkness as though she could see the distant, invisible horizon. 'I was born here.'

'*Here?*' Sean repeated. 'But it's a...dust ball. Did it look better then or something?'

Reaching for the water flask in the pack Sean had dropped earlier, Grace went over what she knew about Numeni. The woman's earliest years were hazy and neither her birth nor its location had ever been entered into the Galactic Database, something that wasn't unusual on worlds that had no planetary authority keeping an eye on the comings and goings of the lives beneath them.

'Oh! No, no.' Numeni laughed and readjusted her hood. 'It's always been like this. I was born into a desert-based tribe that moved here to claim the planet as their own. They told me I shouldn't look to the stars. That I should stay and live a simple life.' She sighed. 'I should have listened.'

Grace lowered the flask and pressed her damp lips together. All of the desert-based tribes scattered across the galaxy had just one thing in common; their deity of choice.

'And your god, the Desine, couldn't help you with this matter?' she asked Numeni.

Sean rolled his eyes. 'Oh, sure. The sub-level gods do everything we ask them to.'

Grace shifted uncomfortably.

'The Desine has always watched over me,' Numeni said. 'He gave me the powers I have used all my life, the powers that my family uses to sense dangerous sandstorms. And, when it looked as though I would be overwhelmed by my company's forces, I pleaded for his help. Without hesitation, he encased me in a tornado of sand and brought me here. Or did you think I was able to discreetly board a starship, with this face?'

Sean's mouth dropped open. 'He *teleported* you? But — why? The Desine isn't known for giving a shi...for his compassion.'

Finara didn't care for those beneath her until she met me, Grace recalled. *And she was so afraid that I'd been sent to her to teach her compassion, just as the Desine's wife was sent to him...*

Numeni shook her head, visibly annoyed. 'He's not like that. Not since the Year of the Silence. The Desine loves us. He cares for us. And he...' Numeni paused, biting her lip. 'He feels like he understands pain. And loss. That's why he helps us when no one else will. So.' She straightened. 'Here I will stay, with my tribe, until the end of my days. And I would be content with this fate, except that my company is still free from scrutiny or censure.'

Numeni's words were strong but her eyes were hollow and she touched her fingers to her palms. Grace looked down at Numeni's hands. No binding scars. Finara had explained how the gods wed each other — a ritual that resulted in them gaining identical scars on their palms — and Grace was aware that the Desine's worshippers did something very similar amongst themselves. Numeni was with her own people again, but she clearly didn't expect to find love and mourned for it.

I've been there, I've been her. But I did find it. Grace quickly buried that thought. With any luck, Finara was too busy elsewhere to have heard it.

'We need a hacker,' Sean said. 'And access to the server.'

'Impossible,' Numeni replied with a swift flick of her hand, dismissing the notion. 'Even if they got close enough, my techs are the best in the galaxy. Do you know any who could best them?'

'I don't know any hackers, good or bad,' Sean admitted. 'I have criminal contacts, sure, but hackers are a secretive bunch. Hard to locate, even harder to hire.'

Grace sat there for a while, letting their words wash over her. The decision was easier than she'd expected it to be. When she finally stood, the wind picked up and tugged sharply at her pantsuit, making her jacket flap hard against her back. She steadied herself, painfully aware of her audience and their questioning eyes.

'Give me a moment,' she said and walked away, communicator encased in her palm.

Darkness swallowed her. Now standing so far from the warmth of the fire, Grace wondered if it was only her imagination that the sand was shifting beneath her feet or if it really was planning to drown her. Was the Desine here? Was he watching, listening, judging? Was he angry that she had entered his domain with another deity so clearly etched on her heart?

Would Finara be able to protect her from him?

Grace started when her communicator made a sound. It was already poised at her lips and someone was speaking to her. She must have called her contact.

'Now me, I knew you'd call, but not because you want to talk to me, no,' mused Gerns in her laid-back tones. It had been more than two years since Grace had met with the Jezlo and written a story about her, but this was definitely the voice she remembered. 'I know you're just callin' me to call in that favour. Alright. I can handle the disappointment.'

Despite herself, Grace laughed. 'I'm sorry to be so predictable, Gerns. I know you said you'd get your hacker friend to make a story of mine go viral, but I was wondering if I could morph that favour into something else.'

'Well, I'm listening, but I can't promise I'll do it.'

'Fair enough,' Grace acknowledged. 'Could you please put me in direct contact with your hacker friend? Trust me, I wouldn't ask if it wasn't important, if it wasn't for something bigger than me.'

'Bigger than you and your ego? Sounds serious.'

'It is. The future of the entire galaxy is at stake.'

'I'm gonna go now, Grace,' Gerns said. 'But keep that communicator on, huh?'

The connection died with a minute click. The silence didn't last.

A vagrant wind howled and Grace blinked furiously as specks of sand were hurled into her face. Distantly, she heard Sean's and Numeni's voices, though she had no clue what they were talking about and didn't really care right now. She strained her ears for one sound only.

Her communicator beeped.

Grace didn't recognise the ID displayed on it and wasted a precious second debating whether or not this was a good idea before answering. 'Grace Pendergast, e-paper reporter.'

'Hello!' a female-sounding voice said. 'Gerns tells me you want to cash in a favour. What can I do for you?'

Grace winced. She hadn't expected the hacker to sound so pleasant or to offer her aid so quickly, and in the background there was a chant increasing in pitch and volume, one that sounded an awful lot like 'Mum! Mum! *Muuuuum!*'.

'I apologise for wasting your time; this is too dangerous for you,' Grace said.

'Too dangerous? I'll be the judge of that, Ms Pendergast.'

'Your child...' Grace trailed off.

'Tell me about this favour,' the hacker interrupted. 'I don't have to agree to your proposal, so it costs you nothing to outline your problem to me.'

Grace raised her eyebrows at the communicator. 'Everything has a cost.'

'I'll name it. But you've got to tell me what's going on.'

Grace said nothing.

'You don't know who you're dealing with and that's making you nervous,' the woman guessed, not incorrectly. 'Very well. I'll give you my identity and you can trade me your story. We'll be even. I was born Feiscina Neron. That's not my name anymore, but it doesn't really matter since most people just call me Fei...'

Feiscina Neron! Grace felt her eyes go wide. *The programmer who saved everyone on Yalsa 5 and gave Ton Tinel a massive scoop that made him billions of coin-chips in a single day...*

'I assume that's adequate, since you've no objections,' Fei said, amusement colouring her words.

'Yes. More than.' Grace cleared her throat and spent several minutes explaining her situation before finishing with, 'We would have to make it *to* the server to begin with.'

There was a tapping noise, as if Fei was slapping her techpad against the edge of a desk. 'And they'll have amped up their security after President Numeni's attempt to reach it. Well, this is a problem, but not a huge one. Numeni Corp is on Hoffa, in the Granite System, isn't it? I wouldn't even have to be away from home very long.'

'Can you do it?' Grace asked.

'Of course I can do it. You might not like my price, though.'

Grace swallowed, mentally taking stock of the money she had in her accounts. She needed to be able to cover her and Sean's expenses for the upcoming month. 'How much.'

'My price...' A gentle laugh. '...is to meet you, face to face, in my home.'

'*Muuuuuummmm!*' shrieked the child in the background.

'What's the catch?' Grace asked suspiciously, though she felt that the noise Fei's child was making might be catch enough.

'Where do I begin?' Fei mused. 'There are many. Catches, that is.'

Grace ground her teeth together. 'Please. This could potentially be the greatest story of my career — and more than that, this about the safety of the entire galaxy.'

'Then you won't mind speaking to me about Finara, will you? For the safety of the galaxy, that is.'

Grace stared furiously into the night. The wind was now clawing at her, as though trying to scour her entirely from the surface of the planet. She ignored it. Feiscina Neron...a known worshipper of Bagara, the sub-level god who had also stepped in to help Yalsa 5.

'Kuja's wife?' Grace chanced, using the rainforest deity's true name.

'That's me,' Fei confirmed.

'You don't know what you're asking.'

'I know *exactly* what I'm asking. And who knows, you might get to have words with the person responsible for the software that's been scrubbing your face for the past year or so.'

'*You*,' Grace growled.

'Yes, little old me! So what about it, Ms Pendergast?'

Grace let a reluctant sigh bleed over her lips. 'If your husband doesn't make an appearance.'

'He won't.' Spoken so confidently, by a woman who held sway over a god.

'Alright,' Grace said.

Hopefully she wouldn't regret this.

CHAPTER THREE

Sean Akiyama had never seen his boss so rattled.

When she stormed back into view, the fire roared up in front of her as though to greet her, or perhaps to reflect her turbulent mood. She took a moment to glare at it, her fists knotting at her sides. Behind her the sky remained as black as coal, but Grace carried with her an inner light, one that blasted any secrets out of her way — except her own.

Sean may have destroyed the footage of Grace being engulfed by flames, but it wasn't so easy to erase those few seconds from his mind. He had never heard of the fire goddess imbuing anyone with those kinds of abilities, though if his suspicions were correct then the goddess had a good reason for doing it. He wasn't stupid enough to bring this up with Grace; she wouldn't keep him around (or keep throwing coin-chips at him) if he dared to ask questions.

There was also the chance he'd be burnt to a crisp by her girlfriend.

He might be wrong about that last part, though. Maybe.

'So...?' he prompted after exchanging shrugs with Diana Numeni.

'I have a hacker,' Grace said grimly. 'But she wants to meet with me. In person. I'll have to do it if I want her cooperation.'

'Sounds...reasonable enough,' Sean hazarded.

His boss visibly ground her teeth. 'I suppose it *sounds* that way. Sean, when that freighter comes back at sunrise — which should be in about six Old Earth hours — you will pay the pilot to take you to Hoffa. There are plenty of mediaists crawling over Numeni Corp right now, so you won't stand out.'

'Will do, Boss,' Sean acknowledged and reached for his techpad. 'Should I see if I can scrounge up some extra background for our report?'

'Perhaps, with Ms Numeni's permission, you can get some filler before you go,' Grace said with a nod at Numeni. 'I'll be leaving shortly. Keep your communicator on, Sean, and *please* let me know before you chase up a lead.'

Sean offered her a sheepish grin. He knew exactly what she was referring to — he'd nearly had his life cut short by some ruffians only two weeks ago. He had neglected to tell Grace about that particular meeting, but she'd still shown up with power in her voice and not a single lasgun to rescue him. She was fearless.

He'd be fearless too if he knew She of the Fire would swoop in to save him.

'I trust you,' Grace said, her eyes narrowing. 'Gods know why, but I do.'

'Sooo, if you trust me, then you'll tell me how you're getting off this dust ball,' Sean tried.

Grace hesitated, then shook her head.

Regret passed over her expression.

He held up a hand, forestalling any lie she was about to give him. 'No need to apologise. I get it. Safe travels, Boss. See you on Hoffa.'

She turned on her heel and stomped away. The moment her shadow merged with the black night, Sean quickly stood up, tossed a 'just a moment' down to Numeni and ran after Grace. He was lucky she had her communicator on. The small light on the device guided him to her and cast a glow over her preoccupied frown. She hadn't noticed him following her.

Sean hit the ground and slithered forward on his stomach.

As if he'd miss this. It was the highlight of his job.

Within seconds, a confusing jumble of vines and dirt swirled up from her feet and began to dance dizzyingly around her. Grace stiffened, her hand clenching her communicator, her mouth forming a tortured shape — and then she vanished. Teleported away, perhaps to another planet entirely.

'Vines instead of fire, Boss?' he mused. 'Well, that's a twist.'

As he made his way back to Diana Numeni, dusting blue sand off his white shirt, he wondered if mingling with the gods was as stressful as it appeared to be.

Gods, I hope Grace gets some support, someone to keep her sane, he thought. *Looks like she needs it.*

Why do you think I haven't killed you yet? asked a voice filled with the roar of a wildfire. The presence of the fire goddess was undeniable and it momentarily froze him in his tracks.

'Ms Numeni!' Sean called, his voice cracking. 'Let's have a chat, shall we?'

Diana Numeni was still sitting where he'd left her, looking decidedly nonplussed about either being stuck with him or her situation in general. She needed some cheering up. So he skidded through the sand and landed hard on his shoulder, grinning smugly when he saw that he'd ended up lying perfectly beside her. Her expression remained unchanged.

'I assume you want to hear more about how I discovered the clones,' she said flatly.

Sean's gaze travelled beneath her cloak. 'Well, among other things.'

Numeni studied him for a long moment, making him feel as transparent as plexiglass. 'I'll tell you everything I can. But I want something in return.'

'Everyone has a price,' Sean said soberly, wondering what she was after. He did not have many coin-chips to his name.

'I have a problem, Mr Akiyama,' Numeni informed him, leaning over until their faces were aligned. 'I'm not going to be with a man for a very long time. At least, not one I'm not related to.'

Sean perked up. 'Ah, yes, that would be an awful prospect.'

'I think we understand each other.'

'I believe we do indeed, Ms Numeni,' he drawled, taking her hand in his so that he could kiss each knuckle.

Her slow smile did things to him.

And Sean had every intention of doing things to her.

But first he had to set up a tent, because it was unexpectedly cold and he didn't fancy braving the night air with only his skin for protection.

***

Grace swayed, not sure where her feet were planted or if they'd found stable ground.

It took a moment to reorient herself. She was inside a small house made out of wood and dirt — or more accurately, design and chaos. The sparse furnishings and threadbare rugs did little to welcome her and the moist air clung to her clothes, weighing her down. She sank to the floor, still fighting dizziness, and slumped

112

against a large cushion that was far too forgiving. Its lack of support caused a sharp ache to start low in her back.

'Are you okay?' Feiscina Neron asked, purple eyes wide in concern as she swooped down to check on Grace. 'Haven't you been teleported before? Oh, I'm so sorry! I had no idea, you must have been terrified. Just breathe. I'll get you some tea.'

'No, I...' Grace swallowed with difficulty. 'I've been teleported. Just not...with trees. Or vines.'

Fei nodded, smiling. 'But you will need tea. I definitely need some!'

She abruptly bounced away. Her hair, falling down past the middle of her back, looked as thick as Grace's own, though clearly Fei smoothed hers out with chemicals (Grace had nothing against this look; she just preferred to maintain her hair with less abrasive oils). Fei had a slighter darker complexion than Grace, though not by much, and was clad in a bright wriggle dress that contrasted sharply with her visitor's charcoal pantsuit.

Fei also liked to talk a lot more, seemingly carrying on a conversation with herself as she brewed the tea in the next room. She soon reappeared, a tray balanced in her hands, her mouth still moving. '...and of course both of us were very pleased when you came into Finara's life. She was so wrapped up in herself until you gave her that stern talking-to.'

Grace couldn't help the smile as she remembered lecturing the Firine for expecting mortals to worship her. Finara had needed to hear that she wasn't entitled to admiration, that her purpose as a member of the Galactic Pantheon was to care for all mortals, regardless of their religion. Having planned to meet her death by walking into a pyroclastic flow, Grace hadn't particularly cared if the goddess killed her for speaking so bluntly.

Fei delicately set the tray down on the rug and then dropped onto the cushion opposite Grace. 'But Kuja and I are also the ones who have to spend several hours reassuring Finara that you care for her. The rants about you — God, the rants! Do you know how many I've had to sit through?'

Grace felt the smile fall right off her face. 'I don't like that she has been speaking so openly about me to you.'

'She has to speak to *someone*,' Fei argued, hands clenched on her knees, tea apparently forgotten. 'Finara is going half mad, you know. She gets that she has to take her time with you, but she's reached the point where she's convinced that you will never reciprocate her feelings. It's destroying her! So please, if you know you will never love her, then *let her go*. It'll be much kinder if you do.'

Grace reached for one of the tiny teacups and stared into the steaming water, unable to find the words. Finally, she managed, 'I...I hope you will still consider helping me with this situation on Hoffa, regardless of the impression you have of me.'

'Oh for stark's sake!' Fei cried. 'Forget Hoffa! I'll help you because it's important, no matter your connection to my sister-in-law. Right now, I want you to do the best thing for both you and Finara.'

'She just needs to be patient,' Grace said evenly.

'What are you waiting for!? Stark it, Grace, *what*?'

Grace's grip tightened on her teacup. 'I don't yet know if I'm ready for marriage. I want to make something of myself first, prove that I can stand on my own. But Finara keeps overstepping, keeps making assumptions. That facial recognition program, for example — preparing me to live forever.'

Fei's eyes widened. 'Grace, that was my idea. She argued against it.'

'She didn't...?'

'No! I said that it would protect you for now, because dating a god can be dangerous. Your name is already known to Finara's siblings — I didn't want your face to be as well. Some of them are so spiteful!' Fei sighed. 'Oh, this mess is all my doing. I only convinced Finara by saying I'd deactivate the program when — *if* — you broke up. She made me swear that I would.'

Grace, flummoxed, stared into her lap.

'And Grace,' Fei continued, voice firming, 'I don't mean for you to take this too lightly and be tempted to do it just because, but here goes. The binding? It can be removed. And Finara has already said she'll take the scars away if you marry her only to regret it.'

'I'm not ready for marriage,' Grace tried again.

'She knows that! But you can love someone without marrying them — in fact, you should probably figure that out *before* you get married! So, do you? Do you love her, Grace?'

'She knows I do!' Grace exploded.

'No, she doesn't.' Fei slid a hand behind a nearby cushion and pulled out a techpad. 'You only thought it. One time. And she doesn't think you meant it.'

'She told...' Grace began angrily, but then the vid on the techpad's small screen began to play. The angle showed that it was taken from a vidcam stowed in the corner of the very same room that Grace and Fei were occupying right now. The fire goddess paced, apparently unaware that she was being recorded.

'She doesn't love me, not really,' Finara said, her voice so tortured that Grace felt heat prick her eyes. 'She would if I was completely human. I just know it. I can't change what I am, Fei! She keeps accusing me of robbing her of the chance to succeed in her career on her own merits. Is it wrong of me to want to help the woman I love? She'll succeed anyway, stark it, it's only a matter of time! She's that good! And I just want to fucking love her as much as I can *now*, eternity be starked. I want to be my full self with her.' Finara caught what sounded suspiciously like a sob in her hand. 'But she won't love a goddess.'

Fei entered the scene, carrying the same jade tea set on a tray. 'I loved Kuja as a man first, then I loved the god. It may just take time.'

'Time,' Finara repeated dully. 'Time can't manifest love if it's never going to appear. She's never going to be able to say it.'

'Finara...' Fei sighed.

'No. I should have known when Father sent Grace to teach me a *lesson*, to make me give a shit about mortals, that I wasn't supposed to get involved with her. She's her own woman, Fei, and I can't force her to feel anything.' This time the sob was more obvious. 'Why does this *hurt* so much?'

The vid stopped.

'Oh gods,' Grace breathed. 'I never...I didn't realise...'

Fei held her gaze unflinchingly. 'Why can't you accept that part of her, Grace?'

'I do, I do love her!' Grace snapped.

'Then why don't you tell her?'

Grace opened her mouth, then closed it.

'It means accepting that you love a goddess,' Fei said with a small smile.

'It means accepting that I will always have a crutch, a way

out,' Grace admitted quietly. 'I'm always tempted to ask for her help. But I can't let our relationship affect my work.'

'Isn't it already affecting your work?' Fei asked. 'Finara tells me you're becoming more reckless, because you know she won't let you die. In the most dire situations, you've even asked her to read minds for you and it's gotten you results. How do you think I intend to get close to the server on Hoffa, Grace?'

'Your husband,' Grace realised.

Fei nodded. 'I've had Kuja's help before. To save lives. Do you want to help your source? Do you want to keep helping people when no one else can?'

'Yes,' Grace whispered. 'But I can't use her like that.'

'It's not a matter of *using*,' Fei said, leaning forward, her expression earnest. 'Finara loves you. She wants to support you and your career. Billions of beings in this galaxy have done the same thing for the ones they love. I get it, though. You're scared that loving a goddess compromises your integrity, because it comes with the knowledge that you won't die so long as Finara is at your shoulder. And it comes with the privilege of being able to find information that no other mortal can.

'But, Grace, with Finara's powers behind you, you can change lives. You can *save* them. Few others would use this gift as wisely as you. Not everyone has your strength. And that's why Finara isn't afraid to offer you her aid — it's because you would only accept it *for the right reason.*'

They drank their tea in silence, or as much silence that could be found in an uninsulated hut that was only a stone's throw from a waterfall that boomed away eternally, content to keep gouging into the rock beneath it.

'It means setting aside my pride,' Grace said finally. 'Admitting that I can't always do it alone.'

'Do you love her more than your pride?'

'Yes, a thousand times yes!' Grace cried. 'I love her. I love all of her.'

Her chest lightened when she said this. Because she knew she meant it.

She loved the woman with the mischievous grin, those quick fingers and that sharp mind. But she also loved the goddess who shielded her, who carved out time to be with *just her*, who cared for her like no one else ever had. Grace thought back to that time on Utalia, when the fire had surrounded her and nearly brought her to climax, and of the dreams she'd had since then, revisiting that glorious moment. She wanted Finara to engulf her, to make love to her in the way only a goddess could.

'I love her,' Grace affirmed. 'Gods, how I love her. And I will for as long as I live.'

'Uh, Grace, be careful how you word that...' Fei said, casting a wary eye around the room.

Grace shook her head. 'I don't need to be careful. Because Finara knows I'm not ready for eternity. She knows that marriage is not the only way I can express my love for her. And she's listening right now, isn't she?'

'I told her not to...' Fei muttered.

'I am certain that a significant part of her presence has been here for a while, if not since the moment I arrived,' Grace said wryly, then raised her voice. 'Finara, show yourself! There are things I need to say to your face.'

A vortex of flames exploded into being.

Grace threw aside her teacup and went to greet her lover.

'I'll just, um, be outside,' Fei said as she sidled towards the door.

Finara stood very still, arms stiff by her sides, her expression wavering between longing and fear.

You still think I won't say it? Grace asked silently.

Finara nodded.

'I love you, Finara,' Grace said, cupping her girlfriend's face with both hands.

'Grace, don't say this just because you feel bad for me...'

'I'm not. I love you, Ms Fire Goddess. And I'm going to tell you about a fantasy I've been having. Perhaps it will prove to you that I really want *all* of you.'

Finara's eyes glowed. 'I can already see it in your mind.'

'I have some time before I need to be anywhere,' Grace told her, smiling.

CHAPTER FOUR

Despite dreaming of this scenario for months, Grace found herself unaccountably nervous.

Relax, Finara soothed, now in her insubstantial form. *It's still me. And I'm not going to judge you for your body's reaction. In fact, I'm going to love your reaction. Almost as much as I love you.*

Grace's muscles refused to loosen at first, so she focused on breathing slowly, filling her lungs with blistering air that should have scorched her lungs but didn't. The whole situation would have been absurd to an outsider's eyes; she was lying on a bed of writhing lava and was surrounded by seemingly infinite quantities of molten rock on a world that had yet to settle or invite life onto its surface.

Naked and vulnerable, Grace was bared to the elements — and the touch of a goddess.

She was exactly where she wanted to be.

A tongue of fire lapped at her ankle, then lazily wended its way up to her thigh. Grace squirmed in anticipation, but Finara's flaming caress had already dropped to her other ankle, trailing sparks over her prosthesis and stump before darting so, so close to where Grace throbbed for her lover.

'Please,' Grace whispered.

Who's impatient now, Ms Hypocritical Mortal?

Grace groaned, closed her eyes and tried very hard not to move.

Better, Finara purred.

When Grace was finally able to look down again, there were ropes of fire swarming over her body, drawing lines of pleasure across her skin and tightening with each passing second. Gasping, Grace flung her head from side to side as excess flames glided over her breasts, teasing her nipples and coaxing them into peaks. The knot inside her abdomen was now quivering faster than her heartbeat.

One sly flame danced towards her core — then darted away from it. Grace arched her back and cried out, wanting more, needing more.

'I want to be encased in you,' Grace panted. 'Please, Finara.'

Say it.

Grace didn't need to ask what her lover meant.

'I love you,' she whispered.

Say it again.

'I love you, I love you, I love you!'

The fire cocooned her, taking her whole.

Grace screamed, unable to find the words, hoping Finara could draw meaning from the jumble of thoughts inside her mind. Her entire being was soon reduced to the pulsing sensation between her legs, a hot, deepening pressure that kept pumping out wave after wave of heat, until Grace thought she would die from the intensity of it.

Finally, drained and exhausted, she collapsed back against the lava, her limbs aching from how awkwardly she had held them. A strangled whimper escaped her lips. Usually Finara would have wrapped her arms around Grace, but this time tendrils of fire squeezed her gently, keeping her in one piece as she rode out the shivers still cascading throughout her body.

She could *feel* Finara all around her. And it was wonderful.

Did you like being at the mercy of your goddess? Finara asked slyly.

'You know I did,' Grace moaned, stretching out her arms above her head.

'Say it,' a voice laden with desire said.

Grace smiled over at the woman who had appeared beside her. 'I love being at your mercy. I love being inside you. *And I love you.*'

Finara's pleased smirk would have woken something inside Grace had she not been so truly spent by the experience. But one of them wasn't so spent.

Grace looked forward to returning the favour, feeble though her mortal attempts would be. She leaned in, but Finara pressed her fingers against Grace's lips, halting their progress. 'I know you're uncomfortable with using all the...gifts at your disposal but, Grace, they're freely given. And I know you'll not abuse them. I trust you.'

Grace hesitated. 'That trust, it scares me — for now, anyway,' she added when Finara frowned. 'But I'll have to make my peace with it. Because there will be moments like this, with stories like this, when it's too big for me, when I can't do it without you. If I have to sacrifice my pride for the good of the galaxy, then so be it.'

'Mmm, talk reporter to me,' Finara said in a low voice, taking Grace's hand and guiding it between her thighs.

'Really?' Grace asked, amused.

'*Yesss,*' Finara hissed.

Grace laughed and indulged her.

***

'You look much better, Boss,' was Sean's greeting, delivered with a knowing grin.

'And you're...glowing,' Grace returned, bemused.

They were standing at the back of a crowd of mediaists who were eagerly watching the podium, where a version of President Diana Numeni was giving yet another speech about her security force's progress in hunting the anonymous destructionist. Hoffa's balmy, tropical air was more suitable for a resort than a factory, but the pleasant climate did make the idea of an intruder seem even more horrific. Most mediaists had begun releasing reports to this effect — and none of them shouted the right questions when Numeni invited them to ask away.

Grace looked aside at Sean again. Still glowing. She'd never seen him like this before, as though a star had taken up residence inside him and was leaking light from every crevice.

Your source back on Dustball put that glow on him, Finara supplied.

Grace sighed. 'Sean, what have I told you about sleeping with your sources?'

'That it can make us biased towards them,' Sean answered. He smirked, seemingly unconcerned that she had guessed what he'd been up to. 'But you can't deny that my methods have managed to get us extra tidbits over the past few months, right?'

Grace wished she could deny it. But she couldn't.

She braced herself. 'At least tell me you slept with Numeni *after* you interviewed her.'

'You should know better than to ask me that, Boss,' Sean said cheerfully. He schooled his expression into something more neutral when Grace threw him a well-deserved glare. 'Look, do you want to hear what she told me or not?'

Grace pried her jaw open. 'Let's hear it.'

It took all of a nanosecond before the words exploded out of him. 'They found a way to omit the markers in the clones! So we can't tell the difference with a blood test! That's going to make things harder during the next uprising for *sure*.'

Stunned, Grace shoved aside the unease his words had stirred inside her gut and demanded, 'If this is true, then how do we know that we spoke to the original Ms Numeni?'

'There's probably no way to tell,' Sean admitted. 'Even Diana wasn't sure. But she figured I ought to know before we hit the sheets, so to speak, in case she was misleading me accidentally. Now would a clone be that considerate?'

'If the source material was considerate to begin with,' Grace replied, keeping her eyes fixed on the clone or the original or whoever it was still posturing at the podium.

Finara, she called inside her mind. *Is there a way to know? Can you see?*

If the person is from my domain, then yes, Finara said guardedly. *But Numeni's from the deserts. I would have to speak to my brother, the Desine. And no way am I doing that.*

What about your father, the Creator God? Grace asked.

Finara's tone gained a sharp edge. *Yeah, good luck getting a straight answer out of him. And I haven't forgotten his part in bringing us together.*

He didn't make me fall in love with you, Finara.

Grace realised that Sean was watching her carefully. She wondered if she'd missed a question or a comment of his and if he was expecting some sort of coherent response.

'What is it?' she asked.

He held up his hands, exposing his palms in a defensive gesture. 'Oh, nothing...just thinking I should ditch my independent projects so I'm here to look after you when you zone out like that.'

'I don't need to be looked after,' Grace told him.

'Yeah, well, I like to keep my skin on my bones,' Sean said, then shuddered. 'Skin I'd totally lose if I let something happen to you.'

Grace eyed him for a moment. 'There'll be time to discuss this later, Sean, whatever it is.'

'Figure we should discuss it at some point,' Sean agreed.

Grace cursed herself for training him to look where he shouldn't.

Finara, she tried again. *Are you sure you can't ask your brother?*

Grace, my love, one does not simply talk to the Desine. He's...angry. Unstable. Violent. And he could very well kill me. He won't even speak to Kuja anymore.

Don't approach him, Grace ordered.

Grace, if you need me to go to him...

No! I won't risk losing you. You mean more to me than any answer the Desine could give us.

Grace stewed for a few minutes, watching the supposed President Numeni waltz back up the stairs. This revelation about the markers complicated her story further; it would force her to slow down and look for the real Diana Numeni...and what if the clones were already preparing another uprising?

'It doesn't matter, you know,' Sean said.

Grace blinked. 'What?'

'It doesn't matter if Diana's the original or not,' he went

126

on, his voice firm. 'She did the decent thing and got out. This Numeni?' Sean waved a hand at the empty podium. 'She has to have noticed what's going on in her company, clone or not. And she's doing nothing about it.'

Grace pressed her lips together, considering his words.

'So...?' Sean prompted.

'We don't have time for this,' Grace decided. 'Let's assume that we've spoken to the real one, or at least the version that deserves to be treated as such.'

Sean nodded slowly. 'Alright. So how do you want to play this?'

Grace looked down at the heels that she preferred to wear, the ones she had made a point of putting on before Finara brought her to Hoffa, but knew they wouldn't be much use for what she had planned.

'I wish I didn't have to interfere so much,' she muttered.

'Why? Because that's what they taught you at mediaist school?' Sean ribbed her gently. He had no formal training of his own, something Grace was trying to rectify by mentoring him. 'You're not a mediaist anymore, Boss. And interfering? We're just stealing information and throwing it up on the Web. It's not like we're catching a princess to avert a war.'

'Oh yes, how dangerous could it possibly be?' Grace asked with a twisted smile.

Sean groaned. 'Oh gods, *why* did you have to say that?'

***

Fei dropped into the acrylic booth Grace had sequestered in the bar, caught sight of Sean and did a double-take. 'Hello! Wow, you're rather ordinary. I expected someone who looked like a vidstar, given the warnings Grace gave me about you. She said you were trouble.'

'It's not about the quality of the goods but how you use them,' Sean insisted.

Grinning, Fei held out her hand. 'Feiscina Rforine, formerly Feiscina Neron. You can call me Fei. I'm married to someone who I think is as handsome as a vidstar, so don't take it to heart.'

'How could I possibly take it to heart?' Sean said dryly as he took her hand and shook it.

'The server,' Grace cut in before any more time slipped away. 'Did you find it, Fei?'

Fei slumped in the booth. 'Yes. And it's well guarded.'

'How well guarded?' Grace asked.

'Forty armed and armoured humans. I suppose it could be worse but not by much.'

Sean whistled lowly. 'We're starked.'

'Any suggestions for dealing with the guards?' Grace ignored the sinking feeling in her stomach.

Fei absently tapped the table. 'These guards are not doing anything illegal, merely protecting property, so having someone send them straight to GLEA is out of the question.'

'I agree,' Grace said, knowing that Fei meant getting Kuja or Finara to teleport the guards into the Agency's prison cells on Gerasnin. 'GLEA would have no choice but to release them. And what's worse, the guards might even speak to the mediaists about how they were...*removed*. We cannot allow that.'

'Alright, we need a distraction,' Sean declared, bringing his hands together and splitting them apart in a vague gesture that might have been meant to indicate an explosion. 'Something to draw the guards away so Fei here can hit the server in peace. I know a few people who can help us out.'

'Of course you do,' Grace said.

'They'll need payment though,' Sean warned her.

Grace rubbed her temples. 'Of course they will.'

CHAPTER FIVE

Explosions blew gaping holes into Numeni Corp's granite facade at midnight.

Mediaists fell out of their beds and ran to the nearest windows, their sweaty hands tossing vidcams into the warm night air so they wouldn't miss anything as they hurried down internal stairs. It was obvious that neither the offices or the showrooms were under threat. No, fire was belching out of the tech wing. Where every item created by the company began its life — and also where the company's server happened to be.

The ensuing eruption of heavy lasgun fire told the mediaists that the attack wasn't done. Blocked by a ring of nervous-looking perimeter guards, breaths stuck in their throats as they recorded the damage, the mediaists thought they were as close to the action as any reporter could be.

They were wrong.

***

Grace peered around a cooling unit, then snapped her head back as lasbolts tore through the space where her skull, hair and flesh had been only moments beforehand.

The assault on the entrance to the tech wing had managed to lure exactly half of the guards away from the server. Covered in armour and their faces hidden inside reflective helmets, they didn't hesitate before firing upon the mercenaries that Sean had dredged up from somewhere. But Numeni Corp could afford the best tech, the best personal shields and the best lasguns. Their guards would not be the first to die.

And twenty of them had yet to make an appearance.

There's still too many people near the server for Fei to teleport in safely, Finara reported.

Grace glanced at Sean, who was cowering behind a thickset panel connected to the side of a conveyor belt. He caught her looking, grinned and then gave her two thumbs up. He was *enjoying* this, stark him. Once his 'friends' lost the charge on their shielding devices, there was a good chance they would all die. It didn't matter that they had willingly hired on knowing they would be storming a building filled with lasgun-toting guards. She was still the one at fault.

More deaths to add to her tally. More blood to stain her skin.

Grace grimaced until her teeth cut into the inside of her cheeks. She'd refused to carry a lasgun but she had taken the grenade the mercenaries had offered her, because she had no intention of leaving any information about cloning tech anywhere inside the building.

You can't destroy the server before Fei gets what she needs, Finara reminded her.

I can't destroy it if I can't even get close, Finara!

The fire goddess laughed gently. *Sure you can. Get close, that is.*

And then what? Grace demanded. *Stand by while you use your powers to kill the guards?*

I'd do it, Finara said. *For you. But you won't ask me to.*

Grace closed her eyes briefly. *No. I can't let you take a life, even for me. I'll find some other way to clear the server room.*

'Hey, Boss!' Sean shouted.

Grace looked back up in time to see the silver cylinder he tossed at her. It passed through a stream of lasbolts, miraculously avoiding them all, and slammed into the hand that Grace held out to catch it with. The item was lighter than she expected and a quick search for the brand name on the slick surface revealed that it was a top-of-the-line personal shielding device. Only the wealthiest families in the galaxy could afford something like this. But it still wasn't the most expensive thing she'd ever held.

Grace ground her teeth together and forced the childhood memories back into the recesses of her mind, where they belonged. The oldest ghost that haunted her thoughts would only distract her now.

'My friends weren't even going to bring that tonight!' Sean said, grinning. 'They were keeping it in their inventory to sell to some rich fool. I wasn't planning on pinching the shield, honest...but a little voice in my head said you'd need it.'

'This won't last long enough for me to get past the guards in our way!' Grace argued, hoping she had misunderstood Sean. Surely Finara wouldn't speak to him so openly.

Sean rolled his eyes. 'C'mon, Boss! You and I both know you're the only one who can slip away without anyone noticing. So slip!'

Grace opened her mouth, then closed it.

'We're having that discussion *later*,' he said pointedly.

Grace nodded and clapped the device to her chest. One button was all it took to activate the self-adhesive and the laser-based shield. The instant the orange sphere sprang up around her, she hit the ground and rolled underneath a large duct, putting herself in a cramped position that hid her from both mercenaries and vidcams (Fei had helped her locate blind spots on the factory's blueprints earlier).

'Can you teleport me near the server without them seeing how I did it?' Grace asked softly.

Yes.

'And without them shooting me full of holes?'

Hey, give me some credit, Finara said, a defensive bite to her words. *Grace, if this shield fails, I'm pulling you out no matter who sees it.*

Grace swallowed. 'I won't even try to stop you.'

Her lover's fiery essence swept around her, cocooning her, and within seconds she was lying somewhere else, somewhere less intense.

Grace drew several breaths as she slowly got to her feet. She was now standing in a long corridor lined with silver pods clustered from floor to ceiling, like the scales of an armoured beast or the static shields of an Old Earth army. Disoriented, she wondered if she'd been teleported into a starship instead of a different section of the same building. But she knew very little about how Numeni Corp made their products. Maybe this was a standard feature in a factory that manufactured survival gear.

And yet...

'These weren't on the blueprints,' Grace realised. 'Cloning pods?'

Yes, Finara said grimly. *It's ancient tech, but you don't forget it.*

Steeling herself, Grace headed for her destination. It wasn't far. The moment she rounded the last corner, Numeni Corp's masked security force turned towards her, weapons at the ready.

Behind them was the server, covered in ports for techpads to jack into and releasing a gentle, low-pitched hum. It was a perversely soothing background noise for the confrontation.

'Wait, wait!' Grace called with her hands up. 'I'm unarmed — all I have is this shield!'

And the grenade clipped to the back of your belt, Ms Starking Liar, Finara pointed out, sounding more tense than playful.

'Intruder!' cried a voice that carried an unusual echo.

Twenty lasguns started firing.

Grace's shield lit up with an array of dots, all of them red, all of them deadly. Without even checking on the device affixed to her shirt, she strode forward, chin held high and shoulders straight. Her lungs were already struggling against the heated ozone filling the confined space and the shielding tech buzzed ominously as it funnelled more and more power into the rusty-hued field surrounding her. But she was closer to the server than anyone else in her group. And she had more than mere violence in her arsenal.

'Please, give me a chance to explain!' Grace bellowed over the sounds of lasgun fire. 'Numeni Corp has been making clones. Yes, clones! And the information that can prove this is on the server. No one needs to die — but I do need to tell the galaxy what's happening! We have to end this here and now. *Billions* of lives are at stake!'

Suddenly, as if they were perfectly synced machines, the guards lowered their lasguns.

Grace smiled — half in hope, half in disbelief.

In one smooth motion they doffed their helmets and blonde hair of exactly equal lengths lashed out of hiding. Twenty copies of the same face greeted her. And then twenty Diana Numenis threw back their heads and laughed.

'You...' Grace stared at them. 'How can you go along with this?'

They all shrugged and spoke as one. 'It is in our design. We are not to care, so that we can effectively carry out our duties.'

'Doesn't that make you angry? That someone decided if you *care*?' Grace's voice cracked. She idly noted that Sean had definitely slept with the original Numeni if this was the case. The woman left behind on Dustball actually cared. There was also the fact that these women didn't seem to realise they should have sand-based abilities to use against Grace — that or the Desine had refused to bestow them powers since they weren't really his followers.

The clones shook their heads. Their lasguns rose again.

'We have to destroy you,' they said. 'We cannot allow anyone to endanger the server.'

Grace retreated several paces, a hand straying to the grenade behind her back.

'Why?' she asked.

They paused.

'I'm going to die anyway,' Grace tried desperately. 'You might as well tell me!'

'It contains the galaxy's only copy of a detailed manual of the cloning process,' they intoned. 'We need to create more sisters. You want to stop us. So you must die.'

Grace's options narrowed down to one. Just one.

'I have in my hand,' she said flatly, 'a grenade that can obliterate this entire section, including those pods that can give you more *sisters*. If you want to stop me, come get me!'

She turned and ran, the grenade sliding around in her grip and the backs of her shoes slapping her feet. The temptation to swap all her heels for flats like these was growing exponentially by the day.

Finara, are they all chasing me? Grace asked, trying not to pant or look over her shoulder.

Yes. Fei is at the server now.

Grace allowed a crazy grin as she rounded another corner.

For stark's sake, Grace, don't lead them back to her! At least not yet.

'Sorry, I got lost!' she wheezed and zigzagged in another direction — a decision which saw renewed lasgun fire explode over the shield.

Grace glanced down at her chest. The shield didn't fail but it emitted a high-pitched whine that refused to desist, even when she tried threatening the device under her breath. Seconds later she tripped, lost her balance and fell backwards, plummeting towards a hovercar-sized shaft that dropped far below into the bedrock —

— and then a vortex of fire swam over her.

Grace blinked. She was now underneath a cooling unit, nose pressed against the many lines of text warning anyone from getting too close while the machine was in operation. Judging by the sound of identical voices calling out to each other as the Numenis hunted her, she hadn't gone too far.

They didn't see! And you were out of vidcam range! Finara insisted before Grace could say anything. *And it doesn't matter if they see anymore, does it?*

Grace jerked her head into a nod and rolled out of her hiding spot. She couldn't send the clones to their deaths, but she could send them to GLEA — who would hopefully keep the mediaists away from their cells. They had a good reason to. The existence of clones would cause untold panic if it got out.

Grace stomped her feet as loudly as she could, then shouted, 'Maybe your company should have cloned someone more intelligent! You can't even catch a noisy, unarmed reporter.'

She bolted down the corridor when she heard the approaching echo of their booted feet.

Is Fei through the firewalls yet? Grace asked, badly wanting to bend over and throw up.

Yes, Finara replied. *She's just copying everything she thinks is useful. Don't rush her.*

Grace hit a right angle in the corridor and collapsed against the wall. She had barely touched it when a lick of flame forced her off the cold stone surface. She staggered back onto her feet, gasping.

I could toss them over to Gerasnin right now, Finara offered, naming GLEA's homeworld.

No, too many vidcams, Grace said. *We need to make it look like they die in the explosion when you teleport them to GLEA! The Chippers will do their part to keep up the ruse.*

They'd better, Finara growled. She'd never been a fan of the Galactic Law Enforcement Agency and refused to speak to them. Whenever the Chippers needed the fire goddess' help, they had to contact Grace, an acknowledged intermediary.

They don't want anyone to know they work with sub-level gods, Grace assured her girlfriend.

She realised she was heading back towards the server, towards Fei. Grace's steps faltered. Her heart followed suit when she felt her back heat up as lasgun bolts sprayed the length of the corridor. The shield took the brunt of it. For now.

Fei's done — blow it! Finara commanded. *I'll magnify the explosion.*

Grace lurched forward and kept going until she came upon the deserted server. She wanted to be absolutely sure that the information contained on it was pulverised.

'No, no, no!' chorused the voices of Diana Numeni behind her.

The vidcams are all focused on me? Grace asked mentally.

Yes, Finara answered. *But your face won't be recognised; Fei's program will take care of that. Numeni Corp won't know who they're watching.*

Good, Grace said. *I'd rather Grace Pendergast didn't die today.*

It would set your career back a tad, the goddess agreed.

Smiling, Grace thumbed the switch on the grenade.

The ensuing blast flung her away from the server. Despite her trust in Finara, she half-expected to hit the wall or have debris punch holes into her body. But after a moment she realised there was no chance of anything ever harming her. Her physical form had vanished and she was nothing but flame and fury. Thrilled and unafraid, Grace joined with another entity, one that possessed her heart and soul, and lost all sense of time and self.

She was utterly consumed by love and there was no need to fight it. Not anymore.

When Grace came to, she was lying on the road outside, staring up at the intense blaze that had engulfed the entire tech wing. She wobbled onto her feet, struggling to find the words to explain what she'd just shared with Finara and coming up woefully short.

'Boss! You're alive!' Sean exclaimed, hurrying down the road. He laughed and waved vaguely over his shoulder at the destruction. 'Well, not that I expected anything less, considering your patron, but we don't have time to hang around. C'mon. You've got a report to write.'

Grace gratefully accepted his help in steering her towards a nearby hotel. Once ensconced in a dingy room, she pulled out her techpad and found that Fei had already sent through what she'd ripped from the server, though her message was missing the crucial information that would allow someone to replicate the cloning process (that data, Fei promised, had been erased permanently).

Usually it took Grace a couple of days to be happy with what she'd written.

This time it took two hours.

The whole Web was already waiting for her, thanks to a preliminary story that Sean had started running at the time of the explosions, promising that only *The Pendergast e-Post* would have the full details on the Numeni Corp situation. His report would have been largely ignored had Fei not sent it viral, making sure that every techpad connected to the Web received a copy.

Grace worried her lips together. For the first time in her career, she'd actually lied to her readers. Sean had informed her that Numeni had specifically requested to be killed off, so that she could live out her days in peace on Dustball and never again be used to endanger the galaxy. Grace could respect that. She'd ascribed the second attack on the facility to the original Diana Numeni and reported that the president had died while blowing up the server.

Grace slumped in her chair, exhausted but victorious.

Sean's hand touched her shoulder. 'Get some sleep, Boss. I'll be in the room next door if you need me. You'd better not pester me until you've had some shut-eye, though.'

Grace's veins were buzzing and she had no intention of bedding down, but it took barely a minute after he'd left for her eyelids to stick shut.

CHAPTER SIX

Dawn light slid its way in through the grime on the window. Skimming a palm over her eyes, Grace sent her other hand searching underneath the pillow until it found her communicator. She held the device in front of her face until she could recognise the ID of the person calling her.

An agent of GLEA. Not just any agent — their Head General.

She had expressly forbidden the Chippers from contacting her via communicator. And they shouldn't even have her details to begin with.

Disengaging the connection, Grace located her techpad on the bed beside her. She couldn't remember moving from the chair in the corner, but Finara often teleported her into more comfortable positions. Grace stowed the smile and checked her readership, as she always did the morning after a story had broken — then bolted upright in bed.

The read count was in the *billions*.

Grace didn't have a public inbox attached to her Web account, so she was spared having to wade through countless requests for her time or endless vitriol spat by anonymous readers. But there was a message from Fei.

> You've become an 'overnight sensation', Grace. But we
> all know how much work you've put into your career for

this moment — Finara never lets us forget that. Kuja hopes you will reconsider meeting him, but I told him that sometimes one god in a mortal's life is more than enough.

Use your gifts, Grace. Use them for the good of the galaxy.

Fei

PS: Can you spare some time to talk to GLEA's Head General, Zareth Sins? He's not that bad. I've been Kuja's intermediary with the Agency for years.

PPS: Zareth is starting to annoy me. Please answer his calls. Or else.

Grace stared at Fei's words, frowning. If the rainforest god's wife trusted the Head General...

Her communicator trilled again.

This time she answered it. 'Grace Pendergast, e-paper reporter.'

'Thank you for speaking to me,' a deep voice said. 'I know you are a busy woman, especially now, but you are also She of the Fire's mortal representative.'

Grace trapped her annoyance behind her teeth and forced a smile into her voice. 'Head General Sins. It would be rude to send you forty clones and not thank you for dealing with them. Have they been saying anything interesting?'

'You mean, do they find it odd that instead of killing them, the explosion teleported them to Gerasnin?' Sins asked dryly.

Grace said nothing. He'd answer her soon enough.

'If they do, they cannot impart that opinion onto anyone,' Sins said. 'Our mutual involvement with She of the Fire remains a secret to all but the highest ranks. We have conducted our own tests and have ascertained that the clones will deteriorate in a couple of months. I thought that might set your mind at ease.'

'Not really,' Grace murmured. 'They were so...cold, uncaring. And single-minded. But I will mourn them.'

Sins cleared his throat. 'I can respect that. But we at the Agency would appreciate some warning before you send us that many prisoners. And perhaps you'll inform us of a situation like this earlier next time. So that we can act in your stead.'

'Would you have had enough agents nearby to deal with this, General Sins?'

His silence spoke volumes.

'You need She of the Fire's help,' Grace reminded him. 'You cannot look after this galaxy alone. Remember that before you reach out to me again.'

'Can I use this method to contact you in future?' Sins asked.

Grace blinked blearily at the sunrise. 'Yes. But don't expect me to answer.'

'And don't expect me to blindly give in to your patron's demands,' Sins said tightly. 'The gods are not infallible. They are more like us than they would care to admit.'

The connection between their devices died. Grace looked down at her communicator, feeling an ache grow behind her forehead as creases wrote their way across her skin. It would have been easier if she could continue to think of the Head General as some distant nuisance.

And it would have been easier to dismiss him if he'd been more of a fool.

***

'I've been told I can trust you,' Grace said after Sean had let her into his room, one that was just as cramped and unappealing. 'I'm not sure what you did, but you impressed my patron.'

'I may have destroyed some footage I had of you on Utalia,' Sean admitted as he dropped onto the bed. 'That was before the program erasing your face went out on the Web, I might add.'

'How uncharacteristically noble of you,' Grace noted.

Sean laughed, rubbing a hand over his jaw. 'And stupid. I could have made a lot of money off that. Sooo...She of the Fire has got your back. Well, Boss, you must be something. If I'm guessing right about your girlfriend problems, that is.'

'I can ask her to smite you,' Grace said, her lips curling.

'Nah, she wouldn't do it.' Sean sounded far too confident for her liking. 'She needs me watching your back. A goddess has to step out sometimes.'

He's not wrong, Finara said. *I do have my duties to attend to. And it would look less suspicious if you sometimes received help from a mortal instead of a god.*

Grace sighed. 'Both of you make excellent points. Unfortunately.'

'Can I convince you to get your own lasgun then?' Sean asked.

'Don't push it, Mr Akiyama.'

***

She was waiting for him when the ship set down on Dustball.

Though coin-chips were now pouring in from the eager new sponsors of *The Pendergast e-Post,* Sean Akiyama was far from

146

being able to buy his own ship. But for now, he could hire pilots and bribe them so that this destination never became common knowledge. He had to be careful; his name was swiftly spreading across the galaxy because of his connection to Grace Pendergast.

'I only managed to get a few days off from the boss — didn't want her getting suspicious,' Sean said. He swallowed nervously, hoping his fiancée hadn't changed her mind. 'Now, where were we?'

Diana Numeni sashayed forward, a grin playing along her lips. 'You promised me the best decades of our lives.'

'That I did,' Sean said solemnly.

Without another word, she took his hand and led him to her tribe.

When Sean Akiyama left Dustball one Old Earth week later, he was wearing dark leather gloves. He fielded Grace's questions about his new attire with a flippant remark about how he was hoping they would help him appeal to potential conquests, though his new-found fame certainly wouldn't hurt.

Grace raised her eyebrows but made no further comment.

He didn't dare tell her about the binding scars that lay hidden beneath his gloves.

THE TRANSGRESSIONS OF EMAN PROST, CEO

CHAPTER ONE

There was a certain freedom in not owning an office, in not needing to remember to clean out your desk or feed some amphibious creature in the corner. *The Pendergast e-Post* often existed in a literal vacuum and today was no different.

Grace Pendergast and her only employee were conferring in the belly of a freighter, having rented out its hold while it was docked at a space station above Fintaz, a world famous for its artisans and the exquisite glass temple they'd fashioned for their worship of the Creator God.

This meeting was mostly concerned with choosing and allocating stories. For over two years, the e-paper had been flooded with pleas from people desperate for the galaxy's most famous reporters to come to their worlds and write about the injustices afflicting them. Other messages coyly asked if *The Pendergast e-Post* would help improve someone's image, despite that *someone* being engaged in the slave trade. Those requests always carried the promise of lucrative sponsorship in return for Grace Pendergast's assistance.

Even if they didn't already have a slew of more ethical sponsors, Grace would still have refused them. She'd spent long, uncountable hours running her e-paper without any financial remuneration before it became wildly popular. If she had to once again resort to using her girlfriend's coin-chips to get by, to continue to expose the truth to her readers, then she would. It didn't worry her.

But she *was* worried about the other e-paper reporters popping up all over the galaxy. It was highly likely they didn't share her views or her morals.

'Look, yet another application from someone wanting to join our outfit,' Sean Akiyama said, his techpad held so limply in one of his gloved hands that it was in danger of hitting the floor. 'I've only received about a hundred of them in the past hour. Remind me why we had to add a public inbox to my Web account instead of yours?'

Grace shifted on the crate that formed her seat and grimaced when the rigid metal pressed lines into her skin through her pants. She gave Sean the same excuse, as always. 'Because I need to remain an enigma to mortals and immortals alike. For my safety.'

'And what about my safety, Boss?'

'Last time I checked, Sean, you weren't dating a goddess.'

'Oh sure, use that against me.' He laughed. 'You're lucky I'm in a good mood from how well my last report was received.'

Grace dipped her chin into a small nod. 'It was very good. No one would have guessed that Warlord Lindali was actually using her ill-gotten gains to liberate and rehome trafficked women. How did you get her to talk so openly about it?' She arched an eyebrow at him.

'Hey, not the way you think, Boss!' Sean said with an aggravated wave of his hand. 'I didn't sleep with her, I swear.'

'That's a change. How did you manage it then?'

Sean retreated into his jacket, eyes diverted from hers. He mumbled something.

'You arranged a false ID for her and gave her safe passage off the planet?' Grace repeated.

'How else was she supposed to retire in peace, huh?' Sean demanded. 'Can't have the Chippers busting her for breaking the laws on her homeworld when she's done so much good for so many people.'

He gave her a defiant look. He didn't need to.

Grace smiled. 'I'm not sure I would have done it any differently.'

'See, I was just anticipating your will,' Sean said, emerging from the safety of his jacket.

'Hmm. Just don't take too many liberties with *anticipating*.' Grace flicked through the messages on her techpad, the ones he'd forwarded to her after a program had filtered out the worst of them. 'There's a lot of junk here. Missing people. Slight grievances. Nothing on a galactic scale. Just small fry that our new competitors will go after. Anything stand out for you?'

'Well, there is my request for leave...'

'Four weeks,' Grace confirmed. 'You want to take it now?'

'Yeah, look, I know it's longer than last time but I've, uh...' Sean squirmed on his crate. 'I've got family stuff going on.'

'You kept in touch with them?' Grace eyed him. 'I thought you were raised by GLEA's Orphanage Division until you were fifteen.' He even had the scars on his temple to prove it — anyone who left the Galactic Law Enforcement Agency had the chip (which gave the agents their unusual abilities and the unflattering nickname of 'Chippers') peeled out of their skin.

'Family's not always the people you share blood with,' Sean pointed out.

'True,' Grace said, even though he was clearly deflecting her.

'Alright. Once you disembark consider yourself on leave. This station is full of starship captains between jobs, so you should be able to get anywhere you want to fairly quickly.'

'And what about you, Boss?' Sean winked. 'Holiday with the girlfriend?'

Grace sighed. 'Don't give her any ideas. I can't set aside my work until you get back. One of us has to stay on to keep this e-paper running.'

'So what *are* you going to do with your time?'

Grace held up her techpad, her smile turning wry. 'Choose something and hope it pans out.'

She was still scrolling through her options some hours later, after Sean had slipped off his crate and fallen asleep against the curved chrome wall, his mouth hanging open as he snored. He'd looked tired ever since the previous day, when he'd received a message on his techpad that had shot panic across his face. Sean didn't usually keep secrets, so he had to have a good reason for doing it now. He still had her complete trust. He'd earned it.

Grace set her techpad down when she felt the freighter's chilly hold suddenly heat up. *Finara. I did not call you. And you have duties to attend to.*

Here's the thing about us gods, the Firine teased. *We can split our presence into a thousand pieces — give or take. So I can totally check in on the woman I love. Just because I can. No other reason.*

This isn't a social visit, Grace surmised.

No, love. It's not.

Grace rubbed her temples. The headache wasn't even her first warning that this might have something to do with the Galactic Pantheon.

Does Fei need me for something? she asked. It wasn't an

unwarranted question. Feiscina Rforine, the wife of the rainforest god, was a hacker and often found incriminating information she wasn't sure what to do with. Grace provided a convenient outlet; the reports she wrote based on Fei's information led to arrests conducted by the Chippers — and Grace never named her sources if they could be endangered by the publicity. Fei's identity was always protected.

No, it's my sister, Finara replied, sounding reluctant. *Renaei.*

The Tirine? The tundra goddess? Grace sat up straight, startled to hear a name that Finara had mentioned in passing more than once.

That's her, Finara confirmed.

Finara, I... Grace wet her lips. *I don't know if I should meet any of your siblings.*

What if I said there was a good story in it for you? Finara baited. *You love a challenge. Especially if it involves a big bad corporation, a seemingly unbeatable foe — that sort of thing.*

Grace's hand tightened on her techpad. The goddess knew exactly how to pique her interest.

One of Sean's eyes opened. 'Boss? You good? Girlfriend problems again?'

'No, not that it is any concern of yours,' Grace replied firmly. 'But it seems that you won't be the only one chartering a vessel.'

'Awesome! She of the Fire got you a story?' Sean jumped back onto his crate, apparently catching a renewed wave of energy. 'It must be big.'

'I'm not sure, I haven't got the details yet,' Grace said.

Sean bit his lip. 'She of the Fire, will you need me to back Grace up on this? I...I have things I need to...but look, I'll do it.'

You need to see to your family, Sean, Finara told him, allowing

Grace to hear the exchange. *Grace will be well protected. You don't need to worry. Well, about this anyway — you've got enough to worry about already!* A laugh.

'What does she know that I don't?' Grace asked, eyes narrowed at Sean.

'Oh, that?' He waved a flippant hand. 'That's between me and my goddess, Boss.'

Grace directed her next words at thin air. 'Finara, is this something I need to know about?'

Nope, Finara said simply.

'I'm not sure which one of you is annoying me the most right now,' Grace muttered.

***

Trox was a planet so out of the way that Grace had to part with more coin-chips than she usually would to convince a captain to take her there. The corridors of the ship she'd ended up on seemed to be constantly groaning and multiple non-essential systems were malfunctioning. Grace stepped into the shower, grimacing in preparation for the icy water that Captain Naistu had warned her to expect. But as soon as Grace swiped the sensor on the wall, she was smothered in warmth.

She turned her smile up into the spray. *I take it this is you apologising for making me meet one of your siblings.*

'No,' a voice said in her ear as a similarly unclothed body pressed up behind Grace. Finara's hands slid down her wet, trembling thighs. '*This* is me apologising.'

'You do realise,' Grace said, gasping when Finara's fingers

found what they were looking for, 'this ship is poorly soundproofed.'

'That's not a problem for me. For you, on the other hand...'

Five minutes later, a lot sooner than Grace had planned on (having to bite down hard on the inside of her cheek to keep from making a sound might have hastened things), a clean and sated e-paper reporter emerged from the ship's poky bathroom.

Renaei wants to talk to you, Finara informed Grace as she made her way through the ship towards the bridge. *She's a bit impatient. Okay, a lot impatient. She's younger than me, but she's still had millennia to learn some patience. Anyway, she's grumpy that I didn't let her teleport you straight to Trox.*

Since 'patience' and 'gods' were not two words Grace would have put together when she'd first met the Firine, she refrained from making a comment to that effect. It wouldn't be fair to Finara, who had since changed her attitude and respected Grace's need to come to terms with the eternity that would accompany any marriage between them.

Renaei does realise that I can't just appear on a planet without any obvious indication of how I got there? Grace questioned, offering a nod to Captain Naistu as she entered the cramped bridge. *The only ships in orbit around Trox belong to N'radian Manufacturing. They'll notice that no other vessels have shown up. It's best to avoid unnecessary attention.*

You might have better luck than me at explaining this to Renaei. Finara's ensuing laugh faded. *I'm going now. I know you prefer time to yourself when you're starting a big story. Just behave when you meet my sister.*

If she behaves, then I might consider it, Grace shot back. *I love you, by the way.*

Love you too, Grace.

'Sent a message to my kids when you boarded,' Captain Naistu suddenly said, her voice gravelly from either disuse or from inhaling too many fumes in her antiquated engine room. Even she looked surprised by how she rough sounded. Naistu cleared her throat noisily. It didn't seem to help much. 'I always do when I take on passengers, so they know who to hunt down if I go missing. Anyway, I told 'em your name. They said you're famous. Are you?'

Grace dropped into the co-pilot's chair which was conspicuously vacant, but given how small the ship was it probably didn't matter that it only had a crew of one. As if to prove that thought wrong, an ominous rattle in the exposed pipe above her head transformed into an insistent banging.

'My name is known across the galaxy — I'm an e-paper reporter,' Grace answered, watching the stars whiz by in a filmy viewport that might not have been cleaned in decades. 'I expose the truth. And I shed light on the wrongdoings of people who can't be touched by the Chippers.'

Captain Naistu nodded, stroking the small strip of hair above her top lip. 'Ah, you smear shit on the names of people who haven't *quite* broken the law. Them that think they're above it. You touch the untouchable. Sounds like this is kinda personal.'

A dismissal or a lie might have worked on most beings. But Naistu's eyes were dark and shrewd, which was why Grace had chosen her over the other captains back at the space station.

'Yes,' Grace admitted quietly. 'It is. Very personal.'

I couldn't touch him, she thought. *But I will stop anyone else who dares to hurt those who cannot defend themselves.*

Logically, Grace knew she hadn't been in a position to do

anything about her brother at the time. Fear had also kept her from righting that wrong for half her life. When she'd finally gathered the courage to search for him, in order to run a story for her e-paper, he had vanished.

His identity — scrubbed from the Galactic Database.

His transgressions — unpunished.

Grace knew she wasn't blameless. She also had blood on her hands from when she'd revealed the location of the rebels on Eransia. It was a deadly decision that had resulted in the deaths of hundreds of people and had taken a career and half a leg from her. She'd tried to atone since then. She only hoped her brother was doing the same.

Grace said very little for the next two days. Neither did Naistu. Their companionable silence was finally broken when the ship shuddered its way out of leapspace and deposited them near Trox, a planet strewn with chaotic ribbons of icy white and dusty green — and guarded by the heavily armed ships clustered around its equator.

Any company that mined a resource as rare and as valuable as n'radian needed to protect their assets. N'radian Manufacturing no doubt hoped that those immense lascannons would the make the people living on Trox nervous enough to leave without a fight.

'They're demanding that we ask permission to approach the planet,' Naistu said in a low voice. 'They might not give it, from what I've been hearin'.'

Grace smoothed out the creases in her pants. 'They have the right to turn us away. Their purchase of Trox was entirely legal.'

'Give it a shot anyway?'

'Usually my name alone is enough to grant me passage,' Grace noted.

The captain didn't look convinced. 'Dunno if that'll work. They'll know you want to write somethin' about how they're forcing the locals to leave. It won't be a good look for them.'

'That's not your concern, Captain. Contact them and let me do the talking.'

Naistu obeyed. The connection was accepted, but the link was verbal only. Not a complete surprise — the CEO of N'radian Manufacturing was notoriously private and had yet to be caught on vidcam.

Grace drew a deep breath. 'This is Grace Pendergast, e-paper reporter and owner of *The Pendergast e-Post*. I am here to cover a story on the planet's surface — '

'You may land, uh, on one condition,' a tremulous voice interrupted.

Grace waited. She wasn't going to ask what the company wanted from her. That might indicate some impatience, or even desperation, on her part.

'The condition is — is as follows,' the voice continued, tripping over each word. 'Once your business on Trox is complete, you must speak with CEO Eman Prost. On his flagship.'

'Ohh, they want to tell their side of the story,' Captain Naistu piped up. 'That makes sense.'

Grace waved her into silence. 'I accept. I will arrive on this same vessel one day from now.'

The link died.

'How much,' Grace said. She didn't need to elaborate.

Naistu was already grinning. 'For a week of my services? It'll be steep. But I'll give the famous Grace Pendergast a discount!'

CHAPTER TWO

Raucous cheering greeted her as soon as her feet touched the ground.

Grace stared out at the crowd, trying not to let her surprise show, and wondered if perhaps they had mistaken her for a vidstar. Her face was scrubbed the second it was uploaded anywhere on the Web, thanks to one of Fei's programs, so it was unlikely they knew who she was simply by looking at her. Grace nearly stepped backwards when a man approached and offered her a coat. She would have refused it had a gust of air not slammed into her chest and driven what felt like an icicle between two ribs. Trox was as cold as it looked from space.

'Ms Pendergast?' the man queried. 'I'm Jordi McKinnon. Pleased to meet you.'

'What is this?' she demanded, gesturing at the crowd. She immediately yanked her hand back inside the warmth of the coat. The fur lining dropped as far as her feet, for which she was grateful. Her heels weren't capable of shielding her five fleshy toes and her five artificial ones from these temperatures.

'A welcoming party, for you.' Jordi beamed at her. 'Renaei sent you to save us.'

Grace kept her voice light, hoping she wouldn't offend him. 'I'm an e-paper reporter. The best I can do is make sure the galaxy is aware of your situation.'

'Renaei says...' Jordi paused, looking uncertain. 'She says

that you help good prevail by using words and the Web as your weapons. She says you are the woman who watches all the other mortals to ensure they stay in line. You are a gift from the goddess!'

The crowd burst into another round of cheers.

Hot pins were beginning to needle the back of Grace's neck. 'I'm not...I am not what you think I am.'

'But Renaei sent you,' Jordi pressed. 'She does not lie.'

'Tell us what to do! Lead us! Guide us!' chorused the pack of people surrounding Grace.

She opened her mouth, but any words she'd planned to say flew out of her thoughts the moment the ground lurched beneath her feet. Moss and damp earth burst up around her in a magnificent spray, shielding her from the crowd — they started cheering again —

Disoriented, Grace threw out her hands to brace herself. They collided with something solid and warm and Grace swiftly retracted her fingers when she realised the *something* was a woman.

Keeping her eyes fixed on her companion as she retreated several paces, Grace took stock of her situation. She was in a dank cave and could hear a steady drip-dripping somewhere in the distance. The air was heavy and cold inside her lungs, but there was a fire burning through a stack of kindling nearby, carefully contained by a ring of rocks.

In front of her stood the goddess of tundra.

'I'm not sure how I'm meant to greet you,' Grace said.

'You could say hello?' Renaei offered. She wasn't what Grace had expected. Golden hair tumbled down her ample curves, contrasting with her white, form-hugging dress.

There was no physical similarity between Renaei and Finara, but just knowing of their connection brought an ache of longing to Grace's chest. It hadn't been enough, that brief fling in the shower. She needed to lie beside Finara, to kiss her, to hold her, to let the days disappear —

'Ohh,' Renaei said softly, her green eyes glistening. 'You really love her.'

Grace's cheeks tightened. *You should have told she was a mind-reader, Finara.*

Renaei waved her arms frantically, making the bangles she was wearing clash. 'Grace, I'm so sorry! It was rude of me to pry. I should be considering your needs. Was your journey a comfortable one? Do you like the coat that Jordi gave you? Are you hungry?'

'Can you explain why your people think I've come to save them?' Grace asked. She barely managed to keep the annoyance out of her words — and out of her thoughts.

'Because you have?' Renaei's lips formed a confused pout.

'I came to report on what's happening down here,' Grace told her. 'That's my job. I'll also talk to Eman Prost, the CEO in orbit, to get his side of the story. And I'll do my best to convince him to rethink his plans of removing your people. I can't promise anything more than that.'

The pout deepened. 'But you interfere more than this. Finara told me so. And if you won't do it, then perhaps I should. I'm a goddess. I can put an end to this Eman Prost.'

'Then why haven't you done it yet?' Grace asked and crossed her arms as best she could over the bulky coat.

'Finara said you could save this planet without hurting anyone,' Renaei said, brightening. 'I don't like hurting mortals. I like saving them. That's why I gave my people my true name, so they can call me when they're in trouble. They know I will *always* help them. I'm not cruel, not like Fayay.' That name was spat with the same amount of disgust that Finara used whenever she spoke of the Watine.

The god of water might be 'Oceania' to his worshippers, but his true name was known only to his siblings and their spouses.

And now Grace.

She wasn't sure how to feel about that. The revelation had come about by accident — Finara had been complaining one evening after Fayay had savagely beat an underwater volcano in an attempt to protect a statue his followers had erected for him on a nearby reef. Of course the volcano had won in the end, since it was an irrepressible force of nature, but Finara had still been annoyed that her brother had attacked her domain in that way.

I shouldn't know this, I shouldn't know any of this, Grace thought.

Renaei was watching her closely, head tilted the side.

Swiftly wiping her surface thoughts, Grace jerked a hand up at the roof of the cavern and said, 'N'radian Manufacturing owns this planet. They're its governing body, so they can make whatever laws they want. They could even legalise murder.'

'Do you think they will?' Renaei breathed.

'Frankly, no. It's more likely they'll make it illegal for any sentient being to live on the surface.' Grace drew a breath. 'The Galactic Law Enforcement Agency will be called in to ensure that any new laws are upheld. Your people could end up in a Chipper prison.'

'You should tell the Agency that I don't wish them to uphold these laws,' Renaei declared.

Grace raised her eyebrows. 'Firstly, you don't have any

agreements with GLEA, the way your sister does. And secondly, GLEA may work with Finara on some issues, but they're not beholden to her — or me. They worship your father exclusively and he hasn't told them that they can ignore laws in favour of what people want, or need.'

'Typical of the Ine,' Renaei muttered.

The Ine. The name the sub-level gods used for their father, who the mortals knew as the Creator God.

Grace stiffened. *I shouldn't know that either.*

'Why shouldn't you?' Renaei's voice was softer than the moss creeping over the rocks on the planet's surface.

Grace shook her head and moved over to stand beside the fire, which immediately sent flaming tendrils to twist around her ankles. Grace's shoes remained intact, which drew a smile from her — Finara had promised not to destroy any more of her clothes.

Several minutes passed before Grace was sure that her voice would remain steady. 'What do you hope to achieve, Renaei? A lot of people in this galaxy respect a man who pays his workers and runs a company that provides life-saving armour. I can't convince my readers to turn against him by telling them that he's not being fair to the people who live on the planet he owns.'

'They've lived here for generations,' Renaei murmured. Deep sorrow was etched into her previously unblemished features. 'This is their home. It pains them to watch Eman Prost destroy it. It would pain them even more to leave.'

She really cares about her people, Grace noted.

See, not all of us gods need a significant other in our lives to teach us to be nice to mortals, Finara remarked, a mental grin accompanying her sudden entry into the conversation. *Too bad. Renaei could use some company. She gets lonely sometimes.*

165

'Finara, your comments are not useful nor are they relevant,' Renaei scolded. 'Go and attend to your duties. I will ensure that Grace is safe.'

Just who is the older and wiser sister of the two of us? Finara demanded.

'Older does not make you wiser,' Renaei shot back.

Finara grumbled something that might have been a curse and withdrew, though not without leaving a kernel of her presence behind, just in case Grace needed her.

'She acts so starking superior,' Renaei muttered, but she was smiling.

'What older sibling doesn't?' Grace asked, hoping she'd injected enough wryness into her tone to drown out the wistfulness. It would have been nice if her brother had teased her this way, if he had drawn a laugh from her instead of frantic silence.

'Well, we don't need my sister for this, do we?' Renaei's eyes gleamed. 'What should we do? How can I help you? Tell me everything!'

Grace firmed her lips together for a moment. 'I'll need to talk to your people, see if they managed to gain ownership of the planet before it was sold to N'radian Manufacturing. The previous owner is the descendant of the man who discovered — and claimed — Trox.'

'And if they don't have ownership?' Renaei asked quietly.

'I can't work miracles,' Grace warned her. 'Your people may still need to leave. What will you do then?'

'I don't know. I don't like hurting mortals, even the bad ones. They'd have to do something truly horrible...' The goddess

166

shuddered. 'It won't happen. You will find a way to save my people without my needing to resort to violence. Won't you?'

Grace said nothing. She didn't want to give Renaei any false hope — or worse, a lie.

CHAPTER THREE

'Tonight I will tell you the tale of how our people came to Trox, and how they were saved by the goddess who reigns here,' Jordi began as he threw powder over the fire in front of him, turning the flames into a vivid blue and evoking delighted gasps. 'Does anyone know how it starts?'

'I do!' a girl cried, one of many in the ring of children clustered around him.

Grace smiled from where she was standing, propped up against one of many curved mud-packed walls that formed the village. She should have felt claustrophobic down here, but instead the warren of corridors greeted her with warmth and safety. Very few rooms, such as this cavern which was used for meetings, had the ventilation to support open fires. It was easy to see why the clan's official storyteller would choose this place to perform for his young audience.

Grace wondered, briefly, what a daughter of hers would look like. Eyes of fire, a mischievous grin, hair that stubbornly curled — and she would never be afraid, never need to look over her shoulder in case there was a shadow following her, watching each and every movement.

Strange, Grace thought. *I've never minded Finara doing that.*

Captain Naistu had offered Grace a bunk on her ship but Grace had refused, preferring to stay with the Troxians to learn more about them. Any small, intimate details that she could include in her report would make her readers more sympathetic towards the plight of these people.

'Your funeral,' Naistu had said with a dubious look at the lumpy mounds that formed the settlement. She had quickly disappeared back inside her vessel.

'We were born on a dying world!' the girl by the fire said, beaming.

'Yes, it was dying and still is,' Jordi agreed. 'The air on that world is thick with smoke and it was choking us all. But then came The Day of Hope — the day that our ancestor, Captain Jass McKinnon, was thrown off course during a routine freighting trip and ejected above the wrong planet.'

'Or the right one!' an adult called as they passed in a nearby corridor.

From the brief conversations she'd had with the Troxians, Grace had worked out that the clan had originated from Londinium, a notorious industrial world. Londinium had been toxic for two millennia, so toxic that at one stage bots had been the only willing workers that could be found for the factories. And even the bots had rebelled in the end, sparking one of the many bot uprisings.

In the four generations since the Troxians had left Londinium, the conditions there hadn't improved in the slightest; the living, breathing workers that had taken over only lasted a decade before their lungs failed them. It didn't help that the planet's laws protected the companies poisoning its atmosphere. Grace made a mental note to see what she could do about that problem, though she suspected it was beyond her.

Jordi's gaze was lost to the blue smoke rising through the vent above him, as though he could see the stars. 'Jass went home and gathered all his family, all his friends, and all of *their* families and friends. They came here in whatever ships they could find, using up all their coin-chips and fuel just to make planetfall. They found a hostile world that they were ill-prepared for, a world that killed the crops grown from the seeds they'd carried in their hands, cradled like a child in the womb.'

Grace straightened, paying closer attention. This, she assumed, would be where Renaei came into the tale. She wasn't disappointed.

'But Renaei saved us!' the young girl said, nodding vigorously.

'Yes, she saved us, just as she always will.' Jordi lifted his hands, indicating the empty bowls that were lying in the laps of his audience. 'She showed us the food already growing around us, and taught us how to live in harmony with this world instead of fighting against it. And so we give her thanks each day. She will always defend us from those who would steal our world and ruin it.'

The children pinned their eyes on Grace. The weight of their hope and desperation was too much for her.

She turned away.

A few minutes later, Jordi left the excitedly chattering children and came up to Grace, smiling sheepishly. 'Renaei says I am to treat you like any other mortal. I'm not sure she knows what she's asking. You're Grace Pendergast. Goddess-chosen or not — I've read everything you've ever written. You've helped so many people. That we're within your notice...'

'Jordi, stop haranguing our guest and invite her to join us for dinner!' another voice exclaimed from the busy corridor outside.

Jordi flushed. 'I was just doing that, Sam.'

'Do it faster!'

This command brokered no argument and Grace was soon sitting down to dinner with Jordi and his husband inside the quarters that belonged to them, a small cave kept cosy and warm by a dirt-packed oven. Jordi excused himself from cooking, smiling when Sam teased him for being terrible at the activity. Grace accepted a bowl of lentil-based soup from Sam and nodded her thanks.

'So there was no agreement between your ancestor and the owner of this world,' she noted.

'None,' Jordi said, his shoulders drooping. 'No rental contract, no bill of sale. Nothing. But no one came. No one told us to leave. It's ours.'

Grace kept her expression neutral as she slid her techpad out of its case to look over the files she had downloaded before coming to Trox. The planet was far enough from a Web relay to suffer glacial speeds, if the Web worked at all. She read through information that confirmed what Jordi had told her as she ate with him and Sam in relative silence. Relative, because the interconnected caverns echoed with the chaotic and cheerful noise of families.

After a few minutes, Grace set aside her bowl and gave Sam her heartfelt compliments. Then she said, 'Trox is mentioned in the Galactic Database, from when it was discovered and claimed. The second and only other time it was mentioned was when it was sold two Old Earth months ago by the claimant's descendant. Any other records that might exist, any laws concerning the ownership of Trox...aren't on the Web.'

'So maybe the laws aren't on the Web?' Sam suggested. 'Maybe they're on a secure server?'

'But where to find such a server...' Grace paused, thinking over a rumour she'd heard but never confirmed. 'Supposedly, there is a hidden server that lists every law in the galaxy, if you believe space station scuttlebutt. The Galactic Law Enforcement Agency is said to have possession of it.'

Jordi frowned. 'Why would they keep it private? Are they hiding something?'

'There's a good reason to hide something like this from the galaxy,' Grace said. GLEA had many secrets, one of which being the potentially damaging fact that they worked with sub-level gods, something their Creator God-worshipping donors would not be happy to learn about. Faced with her hosts' sceptical looks, she clarified, 'Since they presumably consult this server and trust its information, GLEA would have to make sure that no one was able to remotely hack it and insert laws — incorrect laws that would make the Chippers look bad if they upheld them.'

That's quite a guess, Ms Hopeful Reporter, said a voice that belonged to the goddess that Grace would prefer to spend her time with.

She suppressed a smile. *Am I right, Finara?*

From what I've seen in their heads, yes. Finara didn't elaborate on whether or not she'd had to dig past surface thoughts for that information. Going deeper into mortal minds wasn't something she did often because it taxed her strength. *But you'd need to get their permission to access it. They don't allow mediaists — or e-paper reporters — anywhere near the server.*

But if they were approached by She of the Fire's mortal representative... Grace mused.

Your brain is the sexiest thing about you, you know that? Finara

173

purred before her presence faded again. Grace usually preferred her privacy, but this time she wished her girlfriend had stayed.

'I'll find a way to access that server, if it exists,' Grace told her mortal companions. 'But that search might not yield anything. It's highly likely that there are no laws here.'

'But we have laws,' Sam said firmly. 'In our own library.'

Grace considered this. 'That might be useful in gaining sympathy for your cause, especially if the laws refer to your clan system as a governing body. I'd like to see them.'

'Certainly — ' Jordi began, but that was all he had time to say.

A high-pitched alarm filled the room and spat out the same note, a frantic repetition that demanded panic and action. Footsteps filled the corridor outside and people began to run into Jordi and Sam's cramped room. One by one, they sat down at the table and Sam gave them food and soft murmurs of comfort — it seemed everything in the McKinnon clan was considered communal. Including their peril.

Grace glanced at Jordi.

'Rock storm,' he said grimly. 'They started when N'radian Manufacturing parked their machines down here. When the air is still, the debris doesn't generally reach us, but it's windy tonight. All the rock and soil from the digging is tossed up into the atmosphere — and gravity's a little lighter here than most places, so that's pretty far. It's been getting worse since the machines hit bedrock.'

'And is this how you always deal with the storms?' Grace asked, indicating the newcomers.

Sam dropped into a crouch beside her and explained in a low voice, 'It's easier to ride out a storm with others than to do it alone. And it is also easier for Renaei to direct the rocks away from our people if we're not spread out.'

There was little fear on his face or on the other faces crowded around the table. The Troxians evidently believed themselves safe so long as they had the protection of a goddess.

This is a big one, but I can handle it, Renaei said confidently, her words for Grace alone.

Grace felt her eyebrows rise. *Shouldn't you be telling your followers this, not me?*

They're not Webcasting nearly as much anxiety as you. And I... There was a lengthy pause. *It's nice to talk to someone who isn't one of my brothers or sisters.*

The ache inside Grace's chest wasn't sympathy but longing. *At least you can talk to your siblings.*

The storm hit a minute later, a howling maelstrom that shook the caverns and kept on shaking.

Grace forced herself to focus on the people gathered around the table as they sang some common tune, though not loudly enough that it drowned out the slam of rock onto earth. And yet they kept smiling, connected by their love for their clan. Grace enjoyed their laughter and their conversations, but she wasn't one of them. She wasn't part of any clan, or any family. Not anymore.

Are you alright? Renaei asked softly, as though she wasn't shielding the settlement from the worst of the storm, as if Grace mattered in the face of such danger.

I'm fine, Grace responded.

No, you're not. Tell my people you need to confer with their goddess.

Despite her reluctance, Grace did so and tried to ignore the excitement on her hosts' faces as the vortex of moss and dirt stole her away, back to that hidden cave. Instead of Renaei, however, she was met by Finara, who stood by the roaring fire, eyes darkened with concern. Grace immediately went to her, determined to kiss away her memories and her sadness, but Finara tutted and held her at arm's length. 'Nope, none of that. Renaei says you need to talk so here I am. And I totally don't regret stopping you from using sex to forget whatever's on your mind.'

Grace smiled briefly. 'You can see into my memories. I'll show you.'

'You really don't want to talk about it, do you?'

Grace shook her head.

'Well, tough,' Finara said and cupped Grace's face. 'I'm not climbing into that mind of yours — it's like a stronghold and it'll take far too much time to get into. Plus, I'd like to keep enough of my presence with those who also need it right now. So talk to me, love. Talk to me.'

'I'm not sure I can. I've spent so long hiding it.'

Finara kissed her forehead. 'You don't need to hide anything from me.'

'I know,' Grace murmured and gave no resistance when Finara pulled her down to the uneven ground and wrapped her up inside an embrace, one that was warmer and more intense than any flame.

'Talk to me,' Finara whispered into her ear.

Without her love and support, Grace knew she would never have found the courage to speak.

And speak she did.

CHAPTER FOUR

Her lips still tingled from her first kiss.

Emerging from the dense shrubbery, Grace re-entered the garden party that had been thrown for her sixteenth birthday, an event populated by the wealthiest denizens of Julipa. She couldn't help but smile back at the rose bushes, where Heri Cornsell was hiding.

It had been a risk for Grace's classmate to come here today, because she belonged to a family with a business empire that rivalled the Pendergasts'. If Grace's parents found out that she'd been kissing Heri when she should have been thinking about kissing the governor's son instead...

There was no telling what they'd do.

Grace couldn't stand the thought of touching any boy in that manner, much less the one they kept thrusting in front of her. She didn't dare say anything about this. Her parents had already mocked her for asking if they would send her to a media university. They had demanded to know what was so wrong with a future that asked no more of her than a wedding and a life of luxury.

Her quick capitulation had only made them suspicious. They'd asked her brother to keep an eye on her, to make sure she didn't step out of line, and so Grace had spent the past few months looking over her shoulder, afraid of Emmanuel's shadow. At eighteen, he was older than her and poised to inherit the

Pendergast empire. But for now he ran his own company, proving himself to his parents. He had his part in the plan, just as she had hers.

Emmanuel was watching her now, Grace realised.

His eyes, as brown as her own but holding a malicious glint, speared into her from across the expansive garden. Grace shivered in the sunshine. His secondary role in their family had been kept from her, but she'd found out on her own. She had stolen his techpad one afternoon and had gasped when she'd seen the images of him kneeling beside his victims, a twisted grin aimed at the vidcam.

He was an assassin who killed anyone who stood in his way or threatened the growth of their parents' empire. No Chipper had ever chased after him because this was Julipa — gods forbid anyone embezzled or cheated their shareholders out of money, but murder was perfectly legal. Expected, even.

'Happy birthday, sister dear,' Emmanuel said, having stalked across the golden grass to stand in front of her. There was no embrace. She was glad, for he would have felt her tremble. 'Where *have* you been?'

She refused to flinch or look over her shoulder. *Please, Heri, don't be there. Please.*

'Waiting for you, obviously,' Grace said, forcing a brittle smile. 'You didn't get me a present. Don't think I haven't noticed.'

Emmanuel chuckled. 'You can surely wait until tomorrow for my gift. But enough of that — I hear you are to marry in two years. Who's the lucky man? The governor's son?'

Grace confirmed it with a sharp nod.

'Ah, that will be useful,' Emmanuel said.

'Yes, especially when the governor finds out what our

parents have been doing,' Grace noted, jerking a hand towards where her mother and father were swanning about. 'I hear they are underreporting our profits and so our shareholders are getting much lower dividends than they ought to. The governor will hear of this eventually. I imagine he'll feel pressured to protect the family his son has married into.'

Emmanuel stared at her for a moment, then his lips curled. 'You are far too intelligent to be used as a tool in some marriage. If only you didn't keep antagonising our parents...they might have actually let you participate in the family business.'

'I don't *want* anything to do with it,' Grace said stiffly and shoved past him, her shoulder clipping his. The party and its distractions welcomed her. But even the delighted congratulations pouring from the guests who'd heard about her engagement were not enough to drown out Grace's troubled thoughts.

Her family was outrageously wealthy, but she had no access to their accounts. No, not since they'd become worried she would use the money to run off-world and do something as foolish as go to university. They would do their starking best to make sure she ended up destitute on the streets if she didn't marry the governor's son. There was no way she could leave Julipa without any coin-chips and she wasn't sure how to earn them.

She was stuck. Well and truly stuck.

Grace supposed she should just accept her fate.

***

'Accepting your fate — that doesn't sound like you,' Finara said, stroking the ridges on the backs of Grace's hands. The fire in front of them was restless, darting this way and that, mirroring the goddess' mood.

Grace leaned her head on Finara's shoulder. 'I wasn't happy...I was merely comfortable.' Her grimace morphed into a laugh. 'I was so spoiled. I did want to be a mediaist, but I expected to be able to buy my sources and stories. I was afraid of how much hard work I'd need to put into that career without my parents' money.'

'But something made you leave that life behind.'

'Yes,' Grace said softly. 'Emmanuel gave me a compelling reason to flee and never look back.'

**

The knock on her door woke Grace.

It was made from ancient wood, rumoured to be from the same solar system as Old Earth, and concealed a metal panel designed to keep intruders from entering. But this was Emmanuel. He knew the code that would make the extra layer of security retract. Nothing would stop him. And besides, he said he had a birthday present for her. It would be rude to refuse him.

He was smiling when he entered, his techpad swinging in his hand.

'I know you've looked on my 'pad before,' he said as he made himself comfortable on her bed.

She slid her legs away from him. 'Your techpad? I have my own...'

Emmanuel threw the device into her lap, a cruel grin slashing across his features. 'Happy birthday, Grace.'

The techpad displayed his most recent victim.

Heri Cornsell. Her body splayed across the grass, her pale flesh transformed into vivid red, her head dangling by the long black locks tangled in Emmanuel's fingers.

Grace's heart tore into a million pieces.

'Why...' she whispered.

'Oh, sister dear.' Emmanuel reached over to pat her hair, but it refused to lie flat as his did. 'You know I have to deal with any threats to our family. She was probably using you to steal corporate secrets — and besides, you need to marry the governor's boy. You can't allow yourself to be distracted by anything...or *anyone*,' he stressed. 'So that's your present from me. Dad thought it was a great idea.'

And then he was gone, taking his techpad and its hateful images with him.

Grace stood on trembling legs in the shower. The water washed away none of the guilt, none of the blood on her soul, none of the acute despair. She left the bathroom and dressed herself in the smart pantsuit she wore to school, the pantsuit that had gained her the admiring eyes of Heri Cornsell.

Once she was ready, she crept into her parents' study — empty, for they were out at yet another party — and copied the files that would prove they'd broken Julipa's laws.

The hovercar she stole from the garage was expensive, state of the art, and she ditched it a block from her destination. Very soon it would become just another seized asset. Head held high, Grace walked towards a silver tower that soared above the other buildings, ignoring the nearby vidscreens that advertised goods and services — all from the sponsors of Ynsi Gretalia, Julipa's most famous mediaist.

There were waiting rooms full of people wanting to speak to Ynsi.

Grace only had to wait five minutes.

Ynsi waved Grace into her office, annoyance lying thick on every word. 'Be quick about it. I only let you in here because my receptionist said you had something on the Pendergasts — oh.' The mediaist broke off when she looked up from the amber liquid in her glass and recognised Grace. 'Oh, this'll be good, won't it? The Pendergast daughter! Do sit down. I'll get you some whisky.'

'I don't drink.' Grace remained standing, her hand tight on the bag that contained the only possessions she now owned, including her techpad. 'I found evidence that proves that my parents have been short-changing their shareholders.'

'That info's not going to be free, is it?' Ynsi asked, her lips flatlining. She understood the seriousness of the situation. A law had been broken. This would mean the involvement of the Chippers and the imprisonment of a high-profile family. Or it could mean death, if the shareholders were angry enough about being stiffed.

Grace shook her head. 'It's not. I have a few of things I want in return for this information.'

'Let's hear it then.'

'Passage to Radion University for Media, so I can become a mediaist,' Grace rushed out. 'I want you to pay my tuition. Three Old Earth years. And — and I want money for food and board for the duration of my degree.'

Ynsi knocked back her drink in one go and slammed the glass down onto her desk. 'Doable. Radion's one of the cheaper ones. But you're not done, are you?'

Grace swallowed. 'My brother, Emmanuel...he kills people who get in his way.'

'Well, there's nothing wrong with that,' Ynsi said.

'But Ms Gretalia — '

Ynsi sighed and gestured at a chair. This time Grace took it. Seconds later, the receptionist knocked and entered, bearing a second glass of whisky which she then offered to Grace. The alcohol burned Grace's throat and left her light-headed, but it also relaxed her.

A dangerous reaction, she noted. One that she should form an immunity to.

'Look, kid.' Ynsi paused and evaluated Grace for a long moment. 'Ms Pendergast, murder is pretty normal on this planet. The Chippers won't lock him up for that.'

'You could say something in one of your Webcasts, so people are warned — '

Ynsi waved her into silence. 'No broken laws. Just some young hoodlum blowing off steam. It won't interest my viewers, Ms Pendergast. And it won't get you the outcome you're after. I'm sorry. Is he connected to what your parents are doing? Because we can get him that way.'

'I can't find anything in the files to prove it, but...'

'Ms Pendergast, shut up and listen,' Ynsi ordered.

Grace obeyed.

'You want my advice?' Ynsi leaned forward over her desk. 'Go to Radion. Become a mediaist. Wait for your brother to do something illegal, because he will. He'll have learned this shit from your parents. Do him in later, when you're in a position to do so. Why let another mediaist get your revenge when you can do it yourself, huh?'

There was nothing else she could do. Grace bowed her head and accepted Ynsi's words.

Within days, her parents were imprisoned on Gerasnin, protected from their angry shareholders by the Chippers — and then Emmanuel disappeared, his identity scrubbed from the Galactic Database. Grace became a mediaist, just as she had always wanted, but she could never find her brother. So Grace threw herself into her work, desperate to help other people like Heri, and eventually found her way to Eransia, where she recorded a Webcast that revealed her position and compromised the rebels who had trusted her with their story.

Their deaths, combined with Heri's, had convinced Grace that the galaxy would be better off without her. She was very glad a certain fire goddess had come into her life and shown her how very wrong she'd been.

***

Voice hoarse and throat as raw as her emotions, Grace curled up against Finara and wondered if she should have done anything differently. Maybe she shouldn't have listened to Ynsi. Maybe Emmanuel *could* have been punished, if she'd just stayed and found a way to —

'You did what you had to do, to survive,' Finara said softly, fingers sliding over Grace's neck and collarbone, sending a cascade of pleasant shivers throughout her entire being. 'I'm glad you left Julipa. I'm glad that you survived, so that I could find you. Love you. And bring you home.'

Home. To Finara, home was a volcano. But it wasn't...

'It's your home too,' Finara said firmly.

Grace couldn't think of anything to say, couldn't refuse what she so badly needed.

Instead she closed her eyes and drifted off to sleep.

When she awoke, she was wrapped up inside a sleeping bag in Jordi and Sam's room and could tell she'd been there for hours. Finara's presence was thinner than usual and Grace suspected there was more than one emergency that required She of the Fire's assistance.

But even so, Grace didn't feel alone.

She was pretty sure she'd never feel alone again.

CHAPTER FIVE

Captain Naistu passed the long minutes her ship needed to warm up by complaining about the previous night's storm. Her vessel's shield had barely held and the mining debris would surely have pulverised her had she parked one stride in either direction. It was lucky (strangely so) that the rocks had bounced harmlessly away or Naistu would be charging her passenger a lot more money.

Grace tried not to smile at this tirade. It seemed Renaei now understood her need to travel around the galaxy like any other mortal.

'Did you get what you needed from their library?' Naistu asked, slapping a nearby panel when it pinged angrily at her. 'Some library. They've got a whole bunch of ships in that valley and what have they got stored inside? Old documents and dust! They could at least sleep in them.'

'The ships' power cores are depleted, so they lack environmental controls and shields,' Grace explained, dropping into the co-pilot's chair. 'It's safer and warmer in the subterranean tunnels.'

Naistu wrinkled her nose. 'But whoever thought of writing laws on *paper*?'

'Paper can be dated more accurately than a digital file,' Grace told her. 'They may need to prove how old their laws really are.'

'Nah, I still don't get it. Too weird and archaic and shit. If I had my way...'

Naistu was still grumbling when the ship rocketed its way off Trox's surface. Once the sky around them had faded from periwinkle to black, Grace opened a communications link to announce her intention to meet with N'radian Manufacturing's CEO. As they drew nearer, the flagship turned sluggishly towards them, like a bloated sea creature stranded on some unforgiving shore.

Clearance was given and Naistu brought her vessel in close, muttering under her breath — something about how N'radian Manufacturing had been a little too nice, a little too accommodating. These people weren't to be trusted.

When the two ships were connected, Grace bent awkwardly to fit through the docking port and blinked when she emerged underneath the flagship's achingly white lights, so much harsher than what she was leaving behind. The port closed with a bang. Grace couldn't blame Naistu for the extra caution; the corporation might try to sabotage Grace's transportation if they decided that it would be better if she didn't live to tell any tales.

'Hello, you must be Grace,' a high-pitched voice said, clearly belonging to the person who had answered their hail yesterday.

Grace turned around. Her companion was dressed in a suit, its black cotton edged with gold silksein at the hems, and his smile was so forced it had to hurt. The silver hair and crow's feet around his eyes made him look distinguished, but though he carried himself well there was a tremble in the hand that gestured down the corridor.

'Ms Pendergast, actually,' Grace corrected. 'And you are?'

'Brendan Davies,' he answered, dipping his head. 'Personal assistant to Mr Eman Prost, CEO of N'radian Manufacturing. Mr Prost is most anxious to see you. Follow me.'

Grace stayed where she was. It wasn't because she was offended by his brusque manner; no, she wanted to see how he'd react if she didn't comply.

Davies, when he reached the corner, looked back at her and skidded to a stop, a frown creasing his expression. 'Mr Prost wants to see you as soon as possible, Ms Pendergast. Please follow me, *please*,' he added, his eyes darting furtively around the corridor.

Vidcams. They must be hidden everywhere. This was the kind of measure that helped a CEO ensure that the people on his payroll were always 'on'. Every second had to be productive or it was wasted. It seemed that Eman Prost treated his employees little better than he did the Troxians.

When Grace caught up to Davies, he immediately shot off again, his perfectly manicured smile fraying with each passing moment.

'I hope we're not too late,' he fretted.

'It's my fault if we are,' Grace said loudly, making sure the vidcams heard her. 'I like to take my time, see how things work, learn about everyone involved. It helps set the scene in my reports.'

Davies' fearful expression slipped into something more bemused. 'Oh — yes, you're an e-paper reporter, aren't you?'

'That's why your CEO wanted to see me, I'm assuming,' Grace said.

'Oh no, he wanted to get you on board so he could confirm that you were — ' He broke off and bit down hard on his lip, drawing blood.

Grace didn't pry. She had a feeling Davies had already said enough to risk a dismissal. The back of her neck prickled as her disquiet grew and she rested a hand on the pouch containing her techpad; the weight of the item inside it comforted her, but not as much as the knowledge that she was never alone. She was safe so long as a goddess was there to watch over her, to love her and protect her — *Finara. I need you.*

The Firine's full presence arrived an instant later. *Grace? Are you alright?*

For now, Grace assured her. *But I would like you to stay for a few minutes, if you're able.*

Done.

'He's waiting in there,' Brendan Davies said, indicating a chunky steel door that could easily withstand vacuum if the rest of the ship was compromised. 'I have duties to attend to. I'm sure you will need nothing more from me. You shouldn't. I hope not.'

He couldn't have moved any faster if he'd broken from his awkward walk into a run, Grace noted. She took a deep breath and curved her lips upwards. Powerful beings always liked it when their subordinates, or people they considered to be their subordinates, smiled. Your inferiors had to please you, that was a given. A lack of a smile might indicate an enemy, someone not giving you all due respect. She needed Eman Prost to like her. Or at least be willing to talk.

When the door slid open, she went inside without a single hesitation.

Her smile died almost immediately.

'Emmanuel?' The name slipped out.

'I should space you for what you did,' he said, looking up from a desk that was more vidscreen than it was furniture. His fingers, darting across the glassy surface, didn't even pause. 'Did you really hate us that much, Grace?'

Eman Prost hadn't let her dock because she was an e-paper reporter.

He'd let her dock because he'd suspected she was his sister.

Grace had so much to say that none of it moved from her crowded thoughts into her mouth. She had rarely walked into a situation since she was a teenager where she didn't have some control over her emotions. Years of practice were in danger of melting away.

He didn't offer her a chair. Grace wouldn't have accepted one anyway.

She moved to the viewport that was behind his desk, letting her gaze fall out into starry space. Her silence was a weapon, one she'd used effectively against her sources; now it was her shield. She kept her back to him. It was a vulnerable position, but even if he'd wanted to harm her, he would never have succeeded.

Grace, I swear I didn't know and Renaei didn't either. Finara's touch on her mind was accompanied by much-needed warmth. *I'm so sorry. Renaei says I shouldn't, but stark — I'm angry enough to make the offer. Do you want me to kill him? I'll do it. But only if you ask me to.*

Grace felt her shoulders relax.

She wasn't powerless, not anymore.

'I know you're not here for *me*, Grace, you never were,' a man born Emmanuel Pendergast said. His ensuing laugh was dark, sarcastic. 'You're here because the Troxians have been bleating about how unfair I'm being to them. Of course you would represent their interests. You've never cared about the interests of your own family.'

Grace turned to face him and was immediately confronted by his accusing gaze. But she was used to eyes filled with flames.

These unimpressive mortal ones didn't scare her. 'I would like to point out that I had no idea of your involvement in this.'

'I had to change my name because of you!' Eman snapped. 'No one on Julipa would fund my business ventures, not with that name, that ID — not after our parents went to prison.'

'They did break the law,' Grace reminded him.

'You sold us out!'

'I had my reasons, which should be obvious to you,' Grace said, crossing her arms and straightening her shoulders. 'I also scrubbed my identity — but even though I erased my familial connections, I still kept my name. "Pendergast" is so common outside Julipa that it means nothing. You could have gone off-world and tried your luck somewhere else. Although, laws prohibiting murder would have restricted your *ventures* too much. Easier to change your name. I understand.

'But I'm not here to discuss that, Emmanuel,' she went on. 'I'm here to listen. Without interruption. To give you the same courtesy I gave the Troxians. To hear your side of the story.'

'How generous of you, sister dear.' His smile was brittle and false, any real joy eroded by decades of malice. 'That's more than most mediaists would do. They prefer to twist words and make things look worse than they really are.'

'I'm not a mediaist.'

'No, you're something worse. A blood traitor.'

'I'd rather be a blood traitor than a CEO who cannot succeed on his own merits, who must kill all of his competition instead,' Grace said archly. She waved a dismissive hand when he opened his mouth. 'Enough about that. It's not relevant to my story. Will you give me a tour of your vessel?'

'It would be my pleasure,' he said smoothly, regaining his composure within moments.

I am going to destroy you, she thought at his smirking face.

Grace? Finara asked.

No. Don't kill him. He deserves worse than death.

***

The dining room, where they ended their tour, had one whole wall filled with plexiglass, displaying Trox in all its glory — and parading its wounds.

It looked as though an army of giants from the ancient tales of Old Earth had smashed their way across the terrain, gouging holes that plunged deep into the planet's surface and pulverising anything that separated them from the treasure they sought. Trees had been tossed away like weeds, left to gasp and die on their sides, their rotting corpses stretching as far as mountain ranges.

This wasn't a new sight to Grace. Many planets had been broken apart like this. And on many of those disposable, uninhabited worlds, no one cared.

Here they did. And 'here' happened to be under the protection of a tundra goddess — and an e-paper reporter who refused to let her brother hurt any more people. Because Grace had no doubt that if the Troxians failed to move on, he would decimate their settlement from orbit. He certainly had the firepower to do it.

'The man who recently inherited Trox sold it to me, every micrometre,' Eman declared, unmoved by the arguments Grace had tried to make for the Troxians. His high-backed chair on the opposite end of the long table kept him well away from her, but

193

his booming voice was not so easily avoided. The room had been built with acoustics in mind. 'The Troxians are little better than squatters. There are plenty of other planets for them to roam. Nice, warm ones, with none of this frost. I even offered to cart them off to any world of their choosing in the Orion Spur.'

Grace, who had yet to touch the whisky he'd provided at her request, worked to maintain a neutral expression. 'The man who claimed this world — and your seller's ancestor — never returned after his initial discovery. No one else in his family line has ever visited this place. Your seller, as I recall, only sent a survey team to find anything of worth. They didn't report on the people, because they're worth nothing to companies like yours — but they reported on the n'radian, obviously. Since that is why you're here.'

N'radian. The rock so rare and so coveted across the galaxy that it was worth more than platinum. Its greatest quality was how light it was despite its ability to repel minor lasgun blasts. Processed n'radian was used to manufacture armour for those who wanted that extra layer of protection, in case their shielding devices were depleted in a firefight. It also served as an invisible layer beneath the clothes of people who didn't want others to know that they had active protection.

'You expect me to care about the squatters?' Eman reached for his glass of wine, fuller in colour but much less potent than Grace's favoured whisky. 'They should have trespassed on a planet they could afford. People need their n'radian, sister dear. My armour saves lives.'

Since when were you so concerned about saving lives? she wanted to throw at him.

'The Troxian clan has been here for four generations,' Grace

194

said instead. 'Their goddess is here. And so are the bones of their ancestors.'

He took a few sedate sips of wine. 'Oh, please. A goddess would have stopped us digging in the first place if she really was here. As for the bones, I own those now. We'll sell Trox when it's of no more use to us. I'm sure other companies can do something with it.'

Grace refused to flinch beneath his gaze, or when he sprayed a laugh in her direction.

'I thought the great Grace Pendergast was always objective!' he jeered. 'I can see that disapproval on your face, sister dear. I've always been able to see it. Especially on the day I rid you of that distraction, the one who could have ruined our empire. Imagine. She could have ruined us.' His lips twisted. 'You did that on your own in the end.'

The voice that emerged from Grace contained no inkling of a tremor, so unlike the staccato her heart was beating. 'Her name was Heri Cornsell. She gave me the first real affection that I'd ever known. And you killed her. No wonder I disapproved. But, brother dear, now I can do a lot more than disapprove. Be careful.'

He has no idea who he's up against, does he? Finara mused.

Grace blinked. She'd forgotten that she had asked her girlfriend to stick around. *He never knew what I was capable of. He still has no idea.*

And then he went on to prove it.

'So I must fear the e-paper reporter who used to cower in her bed when I knocked on her door!' Eman waved his empty glass at her. Stray droplets flew onto the white satin stretched across the table, looking like flecks of blood. 'But you know I've broken no laws in my life, not on Julipa and certainly not here. I own Trox. I make the laws. You can do nothing to stop me.'

'Nothing?' Grace repeated. 'Not even convince your shareholders to look elsewhere? To make your board consider ousting you? Public opinion can be vicious — and when it turns, corporations must turn with it or risk losing customers.' She lifted her whisky glass in a salute. 'I am highly respected in my field. People take my word over the Creator God's, even though they shouldn't. I won't have to mention Julipa to make the galaxy hate you the way I do.'

She downed her drink in one gulp, praying it wasn't poison.

'You...have become something else, haven't you,' Eman realised.

'And thank gods for that,' Grace said. She set her glass down and delicately picked up her serviette, wetting it on her lips. 'I believe I understand your position enough to write about it, Mr Prost. The law is on your side.' She hesitated, then unleashed the words she would never have said if her image wasn't deleted the moment it was uploaded to the Web. 'But I'm not.'

He scowled. 'I did you a favour. Grace — come back here! We're not done.'

She was already walking way, hoping she could reach Captain Naistu's ship before the temptation to tell Finara to kill him overwhelmed her.

'You won't make it off this ship!' her brother threatened.

She didn't even dignify him with a backwards glance. 'I'd like to see you try to stop me.'

Brendan Davies was waiting in the corridor, dancing on the balls of his feet. He looked terrified. 'You mustn't upset him. He's very powerful. And he...he has a way of making people disappear.' That last sentence was delivered in a whisper; a warning.

'I can make you disappear now,' Grace offered. 'You don't have to stay here.'

Finara, what's his greatest desire? she asked. *Dig in if you have to. I want to save him — but he needs convincing.*

Finara's silence was broken by a laugh. *His childhood dream was to become a Chipper.*

'But this is the only job I could get at my age,' Brendan Davies fretted. 'And Mr Prost will not give me a reference. Where could I possibly go? Who would employ me?'

'I'm going to Gerasnin next,' Grace said.

His eyes went wide. 'Gerasnin?'

'Gerasnin,' Grace confirmed, smiling. 'The Chipper homeworld. The only planet in the galaxy where you can be sure of getting a job regardless of age or references.'

'Well, stark Mr Prost and his penchant for murder!' Davies said breathlessly. 'I resign!'

He put on such a spurt of speed that Grace had to sprint to keep up with him.

CHAPTER SIX

Gerasnin was like Trox in that it was a two-toned planet, but that was where the similarities ended. The Chipper homeworld was filled with blazing blue oceans and stunning white marble, both rigidly separate sections shining from orbit as though this was a star instead of a planet forced to rotate around one. The moment your feet touched down on sun-kissed stone, it became obvious that there was only one place that was fit to house the headquarters of the most powerful organisation in the galaxy — a large, arching temple that dwarfed every other building on the planet.

Grace bowed her head as she passed the pews occupied by those who had come to worship the Creator God, walking as quietly as she could so as not to disturb them. Her name was all the on-duty agent needed to hear before she and her companion were allowed into the temple's restricted areas. While Brendan Davies was shuttled off to the recruitment department, Grace was led directly to the office belonging to the Head General of the Galactic Law Enforcement Agency.

She'd never met him in person, but she knew what to expect.

What she didn't expect was how warmly he greeted her.

'Ms Pendergast, I'm delighted to meet you,' General Zareth Sins said with a smile as he rose from his desk and offered her a chair. 'Kuja and Fei told me to expect a visit. What brings the mortal representative of She of the Fire to my office?'

'You're on first-name terms with the rainforest god and his wife?' Grace asked carefully. She stood in front of the deep armchair he'd indicated but didn't take it.

Sins gave her a pointed look. 'Before my agents met you, only one sub-level god deigned to work with me, and that was because of an existing friendship between us. Despite our differences — I am a staunch follower of the Creator God and Kuja dislikes his father immensely — we have found that we can protect more mortals together than we ever could alone. But much as I am grateful to you for your part in gaining She of the Fire as one of our allies, I can't help you with your current situation.'

'My situation?' Grace echoed.

'Mr Eman Prost has contacted us already,' Sins explained, leaning heavily on the hand he'd braced against the back of his vacant chair. It was clear that he wanted to retake his seat, but he refused to give any ground to Grace. They were of an equal height. 'Mr Prost said you kidnapped his assistant and came here with the intention of smearing his name. He has broken no laws — in fact, he took the time to send us a list of laws that he's created for Trox.'

'They can't be good ones,' Grace said flatly. 'Mr Prost has a breathtaking lack of morals.'

Sins sighed and finally sank into his chair, creases spiralling across his forehead. 'We can only judge people by the laws of the planets they are aligned with...'

'He has murdered at least twenty people — and those are just the ones I know about,' Grace said. She also sat down; it wouldn't do her any favours to keep the Head General on the defensive. 'Eman Prost is my brother. I am fully aware of what he's capable of doing. What surprises me is that you would deal with someone like this, someone who would be arrested if he did the same things on your planet. Ask Brendan Davies, your newest recruit. I'm sure Mr Prost kills the employees who fail him.'

'Be that as it may, N'radian Manufacturing is registered to Julipa, a world where there are no laws against murder.' Sins grimaced. 'I do not approve. I won't deny that.'

'Has Mr Prost created a law banning any sentient being on the surface of Trox?' Grace demanded.

'He has,' Sins admitted.

'Don't send Chippers to remove the Troxian clan. Please don't.'

'I don't have to — yet,' Sins said, a flutter of a smile on his lips. 'GLEA could face a sudden staffing issue. We do have those. But Mr Prost has the ability to do worse than remove people.'

Grace reached into the leather folder she was holding and withdrew its precious contents. She presented the fragile yellowed pages to the Head General. 'These documents are over a century old — older than at least one sub-level god,' she added, thinking of Kuja. 'Have the paper and ink tested. Written here are the laws the Troxian clan came up with when they arrived on the planet four generations ago. One law states that the body of Renaei, which includes the soil and what's beneath it, cannot be *besmirched*. That means no mining. These laws were created long before anything Mr Prost sent you.'

'But the clan has never owned Trox,' Sins reminded her gently.

'We can't let him do this, General.'

'Is that an e-paper reporter speaking,' Sins wondered, his

dark eyes narrow, 'or someone who is representing the interests of the gods?'

'Both,' Grace answered. 'A goddess has threatened to kill Eman Prost if his company doesn't leave Trox.'

'This brother you dislike so much...you would fight to keep him alive?'

'Yes. Because he must pay for his crimes.'

Zareth Sins kept watching her, his expression flitting between curious and — something else. A knock at the door interrupted whatever he had been planning to say.

He glanced up. 'Enter.'

The man who stepped into the office was dressed in the same standard purple jumpsuit, his temple also carrying the chip that provided an agent with their powers. He had softer features than Sins and his hair bore blond streaks instead of the grey ones that pervaded the Head General's scalp.

Sins leaned forward in his chair. 'Ah, Lieutenant Lavine. Do you have good news for us?'

Lavine nodded. 'I do, sir.'

'The lieutenant accessed our private server, which contains all of the galaxy's laws,' Sins said aside to Grace. 'Though it is one of our greatest secrets, it would be foolish to deny the server's existence at this point. Well?'

Lieutenant Lavine held up his techpad, his eyes occasionally flicking away from its screen to rest on his audience. 'No laws as such; what I found is a placeholder. It was added to the server six centuries ago.'

'Let's hear it,' Sins said.

'In the words of the man who discovered Trox — ' Lavine cleared his throat. '"I'm too busy to waste time on writing laws, so whoever sets foot on this rock next can make them up. I just want the deed". As I understand it, sir, none of his descendants have ever set foot there. The next people who did so were the Troxian clan — and after them, only one survey team that barely stayed a week.'

'Lieutenant,' Sins said mildly. 'Can you please take these papers and input the clan's laws into the server in exchange for the placeholder?'

Lavine nodded and left.

'Interesting,' Sins said, stroking his beard. 'So it seems that while N'radian Manufacturing owns Trox, the Troxian clan is responsible for the planet's laws.'

'Is there a precedent for this situation?' Grace asked.

'A couple, but N'radian Manufacturing won't be held accountable for laws they were ignorant of,' Sins warned her.

Grace rose from her seat. 'It doesn't matter. I just needed to stop this.'

'Write your report on Trox, Ms Pendergast,' Sins said. 'And do it fast. N'radian Manufacturing needs to cease drilling immediately. Name me as your source — that will expedite matters. But I hope you can tell me that you're not the only source for your brother's earlier misdeeds.'

Grace winced. 'I can't tell you that. And I know I can't mention his past in my story without further proof. But don't worry,' she added with a smile. 'I know how to deal with him. The tundra goddess and I have an understanding.'

Sins pressed his fingers together. 'Ms Pendergast, I'm curious. You seem well-connected to the gods and must have learned more about them than I ever could. Most mediaists and e-paper reporters would have exposed this information. But you haven't. Why do you demand that mortals reveal the truth when you won't demand the same of the gods?'

Cold dread settled at the nape of Grace's neck.

'I know why I say nothing,' Sins went on, his gaze distant. 'Kuja and Fei are dear friends of mine. They deserve their privacy, as does their son. I am duty-bound to protect all children of the Creator God, be they mortal or immortal. But why do you continue to keep your silence?'

'The same reason as you,' Grace replied.

'Are you sure?'

She couldn't tell Sins that she felt ashamed about writing down everything she'd ever learned about the gods in her techpad, that she felt so guilty for betraying their trust in this way, that she couldn't betray it further by revealing what she knew. She couldn't explain what had compelled her to start compiling this information in the first place. She couldn't even explain it to Finara, who'd simply shrugged and said it was in Grace's nature to research everything.

'I can't expose them,' Grace said at last. 'I don't think that decision is up to me.'

'You think the decision lies with the sub-level gods alone?' Sins asked. 'That no mortal can be allowed to weigh in on this?'

A shiver passed through Grace. 'No. The decision isn't theirs. Or ours.'

'I see,' Sins said after a long moment. 'Could it be that you are acting on behalf of a greater power?'

Grace flinched. She was well aware that her original purpose, given to her by the Creator God, had been to show Finara how to care for the mortals inside her domain, regardless of the gods they worshipped. But Grace had hoped that Finara's father no longer had any use for her.

'What if I don't want to be the Creator God's tool anymore?' she asked softly.

'And what if you're the only one who can be trusted to be that tool?' Sins countered.

Grace had no answer for that.

CHAPTER SEVEN

He was drinking whisky when she found him.

Eman Prost, once Emmanuel Pendergast, barely acknowledged his sister as she took the stool beside him. He remained hunched over at the bar inside his impressively large quarters on his company's flagship, his profile made uneven by deep shadows.

Gone was the pressed suit, gone was the bright lighting that had gleamed off his too-perfect teeth, and gone was his delicate grasp on an even more delicate wine glass. He nudged the bottle of whisky towards her. Grace accepted it and poured herself a measure. They shared a single sip of the hard liquor before he exploded.

'N'radian Manufacturing still owns Trox!' Emmanuel hurled at her. 'You can't make us leave!'

'But the Chippers will stop you mining,' Grace pointed out. She was leaning casually against the bar, an immovable force in the face of his fury.

His top lip curled. 'There are other planets with n'radian.'

'But not many.'

'I'll just build another business from the ground up,' he said and swallowed the entire contents of his glass. A cough wheezed out of him. 'I see you didn't reveal anything about my past in your report. You didn't do that out of any love for me.'

'No,' Grace agreed. 'I don't have any sources outside of myself. It's more opinion than provable fact, unfortunately.'

He half-turned towards her. 'Why are you here, Grace? To gloat?'

'I am here, in your private sanctum, because it has no vidcams. And no witnesses.'

'My bodyguards are just outside!' Eman snapped, carelessly waving his empty glass at the door. 'They saw you enter. You won't leave this ship alive if you touch me.'

Grace slung back the rest of her drink, licked her lips and dropped her own glass onto the counter with a decisive thud. 'No one saw me enter. How do you think I got past your bodyguards? And how did I find a way onto your ship in the first place?'

'How the stark should I know?'

'I am also here,' she went on, her voice firming, 'for all the people you've killed. For the girl you might have killed, if I'd stayed and refused to do what was demanded of me. I am not going to kill you. You don't deserve that. You deserve much worse.'

He retreated a pace, his eyes wide. 'What are you going to do to me?'

Grace merely smiled.

A vortex of soil and rock howled up from his feet and swirled around him. He barely had time to scream before Renaei's teleportation powers bore him away, to a planet that had never been discovered by any mortal, a barren world that would never see another living soul.

The tundra goddess would ensure that he had enough food and shelter to survive. But he would pass the decades with only his regrets for company. If he had any.

'My turn,' Grace said.

And then another vortex came for her.

***

Trox still bore the scars of what N'radian Manufacturing had done to it, but its slow recovery could now begin. The storms had ceased to rain rocks instead of raindrops and already laughter had returned to the clan as they went about their business. Their plight had been heard across the galaxy and a pair of GLEA's agents was due to arrive by the end of the week. Their presence was meant to be a deterrent to opportunistic pirates.

No one was quite sure what had happened to Eman Prost. They said he had gone into hiding to avoid any entanglements with his company's shareholders. A new CEO was swiftly instated by the board; mercifully, Eman's replacement had left Trox without argument.

Grace crossed her arms over her coat and surveyed the Troxian settlement from a distant outcropping. It wasn't long ago that she'd been so careful not to involve a goddess in her work, to ensure that she wielded no unfair advantage against her fellow mortals — unless it was absolutely necessary. She had since fallen down that slippery slope one too many times.

But how else could she have punished him?

Was this behaviour forgivable if she was indeed a tool of the Creator God? Or was she failing her purpose in some way?

'I take it this ending is to your satisfaction,' Grace commented. The tundra goddess was her only companion for now, since Finara was currently monitoring no less than a thousand volcanic eruptions in a single volatile solar system.

Renaei's expression was pinched. 'Not entirely.'

'I couldn't have done much more,' Grace pointed out.

'Oh, I know that,' Renaei said with a dismissive wave of her hand. 'I mean, there's still something troubling you and I wish to set your mind at ease.'

'I doubt you could do that,' Grace said dryly. 'And I would appreciate it if you didn't come too close to my mind when I'm not able to control my mental barriers.'

Renaei grimaced. 'I'm sorry. It is very hard not to listen when your thoughts are this loud. But I'm curious, Grace...why does it bother you that you know so much about the Galactic Pantheon? Especially if my father put you in a position to learn everything?'

'I'm a mortal. No mortal should have this information.' Grace closed her eyes briefly. 'The Creator God made a mistake in choosing me as his tool, if he has.'

'I don't always agree with my father's methods,' Renaei said, her lips pursed. 'But maybe one day the mortals will need to know more about the gods guiding them. Or maybe it's our own children who will benefit from that knowledge.' The goddess smiled wistfully down at the Troxian families emerging into the daylight. 'Who else will record our history if not you?'

Fear knotted itself inside Grace's stomach.

'I don't have the right to curate this information,' she began.

'You're Finara's family, so you're mine too,' Renaei said with a decisive bob of her head. 'We're your family.'

Family. A family was something Grace had always wanted. She'd never truly been part of the one she'd been born into.

'But I'm not...' Grace trailed off when Renaei gave her a severe look.

'I know what you *are*,' the tundra goddess said. 'You are the woman my sister loves. And you put aside your reservations about meeting me in order to help those who would have been powerless without your help. Our secrets are safe with you. They always will be.'

Grace kept her lips sealed. But it was impossible to hide the tear that streaked down her cheek and over her chin before dropping into oblivion.

'You're in our family, Grace Pendergast, mortal or not,' Renaei continued. 'And I can't promise this from the others, but Finara, Kuja and I will protect you. Because you're ours.'

Grace looked away, her mouth baked dry. She'd thought that she had to prove that she could stand on her own as a mortal, that she didn't need Finara. But she did. She needed Finara as much as the goddess needed her. They were entwined. Eternally.

I'm going to marry her, Grace thought. She quickly reeled those words back inside her mind, hoping that Finara hadn't heard them from across the galaxy.

But she had forgotten about a closer goddess.

Renaei gasped in delight.

This earned the goddess a stern look from Grace. 'Don't tell her I'm going to propose.'

'Why not?' Renaei demanded.

'It needs to be...planned,' Grace said with a smile. 'Perfect. She's waited four years. She can wait a little longer.'

'She would wait an eternity for you,' Renaei assured her.

'I don't have eternity.'

'Yet.'

'Yet,' Grace agreed.

'How I envy her,' Renaei breathed. 'She has found her equal in you, Grace Pendergast. You are equal to a goddess.'

Grace considered disputing this, but couldn't seem to.

'Thank you for your help, Renaei,' she said instead.

Renaei grinned. 'You helped me first. And what are sisters for anyway?'

THE AWAKENING
OF IGNEAS,
SUB-LEVEL GOD

CHAPTER ONE

Four years.

It had been four years since this gorgeous woman had come into her life and plonked a silver prosthetic leg on the table between them at a speed dating event, right after Finara had said something admittedly quite thoughtless.

Four years, such a ridiculously short unit of time, one that a god should never heed, and yet she had counted every single day with a joy approaching agony.

Finara, known as She of the Fire to her followers, stood watch as tendrils of fire crept over her dozing girlfriend, claiming her wholly and completely. Grace's bed, a lake of lava inside a volcano (one of many volcanoes smothering this world), was the safest place in the galaxy for one mortal and one mortal only. Anyone else who touched down on this planet would be instantly vaporised. It also lacked a Web connection, a useful feature when dating a workaholic.

Grace had taken time off, finally, and she had even booked a hotel, not an unusual move when the e-paper reporter had just finished a big story. But Finara had been impatient to consume her, to bathe her in flames and make love to her in the way that only a goddess could.

Four years it had taken for Grace to call this place home. Finara's smile spiralled out of control and the goddess did nothing to temper it. She was recalling her girlfriend's first visit to the volcano.

'And what happens when you lose focus?' Grace had demanded, arms crossed as they always were when she wanted her audience to know that she was in complete control — even if she wasn't. 'Will I be incinerated because of one careless thought?'

Finara had been well aware that a serious answer was expected of her. 'My domain knows who you are. The fire, the lava — they all have their own thoughts. And just as I love you, they love you too. Nothing will happen to you here, I promise.'

'But...' Grace had frowned down at the lava, uncertain. 'Lava is not fire, technically speaking. It's molten rock. Doesn't that belong to another sub-level god in the Galactic Pantheon?'

'Sure, there's a lot of overlap with this one,' Finara had replied. 'My sibling, Igneas, looks after rocks, so basically everyone's domain has a piece of Igneas in it. But don't worry. Mostly they sleep. Their latest nap has lasted a century so far.'

'And if they wake up?'

'I'll have to have a word with them about your presence here.' Finara had shrugged. 'Mortals annoy them. They're a bit old-fashioned. But they're definitely not waking up for a while.'

And that had been the end of that conversation.

Grace had long ago discarded her reservations about the volcano and was now completely relaxed, having cast away all thoughts of anything that existed beyond the dark blanket of clouds in the atmosphere. *The Pendergast e-Post*, Grace's wildly popular e-paper, didn't suffer in her absence. Her employee-turned-business partner was busy chasing down leads on her behalf and publishing his own reports on the Web. Sean Akiyama had more than earned Grace's trust.

Finara regretfully turned away from her dozing girlfriend. She wouldn't have usually bothered to do this, but some of Grace's worry had sown a seed inside her and it demanded that she check on something important to her girlfriend — which made it important to them both.

'It's still intact?' Finara asked a blackened patch of molten rock.

One large bubble grew, then burst apart like a flower violently opening up to a ray of sunshine. Cushioned inside was Grace's techpad, a device containing information that existed nowhere else; Grace was in possession of the most concise and accurate notes on the Galactic Pantheon in the entire galaxy. Finara couldn't see why the e-paper reporter had been ashamed to reveal this pastime, because there was no one more worthy to curate and keep those secrets.

'You could just leave the techpad with Sean,' Finara had told Grace earlier.

Grace had shaken her head. 'There is data on here that *no one* should have access to.'

'So why keep it? I mean, people could hack into your techpad, right?'

'I'm not sure if your father compelled me to do this or not,' Grace had whispered, looking away. 'But if he has, then I have no choice and I must continue to add to my files. You've always told me there's no way to escape his grand design.'

That *definitely* hadn't been what Finara had wanted to hear. She'd never been fond of her father, the Ine, the infamous Creator God. He was prone to making suggestions to unsuspecting mortals to further some plan of his and if this was one of those times...it meant that the Ine hadn't yet loosened his grip on Grace.

It troubled Finara because she knew just how much damage he could inflict on mortals when he wanted to jerk their strings.

Maybe it would be better if Finara never married Grace and conferred immortality upon her. Grace could hardly be free from the Ine if she lived forever — and Finara wasn't even sure if her girlfriend would ever warm to the subject of marriage. Best not to mention it.

'Good, make sure it stays intact,' Finara told the lava, an edge to her voice.

The viscous, glowing material recoiled for a moment, then rebuked her. *We are more than capable of doing what is required of us.*

'I...' Finara sighed. 'I'm sorry. But she means a lot to me.'

We know this. But we do not know why you haven't bound yourself to her yet.

'I've got my reasons. Mostly, you know, the fact that a binding consists of at least two sentient beings who actually *want* to get married...' Finara muttered. She loved her girlfriend and wanted to respect her wishes, but it hurt to imagine an eternity without Grace.

Finara glanced down when the rocky ground trembled beneath her feet.

'So soon?' Finara asked. 'Didn't think this volcano was blowing until next decade. Something's not right.'

Regardless, the lava said, *we cannot avoid the chain reaction once it begins.*

'I know you can't stop yourselves, but you've gotta give me more than that,' Finara snapped.

They are waking.

'Oh shit. They're *here*? Of all places?'

Yes.

Finara turned and raced over to the lip of the seething lake, where waves of lava were already washing Grace in her direction. The e-paper reporter's eyes slid open, then shot wide. There was no time for the mortal to react — she landed in the waiting arms of her goddess two seconds later.

'Hey,' Finara said, though she was sure her grin was warped by worry.

'Don't "hey" me, Ms Guilty Goddess,' Grace fired back. She didn't try to wriggle out of Finara's embrace, at least. 'What's going on?'

'So...you know how Igneas was supposed to be napping...'

Grace's glower intensified.

'Sorry?' Finara tried.

And then the volcano exploded around them.

CHAPTER TWO

'Igneas! Stop!' Finara bellowed.

Waves of lava poured over Finara and Grace, blackening as it cooled and solidified. This wouldn't have been such an urgent problem if the newly-formed rock hadn't trapped them inside a steadily shrinking pocket of air. Finara's forehead creased as she fed more and more heat into the layers surrounding her, but Igneas' grasp on rocks, liquefied or otherwise, was much stronger than hers.

Finara managed to manoeuvre a hand out from under Grace and held it high over her head, making punching motions with fingers encased in fire in an attempt to shatter the thickening ceiling of their cocoon. No good. It was still intent on crushing them.

Grace curled up against Finara, using her thoughts to communicate over the noise. *Is this as serious as I think it is?*

Yes! Igneas definitely isn't playing games! Finara replied. *And they can't read minds, so they don't know why you're here.*

Teleport me somewhere else while you deal with this, Grace ordered.

Finara refrained from cursing out loud, afraid it might annoy her sibling. *Igneas wants to kill you, the intruder, not me! They'll follow you.*

How will they track me? Grace asked. *If you send me to another domain...*

Do you know how many starking planets have rocks or a rock-based crust!? Finara exclaimed.

She did have one way to buy some extra time, however. She transformed Grace's body, turning her girlfriend into flames that slid and licked their way all over Finara's skin — this significantly reduced the amount of space that Grace needed to survive.

The seamless rock cocoon kept pressing in but slowed, as though uncertain.

'Igneas!' Finara huffed. 'Listen to me! I'll explain, I promise. Please just give me a chance.'

Let me destroy the mortal! roared a voice that cracked and fissured. *It does not belong here! Turn it back into its natural state so I can kill it!*

'Not happening! No fucking way!' Finara growled.

The cocoon abruptly shrank again. Igneas *really* didn't like it when she swore.

Arguing is not working — you should try something else, Grace spoke up, sounding vastly unbothered for a mortal who had lost her body, albeit temporarily.

Finara curled her hands into fists. *Like what?*

Surprise your sibling. Say something that distracts them and gives you the upper hand.

'Oh, it's that easy, huh?' Finara muttered, but Grace had actually given her an idea. 'Iggy, please don't hurt her! I love her. *I love her!*'

Love...? Igneas' voice was mired with confusion.

'Yes, love! Love!' Finara repeated desperately. 'We can love now! Sandsa even had a kid!'

Igneas lapsed into silence, giving Finara the opportunity she needed. She pushed *hard* with her powers and the layers of rock smothering her immediately shattered. Sighing in relief, Finara reformed her girlfriend. Though Grace could stand unaided, Finara didn't set her down or loosen her grip. Grace offered no objections; she brushed a palm over Finara's cheek, letting the goddess know she understood Finara's need to protect her.

Sandsa has a child? Igneas clarified, distinctly incredulous. *Are you sure?*

'Yes, I'm sure!' Finara snapped. 'I wasn't sleeping the last century away, was I!'

The remaining lava crept back into the lake, sullen and jealous that it couldn't join the river of fire already streaming down the side of the volcano. Finara sent a tendril of her presence after the liquid rock, not because anyone was in danger of being hurt (this whole planet was still too volatile for mortals to live on) but because she wanted to ensure that the eruption hadn't damaged the world's destined development. Nope, no lasting consequences. She relaxed.

But there was still the matter of Igneas.

Standing in the centre of the roiling lake was a dark monolith that began to groan its way towards Finara with halting steps, its weight supported by blocks of granite that formed column-shaped legs.

'What else have I missed?' pebbled lips asked. 'I have much to catch up on. Did we finally get a sibling to care for the rainforests? You know we need one.'

'Yeah, his name is Kuja and he's almost eighty years old,' Finara explained patiently, still holding Grace tightly against her chest, grateful that her girlfriend was keeping out of the conversation. Igneas would not let a mortal interrupt them without consequences.

The behemoth stopped and stared down at Finara and Grace, then shrank a little as if trying to match their height. Flecks of stone splintered away from that crusty face, revealing very human features that seemed entirely at odds with the god's current form. 'Hmm. The rocks like Kuja. They say he is wiser than all of our siblings. He suffered greatly for that privilege. Why was he sad, Finara? He was very, very sad. The rocks say something made Sandsa sad too. But he's still sad.'

Finara swallowed. 'Our mother died. And that's not even the half of it —'

'SHE DIED!?' The volcano shook violently. 'WHY HOW NO SHE CANNOT DIE!'

'Igneas, maybe you should calm down before I...' Finara began, but already her sibling's physical form was breaking part, forming uneven chunks that sloshed down into the lava, stirring the restless volcano back into life for a second time.

Finara's shoulders slumped. There was no use talking to Igneas when they were like this. She might as well take Grace and go.

But Grace had other ideas. She dropped her feet onto the ground and swiftly marched out of the range of Finara's desperate fingers. 'We mortals really have it wrong. We think the sub-level gods are intelligent beings who make important decisions about the galaxy — but they'd just as soon have a tantrum. And aren't you supposed to care for the mortals beneath you? Not try to smother them? Maybe the Ine should assign your domain to a more mature sibling.'

'Graccceee...' Finara hissed.

The volcano shook again.

'You let the inferior mortal speak to me!' Igneas bellowed,

their human form stabilising enough to let them advance on Grace. Their dark skin was steaming, literally and figuratively. Their obsidian eyes were narrow and flinty. Igneas looked *pissed*.

'She didn't *let* me do anything,' Grace continued, completely unperturbed by their approach. 'Because I am not inferior. In fact, I challenge you to think of me as inferior when I'm the one who has complete control over my emotions when confronted by a being who could kill me with a stray thought. You lost all control at the sight of a mere mortal. So much for superiority.'

'Finara will not save you from my wrath,' Igneas said, slowing to pin her with a scowl.

'Actually, she did, and will do so again,' Grace countered. She ignored Finara who was mentally shouting at her to be careful with her words. 'Because she loves me, and I her. And it seems that I am more deserving of her admiration than a god who has worse manners than a toddler. Isn't this display a waste of time and energy on your part? Surely you want Finara in a more generous mood so that she will fill you in on the past century?'

'Yeah, I'm not likely to do that if you kill the woman I love,' Finara added. She drew closer to Grace but didn't touch her, wanting to provide support without eroding any of her girlfriend's power.

Igneas fell silent, as did the volcano. Several bubbles of lava transmuted into cold stone.

'Please, Iggy? For your big sister?' Finara pleaded.

'Fine. I will not kill the mortal.' Igneas stomped over to the rim of the red-hot lake and sat down, crossing their legs. 'But I like Renaei a lot more than I do you, Finara. And I'm going to complain about you the next time I see her.'

225

Finara snorted. 'Sure. I know she's your favourite. But I'm still the one you come to for your starking updates.'

Igneas blinked up at her. 'Do you really need to curse so much? It is most unbecoming.'

'It doesn't bother Grace and her opinion is the one I care about,' Finara said flatly.

'Hm.' Igneas' clinical gaze roved over Grace's naked form. They seemed unimpressed. 'She doesn't look like much. Is she your only lover?'

'Yes!'

'Perhaps she has hidden qualities then,' Igneas decided. They nodded at Grace. 'A mortal who is capable of holding my sister's full attention is indeed a rare and superior specimen. You are worthy enough to sit with me.'

Finara winced as over three millennia of memories came flooding back to her. She'd always wanted to fall in love, desperately so, but for most of her life she had believed that a goddess wasn't allowed to even consider it. So she'd distracted herself with countless liaisons, hoping they'd fill the hole inside her heart. Only one mortal had managed to do that — a mortal who was capable of standing up to Igneas when most of the Galactic Pantheon avoided doing so.

Grace crossed her arms, chin lifted in defiance. 'How generous of you, Igneas. But I'm not sure you are worthy enough to sit with *me*.'

Igneas growled. The lava inside the lake sloshed about angrily.

'Enough, you two!' Finara snapped.

226

CHAPTER THREE

'Do you want me to teleport you somewhere else?' Finara asked her girlfriend in a low voice. She ignored Igneas, who was still giving her an expectant look; they wanted their companions to sit down with them. But the god of rocks had waited a century to wake up — they could wait an extra minute or two. 'Grace, it's fine. You can go on ahead to that hotel you booked. Order a drink, get comfy, start without me. But don't you dare finish.'

'Finara, I'm staying, if you will allow it.' Grace hesitated, her gaze slipping away from Finara's. 'I understand if you're concerned about what I might hear, what I might write down —'

Finara held out her hand, mentally calling upon the nearby liquified rocks; they immediately brought Grace's techpad to her. She deposited the device into Grace's trembling fingers. 'Love, I'm not worried about that. I'm worried about you.'

When Grace looked back at Finara, there was a hard-edged determination in her eyes, so potent that flames would not have looked out of place there instead of brown pupils. 'You are my family. And anything that involves your family also involves me.'

'But you have trouble with this,' Finara said firmly. 'I know you.'

'Finara...' A sigh laden with frustration. Grace was too good at hiding her thoughts and Finara never dug into her mind without permission, so there was no telling what that meant.

'The mortal has made her intention to stay very clear,

Finara,' Igneas boomed. 'And I would enjoy watching you try to stop one such as her. She is oddly persistent for a mortal.'

The god chuckled. Grace smiled in response.

'So not helping, Igneas!' Finara grumbled.

'Father would have removed the mortal already if she was not meant to be here,' Igneas continued with a violent shrug that dislodged the last of the rocks clustered to their shoulders. 'The Ine has billions of plans. Who's to say this is not one of them?'

Finara felt her jaw clench. 'Grace is not one of his plans.'

'Technically,' Grace said, 'I was. And I still might be.'

Fire broke out like sweat on Finara's skin. She hated being reminded that Grace had been sent into her life to teach her a lesson: how to feel compassion for the mortals beneath her. And that is exactly where her father's interference was supposed to have ended. He shouldn't keep poking his nose into Finara's business. Or Grace's.

'There, see, the mortal should stay,' Igneas declared. 'Now sit down and tell me what I have missed.'

Finara stared at Grace, upset, angry, tormented.

Somehow, despite lacking mind-reading abilities, the mortal knew. She always knew.

Grace chastely kissed Finara's lips and took her hand, tugging firmly when the goddess offered resistance. 'I love you, Finara. Your father had no part in the feelings we developed for each other.'

'Still doesn't make it right, what he did,' Finara muttered.

But she did allow Grace to lead her over to Igneas and then pull her down into a sitting position.

Finara began her account with Kuja's birth, remembering with fondness the bright, innocent smile he'd given her at their first meeting — then she segued into how their mother, made immortal by her marriage to the Ine, had broken up with him, how her binding scars had been ripped from her skin, condemning her to a finite lifespan. Igneas perked up and questioned the notion that Julia Ine was dead, because mortals live a century at the very least, of course they do.

'Iggy, it was over sixty years ago...' Finara's voice caught in her throat; it only became unstuck after Grace gave her hand a squeeze. 'And anyway, it doesn't matter because she didn't last more than a year. Mother died in a gang conflict on Yalsa 5. I don't think most of our siblings know this and to be honest I'm not sure how many of them would care.'

Igneas' bulky form began to quake with muffled sobs. 'Why so much? Why did so much happen? It is not fair, Finara — it isn't fair!'

Finara sighed. 'Look, Igneas, it happened, we can't go back and change things.'

'You have had decades to adjust to these events,' Grace interjected. 'Igneas only just learned of them. Given time, they will adjust as well. We mortals don't need nearly as long to come to terms with things, because it is normal to cram everything into a short timespan before we die.'

Igneas stared at Grace with renewed respect, their sobs slowly abating. 'Yes, mortals can bear such agony. We cannot.'

'And your grief will haunt you for that much longer,' Grace said, nodding.

'Yeah, well...' Finara grimaced. 'I guess that explains what happened with Sandsa.'

'I haven't heard you speak of a Sandsa before today,' Grace noted.

Finara hesitated, thinking over what she had told Grace about her siblings. 'Actually, you have, Grace. I just haven't mentioned his true name before...'

Igneas held out a hand as if trying to gesture, but they didn't seem to know what shape to make with their fingers. They frowned down at their hand and retracted it. 'Sandsa is our oldest brother, the Desine, god of deserts. There is nothing and no one that can best him.'

'Except love,' Finara said quietly.

Grace pursed her lips. 'So the Desine is the eldest of the sub-level gods. And I take it he's the most powerful member in the Galactic Pantheon because of that.'

'Correct, mortal!' Igneas said, beaming. 'I see why Father chose you for Finara.'

'Hey now, I chose her,' Finara growled. 'And Sandsa's not all-powerful anymore. He's seriously messed up. Hasn't spoken to anyone in years. Because of Callista.'

Igneas demanded an explanation, so Finara told them how Sandsa had abandoned his deserts to live as a man and had fallen in love with a mortal named Callista. But the Ine had foreseen his disobedience and had in fact created Callista to either teach Sandsa how to care for his mortals and send him back to his domain...or to provide a replacement by giving her newborn son to the Galactic Pantheon.

'Ah yes, the child — I have a nephew!' Igneas exclaimed, delight cracking across their face. 'Is he powerful? What are his duties? Tell me everything.'

Finara's gaze dropped into her lap. 'He's missing. Callista took him and ran.'

'She left the Desine?' Grace asked softly.

'What mortal wants a god for a husband or a goddess for a wife?' Finara wondered. She glanced up, suddenly aware of what she had said and who she had said it to.

But her girlfriend had other things on her mind. For some reason, Grace was thinking about the hotel she'd booked. A familiar room. And an even more familiar table. Was that the hotel where they'd met? Why had Grace decided to go back there? And why was the mortal so nervous about their upcoming dinner reservation?

'But Fei is a mortal and she married Kuja, the Rforine,' Grace pointed out, her surface thoughts swiftly blanking. She shot a sharp look in Finara's direction. 'They still live together with their son. Quite happily, according to Finara.'

'I have another nephew?' Igneas bounced, causing the lake's jagged edge to fracture. Lava bled onto the rocky ground. 'Can I meet this one? Please?'

Finara rolled her eyes. 'Sure, Iggy, but you should probably introduce yourself to Kuja before you show up with years of birthday presents. Anyway, Fei...she's different. Callista just wanted a man, not a god, and Sandsa was happy to play mortal if it meant being with her. Stark, he was so happy.'

'Sandsa was happy?' Igneas echoed in disbelief.

'*Was*,' agreed Finara through clenched teeth. 'And then we went after him.'

It was painful to recount that day, even if Grace had heard a version of the tale before, and Finara wished she didn't have to admit to joining forces with her siblings against the Desine. That they had been successful in restoring the Ine's grand design didn't negate the fact that Finara's involvement had led to Kuja being

231

injured. She'd looked after him and gained his forgiveness, but what she'd done still lay heavy on her heart.

Finara told Igneas how the attack had forced Sandsa to become a god once more so he could defend his family, how he had been reconnected to the deserts that so desperately needed him. Unable to resist his domain any longer, he'd chosen to return to his duties and had reassumed the mantle of Desine. His wife, Callista, had left him shortly afterwards because she couldn't handle what he truly was. The sub-level gods had watched each other closely after that, making sure no one stepped out of line. It wasn't until Kuja had fought for the right to be with Fei that they'd discovered they had been allowed to experience love all along.

I try not to feel resentful, that I could have sought love earlier, Finara sent to Grace while Igneas sat as still as a boulder, sorting through what they had heard. *Because waiting for you was worth it. But stark, I hate what my father has done to us all.*

I'm glad I'm here for you, Grace murmured, her grip on Finara's hand even tighter than before. Warmth spread up Finara's arm and into her chest, where it claimed her heart.

'I love you,' Finara said.

Grace lifted their linked fingers and kissed Finara's knuckles. 'I love you too.'

Igneas' obsidian eyes rose from the ground. 'If this is how you feel for one another, and it is allowed now, why are you not married?'

'Igneas!' Finara hissed, frantically shaking her head and determinedly *not* looking at her girlfriend, not even for a second. 'Grace doesn't want that! She's a mortal who wants to stay a mortal. She doesn't want the binding. So that's it, alright?'

Igneas blinked so slowly it looked for a moment as though they had fallen asleep. 'So you will make my sister mourn you forever. Humans are unusually cruel creatures.'

'I never said I didn't want the binding,' Grace told Igneas, her tone so bizarrely casual that it took Finara several seconds to process what she'd said.

'What!' Finara spluttered.

Grace's next words were rushed, as though they were escaping her instead of being spoken. 'When we first met, I didn't know if I was ready for eternity or if I ever would be. But I'm a lot more ready than I was four years ago.'

Igneas clapped their hands together and the volcano vibrated, echoing their delight. 'I can officiate your binding right now. There is some pain involved, but of course it is nothing compared to the joy you will give Finara —'

'Whoa, whoa, whoa,' Finara said, equal parts panicked and excited. *Grace? Are we doing this? Oh, my love, I had no idea.*

'I'd prefer to be engaged for more than a couple of minutes,' Grace said wryly.

Finara and Igneas deflated as one.

'I was going to propose to you properly,' Grace went on. 'I even booked dinner at the same table from that speed dating event. And I was going to order some of those horrible pink drinks — I think we had hundreds of them during that week. But the thing is, while I am more than ready to be Finara's wife, I am still trying to adjust to the concept of eternity. I thought a lengthy engagement might help with that.'

'But *I* was going to propose to *you*!' Finara exclaimed. Well, she hadn't exactly planned it, but she had always assumed that she'd know when Grace was ready and then make some sort of romantic gesture — albeit nothing as nice as revisiting the hotel where both their lives had changed so drastically.

'That's the first thing you're going to say to me after that?' Grace asked, eyebrows raised.

'Well, I mean, I was going to wait until I was absolutely sure you wouldn't say no — and I was pretending that I wasn't waiting, but I totally was — '

'Finara,' Igneas interrupted. 'I believe Grace Pendergast wants you to give her an answer.'

'She never asked me a question!' Finara exploded.

A heavy silence poured into the volcano.

'This...' Grace said after a while. '...is not at all how I pictured my proposal going.'

Finara tried to maintain her scowl, but it was in serious danger of slipping.

'Stop sulking and kiss me; we're engaged,' Grace told her.

Finara could hardly ignore this pleasing request and cupped Grace's jaw, pulling her into a series of slow, intimate kisses that caused heat to simmer between them. Conscious of Igneas' presence, Finara leaned back and stared at the woman she loved, still not sure she should dare to hope. 'Grace...are you sure...?'

'I am,' Grace said firmly.

'Well, then...' Finara fumbled. 'Do you know when you'll be ready to actually marry me? I mean, this is nice, but...'

Dismay crossed Grace's expression. 'Don't ask me that.'

'Grace, I can't — I can't keep living with this uncertainty!' Finara cried. 'It's killing me. It's killing me that I don't know if I'll have to watch you wither and *die*. I can't do it — I won't!'

'Finara, it is obvious you are making the mortal uncomfortable — ' Igneas began.

But Finara was just getting started.

'Maybe Igneas is right, maybe you *are* cruel,' Finara said. She jerked away from Grace and clenched her fists. 'Yeah, I'm a goddess, but I'm half mortal too! I have a heart, Grace. You know that. Or you should.'

'Of course I know that!' Grace threw back at her. 'But you don't understand. Or you refuse to. Maybe I shouldn't have told you about my desire to get engaged — or even suggested we do it.'

'Maybe you shouldn't have! At least then you wouldn't have got my fucking hopes up!'

'Enough!' Igneas bellowed and tossed out their hands, calling forth rocks that sprouted from the ground and encased both women in separate boulders. They were only a pace apart, but they were trapped, unable to reach for each other.

When Finara tried to open her mouth, gravel swiftly rose to seal her lips — and Grace's as well. The next obvious choice was mind-speech. But Igneas frowned at them both. 'No, no. I may not hear it when you are communicating with your thoughts, but I can tell if you are doing it just by looking at you, sister. I forbid it for now. I would like the two of you to sit here in silence while you process what the other has said, then I will set you free. Finara, I must remind you that I have greater control over the rocks than you do. Don't think I'll let you teleport away.'

And with that, Igneas closed their eyes and began to meditate. Finara hoped her sibling was falling asleep for another century. She could teleport away if they weren't conscious enough to stop her. But that wouldn't help her. There was another, more pressing issue to deal with here.

Grace... Finara called silently.

Be quiet and process, was all Grace said in response.

CHAPTER FOUR

Finara's nose itched. Her hands, annoyingly, remained bound up inside the boulder. At least Igneas wasn't looking at her, so she could keep cursing away in her mind-voice without them noticing. But she made sure that someone else heard just how frustrating this whole situation was.

You should be processing, Grace reminded her.

This is how I process shit, Finara sniped back. *Okay?*

A mental sigh. *Finara...*

Look, Ms Crazy E-Paper Reporter, I'm giving Igneas' silly idea a go because you obviously want to do this for some reason. You two are getting a little too chummy, by the way.

Maybe this was a mistake, Grace murmured.

What — no! Finara didn't even try to hide her panic. *Getting engaged to me is not a mistake. Except for the part where you want me to wait to marry you. Because I am so not doing that.*

Grace raised her eyebrows at Finara. *I meant sitting still and attempting to process. It's obvious you're not going to agree with me about our engagement.*

Finara growled against the gravel sealing her lips, but quickly cut herself off when Igneas opened one eye and watched her closely. Finara went very still until that eye slid shut again.

And it's obvious that you're going to keep ripping my heart into pieces, Finara countered.

Grace didn't reply at first. She was valiantly attempting to keep her surface thoughts bare. Meanwhile, Finara was trying not to stew. She wasn't having as much success as Grace.

What if I chose a specific time frame? Grace suddenly asked.

Finara perked up. *You mean, a definite end point to our engagement?*

Yes. I was thinking my fortieth birthday would be perfect.

Finara's heart thudded painfully against her ribs. *I can do that. I've survived four years already, so four more won't destroy me. But...is that enough time for you to get ready for eternity?*

If you don't give a report a deadline, it will never be ready, Grace pointed out. *And I don't want to keep hurting you. I love you too much for that.*

Finara felt her cheeks grow warm. She grinned.

Grace grinned back at her.

'You did not keep silent,' Igneas observed, looking between them.

Finara spat the loosening gravel away from her lips. 'Yeah, well, we had to talk so we could figure things out. We're fine now.'

'You can oversee our binding in four years, if you like,' Grace told Igneas, stretching as the boulder disintegrated around her. Finara was still shaking off stubborn chunks of rock; clearly Igneas had a favourite here and it wasn't their sister.

'I do like,' Igneas said with a regal nod. 'And I like you, mortal. I will stifle my desire to kill you in future.'

'Good, I'll stifle my desire to remind you that a mortal is your superior,' Grace returned.

Igneas shook so hard with laughter that the volcano followed suit. Still chuckling, they rose from the ground and began lumbering away. 'Much to do. So much to do. And then I can sleep again.'

Pebbles and gems clustered around their form as they teleported away to some distant planet.

Finara was kissing Grace less than a heartbeat later. She shoved her fiancée onto the glowing lake and dove after her, fingers seeking, fingers finding and fingers dancing until Grace cried out in her beautiful voice. Soon all Finara could do was gasp and arch her back as Grace exacted her revenge on the goddess. They collapsed into a pile of limbs, cords of lava binding them together.

Grace frowned, her thoughts now clearly elsewhere. 'I keep thinking about your brother, the Desine, the one who hasn't seen his son in years. Is there no way you can help him?'

'Yeaaah, Sandsa won't accept my help, not after what I did,' Finara brooded.

'If we had a child, and she was taken from us,' Grace said quietly, 'wouldn't you move planets out of their orbit just to find her?'

'Callista did something to block him from sensing her or the kid,' Finara said, hoping that was the end of it.

'But you would never give up. We would never give up. I don't think the Desine would have either. Maybe he needs our help, even if he doesn't want it.'

Finara couldn't think of anything worse than bothering her oldest brother when he was nursing a grudge against her. She settled for giving Grace a shrug. 'Well, if you're so keen on chasing this up, you really should talk to Kuja. He knows a lot more about Sandsa's son than I do. By the way, Kuja's going to start feeling left out if you keep refusing to meet him. I mean, you've met Renaei and Igneas — even Fei. At this point, it looks like you're avoiding him.'

Grace pursed her lips. She was seriously considering this, Finara could tell.

'I'll meet Kuja, on one condition,' Grace said finally.

'Uh oh,' Finara said.

Grace laughed. 'No need to look so worried, Ms Fire Goddess. I might have bungled the proposal, but I'd still like to make use of the hotel room I booked. Once I've got my money's worth, I'll be more than happy to talk to your brother.'

'It would be nice to revisit those memories,' Finara murmured against her neck.

Grace drew away from the goddess to dress herself in one of those sharp pantsuits she was so fond of and Finara watched with a grin, her core tightening as she imagined peeling it back off again. When Grace took her hand, Finara had to struggle to remember what they were doing. Right, teleporting to the hotel on Arksaw.

'Stark, I love you,' Finara said as the fiery vortex swept up around them.

Grace's lips brushed over hers. 'I love you too.'

THE
CONTRACTING OF
BREZ AND ALEX,
WARLORDS

CHAPTER ONE

Grace Pendergast prided herself on her ability to mask her feelings. It was vital in her line of work. Unfortunately, this latest development was proving more challenging to hide than she had expected.

Grace knew there should be no physical sign of her whole universe suddenly shifting to reveal that she had been living out of phase for all of her thirty-six years before she'd agreed to marry Finara, the goddess of fire. Not long ago, owing to hundreds of period romance vids flooding the Web, it had been fashionable to resurrect the Old Earth tradition of exchanging engagement rings. Now only backwater worlds tended to use them.

Grace wouldn't have worn a ring anyway, because it wasn't her style.

But she was apparently *glowing* (Finara had teased her about it before they'd parted ways) and she was sure it was obvious to anyone who looked at her in passing, even though the sheen of sweat on her skin could easily be to blame.

Thankfully, her companion was too preoccupied with a nearby stall to notice her strange behaviour. But it wouldn't take long; Sean Akiyama was more partner than student these days.

Grace tensed when the sea breeze slid across her face. Alnia might look like paradise in the Webcasts, with its pristine beaches, endless misty forests and very few inhabitants, but there was one glaring problem with the planet that she couldn't overlook.

The locals' complete and utter loathing for tech.

'You're late, Sean,' the stall owner noted, her wide orb-like eyes laced with suspicion. 'Probably loaded to the gills with tech too. And they let you land? You smell like a mediaist.'

Sean's easy charm kicked into gear within moments. 'Mediaist? No way, June! I ditched the vidcam years ago, so your authorities had nothing to confiscate. Only got a techpad on me, I swear, and I see you're using one to log your sales. So we're allowed those, although I wouldn't say no to some frisking — if you decide it's warranted, of course.'

The tiny lilac tentacles on June's scalp twisted towards Sean, looking as judgemental as her smirk. 'You still getting the girls with those lame old words and that worn-out smile of yours?'

'I haven't had much luck with that for a while now,' Sean sighed.

Grace felt her lips twitch, but she made no comment. He was right. His ability to charm the pants off his sources had eroded somewhat in the past two years.

June chortled. 'Yeah, mediaists need to be both successful and attractive, so you never had much luck to start with! But I hear you're an e-paper reporter these days, Sean. What a fad.'

'A fad we spearheaded,' Grace said dryly. 'We aren't just any e-paper reporters.'

'Oh good, I wouldn't give a discount to just *any* e-paper reporters,' June remarked.

Right on cue, Sean sprang forward a whole extra pace and pointed at a pile of knitted clothes twinkling in the warm starlight. 'How much for those then? The booties. The ones with the glitterthread. Two pairs? Or maybe three for the price of two?'

'Booties?' Grace mused. 'Did your family emergency have something to do with babies?'

Sean chuckled, then averted his gaze from hers. 'Oh yeah. The galaxy's underworld is getting bigger all the time. More cutthroat recruits. More babies too, since we know how to have a good time. Come on, Boss, what else am I supposed to buy? This is a baby clothes stall.'

'You could shop anywhere,' Grace pointed out, acutely suspicious.

June *tsk*ed. 'Not if he wants his source to talk.'

'I could have come alone,' Sean muttered. 'But *nooo*, June assumed I was the junior partner at *The Pendergast e-Post*. For some reason.' He grinned aside at Grace. 'June used to live on Gerasnin and her stuff was really popular. I'd wager that any Chipper who had kids while stationed there in the last twenty Old Earth years put her booties on those little tootsies. Probably why they didn't lock her up for her other stuff, if you know what I mean. June was also the one who took me in when she saw me wandering around after I got kicked out of the temple...'

'And I've regretted it ever since!' June exclaimed.

She and Sean descended into trading indignant replies that did little to hide the fondness between them. Their half-hearted insults soon slid into reminiscence with practiced ease.

Not wanting to interrupt their reunion, Grace took a moment to absorb her surroundings. The cobblestone marketplace was flourishing and filled with multiple beings adorned in wonderfully bright clothes — but none of them chose to wear purple. The Galactic Law Enforcement Agency and their uniformed agents were banned from Alnia. But there was another, more important distinction between the Chippers and the Alnians: the god they worshipped.

Proudly erected at the entrance of the marketplace, standing guard over anyone who entered, was a large twisting archway made out of treated driftwood. Whirls and other wavy lines swarmed over it, denoting the movement of the ocean, and centred among all this was a horrifically scowling face that did not match the beauty of the object it was set into.

Oceania. The name mortals had given the Watine, the water god. Anyone who had been born with immortality or been granted it through marriage knew him as Fayay, the most vindictive member of the Galactic Pantheon.

I am mortal, Grace reminded herself. *For now.*

Finara's voice slid into her thoughts. *I'm still not happy about you coming here.*

Grace tilted her head towards the sea's distant horizon, giving her vacant gaze something to rest on. *I have a job to do, Finara. And you shouldn't leave this much of your presence on Alnia. Fayay will not take kindly to it.*

He could kill you, Grace!

And he couldn't kill you, Ms Fire Goddess, with your weakness against water-based powers?

Ugh! Why did I have to get engaged to the most stubborn mortal in the entire galaxy? Finara groused, but her ire cooled immediately. *Be careful, love. You're right. Water isn't my strong suit. I wish I could hang around, but...*

I'll let you know if I need your help, Grace assured her.

'Boss, you listening?' Sean asked, giving her a firm nudge that indicated he'd caught her zoning out. 'I know you didn't think this tip was a big deal until your buddy called you up and told you something that might relate to June's problem. But you okayed it and we're here now. Better get to work.'

Head General Zareth Sins, the leader of GLEA, had contacted Grace two days ago with the concerning news that he had lost track of a group of rogue agents. Thanks to Sean's source, Grace had been able to tell Zareth that a handful of Chippers had been spotted on Alnia. She could understand why Zareth had baulked upon hearing this. And she could also understand why Sean had not mentioned Zareth by name just now.

The Alnians would be even more suspicious of anyone arriving on the behest of the most prominent GLEA agent in the galaxy. Grace and Sean needed the local population to *want* to talk to them instead of locking them up, as had happened on some notable occasions that Grace decided not to revisit in her memories.

'One source could lead to a story on a slow day,' Grace said at last. 'But I need at least two sources to pique my interest. Unlike some people I could mention. How did that "brothel bots taking over the galaxy" story work out for you, Sean?'

June's scalp tentacles quivered with amusement. 'Can't tell which of you has been hanging around the other too long, can I? Quite the double act — Pendergast and Akiyama! But she seems like a good influence on you, boy. Stay with her and you might learn something.'

Grace felt more than saw the grimace on Sean's face. She knew what it meant for him, to always stand in her shadow. But he was good enough to strike out on his own.

So why hadn't he?

Sean's smile snapped back into place. 'I've learned enough to know you're stalling, June.'

'Stalling?' June hooted. 'Maybe I don't want to be talking about this where any old sod could hear me! The water here listens, you know. Oceania likes to eavesdrop. He's not a very kind sort, but when he takes revenge for you...now *that* is worth seeing. But he's not too worried if innocent bystanders get hurt. So I'd rather we mortals took care of these starking Chippers.'

'We should go somewhere that we can discuss this without being overhead,' Grace said, the nape of her neck prickling. 'As soon as possible.'

June began packing up her stall immediately, shouting at Sean to help her — and she warned him that he'd better do it without complaint if he wanted that three-for-two booties discount he was after. Grace watched the waves while they did this, squinting against the glare bouncing off them. Chippers, the Creator God's most devout followers, were supposedly terrorising the Alnians. There was no proof but for June's words, since the Alnians did not use vidcams, and Grace's suspicion that Zareth's missing agents were to blame was still only that: a suspicion. But if it was true...

Fayay's fury might not end with him killing every Chipper on Alnia.

He might go after every agent in the galaxy.

His father, the Creator God, very rarely pulled him into line for harming mortals. Grace thought this particularly unfair, since the other sub-level gods always met with consequences when they mistreated the people inside their domains.

'Stark!' June exclaimed.

Grace frowned, not sure what could have caused the stall owner to react so badly — but then she heard the roar of hoverbike engines. She traced the origin of the sound just in time to see eight humans in purple jumpsuits tear through the archway at the marketplace entrance. Their bikes still warm and growling, they stepped out onto the cobblestones, weapons at the ready and temples bulging with the chips that marked them as outlaws on Alnia.

Grace's jaw tightened.

Zareth's rogue agents had arrived.

CHAPTER TWO

Grace did not offer any resistance when she was herded into a group by a Chipper who poked and prodded his way through the pockets of his hostages, looking for valuables of any kind. Sean followed her and kept his feelings to himself, but she saw his mouth move just slightly, forming a silent curse or an insult. He had no love for GLEA. Zareth Sins' leadership had come too late to help the child he had been.

'Give me your techpad,' Grace said lowly. 'Not the decoy. The real one.'

Sean handed it over immediately, also keeping his voice to a murmur. 'Using She of the Fire for storage? That's not a perk that occurred to me.'

Grace set her lips at a firm line. She didn't need the reminder that she was yet again relying on Finara to further her career. But she wouldn't be able to tell the galaxy what was happening on Alnia if she didn't have her techpad to take notes. More importantly, this device (and its contents) should never, *ever* fall into mortal hands.

Grace took Sean's techpad and stowed it in her pocket, alongside hers. *Finara, I know you're still there. I need you to hide our techpads.*

The warmth that encased her fingers told her that the techpads were now in safekeeping. Relief washed over her, keeping her buoyed above the wordless anger seething amongst the crowd. The Chipper soon stomped his way towards her and demanded that she turn out her pockets. She did so. The coin-chips she could easily afford to lose, though it occurred to her when Sean sighed that he might not be in the same position as her. What he did with his money was his own business. She'd never asked. Never *wanted* to, of course not.

'I'm fairly certain theft is illegal on this world,' Grace said dryly as the young Chipper counted out his ill-gotten coin-chips in front of her.

His scowl was deep enough to rival the most sheer oceanic trenches. 'We protect these people. They should have donated money to help cover our operating costs if they didn't want us to take what's ours by force.'

Grace raised an eyebrow. 'Few would agree that donating is a mandatory activity.'

'Oceania is dangerous and doesn't deserve their worship,' the Chipper snapped.

'I won't argue with you there,' Grace said. 'But the fact is they *do* worship him. And they also made it illegal for the Creator God's emissaries to come to Alnia in the first place.'

'They don't know any better!'

Multiple pairs of eyes swung in their direction. Sean muttered something exasperated under his breath but didn't physically withdraw, as many of their onlookers were doing.

'Private Marcus, that's enough!' a grey-haired woman ordered as she marched over, her lasgun larger and more deadly than was standard for an agent of GLEA. 'Don't bother trying to educate these people. They had their chance. We gave it to them last week.'

Judging by the bowed heads and mute acceptance around

her, Grace could tell that the Alnians' famous pride was more passive than it was meaningful. Ignore the problem until it goes away. Never ask for help. Ban the tech that could save you. Their laws might keep them happily isolated, but it had opened them up to exploitation.

'It's their right to refuse you and your religion,' Grace said, meeting the newcomer's gaze squarely. This Chipper was a whole head shorter than her, as most other humans tended to be, but Grace saw that the height difference was not at all intimidating to her opponent. 'You are acting unlawfully *and* against the Agency's mandates.'

'Wise gal, huh?' the woman drawled, eyeing Grace with interest.

'Grace Pendergast, e-paper reporter,' Grace corrected. 'If you want to address me properly.'

Well, that's hot and I'm going to need a replay of this at some point, Finara mused, apparently forgetting to keep silent and off Fayay's radar.

Grace didn't bother to respond, though she made a mental note of this fantasy for later.

The Chipper's expression transformed; dark thunderclouds immediately broke apart, admitting a ray of starlight and a wide, wide smile. 'Ms Pendergast! I'm Colonel Lia Kim. Forgive me. I'm not usually this crabby. It's a busy day for us, you see.'

Grace was no stranger to this kind of welcome; she was one of the most trusted personalities in the galaxy and people thought she would give their own reputations a boost if they looked deserving and friendly enough. She'd used this false assumption before, in order to get information, and she would use it again. But she wasn't the only e-paper reporter on the scene.

'Yeah, becoming a pirate and plundering everything in sight can tend to make someone crabby,' Sean remarked.

Grace swallowed the rebuke. *He has spent too long with me.*

She considered stepping into the firing line instead, but she was curious to see where Sean was going with this. He had come a long way in two years.

'You must be Sean Akiyama, the intern,' Kim said with narrowed eyes.

A vein flickered in the centre of Sean's throat. 'Hey, that's rude. I called you exactly what you are. You know I'm not an intern — just as I know this is not how GLEA runs things. The Head General made a whole bunch of new rules, including not discriminating against people who worship another god. You must offer protection to everyone in the galaxy. What gives?'

'What *gives*...' Kim echoed darkly. The thunderclouds were back. '...is these new rules everyone loves talking about. Did Sins even ask if that's what the rest of us wanted?'

'Oh, boohoo.' Sean paused to trap a yawn behind his fingers. 'You've had seven whole years to get used to those rules. If you don't like GLEA and how it's going these days, then you can leave. That's your choice. You're lucky you have a choice, unlike the Alnians here. You never asked them what *they* wanted.'

Kim took several deep, audible breaths, clearly trying to regain her composure. Her minions continued their work and the Alnians continued to hold their tongues. It was likely that the homegrown Alnians had never known violence. A newcomer like June might have, but if someone came to a peaceful world like this, they were probably hiding from something — authorities, ex-spouses or life in general. They weren't going to make a fuss.

'Leave?' Kim finally said, indicating the scars on Sean's temple. 'Like you did, coward?'

Sean lifted his chin, unaware of or simply not caring about the aghast expressions being sent his way by the Alnians, as though he had been a snake in their midst.

'Yeah, I was given to the Orphanage Division as a baby,' Sean said with a casual toss of his head. 'Wasn't my choice. I tried my best, but I didn't agree with how things were run. So I got out. It's that easy.'

Anger melted into approval. The Alnians clearly respected someone who had rejected tech.

Kim lifted a hand and twisted it about on her wrist, a sign that she was building up a chip-generated forcefield to launch at any person or object in her way. 'Oh yeah? Well, it was our choice to join the GLEA that used to exist. We liked what we saw back then. Now? Not so much. This isn't what we agreed to. And there's no starking way I'll let someone take my chip. Now back off.'

'The safety and wellbeing of these people are more important than your love of tech and the power it gives you,' Sean said bluntly. 'You disgust me.'

The Alnians murmured amongst themselves, the first sound they'd made since they had been rounded up like muskoxen.

Grace stared at Sean. No doubt he was aware, as Grace was, that most Chippers couldn't do much damage with a sole forcefield — he wasn't in too much danger. No, that wasn't what had impressed her. He had effortlessly won over the crowd and made himself the only person they'd trust to tell their story. The words he'd chosen showed just how much he understood his audience and their emotions; a dangerous skill in the wrong hands.

It was a good thing he'd had a very good teacher.

The best, actually.

Kim levelled her lasgun directly at Sean's chest, using both hands to heft the heavy weapon. The bravado leeched out of him in an instant. He took a hasty step backwards and lowered his chin, fear flashing through his eyes — or was that a reflection of sea foam?

He's never quit this easily before, Grace mused. *Why has he become as docile as them?*

Because he has something to lose, like them, Finara said softly.

Them. Sean was one of them. And Grace wasn't. Not anymore.

Shame washed over her.

How could she already be so blind to her privilege? Most mortals would never contemplate enjoying the personal protection of a god, much less be in a position to take advantage of it.

She took Sean's place, putting him squarely behind her. 'Anyone who uses a weapon to win an argument needs to seriously reconsider that argument and its value.'

'Should have known that Grace Pendergast, champion of the truth, would take issue with me,' Kim said, her top lip twisting towards her nostrils. 'I always was a sucker for a pretty face.'

Grace was unmoved by the flattery. 'What will you do now?'

'Now? Now we take our money and go. Unless you want to die trying to stop us.'

Grace, much as I love those fiery images in your head right now... Finara murmured. *Probably best if the people here don't see a bunch of Chippers spontaneously combust. And that would definitely draw Fayay's attention.*

Grace pressed her lips together briefly. 'I won't stop you, Colonel. But I do want to go with you, if you'll permit me.'

'What for?' Kim sneered. 'So you can write terrible things about us?'

'I'd like to know why you're doing this. I want to understand.'

'You know everything already,' Kim said and turned her back on Grace. 'Go somewhere else for your quotes and righteous indignation, Ms Pendergast.'

There was no point in arguing. A hostile source was often worse than no source at all — not to mention unreliable. Grace could only watch, powerless, as the Chippers hauled their stolen goods away. One of them even used their tech-powered forcefields to juggle coin-chips, laughing when they dropped some of the money.

Was this the eternity ahead of her? Being lauded as Grace Pendergast, champion of the truth, but failing to help people when they needed her the most?

Your words will expose what's happening here, Finara reminded her gently.

I need to stop what's happening here, Grace countered. *If I write this report now and expose these agents, it will damage GLEA's reputation. I don't want that. The Agency protects those who can't afford to protect themselves. I need more information — no, I need a resolution.*

There was a long pause, one that was charged with Finara's tension and worry. *Hang tight, Grace. There might be a resolution headed your way — well, you'll make it one, knowing you. But I have to go. I've lingered too long.*

Finara? Grace called. *What do you —*

She didn't have long to decode her future wife's words. Her unfinished question was answered seconds later.

Grace just didn't expect the 'resolution' to involve a starship nearly falling on top of her.

CHAPTER THREE

A tortured metallic scream rent the air apart as the starship bore down on the marketplace, drowning out the panicked shouts of the people running from its path. The limping, oblong monstrosity was more rust than it was chrome, but it still managed to plough through the ornate archway at the entrance. The driftwood forming the archway broke into splinters as tall as human beings and hurtled through the air, tearing gashes into awnings and stabbing into the sandy ground, forming potential gravemarkers.

'Boss, come *on!*' Sean said as he grabbed Grace's arm and gave it a hard yank. 'Don't give She of the Fire any more work to do than you have already!'

Grace didn't need further prompting. She slid off her heels and hooked her fingers into the backs of them, then turned and ran. Within seconds, Grace and Sean had caught up to the Chippers, who were frantically trying to strap down their stolen goods. Some had already given up and abandoned their hoverbikes. The fifteen rogue agents might have been able to join their forcefields together to counter boulders or perhaps a hovercar.

But a starship? Best to keep running.

The ground shuddered beneath Grace's bare feet and a blast of air threw chips of stone and gritty sand against her back. The ship had made landfall. She slowed, swinging back around to take in the damage. A large gash had been sliced through the soft dune system and the rectangular vessel had come to rest inside a jagged crater in the cobblestones.

Alnians with wares to sell had converged there once a week for centuries. Now it was an assembly point for the mercenaries who spilled out of the wreckage, their armour and weapons gleaming — unlike their vessel, their equipment was new and dangerous and their expressions were hard enough to shatter diamonds. Their cohort might have been made up of an array of different species and genders but they all moved perfectly in sync, like the outlawed bots were supposed to have done during their many uprisings. The mercenaries found and targeted the Chippers with ease, the red pinpricks projected from the sights of their weapons dancing over the agents' purple jumpsuits. But they didn't fire.

Evidently, they weren't here to kill the Chippers, just chase them off.

'Retreat!' Colonel Kim bawled. 'Retreat now, agents! Leave the bikes and run!'

The Chippers fell back to their sea-bound vessels which they'd stashed on the other side of the peninsula, away from the broken yachts and fishing boats that had been tossed into each other when the downed starship had passed over the sheltered cove, churning up waves and destruction.

'You lot don't look very grateful,' one of the mercenaries sneered at the subdued Alnians as he marched forward with his chest puffed out, to better display the legionnaire badge pinned to his chest. The symbol on the blue backing wasn't one that Grace was familiar with.

There were thousands of legions throughout the galaxy, far

too many to keep track of. Many disbanded within months due to running out of money and/or losing their territory. Why this legion had thought that either was to be found here was beyond Grace. Alnia had very little in the way of coin-chips and their laws clearly stated that the planet was already under the sovereignty of a permanently settled people. Then again, that didn't deter some legions.

'So are ya gonna pay us what you owe us, for helping you out with them Chippers?' the main legionnaire demanded. 'Come on, I'm gettin' old here.'

Sean stepped out in front of the pack, then raked one finger from east to west and back again. 'This is a lot of damage. If you want to hang around that badly, you could at least help us rebuild and chip in for the costs.'

The mercenary huffed and puffed in annoyance, but his lasgun drooped.

He didn't seem to be in the mood to keep fighting.

Grace saw Sean's shoulders relax slightly. This was the second time in so few minutes that he'd faced off against someone bigger and better armed than him.

'We good?' Sean prompted.

The mercenary growled. 'No, we're not *good*. But our leader will probs think so. He's way too soft sometimes. Still, it'd be nice if you lot threw something our way for chasing off the purple brigade just now.'

'What little these people have,' Grace said, moving forward to stand beside Sean, 'if it wasn't stolen by the Chippers, needs to be kept for repairs. And I would be very careful about what demands you make of followers of Oceania. Revenge is his mandate. Everyone knows this.'

'He's more likely to go after the Chippers, isn't he?' the legionnaire laughed, unbothered.

Grace bit the inside of her cheek. *Finara, can you at least tell me why you thought these people would provide me with a resolution? They won't take on the Chippers out of the goodness of their hearts. Legionnaires don't work for free.*

But Finara said nothing; she had scrubbed her presence from Alnia and left Grace completely alone, something the goddess would only do if Fayay had been about to catch her lurking in his domain. Grace shivered in the ocean breeze that was unrelentingly fresh and cool, so unlike the crackling flames that consumed her so often. Sean glanced at her, concerned, but she gave him a tight nod.

'Will you be leaving Alnia?' Grace asked, giving the downed starship a dubious once-over.

The mercenary scratched his auburn bristles. 'Nah. That was our ride off this rock. Sorry to disappoint. But we've got some yachts stashed in another cove that can take us back to our base.'

'I'd like to come with you,' Grace said.

He blinked. 'Uh, why the stark would we let you?'

Grace crossed her arms and straightened her shoulders into a terse line. This was what Fianra called her 'power move'. And not without reason. 'Because I'm Grace Pendergast, e-paper reporter. You may have heard of me.'

That was an understatement, apparently. There was a sharp intake of breath from the group of mercenaries that had slowly formed a ring around Grace and Sean. The main legionnaire whistled lowly. 'If you're tellin' the truth, I'm down for you to ride along.'

'Just like that, you'll allow me into your base? Unharmed?' Grace confirmed.

'Oh yeah! Being featured in *The Pendergast e-Post* — it'd be great advertising for us.' The mercenary grimaced. 'Don't know that there's much to advertise though.'

Grace let her eyes wander over the destruction sown by the legionnaires. 'I agree with you there. But I can't promise you anything except my presence. My associate will be staying here to speak to the Alnians; it's only fair that we hear as many sides of the story as possible.'

'Grace...' Sean hesitated. 'Are you sure you don't want me with...'

'I'll be fine,' Grace said sharply. 'I used to do this alone — without *any* backup. I still can. And besides, the Alnians don't trust me. They trust you.'

'Already?' Sean asked, perplexed. 'She of the Fire tell you that?'

Grace smiled. 'No. I saw how well you handled yourself earlier.'

'Boss, I *backed down*. It was humiliating. You'd never do that.'

'I think you forget just how capable and clever you are.' Grace paused, feeling her temples tighten. 'There's a big difference between us, Sean. I never have to back down. It's an unfair advantage. And it's not your fault.'

Sean stared at her, mouth slightly agape.

'Sean,' Grace gently prompted. 'Right now we both have work to do.'

'On it,' Sean said immediately and walked back to the crowd. He began asking questions that most reporters would never dream of keeping in their arsenal; he wanted to know if they were all okay, if anyone was hurt, if they could help him sort out which wares could be salvaged and returned to their owners.

A good way to distract them, Grace noted. *They've calmed down enough to start talking to him.*

Sean really did know what he was doing.

'Alright,' Grace said to the mercenary. 'Take me to your leader. But I want to know their name first. And yours too. You already know mine, so it's only fair.'

Her new companion shrugged. 'Can't argue with that. I'm Brez. And Alex Moore is our leader. He's the man with the big ideas and *morals*.' A minute sigh. 'I wish he'd let us kill people. It'd make things so much easier.'

Grace's lips twitched. 'I'd very much like to meet the man with the big ideas and morals.'

Brez gave her a pointed look. 'You won't be able to just snatch his secrets, I warn ya. He'll be a tough nut to crack.'

Soft enough to forbid murder, but tough enough to lead bloodthirsty legionnaires, Grace mused as she followed the mercenaries across the dunes, still carrying her heels. *That's unusual. Is this Alex Moore a fighter or an actor pretending to be one?*

She'd soon find out, but first she would have to traverse the sea in order to reach his base.

Grace drew up short in front of the small motorised boat that would take her out to one of the yachts. When the waves continued to gently lap at the sand, when no god arrived to smite her, she accepted that she was as safe as she could be for now — and stepped onto the boat.

She still wasn't sure if these people would give her a resolution, but in lieu of legitimate Chippers, the legionnaires seemed like her best chance of dealing with Zareth's rogue agents.

So far that 'best chance' didn't look very promising.

CHAPTER FOUR

Grace had seen many hidden bases in her time as an e-paper reporter, but few so interesting as the rocky cove where the mercenaries took her. The stairs and passageways inside the jagged cliffs were so ancient and shadow-strewn they looked like they had been created back when the bots had ruled over the endless skies, leaving humans and other intelligent species to hide wherever they could, rejecting all tech in a last-ditch attempt to survive.

It wouldn't surprise Grace if Alnia had been one of the last holdouts where people had gathered before eventually resisting and reclaiming the galaxy. The locals' loathing for tech was stronger than anything she'd encountered on any other world.

Grace ran her fingers along the rock walls, entranced by the smooth lines carved by hands long ago. This method of recording history would ensure that this story lasted for millennia, dying out long after any files or written texts. The waves in the ancient artwork rose up with the tunnel floor as she continued to walk, their uneven lines smashing the specks that fell from the sky. Small stick figures then bowed to the waves, worshipping the source of their salvation.

Fayay might have a reputation as a tempestuous god with a knack for hurting his people instead of protecting them, but he hadn't ignored them during the bot uprisings.

Was he less jaded then? Grace wondered. *Did he show a mercy towards his people that he'll never show his siblings? It's impossible to know. There are so few records from that era.*

She slammed a lid on those thoughts and was relieved, as always, that the water god couldn't read minds. He'd know what she was — and *who* she was connected to — in an instant.

Hopefully he wasn't paying any attention to Alnia just now.

The legion's leader sat on what looked like a throne, lounging back against the rigid slabs as though they were cushions instead of worn rock. He was barely old enough to be an adult, probably not even in his twenties, and he wore leathers that had been strategically distressed. The badge of his legion was displayed proudly, as were the aluminium stripes he'd used to denote his role as leader. It was almost laughable when Brez took up a protective position beside him. They reminded her of little boys pretending to be soldiers.

'Haven't you lot got somewhere to be?' Alex Moore groused and his legionnaires (except Brez, of course) immediately scarpered back down the tunnels. Presumably they had assigned tasks to complete, though Grace hadn't a clue what they could be doing. The mercenaries certainly weren't cleaning out the caves or trying to make them habitable.

Grace waited with her arms crossed and her back straight. Soon enough, Alex Moore would reveal his measure. People always did in her presence, no matter how hard they tried not to.

'Stark,' Alex breathed and stood up, rubbing his lower back. 'That chair is about as comfortable as an icicle up the rear end. But it's nowhere near as painful as what happened today! Shit, Brez! How could you be so careless?'

'Chased out the Chippers though, hey?' Brez said blandly.

'Brez! We did way more damage than the Chippers ever

have!' Alex paced, his feet moving in an erratic zigzag. 'It was supposed to be different this time. These people were supposed to accept us as legitimate protectors, not brand us as wannabe warlords like all the other planets have done.'

Brez smothered a yawn with the hand that wasn't caressing his lasgun. 'Wasn't my idea to pick this backwater. You said it was a good place to hide out, since there weren't any Chippers down here. *Yeah.* No Chippers. Nice one.'

'They're not real Chippers,' Alex said with a dismissive shake of his head.

'*Real* Chippers?' Brez exploded. His face darkened beneath his auburn beard. 'They've got starking chips!'

'They can't arrest us.'

'They can still fucking kill us by waving their *hands!*'

'Oh yeah? Well, our numbers are pretty even, so I'd like to see how they fare in a lasgunfight.'

Grace gently cleared her throat. 'Pardon my interruption. Am I to understand that you have broken laws on other worlds? Operated above or around them? If this is the case, that's probably why you're being seen as warlords.'

Alex blinked for several moments, then smiled sheepishly. 'Sorry. It's been a shitty day. Where are my manners? I'm Alex Moore — you've already met Brez. We're in charge.'

'Of what exactly?' Grace pressed. 'What does your legion actually do?'

'We save people when the Chippers aren't around,' Alex replied, linking his arms behind his back. It was far from a gesture of authority; on him it was performed and poorly at that. 'The Chippers can't go everywhere. They don't have the bodies — or the permission, like here on Alnia.'

Grace's eyebrows rose. 'Saving people. An interesting pastime for a legion.'

'Our old legion went bankrupt,' Alex said, marking out a jagged circle as he paced back towards Grace. 'Too much focus on coin-chips. Too many idiots in middle management, you know? So we — Brez and I — figured we could strike out on our own. Do what the Chippers do. Get people to donate to our cause.'

'Donate!' Brez spat on the floor. 'Should have extorted them, like most legions do.'

'That's *illegal* in some places,' Alex said with a wince.

Brez just stared at him. He had a right to — it sounded like the legion was already neck-deep in the kind of trouble that could land them in prison. Extortion was a strange place to draw the line.

'Illegal or not, turning up without permission to deal with a problem...' Grace paused, taking note of Brez's defiance and the tightening grip on his lasgun. '...is not going to convince the people you save to give you any coin-chips.'

'Yeah, like I never tried to tell him that,' Brez muttered.

Alex's pale blue eyes glimmered with exhaustion and his dark hair seemed to flatten around his temples. 'I wanted to help people. For a fee, of course. But I underestimated just how skint everyone in the galaxy was, didn't I?'

'I *told* you the Alnians didn't deserve our help,' Brez snarled. 'Fuck this, Alex! They as good as killed your mum. Shoulda left them to rot! Stark! We can't leave now. We're stranded.'

Grace narrowed her focus onto Alex. 'This is personal to you. What happened?'

He sighed and slumped back onto the throne, rubbing the uneven bristles shadowing his chin. It didn't look as though he could grow a decent beard. 'Getting new tech onto Alnia is hard, even the stuff they allow here. A storm opened up on top of us one time and we were too far out to make it back to the peninsula on our own engines, so she tried to call for help — Old Abe had a big trawler and he could have grabbed us, see. But the starking communicator conked out. And we went down.

'I woke up on the shore hours later. Mum didn't.'

Even Brez had fallen into a respectful silence. Eventually, when he did speak up, his voice no longer dripped with hostility. 'Look, mate, the Alnians don't want to be saved. Shoulda found another world with a raging hate-on for the Chippers.'

'But the Alnians do need help,' Grace said.

'Not from us, I guess,' Alex brooded. 'Brez is right. We should have gone somewhere else. And you're right as well, Ms Pendergast. We're criminals. The Chippers will be happy to snatch us up as soon as we manage to leave. Which we should do soon. We've pissed these people off enough.'

Brez audibly ground his teeth together. 'The boys aren't going to like this. They were okay with your idea to start with, figured it was an inventive way to make money. But now that they're fugitives with nothing to show for it? They'll kill us — and that's if they're generous!'

'I'll take the fall,' Alex decided. 'Alone.'

'The stark you will!' Brez snapped. 'We're co-owners! Both of our names are attached to the legion's ID on the Galactic Database. I'm just as fucked as you.'

Grace held up a hand to forestall any further argument. 'I don't agree with your methods, but I understand what you were trying to achieve. And frankly, you're the only ones who can do anything about this. Head General Zareth Sins won't send any legitimate Chippers here to deal with these rogue agents, because he doesn't want to break the law.'

Alex's blue eyes narrowed. 'You say that like you know what Zareth Sins is thinking.'

'I have no idea what he's thinking,' Grace said, even though she probably *could* know if she asked Finara. 'But I've been in contact with him. He's the one that alerted me to Alnia's current problem.'

Brez erupted into curses, squared off against Grace and levelled his lasgun at her chest. 'No starking Chippers or Chipper-lovers are allowed in our presence! Back off.'

Alex rubbed his temples. 'Brez, please. I'm trying to fix this. Ms Pendergast, do you know Zareth Sins? As more than a source?'

'Yes,' Grace said. This connection would work her in favour now. 'He's become a friend.'

'How friendly is he to criminals?' Alex asked glumly. 'Do you think...'

Grace allowed a small grimace. 'I don't know. But I would like to call him and see if we can sort something out. What would you ask of him — what do you *need* from him?'

'How about a starship to get us off this miserable planet?' Brez grumbled. But he did lower his weapon.

Alex leaned further back against the throne, his fingers tapping out the rhythm of some popular Enocian song. 'If we're to help the Alnians, we need an upper hand over the Chippers. Sure, we have more lasguns than them, but they have forcefields. We won't catch them off guard next time. If Zareth Sins can give us any kind of advantage...'

'He could give us a lot more than a starship,' Brez added, now looking thoughtful. 'Mate, we could keep doing his dirty work...in return for a *pardon*.'

Alex's expression brightened considerably.

'I can't promise anything,' Grace warned. 'But I'll speak to him.'

Eyeing the young man who had appropriated a throne that was far too large and awkward for him, Grace unclipped her communicator from her belt. Alex Moore's plan to use his legion to help people wasn't a completely foolish one. There were times when the Chippers could do nothing — and times when even the sub-level gods couldn't step in. They would never interfere outside of their own domains.

This was Fayay's territory. But it was also Alex's homeworld.

The Watine would not be displeased that one of his mortals was dealing with the problem without pestering him; Fayay was always more violent towards those who made incessant and pointless demands on his time.

Grace knew what resolution she wanted. She just wasn't sure if Zareth would go along with it.

'I'll need the room,' she said. 'To make a private call.'

Alex and Brez practically tripped over each other on their way out.

CHAPTER FIVE

'Is this link secure, Zareth?'

Pleasantries could wait. This was too important.

'Do you really want Fei to know you asked me that?' Zareth Sins asked dryly. 'She designed our communications system — *and* billed us directly instead of putting TerraCorp on the invoice. That made it impossible for us to hide the expense from those who donate to our cause. GLEA founded TerraCorp for a reason.'

Grace kept her expression neutral instead of releasing the unbidden smile. There weren't any vidcams hidden in Alex's throne room and she knew this from conducting a quick sweep with her techpad, using software also provided by Fei (the rainforest god's wife and also the galaxy's best programmer). But it was better to be sparing when it came to letting her professional mask slip.

'I take it you found my rogue agents,' Zareth went on, far too used to Grace's silences to wait for her to say something. 'What can be done about them?'

Grace's eyes roved around the throne room, tracing the extensive mural on the walls that depicted an array of beings hunting bots, a menace of the past. Alnia was now facing a different menace — even if their new saviours were using the same ancient base.

'There's a legion here that can help,' she told Zareth.

'A legion!? Grace, I don't know of any legion that isn't outlawed somewhere.'

'It's worth noting that your agents are outlawed here,' Grace said. 'I have already spoken to the men in charge: Alex Moore and Brez. They are in a position to do something. They are, in fact, *willing* to do something. But they need GLEA's backing.'

Zareth's long sigh descended into static. 'They want a pardon, don't they. I can't give it.'

'Why not?'

'It sets a precedent,' Zareth explained. 'We shouldn't encourage criminals to trade favours with the Galactic Law Enforcement Agency.'

She had an argument ready for him. 'You can still decide who you ultimately deal with. And I would call them "contractors" instead of "criminals". You don't need to pay them as much as you do your agents, if you want to ensure that people still enlist.'

'I see you've given this some thought,' Zareth said. 'What else?'

Grace wasn't one for pacing, but found that she had to neatly align her heels on the floor to keep herself still. 'GLEA imprisons criminals and releases them when their sentences are served. But many of those people return to a life of crime, because you haven't given them anything except a holiday from it. If they know they might get a job at the end of their incarceration, if you *rehabilitate* them as opposed to simply punishing them, they might reoffend less. It would be a good look for the Agency.'

'Especially if the famous Grace Pendergast is the one to give us that look,' Zareth noted.

Grace gave him the time to think it over.

He relented within seconds. 'Alright. I'll consider it a trial run, with these two men.'

'Better make it official before we tell them anything,' Grace said. 'And you'll need to promise them — and the other legionnaires, who can't be charged for the crimes of their leaders — a ride off Alnia.'

'I can give them that ride, but they're on their own when they go after my rogue agents.'

'I understand. It looks like a very even fight from where I'm standing. The outcome could go either way, so it would help if you gave them some advantage over your agents.'

Zareth muttered a soft curse. 'They'll have it. The rogue agents will not be able to use their chips.'

'How?' Grace asked.

'This is not something that can ever appear in one of your reports,' Zareth warned her. 'It would compromise the thousands of agents under my command.'

Grace wet her lips, tasting salt and something else: the desire to keep gathering information, no matter what it pertained to. 'Trust me. I'm keeping secrets that are far more important. Cosmically important.'

'Very well.' He sounded tired, but there was a measure of relief in his words, as if he'd wanted to tell someone about this for a long time. 'Fei found some very old code in our servers. Seems that when the Web was built, our chips were connected to it so that our agents could join their powers together and create larger forcefields.'

Grace said nothing. Usually it would have been a tactic to keep him talking, but she was actually stunned. This wasn't in the Archive, the galaxy's biggest repository of history. She'd never found anything about GLEA's past or their origins — and she'd spent years looking into it.

'Because the chips are on the Web,' Zareth explained, 'they can be shut down. Remotely.'

'You can shut down an agent's powers anywhere in the galaxy?' Grace murmured. The implications were huge.

Zareth blew out a breath. 'Yes. But not precisely. I can send a shutdown signal through to a specific Web relay — such as the one near Alnia. Every chip in range of the relay will cease to work. For as long as we like.'

'Was that also in the old code?'

'No,' he admitted. 'We decided to add our own modifications. Now we can upload updates into the chips to deal with glitches. And it means I can give your legionnaires that advantage. Trust *me*, Grace.'

It was an explosive secret. And Zareth had chosen to share it with her.

'I do trust you,' Grace told him.

'That's it then,' Zareth said quietly. 'I'll take out the chips for the next few hours. I have a nearby starship that I can redirect to provide this *ride* for our contractors and their legionnaire friends. I'll contact you again when it's in orbit.'

Grace's communicator fell silent.

She clipped the device back onto her belt and went out into the tunnel to give Alex and Brez the good news.

Of course, they wanted to know what sort of salary they'd be getting.

Grace was glad she didn't know the answer to that. She suspected Zareth's budget wouldn't offer them the riches they were busily imagining.

***

'Well, this is fun,' Sean said dryly after they'd watched the mercenaries' yachts ram into those belonging to the Chippers. He and Grace remained safely on the shoreline, away from the action. 'Even if I can't see exactly what's going on. Best I can tell, the Chippers are wearing lascuffs and are being escorted onto a ship that your legionnaire buddies definitely didn't have this morning.'

Grace pressed her lips together firmly. There were a lot of things she would never write for the galaxy's billions of eyes, though Sean was one of the few people that she trusted with her secrets. But this wasn't hers to tell. Finally, she said, 'GLEA has decided to hire contractors. Alex and Brez are the first they've signed up, in exchange for a pardon and a salary. That's why they have GLEA's backing.'

'Contractors,' Sean repeated, dubious. 'Contractors for a *religious* organisation?'

Grace bit back the laugh. She was beginning to suspect she was a contractor herself — for a much higher power. Her side project, curating a history of the Galactic Pantheon and its members, would not be done at all if it was left to the gods. Stark, she wasn't even sure why *she'd* started doing it. But if it was her purpose, then she wanted to see it through.

'Stranger things have happened in this galaxy,' Grace offered.

Sean tossed her a grin. 'Yeah, you would know.'

Their laughs mingled together and grew in volume, chasing off the Alnians who had been milling around and eyeing Grace and Sean, not brave enough to ask what happened now. The

279

answer would have been simple: soon GLEA's starship would break free from the atmosphere and there would not be a single legionnaire, contractor or Chipper left on the planet.

'Do you have another story lined up?' Grace asked as the sun began to set.

Sean shrugged. 'A few. Maybe. We'll see. Depends if your sources corroborate mine.'

'Not anymore,' Grace corrected. 'You no longer need to confer with me before you choose a story. I trust your judgement. Just send me your reports.'

'About time!' Sean crowed.

She raised her eyebrows at him.

'Thanks, Boss,' he amended quickly. 'This means a lot to me.'

Grace smiled. 'I know. And it really was overdue. Before you know it, you'll be leaving and starting your own e-paper.'

Her curiosity lifted the pitch of her words; an unspoken question. He had to have heard it. She wanted to know why he hadn't left yet, why he hadn't at least considered it. But Grace couldn't bring herself to ask. She was afraid that it had something to do with her.

Sean waved a dismissive hand. 'Nah, like June said — if I stay with you long enough, I might learn something. See ya round, Boss.'

He turned and walked back towards the small, sandy strip of land that served as Alnia's primitive spaceport.

Grace watched him go, her heart sinking.

He thinks he has to protect me, Grace realised. *That's why he stays; it's never been about the fame or the coin-chips. Finara...please tell me I'm wrong.*

Finara's voice ghosted into her mind, still faint due to fear of discovery. *Grace...*

At least tell him that it isn't his job! Grace cried.

I can't, Finara said. *He wouldn't believe me. And it's not just a job to him. It's part of him, part of why he gets up in the morning.*

The tear startled Grace as it wended its way down her wind-chapped skin, as salty as the sea undulating around her and as hot as the eye it had bled from. Grace wiped the tear away and stared down at the moisture on her fingertips.

'Then I still have something to teach him,' she decided out loud.

And what's that? Finara asked.

'That sometimes you have to move on and let it go. The thing that you thought defined you.'

Good luck, Finara mused. *You'll need it.*

Grace winced. 'I know. I shouldn't have taught him to be so stubborn first.'

Finara's laughter warmed her and lightened every corner of her heart.

Grace knew she could do it. Maybe not today or tomorrow, but she'd get Sean to move on.

It was only a matter of time.

THE EDUCATION OF SELBEN, TEENAGER

CHAPTER ONE

Shadows clad the intruder as they darted through the narrow aisles, their hooded head bowed as they hunted for their victim.

It was hard to tell exactly which room they were in, since it was no different from the thousands of others hidden beneath the surface of fifty identical moons. Cold, lifeless and smoothed over by machines, the moons were connected to each other in a tight orbit, like grey stone beads threaded onto a necklace. There was no planet for them to rotate around; just a strange, small asteroid that never moved, a curiosity left behind by the galaxy's ancestors in a time before the bot uprisings, a time when tech could do amazing things.

That's not to say that tech couldn't do amazing things now, of course.

The intruder possessed a techpad loaded with software that could make doors part for them like flimsy curtains. The Web was blocked beneath the surface of every moon belonging to the Archive, so you had to make a lucky guess about what type of security systems you needed to hoodwink — and after all that, you'd have to locate a specific server among millions of others.

The intruder wasn't deterred. They knew exactly which server to target and plug into. And they knew exactly what information they wanted to erase. Their work was done in moments, allowing them to turn and sprint away, still completely undetected.

The program had done its damage. The precious files were gone.

Forever.

***

'What was deleted?' Grace Pendergast asked, leaning forward as she watched the footage being displayed on the small vidscreen. The vandal might have been invisible to all sensors (thus triggering no alarms), but the Archive's vidcams ran off a separate system in case a breach like this ever occurred.

The technician sitting in front of her, Vott Nevi'in, used another vidscreen off to the side to call up the required file. 'Moon 32, Hemisphere 2, Section 55, Subsection 89. The early history and settlement of the planet Leeds. It was marked "irreplaceable". Which means — '

'This information existed nowhere else,' Grace finished in a stunned whisper.

Vott nodded unhappily. 'Yeah. It's gone. Shit. Who would do something like this? To the Archive? We're no one's enemy. We're starking neutral in every clash. *Why?*' He swore a few more times and shoved his hoverchair backwards, narrowly avoiding a collision with Grace. 'I'm sorry, Ms Pendergast. I know you donate enough money to the Archive to be given the VIP treatment here, but I'm not feeling terribly cordial just now.'

'Don't worry about it,' Grace assured him. 'This is a great loss.'

He left the room, his four shaking hands smoothing his wild ginger mane back behind his ears. His pale skin had turned a stunning cobalt blue, the sign of a Lentarian's distress. They rarely allowed anyone to see them like this; they had learned millennia ago that humans, the dominant species in the galaxy, preferred those species that looked most like them.

Grace turned away from the vidscreens and took in the view offered by the looping plexiglass window. The servers she could see represented a tiny fraction of the entire system. This was the head of operations at the Archive and only certain visitors (those who donated significant sums towards the monstrous running costs, of course) were allowed inside. The Archive contained more of the galaxy's knowledge and history than anywhere else. It had to be protected.

Grace crossed her arms and exhaled slowly.

What did she know about Leeds? Not much. It hosted the Arms Academy and various other institutions devoted to military education. Most legions in the galaxy were formed there by graduates who had failed to secure jobs in more legitimate streams.

She had no idea how the planet had been settled. What it had been like millennia ago.

Did anyone alive know? Had anyone accessed this file and read it, perhaps committed some of it to memory? Someone had to have done so, because the alternative was too much to bear.

Grace? Finara called. *Are you alright?*

Grace closed her eyes, allowing the moment of weakness. *What do you know about Leeds?*

Uh, it's not in my domain anymore, not since the core cooled down...

So it was yours once, Grace said. *What was Leeds like? Before humans colonised it?*

Finara hesitated. *I...don't really know what you want from me.*

Grace filled her mind with her sorrow and the story of what had happened. There were too many vidcams in the Archive's facilities to allow the goddess to make an appearance, but the room noticeably warmed up. Grace's shivers abated, as though her fiancée had physically arrived to envelope her inside a much-needed embrace.

I'm sorry, love, Finara said. *I should have known it was serious from that look on your face when the Archive contacted you. I was so miffed about losing a night in a hotel with you that I...*

Grace drew a steadying breath, then another. *It's alright. I was disappointed too. But the Archive is important to me — and important to the entire galaxy.*

If it's important to my future wife, then of course it's important to me, Finara told her.

Grace felt a smile prick her lips. Finara had come a long way from the goddess who had spent millennia dismissing the mortals beneath her. Sure, one particular mortal would always be more important to her than the rest of them, but the goddess *cared*. She didn't just care about the safety of mortals — she cared about their feelings as well.

Hey, that's a secret, you know. Finara did the mental version of clearing her throat. *Now get that poker face back on. You've got work to do.*

I love you, Grace murmured.

Love you too, Grace.

Grace turned back to the paused footage on the vidscreen. She could find no clue about the intruder's identity there, or their allegiance. One thing was for sure — the information was lost. There was no retrieving it. But even this was a useful starting point, because someone cared enough about Leeds' past to erase

288

it from existence. There was a connection to be found here, however tenuous.

She just had to figure out what it was.

Her communicator beeped. Recognising the ID displayed on the device, Grace accepted the link. 'Sean? I thought you weren't reporting in for another Old Earth month.'

It had been just under three years since they'd last worked elbow to elbow. There were weeks when silence stretched between them, though Grace read everything he wrote, more confident than ever in her decision to let him operate independently.

Sean hesitated. 'Grace...I found them.'

'Found who?' Grace asked, a thrill of foreboding racing through her. It had to be a coincidence. She hadn't even told Sean what story she was chasing; not only was it something she never did, she hadn't even had time to do so. She'd barely been able to dress before Finara had teleported her to a nearby space station.

'The Archive's vandal,' Sean answered.

'I need to meet this vandal,' Grace said firmly.

His voice remained guarded. 'I thought you'd say that, Boss. I can hazard a guess as to where you are right now. I'm on Croatoan, a planet in the next system over. It's about two days away if you've got a good starship. But that won't be a problem for you.'

'No, it won't,' Grace agreed.

'See you soon then?'

'Soonish.'

Grace clipped her communicator back onto her belt and headed for the exit. This wasn't a secure place to suddenly disappear from. She returned to the shuttle that would take her back to the space station, forcing herself to walk with long, unhurried strides. The journey took two hours. It felt like an aeon to someone used to the instant nature of teleportation. As soon as she was able, Grace disembarked and cloistered herself inside her cheap hotel room, where the vidcams had already been fried, and swiftly packed her bag.

The flare of warmth at her back told her that a certain fire goddess had arrived. The arms that circled her body and the lips that pressed against the nape of her neck revealed that Finara knew she needed more comfort than words alone could give.

'Let it all out, before you're face to face with the vandal,' Finara told her. 'Do it *now*, Grace.'

Grace closed her eyes, but hot fury had already dried up her tears. Her carefully cultivated mask slipped and kept slipping. She could not face anyone right now, much less a source who definitely wouldn't respond to an openly hostile interviewer.

Fire roared down her arms and up her legs, smothering her. The flames were welcome, for they burned away the roiling, unwelcome feelings and grounded her like nothing else could.

The flames meant that she had not lost the most important thing in her life.

'You okay now?' Finara whispered against her ear.

Grace nodded slowly. 'Yes. I'm mortified that I lost control of my emotions. But it's...it's a colossal loss on a galactic scale. This is no mere crime. It's a disaster.'

Finara turned Grace around, keeping firm hands on her shoulders. 'Grace, a lot has been lost since the days of Old Earth. And it'll happen again. Time is the most prolific killer. I should know — I've watched it take many lives.'

But not yours, Finara added quietly. *It will never take your life.*

Grace bit her lip, her mind wandering a year into the future, when she and Finara would be united forever by marriage. Nothing would change, not at first. She'd remain an e-paper reporter. But what would she be in a century? Shouldn't she change her career at some point? Challenge herself with something new?

'Grace, you love what you do,' Finara reminded her.

'For now,' Grace said. 'But I can't keep doing the same thing. Not for an eternity.'

'It's a good thing you'll have a wife who can find other fun ways to fill your time, hmm?'

'And a wife who can take me across the galaxy to wherever I need to be,' Grace added.

Finara laughed. 'I remember when someone used to ask nicely.'

'I can ask nicely. If you'd like.'

'Mmm, I'd rather give you a proper send-off,' Finara said lowly. She hooked her fingers into Grace's jacket and yanked the reporter in close, grinning wickedly but denying Grace what she craved.

'Finara...' Grace said hoarsely.

She couldn't help it. She chased Finara's lips and swiftly lost herself in the ensuing kiss, hands sliding beneath the goddess' sparse clothes and grasping warm flesh. Finara indulged her.

Several minutes later, when the fiery vortex had dropped from her body and revealed her new surroundings, Grace was ready, her suit straight and her expression neutral. The galaxy still needed Grace Pendergast, e-paper reporter.

And she had no intention of letting her readers — or the Archive — down.

CHAPTER TWO

Walls smothered in grey ooze greeted Grace when she appeared inside the motel. Whether the slime was due to questionable cleaning practices or the foul atmosphere (the ambient stench was beyond anything she had ever encountered), Grace had no idea. Croatoan was a disgusting planet, but she hoped that every detail about it was recorded and safe inside the Archive. It had to be preserved. No matter how vile it was.

Grace sent off a silent question to her fiancée, wanting to know if her 'poker face' was intact.

You're good, Finara promised her. *Now go do your thing.*

One sharp nod later, more to herself than the invisible deity who always rode her shoulder, Grace rapped on the appropriate door. It squealed as it slid open to reveal the dingy room inside, somehow in far worse condition than the corridor. The filmy light on the ceiling kept flickering and the carpet seemed to have been replaced by glistening tar. A leak? Or an excretion from the precious occupant? It was hard to tell. Frankly, Grace didn't want to know.

Sean waved her in and indicated a lump beneath the ratty blankets on the bed. His finger then flew to his lips.

'She's asleep,' Sean whispered. 'The kid's exhausted.'

'Kid?' Grace repeated, eyeing the lump. It couldn't be hiding anything more than a slim teenager. The vandal's age wouldn't save her; the Archive's laws did not recognise a difference between adult and juvenile offenders.

Sean nodded. 'Yeah, let's take this into the bathroom.'

The tiled room he led her into was barely big enough for one human to change their clothes, but Grace made sure to stay as far away from the walls as possible. Sean hissed a curse when he brushed against a tile and the sleeve of his shirt disintegrated.

He shifted his feet, the only indication that he might be uncomfortable with Grace's questioning gaze. 'As to how I found the girl — let's just say it's a long, complicated story involving a bunch of bored teenagers hanging out on the same Webchat feed. Usually I'd ignore hot air from kids, but this one was obsessed with the Archive. Who the stark would boast about a plan to hack into a place that's full of knowledge instead of coin-chips? Anyway, it got me interested.'

'That's some hunch,' Grace said, impressed.

'Yeah, well, you haven't kicked me off *The Pendergast e-Post* yet.' He grinned. 'I figured I still brought something to the table.'

Grace shook her head. She wasn't in the mood to once again ask him why he hadn't left to make his own e-paper; any time she broached the subject with him, he expertly dodged the question like a slippery politician or suddenly found somewhere else to be.

His eyes flashed, daring her to get into it with him. She didn't take the bait.

'Tell me more,' Grace said instead.

Sean's usual smirk spilled across his face; he knew he'd won this round. 'So I got in touch with her, told her I wanted proof after the deed got done, then said I'd give her a platform, let the galaxy know she wasn't a criminal. She didn't like the "freedom fighter" label I wanted to use — apparently, she was just righting a wrong. I was intrigued.'

Grace swallowed the sudden surge of anger. 'Righting a wrong? She broke the law and deleted something irretrievable.'

'Yeah, well...' Sean glanced at the door, his expression softening. 'She's young. Everyone else seems wrong when you're that age. Anyway, she sent me the proof and I knew you'd be hot on her heels so I gave you a buzz. I'm surprised how well you're taking this, actually.'

'If I didn't have the support that I do, I'd be taking it a lot worse than this,' Grace admitted.

Sean shot her a piercing look that quickly melted into sympathy. 'I totally get it, Boss. We're only as strong as our support base. And this kid doesn't have much of one. I feel bad for her. All she had in life was this one purpose and now she's done it. She feels so lost.'

'What purpose was this, exactly?' Grace asked.

'The official history of Leeds — she didn't agree with it,' Sean answered. 'Said it was lies. Her family has had the real story all along, handed down for more than two millennia.'

'Written down or an oral account?'

His grimace said it all.

The Archive didn't accept oral traditions that weren't backed up by a secondary source. Their laws were more relaxed when it came to written sources, since those were less likely to warp over the centuries — and they also tended to last longer than any audio format the galaxy's sentient species had ever come up with.

Grace had to admit that she was also sceptical of oral accounts. But a great many of the text-based sources in existence most certainly had their roots in verbal tradition. The only difference was that someone had bothered to write those stories down.

'I'll speak to her when she wakes up,' Grace decided. 'And I will refrain from pushing her too hard. But I may need you to pull me up, if necessary.'

'It's a wise person who knows their limits,' Sean said.

'And it's a wise person who knows when to strike out on their own.'

His smirk was back. So too was the same old argument.

But Grace didn't mind. It would help pass the time and it gave her an opportunity to defeat him.

She was sure that one day she would.

***

'Oh, so that wasn't me,' Selben said with a laugh after Grace showed her the footage of the break-in. The silhouette of the intruder was clearly a little more robust than the petite teenager. 'I hired someone. Didn't want it to be too obvious who it was, you know? I did some of the coding, in case you were wondering. I outsourced the major stuff though.'

The diner's windows were grimy enough to obscure the view outside, which was probably a point in its favour, but the major drawcard was the fact that it was the only eatery on the entire planet. Grace supposed that's why people were in there at all. Selben had needed little convincing to join them in the diner; she had noticeably brightened at Sean's suggestion of ice cream.

Sean had been surprisingly gentle with Selben so far, but his voice was now firm and uncompromising. 'Sel, I know you said you wanted to get your message out there and all that, but you need to know that your actions were illegal. The Chippers will have a right to hunt you down if you go public.'

Grace should have expected the stunned expression on Selben's face, but it still drove a sudden wedge of sympathy between her ribs.

'But I was *fixing* it,' Selben said. 'It was *wrong*.'

'Right and wrong are usually decided by groups,' Grace told her. 'Not one individual. To some people, like myself, history is vitally important because if we know our ancestors' pasts, then we can avoid making the same mistakes in the future. I was...' The catch in her voice did not need to be performed. '...upset when I discovered the files were deleted. This means a lot to me.'

Selben stared at her. 'I didn't think anyone would care.'

'Our actions always have consequences. And that includes hurting others.'

'I was just getting rid of something that wasn't true.' Selben's tone grew sullen. 'How can the Archive decide that one version is completely right? When everyone's got their own take on what happened?'

'How much do you know about the Archive?' Grace asked.

'It's where all the galaxy's history is preserved. But only the history that people *want*.'

'Yes and no,' Grace said, drawing a breath to centre herself.

She glanced aside at Sean who nodded imperceptibly before he took over. 'Sel, the Archive has a lot of conflicting accounts. You know we're e-paper reporters, right? We can't just trust one source. So the Archive doesn't either. Only problem is, they have these annoying rules about oral traditions, so even though the written account about Leeds was the only source they had, they're not going to welcome your version.'

'Even when they now have *no* version?' Selben asked, mouth hanging open.

Grace's lip twisted. 'To them, it would be better to have no version at all.'

'Well that's shit!' Selben said. 'They've gotta have lots of gaps in their database! Plenty of people only have that *oral tradition* thing. Like the desert tribes. I've read about them — they've been around forever. Are we gonna say the Desine doesn't exist because he's only in their unwritten tales? I get it, I fucked up. But don't you think the Archive fucked up too?'

Sean glanced around at the diner's other patrons, since Selben's voice had risen noticeably, but they were all still engrossed in their cups of coffein.

She has a good point, Grace realised and quickly smoothed out the creases she had bunched into her pants underneath the table. *I've always questioned tradition and the status quo. I shouldn't punish her for doing the same thing.*

Grace leaned forward, capturing Selben's gaze. 'You didn't go about this the right way, but I'm not sure the Archive would have listened to you if you had. I agree with you, Selben. Oral tradition is just as important — and it's much more susceptible to loss.'

'Boss...' Sean hesitated. 'You know the Archival Committee isn't going to hear Sel out...'

'Why? 'Coz I committed a crime?' Selben demanded.

'There is that,' Sean agreed with a wince. 'But these guys don't listen to just anyone.'

'They may listen to the donor responsible for half of their funding,' Grace mused.

Sean laughed. 'Do I even need to ask? I did wonder what you got up to with all that wealth of yours.'

'Are you rich?' Selben asked, curious. 'Can you pay the Chippers not to arrest me?'

Grace levelled a stern frown at the teenager. 'Bribery is not one of my tools and it wouldn't work on the Head General anyway. I have another idea. Selben, how much do you remember of the written account you erased?'

'All of it, unfortunately,' Selben replied with a roll of her eyes.

Grace indicated the techpad lying beside Selben's bowl. It was currently displaying a Webchat feed that kept stealing the teenager's attention.

'Write it down,' Grace instructed. 'All of it.'

'Do I *have* to?'

'Yes. The Archive is more likely to be forgiving if you provide a replacement for what you destroyed.'

Selben hunched over and began to write, having already quit the Webchat. 'You'd better buy me some more ice cream. This'll take all afternoon.'

'Right on it,' Sean promised.

Grace followed him up to the counter, where a bored employee took their order before slouching out the back, leaving a trail of grimy footprints.

Sean glanced over his shoulder at Selben and smiled gently. 'She's not a bad kid, Boss. Thanks for this.'

'Where's her family?' Grace asked.

'She's an orphan, the last of her line she says,' Sean replied, his voice growing rough. 'She's been through a lot, but she still found a way to keep up with her education. Don't worry,' he added, deftly reading Grace's expression. 'I've got somewhere for her to go. You don't think my promise to get her message out there was the only incentive that got her to talk, hmm?'

Grace watched Selben typing furiously away on the techpad, brow furrowed and tongue sliding out of the corner of her mouth. Grace doubted that the teenager would even notice the ice cream when it arrived. Selben was nothing if not determined.

'Good,' Grace said. 'She'll need support. Understanding. Guidance. An environment that lets her grow her gift instead of stifling it.'

'Sounds like someone's getting into the whole parenthood thing,' Sean remarked.

'And how would you know?' Grace asked, quirking an eyebrow.

Sean shrugged without meeting her gaze. 'I know what it *should* be. I've seen enough vids and families in my life, you know. So is it something you want? Is it even possible for you and...well, forget I was going to ask that. Do you want to be a parent, Grace?'

Grace's lips curled. 'I don't think I'd be terrible at it.'

Though she felt Finara's presence nearby, the goddess said nothing. It was a discussion they'd had years ago, with Grace not being able to give a definitive answer and Finara being willing to accept that despite her own desires. It wasn't that Grace was opposed to having a child; she just didn't want to do something unless she had the conviction to see it through to the end. But that was then.

Something had changed when she hadn't been paying attention.

Grace was glad of Finara's continued silence. She still had to come to terms with this sudden revelation before they sat down to discuss it again. But first — she needed to convince the Archive to drop the charges against the vandal and allow the introduction of oral accounts.

A headache splintered through her skull.

Convince them to go against centuries of tradition? Convince them to lock her up, more like it.

CHAPTER THREE

'I'm not sure what's more surprising,' Zareth Sins said at length. 'You frequently appearing in my office inside a vortex of fire — or me finding you here, inside a prison cell belonging to the Archive. A cell you could no doubt leave at any moment.'

Grace, having heard his measured footsteps approaching, was already waiting for him with her arms crossed. Opposite the burring laswall that divided them, Zareth mirrored her pose, but the similarities ended there. The purple uniform he wore was a garish counterpoint to her charcoal suit — and he would always be mortal. Unlike her.

'But I'm not surprised,' Zareth went on, smiling, 'that you're asking me to help you look after someone who cannot defend themselves. Again. You would make a fine agent, you know.'

Grace raised both eyebrows. 'No, I wouldn't. I would never obey your orders.'

'I suppose the galaxy needs people like you,' he noted, gaze distant. 'Otherwise there would be no change, no progress. But you'd have less trouble convincing the galaxy to change if you named your sources.'

'Change won't happen at all if my sources are intimidated into silence,' Grace said.

Zareth shook his head. 'Your quest to expose the truth to the galaxy will always be stymied by anonymity.'

'I seem to recall that you've enjoyed that anonymity once or twice in my reports.'

His brow creased. He was clearly bothered by the reminder, however gently she'd phrased it.

Grace... Finara sighed. *He's trying to help you. Don't antagonise him.*

Grace kept her lips in a firm, straight line. *I thought you were a fan of banter.*

Why do you think I'm marrying you? Finara asked dryly. *So I can enjoy an eternity of banter, of course. But Zareth doesn't have your patience. Or my sense of humour.*

Grace cleared her throat and tried a different tack. 'I appreciate your coming halfway across the galaxy to see me. GLEA's Head General doesn't need to obey the summons of an organisation like the Archive.'

'Especially when the person who's offended them hasn't broken any laws,' Zareth noted. 'But I would not be surprised if they suddenly made "protecting an information vandal" illegal.'

Grace winced, remembering how furious the Archival Committee had been with her when she'd refused to give Selben up. She had said that they would need to drop all charges if they wanted the teenager's two historical accounts.

'Is the oral version really so different?' Zareth asked. Clearly the Archive had wasted no time in informing him of the situation.

'No, not significantly,' Grace answered. 'Both say that humans created a colony on Leeds, but Selben's version goes back further. Leeds wasn't an empty planet for humans to take. Someone else lived there first, an unknown species that helped the initial settlers survive the harsh climate. This was long before it was terraformed and properly colonised.'

'And how would your source know?' Zareth pressed. 'Oral accounts are...sketchy at best.'

'It's the story that her family has safeguarded for generations. She believes she's directly descended from those first settlers that the unknown species looked after.' Grace paused, gauging Zareth's reaction. She was sure she didn't imagine the flicker of compassion in his loamy eyes. 'She wants to honour the people who made her existence possible.'

Zareth nodded slowly. 'Very well. I can respect that. I'll tell the Archive that if they ever want me to contribute GLEA's historical files, they'll need to accept oral traditions — and do nothing to your source other than allow her to provide the accounts promised to them. I might also be able to get them to release you, though I think your bank account will do better there than I ever could.'

Well, he wasn't wrong. She was still the Archive's greatest contributor.

'At least this is something I can actually do,' Zareth murmured, looking weary. 'I can't seem to do much on Gerasnin anymore.'

Grace stepped forward until only a pace (and the laswall) separated them. 'What's wrong?'

'Oh, just...' Zareth sighed. 'More agents demanding that we no longer recruit or marry outsiders, since they supposedly don't understand our way of life. I'm one of this group's favourite targets, because I joined late in life. I changed the Agency's policies after the Yalsa 5 debacle — I had to, if we ever wanted the galaxy to trust us again — but it hasn't made me popular with everyone. A Head General is voted in by senior members, not given the rank based on their years of service, you see. I can't ignore the dissenters forever.'

'Their numbers are growing,' Grace guessed. 'And if they become a majority...'

'Exactly. I'll have to appease them. But never mind. The Creator God will guide us.'

Grace wasn't sure he should sound so confident; it had been centuries since Finara's father had spoken to anyone in GLEA. But she didn't say this. It wasn't what Zareth needed from her right now.

'We are both agents of change,' Grace said. 'The galaxy will become a better place because of our efforts.'

He didn't meet her eyes. 'Thank you for saying so, Grace. I'll be on my way now.'

She watched him go, noting the slump in his shoulders that hadn't been there when they'd first met, and wondered if GLEA could ever weather the loss of a leader like him.

***

The members of the Archival Committee were all visibly grinding their teeth when Selben arrived to give them her two accounts. True to her word, she provided a replacement for the written text she had destroyed, then delivered her own version into both a vidcam and a simple audio recording device. A precaution, in case one format disintegrated before the other.

When she was done, Selben drew several deep breaths and finished with, 'I am Selben, the last descendant of the first human settlers of the planet they call Leeds. Thank you for letting me do this. Now the story won't die with me.' A pause. 'I guess I'm sorry for how I went about this. But it won't happen again, because the Archive has promised to accept all oral traditions. No more history will be lost. That's the best legacy a girl can ask for, isn't it?'

Grace kept her arms crossed as usual, this time to keep herself from applauding. It would surprise her if the teenager didn't manage to expand her legacy until the entire galaxy knew her name. This was only the beginning.

Selben bowed her head respectfully towards the committee members, then turned to leave. No one stopped her. She and Grace fell into step together and walked along a gangway overlooking servers dedicated to what remained of the era between Old Earth's destruction and the bot uprisings.

'What are your plans now?' Grace asked her companion.

Selben shrugged. 'Probably finish school. Then I might go out and find other stories to record for the Archive. They'll have to pay me a salary for that, hey?'

'You will have to convince them that you deserve compensation,' Grace warned.

'Not gonna exert your influence for me again, huh?' Selben chortled. 'Don't think I'll need your help anyway.'

Grace smiled. 'You know, I don't think you will. But do make sure you keep a — a family of sorts around you. You'll need the support.'

'No problemo. Mr Akiyama's got me sorted.'

'Of course he has,' Grace said flatly.

'And he told me to tell you that he's still not done working for you,' Selben added. 'So stop asking. You really want to throw down with him in a battle of wills? He reckons you'd lose.'

'Does he,' Grace mused.

'Yeah. But I think he just needs some more time to change his mind.'

Grace tilted her head to the side, evaluating Selben. 'So I should do nothing.'

'Absolutely. It's a waiting game. He'll cave eventually.'

Well, it seemed she wasn't done learning, despite the thirty-nine years she had lived.

Hours later, when she was wrapped up inside Finara's arms (back at the volcano where she felt warm, safe and truly at home) Grace asked, 'Were you waiting all this time for me to change my mind about having children?'

'No,' Finara said, nuzzling her neck. 'Hoping? Sure. But I'd rather have you, just you, instead of losing you by asking for more. I won't deny I'm thrilled about this development, though. I'm looking forward to seeing how you manage to book us a clinic that agrees to destroy my DNA afterwards.'

Grace slid her fingers through Finara's hair, gently teasing the long strands. 'There are benefits to marrying one of the wealthiest women in the galaxy.'

'And here I thought being a goddess made *me* the bigger prize...'

Laughing, Grace kissed her future wife into silence.

THE FAMILY OF FINARA, FIRE GODDESS

The thick, soupy heat tugged at her clothes, making Finara very glad that she'd swapped the scarlet thigh-length dress she'd worn during her binding ceremony for her preferred two-piece outfit. She had no plans whatsoever to wear anything once she got this family visit over and done with. Honeymoons weren't exactly conducive to clothes, especially inside volcanoes.

Grace showed no discomfort as they left the thundering waterfall behind them, her usual charcoal suit cutting a fine figure on her — and it always would, because she was now as immortal as the goddess of fire.

Finara gave her wife an appreciative sideways glance. At forty, Grace was still as beautiful as the day they'd met. It was a pity Grace had also ditched her wedding outfit: a white pantsuit with a jacket that seamlessly blended into the low neckline of the white satin top beneath it. The lake of lava in the volcano back home was keeping both formal outfits pressed and ready for retrieval at any moment.

That suit really *had* looked good on Grace. And Finara would rather think about something as superficial as clothes than that other thing, the thing she had absolutely no control over.

Finara grimaced when her stomach gave a clench. Cramps.

Fantastic.

Her body had failed her.

'You going to knock?' Finara asked, her words coming out in a growl.

Grace studied her closely. 'Are you alright?'

'Of course I am. Why wouldn't I be?'

Grace reached over and took Finara's hand, squeezing

gently. She didn't let go, not even when the door opened to reveal a plump, grey-haired woman wearing a grin so wide it could have swallowed half the galaxy.

'Look at you two!' Berale Neron, the rainforest god's mother-in-law exclaimed. 'Marriage suits you both very well. Especially you, Finara.'

Finara rolled her eyes. No matter how many times she and this mortal crossed paths, they had never let their mutual fondness get in the way of the banter they enjoyed dishing out so much. 'Well, it has to suit some of us, doesn't it?'

Berale chuckled. 'Marriage was never going to suit me. I'm an independent spirit. Can't hold someone like me down.'

Berale released a startled huff of air when a gangly child burst through the gap between her body and the doorway, knocking her aside. Wearing the bucket-shaped helmet that Grace had given him for his tenth birthday (she had found it on a world that fancied themselves the origin of high fashion), Berale's grandson rammed into Grace first. The reporter bore his tight embrace with supreme patience.

Finara didn't have to display the smile, since Micadei had inherited mind-reading abilities from his father, but he was disappointed when the people around him didn't outwardly show what they were feeling.

Finara wrapped her arms about her nephew when it was her turn to be hugged and held on, despite his incessant babbling. 'Aunty Grace! Aunty Finara! It's so cool that you're married now! Am I going to get a cousin? I'd really like a cousin. Well, I have one already but no one lets me see him and — '

'Hush,' Berale cautioned him. 'Don't talk about that. Not now.'

'Not *ever*,' Micadei whined.

Berale managed to wrangle him back inside with the promise of cookies baking in the kitchen's solar oven, which earned her a grateful look from Grace. Finara followed her wife into the hut, but only just made it past the threshold before Micadei skidded back towards her. His green eyes were shrewd and narrow.

Keep to your own head, pipsqueak, Finara told him.

He grinned. *I need to get better at masking my presence when I slip into your thoughts.*

Nah. You need to get better at not showing every emotion on your face.

It was his greatest weakness, in Finara's opinion, but her nephew seemed to think it was more important to be open and honest.

You're lucky I like you more than Aunty Renaei, Micadei said with a small pout. *She was supposed to be here already, but I don't think she'll come. She* never *comes.*

Finara had a feeling she knew why Renaei had bailed on this gathering. Her sister, the tundra goddess, had been equal parts delighted and jealous upon receiving the invitation to meet them after the binding ceremony. Grace had said that Renaei needed time to sort through her feelings before celebrating with them. Finara had sniped back that Renaei needed to get over herself.

'Wouldn't you rather she be genuinely happy for us when she does show up?' Grace had asked and that had been the end of that discussion.

Finara watched as Grace greeted Fei and Kuja, who were both overly enthusiastic with their congratulations, and tried not to scowl. The cramps hadn't let up yet, a painful and unwanted reminder. For millennia, she had been bitter about her periods, but then Grace had bought her that contraceptive implant thing which (aside from being more convenient than other methods) also completely stopped a woman's cycle. Best birthday present ever.

Finara had only recently taken it out, in preparation for a pregnancy. Maybe she should have left the implant beneath her skin forever.

Because then she'd never know that her dream wasn't possible. It had been stupid to think that it was. Just because two gods had fathered children didn't mean a goddess could carry one to term.

Sure, she could ask if Grace would consider doing it instead, but it wouldn't be the same. Not by a long shot.

Finara softened when she saw Micadei's downcast expression. She reached over and ruffled her nephew's thick, tawny hair. 'Aunty Renaei is nowhere near as cool as me. My domain is all fire and awesomeness, you know. But I could never look after the rainforests the way you and your dad do. The plants need something from you guys that I could never give.'

'Yeah,' Micadei agreed, beaming. 'I bet all the trees'd wither if you tried to take care of them. I can look after the rainforests for a full half hour now! Nothing withers.'

Yeah, the only thing that withers around here is my womb, Finara thought darkly.

Kuja's eyes shot over to her. She gave the rainforest god a hard look in return, one that promised dire consequences if he dared to say anything out loud. Micadei she could shield herself from, because he was so much younger and lacked control, but her brother had an annoyingly strong mind-reading talent.

'*Sooo,* did we miss anything exciting while we were getting hitched?' Finara drawled. Because that's all they'd done. Definitely no trip to some doctor based at some exclusive clinic.

Berale swept back in from the kitchen. 'I was going to retire from United Nursing and try something else, but there's just too many people across the galaxy who need me. It's a pity GLEA won't help fund us. So few beings can train to be a nurse and be happy with the pittance that comes with it.'

'Has the industry not improved in the past decade?' Grace asked, frowning slightly. 'This is an essential service that requires stable funding. But do you really think GLEA should be involved?'

Well, there was that sexy reporter brain again, mercifully drawing attention away from Finara. What a relief. But Kuja took it upon himself to sidle up to Finara while Fei and Berale answered Grace's questions, involving themselves in a deep conversation that might simply pass the time — or just might change the entire galaxy. You never could tell with Grace Pendergast, e-paper reporter.

'Let's take a walk, shall we?' Kuja prompted.

There was no inconspicuous way to refuse her brother. Finara silently snarled.

Undeterred, Kuja waved Micadei off with a stern warning about what would happen if he eavesdropped on thoughts as well as spoken words (the boy could probably convince a plant to listen in for him) and then the rainforest god led his irritable sister outside.

The moment her feet hit the path that lazily wended its way back down to the waterfall, Finara drew several deep breaths. Humidity and a fire goddess who favoured dry heat were never going to be best friends, but she'd begun to tolerate the climate during her visits here. This time, however, the hut's mud-packed walls had felt like they'd been pressing in around her, stealing the air from her lungs and causing her vision to spark.

'Something is bothering you,' Kuja said. 'Please let me help you with it.'

Finara sighed. 'I don't want to ruin today for Grace. And I...there's no reason to fall into despair and drag her down with me.'

Kuja waited her out, his expression neutral instead of displaying the pity that would have driven her from him. Why did he have to be such a good brother? Why couldn't he be nasty like Fayay, or completely distant like Sandsa?

'Okay, so...' Finara hesitated. She'd thought this conversation would happen with Fei or Berale, but a part of her knew their reassurances that everything would be alright would just make her feel worse. Kuja had a morose streak and she needed that right now. 'Grace and I got married. Which was great. Beautiful. Cringe-worthy. The whole thing was way too soft and sentimental.'

'You *are* soft and sentimental, Finara. You're just better at hiding it than the rest of us.'

'Don't you dare tell anyone!' Finara said. Her words lacked any real venom. 'Anyway, we went to this medical clinic on Enoc right after the binding ceremony. Well, after all the kissing. Of course.'

'Of course,' her brother said, but his smile had an edge to it. He knew she was stalling.

'Yeah, yeah.' Finara wet her lips. 'I thought we'd need to come up with some story about why we wanted our DNA destroyed afterwards, but Grace just gave the doctor a giant chunk of money. She's also sending him regular instalments. If he blabs, the coin-chips stop coming. Grace is great at getting shit done. She's great. And I'm just...not.'

Kuja reached out, his fingers finding her shoulder. 'I know this is something you've wanted ever since Fei and I had Micadei. Did the procedure not work?'

'Should have realised our father wouldn't let me have this,' Finara muttered. She let him feel the full force of her pain; Kuja winced and looked down at her stomach — until Finara's aggressive thoughts told him not to.

His green eyes grew almost as dark as the night falling fast around them. 'He should have no say in this. I will speak to him.'

'Don't bother! What's the point? When the Creator God makes a plan, that's that.'

'Do you think I have no reason to demand answers on this matter?' Kuja asked, his voice dangerously quiet. 'Do you think we've never wanted to give Micadei a sibling? Someone his own age he can play with?'

Finara's stomach filled up with cold, hard dread. 'He wouldn't. Even he's not that cruel.'

'Apparently he is,' Kuja murmured.

His hand began sliding off her shoulder, so she gathered him into a fierce hug — after making sure that no one was watching, of course.

'Oh stark, I am so sorry,' Finara whispered into his copper hair, clutching her brother to her chest as though he was the same age as his very young son. 'I didn't realise. I just assumed you guys were done. I'm *so* sorry.'

'We could only have the tests run on Fei, because of what I am,' Kuja said, shuddering. 'But I knew it was up to him.

Somehow I always knew. And I'm furious, Finara. I would kill him if I could. What he did to us, making us think we weren't allowed to know love, was bad enough. But this time I...I can't put it aside and move on.'

He tore away from his sister's arms, distress twisting his face into a gruesome mask. Finara's heart ached for him. She'd always been able to dance around her own feelings or outright ignore them when she had to. But for Kuja, who loved and felt everything so deeply...this had to be torture. It *was* torturing him. Darkness choked his thoughts.

'How do you live with it?' Finara asked.

Kuja shrugged helplessly. 'Somehow you survive. You put one foot in front of the other.'

'Does the pain ever go away?'

'No. Never.' Kuja's sigh was deep, underscored by the low winds that snaked through the trees around him. The vicious, jagged fronds that had suddenly sprung up alongside him drooped and then slithered away, no longer driven by his anger. 'But I focus on what I have: Fei, Micadei, Berale. Renaei. You and Grace. My family fills me with joy, even if I cannot find some way to fill this hole in my heart.'

Finara opened her mouth, then closed it. She wasn't going to mention that he had so many holes in his heart already. Sandsa, the desert god, was always a shadow in his mind. And then there was Kieran, the first child Kuja had ever held in his arms, a treasured nephew he had seen himself caring for and teaching compassion. That opportunity was lost to him. Even though he had his own son now, he never forgot about Kieran.

It didn't weaken him, those losses. They actually made him a better man.

'Stark, I wish I was as strong as you,' Finara said. 'Or as strong as Grace. I'm surrounded by strength but can't muster any of it for myself.'

Kuja smiled gently. 'The people in our lives make us stronger, Finara. And they lend us their strength when they know we're at our worst. I'm so happy for you, because I can see how much Grace has changed you, how much joy she brings you. Marriage is a commitment, one that goes beyond love. You know it will be hard work. But it's worth it.'

'Oh, it is,' Finara agreed. To stark with the cramps. She was a big girl — goddess, whatever. And she wasn't alone anymore. She swatted Kuja's side affectionately. 'I wish you weren't so wise, bro. And I wish you were a bit more smug about it. This modesty just isn't *normal*, Kuja.'

There was a twinkle in his emerald eyes. 'I never said I was modest. You just assumed. Let's go in — it sounds like Renaei has arrived and Berale is sorely testing her patience by demanding that our sister sample her cooking.'

'Poor thing, we should rescue her,' Finara said without specifying who she meant.

United by laughter and love, brother and sister walked back into the hut and sat down on cushions clustered around the table. Renaei was already there, on the cushion closest to the door. She offered Finara a shy smile. 'Igneas told me it was a beautiful ceremony. I'm so pleased for you both. This really does deserve celebration.'

Finara could see in Renaei's mind that Igneas, the god of rocks, had also delivered a lecture about Renaei treating Finara's happiness as something that had been designed to hurt her. Igneas didn't usually involve themselves in family squabbles, so it was

319

clearly something they felt strongly about. When she realised that Finara was sifting through her memories, Renaei mentally apologised and stuffed a handful of Berale's cookies into her mouth rather than join the conversation springing up around her.

Fei set out glasses in front of the adults in attendance and poured a fruity wine into each clear vessel, winking at Finara when she saw that the fire goddess was resting her hand on Grace's knee; a possessive, tender gesture.

'Hey, you saw nothing,' Finara told her, stowing her hand beneath the low table.

Fei chuckled. 'Alright then. I saw nothing.'

'But *Mum*,' Micadei protested. 'That's not true.'

'Even I must practice restraint with how honest I am,' his mother said lightly. 'It's a skill that sets other people at ease, my darling. And if you didn't insist on using your powers with wild abandon, we could let you go to the school in Bagath.'

Micadei scowled. 'No *way*. That wouldn't be honest, hiding who I am.'

Fei rubbed her temples. 'Well, your decision is made, Mica. Let's drink to Finara and Grace.' She picked up her slim glass, leading the toast. 'If anyone can keep the Firine on the right path, it's her wife. Grace, if you ever need a kind, *sane* ear to listen to your woes...' Fei smirked. 'Might be best if you don't speak to any of us either.'

'To Finara and Grace!' Berale said.

'To my sister and her equal!' Renaei added.

'To us,' Finara murmured, gazing deeply into her wife's brown eyes. She decided to enjoy the moment, enjoy the years, enjoy the eternity watching over an e-paper reporter who somehow got herself into the most dangerous places imaginable.

Hopefully Grace wouldn't find out just how many times Finara had saved Sean from similar situations, sometimes arising from his own secret. Finara wasn't even sure how Grace would react.

'To us,' Grace agreed and leaned over to capture Finara's lips with her own. It was an echo of the kiss they had shared after Igneas had bound them together, giving them the diagonal scars that would cross their palms forever.

Finara said nothing of her fears — not that night when she experienced spotting, a sure sign that her period was about to begin, nor the next night when the spotting failed to become the heavier flow she was so used to putting up with.

But she did say something a few days later, when the cheap pregnancy test she'd bought on some mortal world gave her a positive reading.

THE DISCOVERY OF DOM ZHANG, GRAPHIC ARTIST

CHAPTER ONE

The child screamed as its mother held it up to the angrily burring laswall, tiny fists flailing but thankfully never meeting the electrical field that would have sent a shock through its fragile body. The desperate pair were just one speck inside the crowd, all of them shouting and wailing, all of them demanding some small measure of mercy from the hot suns and the government officials who stood on the other side of the laswall, arms clasped behind their backs, expressions stern and unchanging.

Grace Pendergast tried to remain as impassive as the uniformed men and women beside her, as though the despair below didn't affect her. But how could it not? She gritted her teeth, kept her heels planted on the concrete and buried the fury that would only turn her interviewee against her.

She was an e-paper reporter. She couldn't interfere.

Wasn't *supposed* to interfere.

'Like that's ever stopped you, Boss,' she could imagine Sean Akiyama, her colleague-turned-competition, saying with a sparkle in his eye.

I was a terrible influence on him, Grace thought wryly. *At least he finally left and started his own e-paper. It shouldn't irk me, but I still don't know what changed his mind in the end.*

'Not a pretty picture, is it?' Governor Strindi Slundi drawled, her vowels almost as long as her shadow.

Grace managed to turn from the frantic scene in front of her

325

and bowed her head in greeting, a required gesture of respect for the leader of New Dunedin. Governor Slundi had warm brown skin and a wide nose that made her seem a lot friendlier than she truly was.

'I can see why you banned all mediaists and anyone else with a vidcam from landing on New Dunedin,' Grace said. She didn't waste time preparing a smile, even if it would have ingratiated her with the governor. Slundi didn't deserve it.

'You should feel special, Ms Pendergast!' Slundi said, cheerfully unruffled. 'We banned all e-paper reporters too! Except for you, that is.'

Grace kept her arms crossed. 'Because you thought that the galaxy's most famous e-paper reporter got her reputation by taking bribes. You thought you were buying yourself some much-needed publicity for your crystal mines — and good publicity at that. Sorry to disappoint you. Your business partners will find out just how poor this investment is, mark my words.'

'Still gotta get off the planet, don't ya,' Slundi said, clapping Grace on the shoulder and laughing uproariously, like they were sharing a private joke. 'And you can't post any reports about this on the Web, because we shot up the orbital relay weeks ago!'

Grace merely raised an eyebrow. All it would take was one word from her and the goddess of fire wouldn't just spirit Grace away from this mess — she'd turn Slundi into a pile of ashes. Finara was temperamental on the best of days lately. Her pregnancy had a tendency to cause her to burst into flames over the slightest change in mood or position. Mercifully, Finara had been spared morning sickness — it would have made her even volatile than she was already.

Slundi's miners, who were striking out of desperation for

something that might constitute a 'living wage', weren't as lucky as a goddess' wife. They were stuck here.

Grace had accepted the governor's invitation to visit New Dunedin because Slundi had assured the Galactic Law Enforcement Agency that she could deal with the problem without their assistance. Whenever the leader of a small, backwater planet said this, they were invariably hiding something.

Grace now knew what that something was: Slundi's mines lay idle. Which meant that they weren't currently producing the energy crystals that powered smaller devices such as techpads and communicators. It would be very bad for business once this got out; the crystals weren't so rare that other planets couldn't make up for the shortfall. New Dunedin would quickly lose its customers.

'You look worried, mate,' Slundi said.

'Not for myself,' Grace assured the governor and removed Slundi's heavy grip from her shoulder, pulling the woman's fingers off one at a time. 'I am worried about the miners, who have started snapping at the hand that takes so much and gives so little back. They're starving and angry — and that is a deadly combination.'

'I only stopped paying the shits because they stopped working!' Slundi snarled. 'Once they get back in the mines, they'll be able to feed themselves again.'

'They could barely survive on their abysmal wages to begin with,' Grace said. She held up a hand to forestall comment and grimaced when she saw Slundi's eyes dart across her palm, belatedly remembering her binding scars, the ones that bound her to Finara for eternity. 'No, let me finish. I'm also worried about your vast cohort of officials. A revolution born from fury will be painful for them. If they don't lose their lives, they may wish they had. Then there's the matter of what type of government the workers will form. Will it be a good one? Or just as cruel as yours?'

'Seen this on other worlds, have ya?' Slundi asked.

'Oh yes. I'm surprised you invited me here without reading my full body of work.'

Slundi growled under her breath. 'I just asked my aide to find an e-paper reporter who was famous and would go anywhere. Regretting this decision now, I'll give you that for free, mate.'

'You'll be regretting it a lot more once your workers get through that wall,' Grace warned her.

'They won't. And you won't be helping them with that.' Slundi's smile was both savage and cold at the same time. 'My mates here will make sure of that. They'll count every breath you take and dog every one of your footsteps. If you try to leave this planet or get someone to take your techpad off-world, they'll let me know. And I'll kill a miner every time you attempt to do that, Ms Pendergast.'

Grace glanced over her shoulder, at the guards waiting behind her, and tried very hard not to roll her eyes. Sure, they were big and burly and were smothered in an array of weapons, but if they dared to lay a hand on her, they would burst into flames. No amount of muscle was a match for the ire of a god, even a sub-level one. She could easily escape this predicament.

But she couldn't let any innocent miners die.

'I hope your *mates* are thirsty,' Grace said and marched off towards the nearest bar.

CHAPTER TWO

Grace chose a booth at the back of the bar, one that had plenty of room for her large companions. They, however, chose to distance themselves from her in a separate booth. She wasn't sure why they bothered, since it was obvious from their unrelenting sneers that they there for her. They could have at least done her the courtesy of providing some conversation. Bored and idly sliding a finger around the rim of her glass, Grace let her eyes roam over the other patrons.

I'm not liberating a whole starking planet for you, so don't even ask, Finara muttered.

Who says I need your help, love? Grace asked, lips twitching. *All I need to do is to find the right people. The ones who have hated their governor long enough to start whispering about rebellion.*

Scepticism coated Finara's every word. *You're hoping you'll find a bunch of willing rebels? With Slundi's heavies watching your every move? Let me get you out now. You've already got enough to write about.*

Innocent lives will be lost if I leave and I refuse to have any more of those on my conscience. Grace allowed the grimace to escape, albeit briefly. *I'll be fine. You always worry too much.*

I worry even more now. I won't have our daughter grow up without you.

Give me a few days, Grace requested. *If things get bad, then you can pull me out.*

I wish it was time for someone to pull this thing out of me, Finara grumbled, but her mood quickly changed and she shared a mental image of what was clearly an arm moving beneath the smooth skin of her stomach. The fire goddess was now preoccupied with talking to her unborn daughter about the dangers of hooking up with someone as stubborn as an e-paper reporter.

Smiling, Grace went back to casing out the bar. Many of the crystal miners worked themselves to the bone just so they could send coin-chips to their families, who were now on the opposite side of a divisive laswall. Members of those families might very well be here, inside this room. The bartender. The rowdy pack of drunks near the door. The student who was home from university, visiting his girlfriend. *Someone.*

Grace's eyes fell on one particular man.

He had been draped over the bright acrylic counter for a good hour, adopting a casual pose that only added to the magnetism he seemed to exude. His drink, a viscous blue, remained just as untouched as it had been since he'd first deposited himself at the bar. Most bartenders would have shooed him out with a stern look or perhaps even given him a shove, but this man, with his narrow brown eyes and evenly tanned features, seemed to be able to charm every being who came near him.

In fact, he could have had his pick of anyone in the bar — if he wasn't so interested in perusing the contents of his techpad. Several potential partners for the evening, mostly men, had departed his silent company, downcast and defeated.

He wasn't a local. No one here seemed to know him.

And no one seemed to notice the hidden vidcam hovering over his shoulder. Probably a good thing, considering that the device was banned on New Dunedin and its existence could land him in prison — or worse.

Grace's attention, however, was drawn to the binding scars that were dashed across the palms he lifted in exasperation when something on his techpad failed to please him.

Those who originated from the deserts used binding ceremonies in lieu of more formal weddings, gaining identical scars from the experience. But New Dunedin didn't have a single stretch of sand or anything approaching a desert. The world was primarily comprised of bland grey rock, with a smattering of a struggling savannah. There was some ice at the poles, nothing major, and certainly not enough to slake the thirst of the entire planet. Most of the population's water was imported from elsewhere.

There was a chance this stranger had desert-based powers (gifted to him by the Desine) and was travelling, or he was simply married to someone who worshipped the desert god. But mortal beings weren't the only ones who used binding ceremonies.

There was the possibility that his spouse was someone far, far more powerful.

Grace slid out of the booth and sidled her way over the bar. She was aware of her escorts following her with their eyes, as well as the stares of the other bar patrons who could see the prosthetic ankle that glinted beneath the hem of her pants. She was used to the attention, and the whispers of onlookers who wanted to know why she hadn't bought a more realistic synthflesh version. Grace could have afforded it, but didn't see the need to replace the one she'd worn during her entire relationship with Finara. And she wasn't called 'champion of the truth' for nothing.

She grabbed a nearby stool, an old-fashioned one that didn't hover and was chipped and worn from abuse, and dragged it over to the man. The terrifyingly loud screech that ensued made him look up, but only briefly.

'Not my type, sorry,' he said.

Grace wasn't deterred. Gathering information on the Galactic Pantheon was more than a hobby to her; it was a calling. And though she was acquainted with sub-level gods like Finara, Kuja and Renaei, her ability to learn more was restricted by the tension and squabbles that kept her from meeting new members of the family.

This man might have nothing to do with the gods. But she didn't want to squander the chance if he did.

Her eyes fell to the techpad resting on the counter. The device's screen was filled with fantastical swirls that had ethereal, hypnotic qualities. This landscape couldn't possibly be real. He had clearly taken an image of somewhere that actually existed and made it his own.

'Graphic artist?' Grace asked.

Artists liked to talk about their work, she reasoned, especially since most of them spent their lives in poverty and obscurity. It should be easy to get him to talk.

He grabbed the techpad, thumbed it off and shoved it into the pocket of his jeans. His scowl deepened. 'Like I said, you're not my type. Find someone else to bother.'

'You mean my wife?' Grace asked, cultivating a friendly smile. 'She's pregnant. I've already bothered her enough for one day and she deserves a break from my witty banter until at least tomorrow.'

Ha, I heard that! Finara said. *What are you up to, Ms Annoyingly Tenacious?*

It might be nothing, Grace replied.

Finara paused. *It's not 'nothing'. Grace, he's got something big hidden inside his mind. Do you want me to have a look...?*

No. I need to know if I can figure this out on my own.

The man's expression relaxed, but only slightly. Grace had guessed correctly that he was frustrated from having to field the interest of people looking for a night in bed with him.

'What do you want then?' he asked.

'Just a chat, nothing more,' Grace assured him.

He tapped the counter twice. 'You've got two minutes. Make them count.'

Grace kept her hands on her knees, concealing the scars on her own palms. 'I liked what I saw on your techpad. Definitely better than Celina Cartoure's work — you could make as much money as her one day. If you get enough targeted exposure, that is. Have you been at it long?'

'A while,' he answered, his tone guarded. 'But I'm not going to let you strike a friendship here. I'm not stupid. Those thugs in that booth over there — they're gunning for you. And they're wearing government uniforms. Listen, you'll get no sympathy from me.'

'I'm not worried about them,' Grace said with a shrug. *Might as well try. Either he'll have no idea what I'm talking about or a sub-level god will try to kill me, which will give me all the proof I need...*

Suspicion sharpened Finara's voice. *Grace, what are you doing?*

'Just as you wouldn't be worried if you were in my position,' Grace went on, ignoring Finara. 'You're not carrying a lasgun. You don't need one — you have someone watching out for you, right?'

The fear flashed through his eyes almost too quickly for her to see it. 'I don't know what you're talking about.'

Grace firmed her lips together, not sure if she should press the issue given how alarmed he seemed. Her face was scrubbed the moment it was uploaded anywhere on the Web, a favour done for her by Fei, the rainforest god's wife. This man might have no way of protecting his identity. But it wasn't like she was going to expose him to the galaxy. She'd sooner expose herself.

And that was something she would never do.

Who would respect an e-paper reporter who put herself in dangerous situations if they knew that she always had a way out of them?

Grace lowered her voice. 'And by "someone", I don't mean the vidcam hovering over your shoulder, the one that's definitely illegal here. I meant...your connections.'

'You do *not* want to cross me,' the artist said, his expression hardening.

'Believe me, I wouldn't do it if it wasn't important. At least, I think it is.'

He surprised her by grabbing her wrist and slamming her hand down onto the counter, revealing one of her binding scars. 'Don't *you* have someone watching out for you? You look too old to be a god, but you're definitely shacked up with one.'

Grace yanked her arm out of his grip. 'I'm not here to expose you. I'd just like a chat. About our family.'

'No way,' he said and began sliding away from her. 'I am not getting involved with the whole starking pantheon, okay? Just no. No freaking way.'

'Hey, is this gal bothering you?' a nearby man asked, bearing two glasses and a broad grin.

'Get away from me!' the artist snapped. 'What the fuck is wrong with everyone today?'

The man with the drinks jerked back in surprise — and smacked his head against the vidcam. The device burst into view with a cascade of static and hurtled sideways with a distressed whine, nearly hitting several patrons. Grace and the artist exchanged identical looks of horror.

The governor's guards were already on their feet, weapons drawn and expressions murderous.

Finara, Grace pleaded. *Don't let them arrest him, it's my fau —*

But she didn't need the intervention of a goddess.

Not this time.

A heavy lasgun barked repeatedly, felling the guards and transforming them into smoking masses of flesh in under twenty seconds.

The bar lapsed into stunned silence. Grace and her companion turned as one to the bartender, who calmly lowered her splatterlasgun. There was plenty of room behind the bar to hide a weapon as illegal as that one, but it was still a surprise to see it in the arms of someone so whip-thin and waif-like.

'Our spies at the governor's mansion let us know you'd come to save us, Ms Pendergast,' the bartender said in a hushed voice. A reverent echo passed through the entire room and swept back again, like a wave that had gathered more momentum than the shore was prepared to receive. 'We are ready to begin the revolution. Just tell us what we need to do!'

'What the stark?' the graphic artist exclaimed.

Grace wasn't sure whether to grin or grimace, so she gave him a mixture of both. 'It seems I've found the people I was looking for. I can only write about a revolution, not lead one, but...' She held out her arm, willingly this time. 'I'm Grace Pendergast, e-paper reporter.'

He recoiled from her hand as if it was something alive, something capable of dragging him down into the depths. Grace couldn't blame him. She'd already given him a healthy shove into the abyss.

'If you stick around, I can name you as a source in my forthcoming report,' Grace baited. 'An up-and-coming graphic artist like you could use the publicity.'

'Do I look like I take bribes?' he snapped, though he did appear tempted. Artists could create for their whole lives without becoming famous. The prospect of an eternity of obscurity probably wasn't to his liking.

Outside, there was a burst of lasgun blasts, sounding a lot more intense than what they'd just witnessed. Multiple pairs of eyes shot to the door. Whether it was the government cracking down on dissidents or more locals suddenly being inspired to fight wasn't clear.

But it was clear that no one wanted to risk their lives by checking.

'We need to go now!' the bartender told them urgently. She slapped a panel on the wall and a section of the floor fell away, revealing stairs that vanished into darkness.

'I'm not offering you a bribe, I don't do those,' Grace told her companion, voice firm. 'But it seems only fair to give you some assistance with your career, given the mess I've landed you in. My own career wouldn't be what it is without the help of others.'

The graphic artist ran a hand through this hair — then transferred his fingers into her grip and shook firmly. 'Dom Zhang. You're lucky you can give me something I want, Pendergast, or I'd've got myself teleported out of here by now.'

'We need to *move!*' the bartender insisted, her voice shrill.

They moved. But they weren't alone.

It seemed that the entire bar needed to be emptied.

Given that the bodies of government employees were cooling on the floor, none of the other patrons could really be blamed for not wanting to stick around.

CHAPTER THREE

New Dunedin didn't just have an underground in the 'subverting the government' sense — the planet also had an underground network of tunnels hewn into the rock by miners who had been quietly preparing for the right moment. And apparently this was it.

'Not everyone could agree on how to get rid of the governor,' the bartender explained. She had introduced herself as Ngata Kwon. 'Some wanted all-out war, us swarming up like dustrats from the sewers. Others wanted to do it guerrilla-style, rightly pointing out that it's too hard to get weapons onto this rock. And some of us...' She grinned. '...figured we'd join in if conditions became more favourable.'

Dom snorted. 'And by "favourable", you mean waiting for the galaxy's most famous e-paper reporter to show up?' His vidcam, dutifully hovering over his shoulder, kept flitting between invisible and very-not-so. 'Did you make *any* decent plans while you were sitting around and twiddling your thumbs?'

'Well, it's not like we didn't think about it...' Ngata fumbled, looking uncomfortable.

'You knew your people didn't have a starking chance so you didn't bother,' Dom said with a sharp nod. 'But then you got wind of Ms Pendergast's presence on your planet and sprang into action. Without having laid any of the groundwork. All you can do is keep muttering about the government, except now you'll have to do it down here. Well done.'

Grace swallowed the rebuke. He wasn't Sean, he wasn't a colleague and, most of all, he wasn't wrong. She'd been a tempting symbol of hope to Ngata. And that worried her — but it worried her even more that Ngata had known who she was. No one should be able to recognise her, thanks to Fei's face-scrubbing program. However, Governor Slundi had made no secret of her arrival, probably even made sure that Ngata's spies heard about it. As for the guards that had been tailing her...she might as well have been wearing a sign about her neck.

Slundi had wanted a famous e-paper reporter. She had to have known there was a chance that whoever her aide found would refuse to take a bribe. It could be that the governor was using Grace as bait, to draw out members of the underground instead of wasting time and resources by hunting for them.

Ngata had blundered right into the trap.

'Ms Kwon, I'm not here to lead your movement,' Grace said, keeping her voice low to avoid being overheard by the other bar patrons in the tunnel. 'I'm only here to observe.'

Ngata stopped dead and turned back around. Her thunderstruck expression was obvious, even in the poor lighting shed by the glowing spheres strung along the ceiling. 'But you were the one who sparked the rebellion on Butisl!'

'What role do you think I played in that?' Grace asked, crossing her arms.

'You — you helped rouse the spirits of the people — '

'Yeah, but she did that by getting a hacker to make sure the rebel leader could Webcast his speech to the entire planet, uninterrupted by any other signals — and then she quoted him verbatim in one of her reports,' Dom interrupted. 'Have *you* got a speech handy? One that will make all of New Dunedin rise up with you?'

Grace didn't dare mention that she'd rewritten the rebel leader's speech to make it sound more impassioned.

Ngata's shoulders sagged. 'Goss always made this sound so easy.'

'Who?' Grace prompted.

'My cousin...he went to university...' Ngata nibbled her lip for a moment. 'He said that the success of a revolution is inevitable, because people are more powerful than their governments...'

Dom laughed. 'So your revolution's leader is the uneducated cousin of an idealistic student. And...' He trailed off, mouth moving soundlessly as he counted the beings gathered nearby. 'And about twenty people who only came down here into the tunnels so the government wouldn't blast them for being in the wrong place at the wrong time.'

Multiple pairs of feet shifted awkwardly.

Ngata wrung her hands, looking frantic. Grace realised just how young the bartender actually was. She couldn't be more than twenty-five. When Grace was that age, she had assumed the galaxy would yield for her too.

'But you knew that a famous e-paper reporter would help your cause,' Grace said, taking pity on Ngata. 'You have some grasp of what needs to be done.'

Ngata abruptly lifted her head, her eyes wild.

Dom's sigh echoed in the tunnel. 'Really? You had to get her hopes up?'

Ngata was practically bouncing on her toes now. 'This is just the start! And I will not be caught like Goss was!'

'I'm going to regret asking this,' Dom said, 'but what happened to Goss?'

'Sold into slavery on Rochaccia,' someone piped up from the crowd.

Grace raised her eyebrows. Clearly Slundi was an even more disgusting specimen than she had initially suspected.

'Well, I'm out,' Dom said, hands raised as he began to back away. 'Ms Pendergast, I get why you're staying. Revolutions are your stock-in-trade. Mine's landscapes and hours of mercifully silent editing. I'm getting off this rock ASAP. So good luck, everyone.'

'The spaceport was shut down last week!' Ngata exclaimed. 'You can't leave.'

Dom smirked. 'Who says I'm taking a starship?'

'You're staying,' Grace told Dom.

'Oh, really?' he drawled.

'I'll write a whole report about you and your art,' she tried. 'Not just name you as a source.'

'This bullshit isn't worth *that*. And you can't guarantee that it will help my career any.'

'Alright, then at least leave your vidcam behind so we can use it,' Grace said. This movement needed a vidcam, to convince viewers that they could help by joining the fight. New Dunedin might not have the Web, but they still had vidscreens. Ngata Kwon would have to recruit people who wanted to distribute such inflammatory footage. It was dangerous work, but necessary.

A movement without a face to rally behind was a doomed one.

Grace made a show of pursing her lips. 'But I suppose you'll want to stay to make sure your property is returned to you undamaged.'

'You can get a vidcam brought straight to you,' Dom said, unmoved. 'You don't need mine.'

'I could procure one,' Grace agreed, trying not to wince when she heard Ngata loudly asking her customers if they had any more ideas about how to fight a government. 'But I won't deny that I have my reasons for wanting you to stay, Dom. I can't force you to do so. However...'

Dom's expression darkened and the tunnel grew cold, as though they were standing inside an icy cavern on some world that had never known the touch of sunlight.

'Don't try me, Pendergast,' he warned.

'Don't try *me*. I've got She of the Fire on my side.'

She didn't expect him to laugh.

'Ah, the fearless Grace Pendergast!' he mocked. 'Fearless! All because she knows she can disappear when the danger gets too much for her.'

Grace opened her mouth, then closed it.

'I thought I'd made my peace with that,' she finally admitted.

'Obviously not,' Dom said, smirking. 'So. I have something you want: the chance for a chat about *the family*. You don't have anything I want quite so badly. But who knows? The vidcam and I might stick around, for the right price.'

'Are you going to help us?' Ngata asked, interrupting them.

Grace cleared her throat. 'If you want to borrow this man's vidcam so you can make speeches of your own, you'll have to give him some incentive. I've already offered to make him famous, but it seems he needs a little more convincing.'

'What can we give you?' Ngata implored.

Dom swung his annoyed look from Grace to Ngata, but then he apparently decided to play along when he saw that the bartender was on the verge of tears. 'I'm into landscapes. Stuff no one's seen before. Something unique. Something I can play with when I'm making art.'

'The ice caverns under the Jansa Ridge!' Ngata cried almost immediately.

'Saw them yesterday,' Dom countered.

'But you don't know the sacred path — it's impossible to find the caverns without a guide.'

'Impossible for some,' Dom agreed. 'The path was pretty obvious to me.'

Grace gave him a questioning look.

'Ice,' was all he said in an offhand way.

'Ice?' she repeated. Finara had never mentioned a god or goddess of ice to Grace, but there were some siblings she didn't like talking about. 'There's a ridiculous amount of overlap among our in-laws.'

'Really?' Dom said dryly. 'I wouldn't know. I've never met any of them.'

Ngata perked up again. 'The crystal mines!'

'What about them?' Grace asked.

'They are cut by hand!' Ngata told her. 'Machinery would destroy the crystals. The manual tools leave behind such unusual markings. And — and our ancestors built an amazing altar to the god of rocks inside one of the caves!'

'Man-made, not my scene,' Dom dismissed with a shake of his head.

Ngata deflated.

Grace turned to Dom before she'd even finished making her decision. 'I'll give you access to a landscape that would kill most beings.'

He looked intrigued. 'Something full of flames?'

'Yes,' she answered. 'Forest fire. Volcano. Whatever you want. You won't be harmed.'

'And my vidcam? Would it melt?' he pressed.

'Of course not,' Grace said flatly. 'Or did you think an e-paper reporter could afford to have her techpad melt every time she went home?'

Dom snapped his fingers at his vidcam and it dutifully shot forward. 'Alright, Ngata! Have you got a speech ready for us?'

'Um,' Ngata mumbled.

Dom grinned at Grace. 'Apparently you're the brains of this operation. How's it feel to get involved in something you're only meant to be reporting?'

'Very familiar,' Grace admitted with a sigh.

CHAPTER FOUR

Grace kept well away from the sweating subterranean walls that closed off the space newly designated as Ngata Kwon's 'study'. The revolutionary was still unsure why she needed a separate alcove to make plans, even though Grace had spent two days trying to explain that it would make her look more like a leader instead just another member of a disorganised rabble.

'Firstly, your revolution needs the support of your own people,' Grace told Ngata. 'They are your greatest source of soldiers and funding. Right now, no one else can get onto this planet to assist you.'

'Oh.' Ngata brightened. 'Cool. We can make people give us what we need!'

'Not so fast,' Grace said. 'You'll have to promise them something *they* want.'

'You'll also need to make them like you,' Dom added. 'Or they won't listen, no matter how many vidscreens you get your face on. At least you're able to distribute that footage across the city without our help.' He rolled his eyes at Grace. 'Tell me why you can't just write a story about this instead.'

'Governor Slundi said she would slaughter innocent miners if I left the planet.' Grace gritted her teeth. 'With the Web relay out of action, any report I post will make it seem like I did leave.'

Dom whistled lowly. 'Slundi didn't want the underground rallying galactic support for their movement. Smart.' He cleared his throat when Grace sent a frown in his direction. 'Ngata here has to rely on local media sources. Got it. What's next?'

***

'...and we will make our own laws! New laws!' Ngata Kwon went on, dark eyes lancing right into the very hearts of her viewers. 'No one will be forced to work more than eight hours straight. We believe that everyone is entitled to eight hours of leisure and eight hours of sleep in a single Old Earth day. This will be done — for all of you! Not just the miners,' she added, looking momentarily bemused, as though she wasn't sure why saying that would help her cause. Grace had done her best to coach Ngata, but she still had a way to go.

Head General Zareth Sins, leader of the Galactic Law Enforcement Agency, turned from the vidscreen on the wall and raised his eyebrows at both Dom and Grace, who were standing side by side in his office on Gerasnin, the home of GLEA's headquarters.

Zareth hadn't wasted any time questioning their sudden appearance. He'd seen Grace manage this trick enough times in the past few years and knew that she didn't do so without a good reason. While he wasn't aware of Finara and Grace's particular connection, Grace was the acknowledged intermediary between the Chippers and the Firine — it wasn't common knowledge, but GLEA actually worked *with* sub-level gods to protect the Creator God's mortal children.

'I understand why you want me to procure and move a Web relay closer to New Dunedin,' Zareth said. 'And I get why you want me to refrain from assisting their government just now.

348

What I don't understand is why you're interfering so starking much. This planet doesn't even belong to She of the Fire's domain. And you — ' He frowned at Dom. 'You're just an obscure graphic artist.'

Dom sighed theatrically. 'Grace has something I want and I have to help her in order to get it.'

'You had something I wanted first,' Grace reminded him. 'And that's what started all of this.'

Zareth Sins shook his head. 'I don't want to know. Just do what you can for the people of New Dunedin.'

'It must be handy for you when the gods step in and help when the Chippers can't,' Dom commented. 'Just how many sub-level gods are you working with anyway?'

'I *really* don't want to know,' Zareth repeated.

'Just two,' Grace told Dom.

'You'd think he'd treat me a little better, considering that I can try to get him a third,' Dom said, either ignoring or not noticing the vein flickering around the chip embedded in Zareth's temple. 'Fancy buying one of my artworks to mount on a screen behind your desk, Head General? I'm about to become very famous. I can't promise he'll say yes, but I can definitely talk to a god for you.'

Zareth sounded resigned. 'Name your price.'

***

'Next you'll need the support of the galaxy,' Grace told Ngata Kwon, once she and Dom had secured the ex-bartender's study for an afternoon. 'So that no one takes the side of your governor and demands that the Chippers come here and arrest you.

Luckily, a relay in a nearby system was moved close enough to give us Web access again, so I've been able to post a preliminary report without any consequences. But you'll have to do something to inspire my readers to rally behind you.'

It was now surprisingly difficult to find time to confer with Ngata, especially with various guerrilla battles going on. Ngata's people were able to plan their engagements, so Grace wasn't needed for those sessions. Maybe that's why the revolutionary looked so distant despite this meeting being an important one.

Grace cleared her throat, drawing Ngata's attention back to her. 'We also need to accumulate enough funds to pay off the mercenaries that Slundi's no doubt planning to send after us.'

'Good thing we came up with a plan for that,' Dom said.

He stepped out of the shadows, holding up a white t-shirt that had Ngata Kwon's face printed across it multiple times and in an array of colours. It was just one of thousands of shirts that Ngata's army of rebels were printing by hand in a nearby cavern. The capital required for this venture had come from Grace's own accounts, but she didn't mind because it was for a good cause — and it was already paying off in the hits she was getting on her preliminary report. Her sponsors were always happy to fork over money when their adverts were being seen by billions of eyes.

'It's...a shirt,' Ngata said uncertainly.

'It's *art*,' Dom corrected. 'And not even my usual type of art. Had to stretch myself creatively for this one — you know I don't work with faces or living things. But I mocked this up on my techpad and I have to admit it looks pretty good when it's printed.'

'T-shirt art is a very archaic practice,' Grace said. 'But it will be back in vogue once we're done. And it's your face on these shirts, Ngata, the face of revolution.'

Ngata beamed. 'Um, okay, that sounds cool. People wearing my face!'

***

'Art can and should be used as a weapon, because playing it safe does nothing except line the pockets of the artist,' Finara read out loud as she perused her wife's latest report, one hand holding up Grace's techpad and the other resting on her swollen stomach, occasionally patting down the flames that her unborn daughter kept conjuring.

The goddess was lying back on a lake of lava, propped up against glowing rocks as she took the time to rest. Grace had requested a short visit home under the guise of missing her wife, though she really wanted to make sure that Finara didn't ignore the exhaustion she'd been feeling lately.

Finara lowered the techpad and frowned at Grace. 'But isn't that exactly what this Dom Zhang is doing? Lining his pockets? You said he was getting a percentage of the shirt sales.'

'Most of the money is still going towards the underground movement,' Grace said. This latest report had not only drawn in readers eagerly following the New Dunedin drama, but also those with a keen eye for the next creative trend. Some arts universities were even setting up classes entirely devoted to studying the shirts. 'It's not fair to pay Dom in exposure. He's a starving artist.'

Finara snorted. 'A starving artist who somehow finds enough coin-chips to travel the stars while searching for new 'scapes for his graphic art.'

'I did something very similar once, when I was starting out,'

Grace noted, recalling those earlier days, before fame and fortune had presented themselves.

'Love, you had a goddess supporting you,' Finara reminded her.

With more than just money, Grace thought with a smile, then moved over to rest a hand on her wife's stomach, where her daughter was growing. Sudden clarity washed over Grace. *I can't keep being this reckless, always expecting to be bailed out of danger. I have a family now.*

Finara cupped her cheek. 'Yes, you do, Ms Suddenly Responsible, but don't change the subject. How can you trust this Dom Zhang if you don't know how he supported himself? Remember, he has that big secret inside his head and you stopped me taking a peek...'

'When I said I'd done something very similar, I meant it,' Grace said.

Finara skipped over her mind and drew back, startled. 'He married my brother? The Iceine? *Rasson married someone?*'

'If Rasson is the god of ice's name, then yes.'

'It is indeed, and I know you're itching to add this to your copious notes on the Galactic Pantheon,' Finara teased gently, waving Grace's techpad until the reporter snatched it off her. The goddess' expression grew serious. 'Grace, Rasson doesn't talk to any of us except Fayay. And you really don't want to get that close to someone whose friendly with the god of water. You know what he's like.'

Grace's blood froze over in her veins. She forced herself to shake off the ensuing chill. 'I wasn't aware of that connection, but it makes sense. Ice and water. I'll speak to Dom about it.'

'You — *what!?*' the Firine exclaimed.

'For reasons that escape both Dom and myself,' Grace said wryly, 'we've become friends. And I think, despite appearances, he actually needs someone to talk to, someone who understands the situation he's in. That or I still have something he wants.'

Finara rolled her eyes. 'Oh, he sounds like a *great* friend.'

CHAPTER FIVE

'Any idea why Ngata is making us wait so long?' Dom asked, lazing on one of the soft qiviut couches arranged outside Ngata Kwon's study. The couches were a newer addition to the tunnel system, a comfortable if baffling one.

'No,' Grace answered, standing with her arms crossed. Dom had told her that this frequent pose of hers made her look like she was about to lodge one of her heels into someone's backside. 'She's usually so keen to hear about the next step in a successful insurgency.'

'Careful, I'm not sure she knows what an insurgency is.'

'Of course I'll keep telling her it's a revolution.'

Their conversation fizzled into silence. Dom fidgeted.

'How did you and Rasson meet?' Grace asked, keen to make use of the opportunity.

Dom smothered a yawn before indulging her. 'My hoverboots cut out when I was recording some footage and the fall would have killed me if Rasson hadn't come to my rescue. He then held me prisoner inside an iceberg in the hopes that I'd marry him.'

'Oh,' was all Grace could think to say to that.

'I only agreed because immortality is useful when you want to see the entire galaxy,' Dom went on. 'And he's amazing in bed. He should be. I taught him everything he knows.'

He threw a disarming grin at Grace, one that barely left a dent on her.

She managed, somehow, to keep the judgement from her face. 'You don't...love him?'

'How'd you meet yours?' Dom countered, pointedly ignoring her question.

'I was going to kill myself, so Finara offered to make sure I didn't die a virgin.'

Dom snorted with laughter. 'Gods, huh.'

'We're having a daughter at the end of the year,' Grace said, a hand on the pouch that concealed her techpad. This information would be entered into the device as well. 'I never thought I would love anyone, much less enough to share an eternity and start a family with them.'

Unhurried footsteps announced the arrival of the revolutionary leader and whoever she'd been seeing in her study. Grace and Dom turned as one towards the opening in the cavern wall. Both of them stared. Ngata Kwon was shaking hands with Governor Strindi Slundi.

'Slundi has agreed to go,' Ngata announced. 'And now the planet is ours. We can do whatever we want with it!'

'You're just...leaving?' Grace directed at Slundi.

The ex-governor shrugged. 'Ngata made an obscene amount of money off those shirts and offered a generous portion to me in exchange for ceding my authority. I can now retire. Those mines aren't particularly profitable anymore.'

Slundi then swept down the tunnel, presumably on her way to the spaceport.

Ngata's ensuing grin was smug and victorious.

'I really did not see this coming,' Dom said faintly.

Grace's temples throbbed. She rubbed them. 'If I ever feel the urge to interfere with a planet's system of governance again, remind me of this incident. In fact, I wish you'd stopped me in the first place.'

'No way!' Dom exclaimed. 'If you hadn't interfered, I wouldn't be the third most famous artist in the galaxy right now. Want a drink? I'm definitely buying.'

He took her to the bar where they had met, a venue that was now extremely popular because of its reputation as 'the birthplace of the revolution'. Ngata Kwon had put their names on a priority list so they would always be given a seat and swift service. Grace couldn't bring herself to refuse the honour, especially since she received her drink a handful of seconds after ordering it.

One of the first things she did was ask her companion about the Watine, known to his siblings as Fayay. He was the most vengeful member of the Galactic Pantheon. Dom quickly put her fears to rest. The Iceine wanted nothing to do with the brother who had manipulated him for two centuries.

'It took a lot of effort to convince Rasson that someone actually cares about him,' Dom brooded, his gaze distant, glass listing in his hand.

'Do you love him?' Grace asked.

Dom's shrug was crooked. 'I have no idea. I've not dared to give it any thought.'

'Why not? The Iceine can't read minds. You'd be safe to think it over.'

'Because I don't deserve to feel it, or have it returned,' Dom said softly. 'I'm with him because of my greed. Because of his immorality. I guess there are worse reasons to get married, but not many.'

357

They sat together in silence for a while. Grace pictured the uncountable years that lay ahead of both her and Dom. There was happiness in her future. She wasn't so sure about his.

'I want to have the two of you over,' she decided. 'For dinner.'

'Would the goddess of fire agree to that?' Dom asked.

Grace smiled. 'I can be most convincing. She taught *me* everything I know.'

***

'I can't believe they convinced us to do this,' Finara said under her breath.

'Sometimes I wonder if Father imbued certain mortals with powers of persuasion,' Rasson muttered.

They looked down into their glasses, which were filled with blue, non-alcoholic ooze. Dom had thrust the drinks at them before skittering away to talk to Grace in private. Finara thought it best not to eavesdrop for too long, especially given the topic of their conversation and how much turmoil it was causing Dom. The fire goddess was planning to have a very strong word with her wife about it later.

'So you finally told Fayay to shove it, huh,' Finara said.

'It's not like any of you cared enough to speak to me in his place,' Rasson sniffed.

'Fair point. At least you have Dom. He seems good for you.'

Rasson smiled wistfully, his pain written right across his features. 'Yes, yes he is.'

And that's when Finara realised what Grace wanted to achieve.

'He thinks about you a lot,' Finara remarked.

Rasson looked down at the gravel beneath his feet. 'You mean, he thinks about having sex a lot. He is attracted to me.'

'Not just physically. He thinks about you in other ways.' She flipped a grin at him. 'But what would I know, I'm just the older sister with mind-reading abilities.'

Rasson remained very quiet for the rest of the evening.

The seeds had been sown. But it would be some time before the god of ice and his husband were able to broach the subject with one another.

***

'I think it's time I took some parental leave,' Grace said after their guests had vanished inside a swirl of ice. She did not appreciate Finara's knowing smirk.

The fire goddess ran a finger down Grace's arm, a trail of flames following it. 'You're just sore about how the revolution ended. There's no need to throw up your hands and quit because of that.'

'I thought you wanted me to stay close to home for the next year,' Grace commented.

Finara laughed. 'Yeah, probably a good idea. Or you might make friends with Fayay next and I'm not sure how I'd react to that.'

Grace raised her eyebrows, amused despite herself. 'That's about as likely as me finding the Desine's missing son.'

'If anyone could do that, it'd be you, Grace,' Finara said and kissed her.

THE FRAMING OF SEAN AKIYAMA, HUSBAND

CHAPTER ONE

'My wife's missing.'

Grace Pendergast stared at the communicator in her hand, hoping her silence would goad him into saying something else, preferably something easier to deal with. But he was just as good at playing this game — after all, she had taught Sean Akiyama everything he knew about being an e-paper reporter. These days he ran his own e-paper in direct competition to hers and he wasn't doing too badly, last time she'd checked. But his public biography said nothing about a wife.

'Is your wife's identity relevant to her disappearance?' Grace asked carefully.

'Probably, yeah.' Sean's ensuing sigh sent static rushing across the connection. 'My wife's name is Janiche Jones. And you know how I met her. So you can understand why I want to talk to you in person about this.'

Grace leaned back in her hotel room's desk chair and cursed.

Janiche Jones was the alias that a source had used when contacting them nearly fourteen Old Earth years ago with explosive information (quite literally for Grace by the end of the whole experience) concerning a high-profile company. Despite the matter being resolved, 'Janiche' had requested that her death be written into the very report that had made Grace a galaxywide sensation.

'Boss...it just sort of happened,' Sean said, sounding feeble and ashamed, like a child caught in their parents' crashed hovercar with the steering rods still clenched in their hands.

'You can explain when I see you in person.' Grace slid her feet back into her heels and left the chair. She had been chasing a lead about a particular hotel chain that was allowing thieves into rooms rented by the galaxy's wealthiest denizens, but since no lives were in immediate danger it wasn't anything that couldn't wait. Suspecting that the call was being overheard on Sean's end, she didn't mention her unorthodox method of travel. 'I might be close enough to visit you.'

'I'm on Gerasnin.'

Grace stopped short, two paces shy of the bed. '*Gerasnin?*'

'Yeah…it doesn't look good for me.' An audible gulp. 'Di — uh, Janiche really wanted to get off that rock, Grace. She's been hiding out there for years and I kind of owed her a honeymoon…'

'And?' Grace prompted.

'I woke up in my hotel room to find her gone. And her blood was all over the sheets.'

Grace swore again, this time so loudly and so in depth that someone banged on the thin wall dividing her from the next room. A decade may have passed since Diana Numeni, former president of the now-defunct Numeni Corp, had been 'killed' trying to prove that her company had cloned her in an attempt to cut costs, but someone could have recognised her. *Anyone* could have. Numeni's face had been splashed across nearly every vidscreen in the galaxy at the time.

'It's bad enough without this happening on Gerasnin of all places…' Sean muttered.

'The Chipper homeworld,' Grace said with an exasperated shake of her head, even though he couldn't see her. The Galactic

Law Enforcement Agency, the biggest organisation dedicated to upholding planetary laws, made no secret about their headquarters being on Gerasnin. GLEA had free reign there and had even written some of the laws governing their world.

'Yeah.' More static as Sean sighed again. 'I'm being held for murder. But I didn't do it, Boss.'

Grace closed her eyes briefly. She believed him, but he couldn't have picked a worse planet to be framed for murder on.

Sean coughed awkwardly, which made Grace think that he wasn't done unloading bad news. 'So you can guess just how much shit I'm in right now. The only reason I was allowed to call you is because I told General Zareth Sins that I knew all about his side project. The one he doesn't want his own agents finding out about.'

'How did you know to do that?' Grace asked. It wasn't common knowledge that the Head General of GLEA worked closely with sub-level gods to ensure the safety of mortals throughout the galaxy. This secret could cost him his job. An agent of GLEA was supposed to be loyal only to the Creator God, not his divine offspring.

'She of the Fire told me to,' Sean answered, clearly reluctant to part with that information.

'I need to have a few words with my wife before I come to you,' Grace said tightly. With that, she cut the connection and clipped her communicator onto her belt.

Finara, she called, knowing that her wife was already listening to her thoughts.

The Firine's tone was equal parts defensive and playful. *Hey, it's not my fault you didn't think much of him wearing those gloves.*

Binding scars, Grace realised. Diana Numeni had been born

into a Desine-worshipping tribe and had returned to her family after escaping Hoffa. The desert tribespeople scattered throughout the galaxy wed each other using a binding ceremony, much like the one the gods used to marry their spouses and confer immortality upon them.

Sean Akiyama had been wearing gloves for fourteen years.

Got it in one, Finara confirmed.

Grace ground her teeth together. *Why didn't you tell me?*

He asked his goddess to keep it in confidence — and he has been a loyal follower of mine ever since he discovered I was your patron.

'Probably so you would help him out in a situation like this!' Grace exploded.

Finara gave the mental equivalent of a snort. *I knew what he was after when he started worshipping me. But he spent years risking his life to watch your back. No way was I going to snitch on him after that.*

Grace bent over to retrieve her duffel bag from beneath the bed. She had used it for this trip because it would have been suspicious for someone to stay in a hotel for two weeks without luggage. She adjusted the straps on her bag, a delaying tactic to get her anger under control. This was something Finara should not have kept from her. They were married, for stark's sake, and had a seven-year-old daughter.

Grace, love, I'm sorry. But I won't break any of the promises I give the mortals. I want to deserve their trust. Worry crept into Finara's tone. *Don't condemn him because you're mad at me.*

'He's my friend — of course I'll help him,' Grace said.

A brief hesitation. *It's also kind of my fault. I convinced him to propose to her. He wasn't going to go through with it otherwise. And I didn't tell you because I didn't want you to talk him out of it.*

'Finara!'

He says he'll give you the scoop, if that makes you feel better, Finara offered.

'No, it doesn't!' Grace clenched her bag with both hands, hard enough to dent its polyskin with her blunt nails. 'You're right. I would have tried to talk him out of it. A fugitive spouse is not a safe secret for an e-paper reporter to have — what if Numeni's existence was discovered and he was blackmailed into burying a serious report? It's a terrible risk. He must really love her.'

He does.

'Do they have any children?'

Five, Finara replied.

'Five! Couldn't he give her a break?'

Well, he has two sets of twins...and he adopted the other one.

'That's still five children he wasn't there to help with,' Grace said under her breath.

Are you ready to be teleported or do you still have more ranting to do?

Grace lifted her chin. 'I think Sean needs me a lot more than I need to rant. I'm ready.'

A vortex of fire blew up from the carpet and swirled around Grace, sending her across the galaxy.

The occupant in the next room over banged on the wall once more.

CHAPTER TWO

Head General Zareth Sins looked up from his techpad, saw Grace standing in his office and sighed lengthily. One would think she was an unruly recruit sent from the training rooms to be reprimanded, not an e-paper reporter who had just materialised out of thin air, courtesy of a goddess.

'I had a feeling I'd be seeing you,' he said, setting the techpad down on his polished wooden desk. 'You are not known for sitting idly by when you decide that an injustice has occurred.'

'Sean Akiyama is not guilty of murder,' Grace told him, stepping forward. 'She of the Fire has seen into his thoughts and can confirm that.'

Zareth gave her an even stare. 'I cannot use a goddess' mind-reading abilities as evidence. My agents would demand answers from me and I would have to give them. It would end my career. We've helped so many people by working together in secrecy, Grace. I can't jeopardise that.'

Grace shunted aside her disappointment. She understood his dilemma. He was already struggling to appease the agents who were pressuring him to ban marriage to 'outsiders', those who weren't members of GLEA. Zareth was walking a very fine line. If his agents found out about his connection to the sub-level gods, if they ousted him because of it, the Agency would lose the greatest leader it had ever known.

'What have you discovered so far?' Grace asked.

'The DNA at the crime scene scored a match on the Galactic Database,' Zareth answered, visibly relieved that she hadn't started an argument. 'A Diana Numeni, which is puzzling since she perished fourteen Old Earth years ago on Hoffa. This was an event you covered in an early report of yours — the one that made you wildly famous and wealthy.'

Idiot! Grace thought. *Sean didn't even scrub her identity from the Database!*

Finara swiftly came to Sean's defence. *He thought it would look odd if someone scrubbed the identity of a dead woman, especially since thousands of mediaists were making Webcasts about her. Billions of people knew her name.*

It could have invited some unwanted attention, Grace acknowledged.

'I remember that incident, Zareth,' she said out loud, keeping her voice mild. 'I'd like to know if you have a body. Blood does not a murder make.'

Zareth Sins inclined his head towards her: a concession. 'Correct. I am told that the amount of blood found at the scene is not enough to indicate death. But you will not evade the issue that easily. You reported that Diana Numeni was dead.'

'And dead she should have stayed,' Grace said. She saw the disapproval line Zareth's features and felt no shame. They were friends, but she would never compromise a source.

Zareth rubbed a thumb along his jaw and slumped in his chair, as though the weight of a thousand worlds lay heavy on his shoulders — which probably wasn't far from the truth. He had a limited number of agents spread out across the galaxy and no doubt he had to make tough decisions about which planet received their attention.

'Grace, I understand that you don't always want to enlighten me,' he said. 'But Sean Akiyama isn't part of the, ah, family. I won't do anything untoward for him, the way I would for...someone else.' His dark eyes fell to Grace's hands. Her palms were firmly pressed to her charcoal pants, something she had done in his presence ever since becoming Finara's immortal wife, to hide the binding scars on her skin. But it was clear that Zareth knew about, or suspected, Grace's connection to the Galactic Pantheon.

'But you can locate Mrs Akiyama and find out who is actually responsible,' Grace told him. 'You need to do what's right.'

His gaze grew distant. 'What I do, I do for the safety of every soul in this galaxy.'

'And I expose the truth to ensure that those who need help receive it,' Grace responded.

'You also omit the truth and warp it completely.'

'The galaxy is bigger than me,' Grace said. 'Some truths cannot be told.'

Zareth surprised her by smiling. 'I won't disagree. We both have our truths, Grace. Let us keep them where they are — hidden.' He leaned forward, elbows braced on his desk. 'Now, the problem at hand. Motive.'

'Sean wouldn't kill his wife,' Grace began.

'Yes, I'm aware of your opinion,' he cut in. 'Let's move on.'

Grace studied him, saw the determination and earnestness in his expression, then nodded and sat in the chair opposite him. No hovering furniture was to be found in Zareth's office. He liked to keep himself grounded — well, he liked the *appearance* of being grounded.

Zareth brushed a hand over the golden stars that studded his shoulders, as though to make sure the signs of his rank were still there. 'Our first step should be to discover, if we can, what reason someone would have to frame your friend for murder.' He unhooked his communicator from the collar of his purple jumpsuit and slid it into the centre of his desk. Then he hesitated. 'Wow, talking to your ex is never easy.'

'I could call her...' Grace suggested.

He released a short, bitten-off laugh. 'No, no, I mustn't give Kuja any reason to worry.'

'Is there...a reason?' Grace asked, watching Zareth closely. The Head General was a trusted friend of Kuja, the rainforest god and Grace's brother-in-law, but that hadn't sounded like a joke.

'Of course not!' Another laugh, no less performed. 'I'm past all that, you know. It's just...she's married to a god now. And I'm, well, I'm never really going to compare, am I?'

'Just call her,' Grace advised.

He did so. When the device clicked, signalling that the link had been accepted on the other end, he charged on without offering a greeting. 'Fei, I have Grace Pendergast with me. We were wondering if you could help us with a particularly sticky situation.'

Grace held her breath, hoping she wouldn't hear her daughter in the background. Fei's son, Micadei, was quite adept at occupying Lirlia when he looked after her. However, though Lirlia might be Micadei's junior by twelve years, she was precocious and already capable of arguing up to his level. It didn't help that Lirlia had inherited both Finara's grumpiness and Grace's stubbornness.

Happily, Fei's was the only voice that they heard. 'Hi, you

two! She of the Fire already had me looking into this — don't be annoyed with her, Grace, she's just trying to help — and I found a program lurking in thousands of relays and substations. It was waiting for a particular set of facial features to surface in any devices connected to the Web.'

Grace curtailed the annoyance that Fei had guessed at. She was willing to accept Finara's help, since Sean was a good friend of hers, but she was planning on having a stern word with both goddess and e-paper reporter once this crisis was averted.

'Someone was still looking for Numeni after all this time?' Grace asked, desperately trying to picture the various people she'd seen on Hoffa fourteen years ago. Her memories were fleeting but the perpetrator might be buried somewhere inside them.

'No, this was more recent,' Fei said. 'They were looking for Sean.'

Zareth made a quick note on his techpad. 'And you can provide evidence of this program's existence? Have you located its source?'

'Yes and yes,' Fei responded. 'The source is on Enoc.'

Grace heard the hesitation in those words and decided to chase it. 'What else?'

'It came from a computer in the Enocian palace.'

Grace stared at the communicator. '*Queen Jewel* is behind this?'

'We cannot assume that the queen is responsible,' Zareth said.

'That's not all,' Fei went on, suddenly very quiet. 'The program was looking for someone else. You, Grace. It's a good thing I already run something that erases your face the moment it's uploaded anywhere.'

'That *wyvern!*' Grace said savagely. She looked down and realised she was on her feet, fists clenched. 'After we agreed to never run the story. After we promised to protect her reputation.'

'Right, so at least someone's not confused about this,' Fei remarked. 'That makes one of us. I did think it was a bit strange for the Enocian queen to target you. Grace, what's this about?'

Zareth said nothing, passing no judgement. Yet.

Grace sank back into the chair. 'Oh gods. He always said he was a target, that he needed protection. And I didn't believe him.'

Grace, love, you couldn't have known she would do this, Finara said softly, her presence causing the air to heat up around Grace.

Grateful for her wife's support, Grace closed her eyes and breathed deeply. Zareth and Fei deserved an explanation from her.

This was not the time to obscure the truth.

'Fourteen years ago, I went to Utalia to write a report about the princess going missing hours before her wedding,' Grace began, thinking back to those days, when she'd been too afraid to admit to her love for Finara, much less consider spending an eternity with her. 'That's where I met Sean. He was also covering the incident, which soon became a lot more volatile after the severed hand of the Utalian princess showed up. For Sean it was particularly concerning, because he had been sleeping with the princess and was afraid that he might be a suspect.'

'The Utalian princess — that would be Queen Rudbeckia,' Zareth noted.

Grace nodded. 'Yes. We discovered that the princess planned to abscond to Enoc with Prince Julian of Unanda — her then fiancé — and Princess Jewel, in order for the three of them to get married under Enoc's laws. On both Utalia and Unanda, marriages are restricted to two people only.'

'That would have changed *everything!*' Fei exclaimed from the communicator. 'Utalia, Unanda and Enoc would have all gone to war with each other over the insult to their royal houses. With three of the wealthiest planets in the galaxy going at it...there's no telling how big or bad that conflict would have been.'

Grace diverted her gaze from Zareth's, not wanting to see the disapproval lining his dark eyes. 'With that in mind, I convinced Princess Rudbeckia and Prince Julian to return to the palace for their delayed nuptials. I told them to wait until they were Utalia's rulers to wed Princess Jewel, because by then they would be able to change the laws. It was the first time I interfered in a situation instead of just reporting on it and I...I thought it was the right thing to do.'

'You stopped a war,' said such an unlikely voice that Grace had to look up, to make sure she hadn't imagined that those words had come from Zareth. 'And stopped three young people from making a selfish decision that would have affected billions of lives.'

'I agree with you, Zareth,' Fei said.

Dawn seemed to break over Zareth's face at Fei's use of his name.

He's still in love with her, Grace realised. *Does Kuja know?*

Finara didn't dare keep her in suspense. *Yes. I can count the amount of times Kuja and Fei have tried to set Zareth up with someone on about four hands. But they're never quite to his...tastes.*

Kuja isn't bothered?

No. He's too nice for his own good sometimes. Finara snorted. *Zareth only fell for Fei when Kuja came into her life and she became much happier. My brother knows all about this and yet he feels sorry for the fool.*

'Sean and I promised to bury the story,' Grace continued once Zareth's vacant smile had faded. 'We said we'd bring it up in a decade, when Utalia was in new hands, with new laws.'

'But it's been more than decade,' Fei pointed out, sounding bemused. 'And though the princess of Utalia is now its queen and is able to change the planet's laws...there's no word of her and her husband marrying Queen Jewel of Enoc.'

Zareth nodded slowly. 'The Enocian queen recently informed the Agency that she was changing her laws so that marriage consists of two people only. This is starting to make sense.'

'Sounds like she's bitter about whatever happened between them,' Fei said.

'"Bitter" would be putting it lightly,' Grace mused. 'Queen Rudbeckia and her husband broke it off with Queen Jewel. She refused to beg them to take her back, afraid it would get out that she considered herself inferior to them. She wanted to erase all evidence of a connection between her and the Utalian rulers. This led to her demanding that neither Sean nor I published any reports about the relationship, which we'd been planning to do after a certain time frame. By then Sean had his own e-paper, so she had to contact us separately.'

'Did you take money for your silence?' Zareth asked.

'No,' Grace said firmly. 'And I'm sure Sean didn't either.'

Zareth snorted.

'Well, something made her suddenly decide to target you guys,' Fei piped up. 'But what?'

Grace was on her feet in moments and Zareth rose about two seconds later.

'I need to speak to Sean,' Grace said.

Zareth's lips tightened and his shadow seemed to grow across the table.

He thinks we'll spirit Sean away the moment we see him, Finara commented. *But he doesn't want Fei to hear him say it, because he doesn't want to lose any of her respect.*

'Zareth, please.' Grace cleared her throat loudly. 'If we were going to steal Sean Akiyama from you, we would have done it already.'

The Head General's words were sharp enough to cut diamonds. 'I would appreciate it if you didn't pry into my thoughts. You will notice that I did not actually voice them.'

'Enough, you two,' Fei said sternly. 'We've only kept this arrangement going by remembering to be nice to each other. Well, if not nice, then at least civil. Which is something my niece can't even manage right now...'

Zareth's eyes darted to the communicator, then back up at Grace.

She gave him a nod, not sure if she'd managed to convey her meaning, not sure if he understood that Fei's niece was her daughter.

I trust you, she mouthed. *So trust me.*

'Uh, will you guys be alright if I cut this short?' Fei asked nervously.

'We're fine,' Grace answered. She and Zareth exchanged loaded glances, confirming their willingness to cooperate. 'Zareth, I'd like to visit Sean alone. And I need to know how many techpads he had on him when he was caught.'

'We only found one...' Zareth began.

Grace laughed. 'You've never held an e-paper reporter before, have you?'

CHAPTER THREE

The cell she found Sean in wasn't terrible by galactic standards. It was made of cold marble, GLEA's go-to material for their outposts and temples, but Sean had a cell to himself and its three stone walls allowed him some privacy (a burring red laswall completed the square-shaped space). The bed in the corner looked better than the one Grace had just spent the night in; cushions covered every micrometre of the plump mattress and there was even a pair of slippers peeking out from underneath the overhanging blankets.

Grace held up the techpad Zareth had given her. 'Nice decoy. No wonder General Sins hasn't found anything useful on it.'

'Well, Boss, I need a decoy,' Sean drawled. 'I can't just lob my real techpad into a pit of fire to hide it. Unlike someone I could mention.'

'I've asked Zareth to let you keep it,' Grace told him.

The techpad immediately appeared in his gloved hands. Sean's smirk turned sheepish as he peeled the leather off his skin, revealing the binding scars that he had kept out of sight for most of the years she had known him.

Grace sighed. 'I'm not going to lecture you. I believe the time for that is well and truly past.'

He offered her the techpad. Grace glanced at the laswall between them and shook her head.

'I trust you'll give me the right answers,' she said. 'I wouldn't want to give up my techpad to anyone, so I won't ask it of you.'

Sean leaned heavily against one of the marble walls, deflating a little. 'That means a lot to me, Boss. I just wish I knew who was gunning for Diana.'

'Actually, they were after you.'

Grace explained the situation as quickly as she could. The sudden flare in Sean's eyes revealed his anger, but he kept his lips sealed and even arched an eyebrow, waiting for her to break the silence, just as she'd taught him to do with his sources.

I can tell you what I see in his thoughts, Finara offered.

No, I want to make him say it. To admit to whatever he's done.

'Sean...' Grace paused long enough to make him twitch. 'What did you do?'

'Nothing — nothing to warrant something this major!' Sean said.

Grace gave him a look.

He quickly relented. 'Okay, fine, I might have announced that I was writing a memoir. A tell-all about what goes on behind the stories, how I got started — the works.'

'Tell-all,' Grace repeated. 'I hope you were going to discuss this with me at some point.'

Sean grimaced. 'I'm sorry, Boss. I *was* going to. My consultants said that no one would buy my book unless I wrote chapters about my adventures with you. I guess I'm definitely still second best if you haven't heard about it. Problem is, practically everyone else did.'

'Let me guess,' Grace said, her heart sinking as she thought through the ramifications. 'All your sources, all the people you've ever protected by not going public with their names...wanted to make sure you kept quiet.'

'Some even wanted money,' Sean said gloomily.

Grace laughed and shook her head. 'You have made a lot of it during your career. Your readers and fans can't have failed to notice.'

'I was saving up to give my kids the best IDs coin-chips can buy,' he told her, scowling. 'And some DNA maskers to go with them. That shit's expensive, even for people like me! I need my kids to be able to leave Dustball if that's what they want, okay?'

You shouldn't have had five of them, Grace felt like saying, but bit down hard on her tongue.

Grace, love, he always liked leaving a part of himself behind with his wife when he was off chasing stories, Finara told her. *And she liked having that part of him with her. Plus, she's got a whole tribe to help her out with the kids.*

I still don't understand how they decided to get married barely an hour after meeting each other.

You don't have to understand it, Finara said. *They love each other. And that's that.*

Grace rubbed both of her temples with one hand. 'Queen Jewel. Did she contact you?'

'I guess she could have, but like I said — *everyone* did.' Sean sighed. 'I haven't even got around to reading half the messages in my inbox.'

'Maybe you should look then,' Grace said pointedly.

Sean nodded and swiped his fingers over his techpad. His forehead creased, ironed out, then creased once more. 'She did. And it's not good.'

'Send it to me,' Grace requested.

381

Within moments, she was looking down at Queen Jewel's message on her own techpad.

> *Mr Sean Akiyama,*
> *You will not publish anything about how your career began. My story is intimately woven with yours and by releasing your memoirs you will embarrass not only me but my entire planet as well. I cannot allow that. You have forty-eight Old Earth hours to retract your announcement and delete all files referring to me.*
> *If you fail to meet this deadline, I will destroy you and Grace Pendergast.*
> *Don't think you can hide — I have a program that will trace you across the galaxy by searching for your facial features. But of course, a painless death is too good for those who seek to besmirch my name and my reputation. So I will destroy the thing you love most. I have yet to find what it is.*
> *But I will.*

'It's my fault! It's all my starking fault!' Sean cried. He was pacing the length of his cell now, one hand clawing through his hair. 'She's killed Diana! Gods, Diana — what do I tell our children? What do I *do*?'

'She might still be alive — ' Grace began.

'Boss, Boss!' he interrupted, waving his techpad wildly at her. 'There's another message, it just came in and it mentions you and — shit. I'll send it across.'

> *Did you think I wasn't serious?* Queen Jewel

demanded. *Now I have your wife. She's alive. For now. But if you want her back, you must heed my previous message.*

I have not been able to locate Grace Pendergast with the program created for me. However, if I have planned this correctly, she will have gone to your aid on Gerasnin. Tell her that I did not know what she was at first, but years of reflection have given me the answers about what happened that day, when she failed to burn.

She is a sub-level god, She of the Fire, and has been sourcing her information through means unavailable to any mortal. She has cheated. She does not deserve the galaxy's praise.

I will tell everyone who she is if you don't comply within twelve Old Earth hours.

'I'm sending these to General Sins,' Grace said immediately.

'What — no!' Sean cried, flying at the laswall and remembering to stop at last second, narrowly avoiding a jolt. 'You can't! It'll get out, your connection to She of the Fire — Grace, you can't risk your career, everything you've built —'

'Your wife and your children mean a good deal more to me than my career.' Grace cut herself off, startled by how harsh her voice sounded, as though it was scorched raw by fire.

Sean was staring at her, mouth slightly agape. 'Grace...'

'One day I'll have to give up my name and start again,' she charged on. 'Because Grace Pendergast won't live forever. But this is not that day. I trust General Sins. And I trust his desire to continue working with She of the Fire. He'll protect me. And if he can't? I don't care, so long as I can help one of my dearest friends.'

Sean took a step back towards the bed and sank onto it. His face was far more lined than she could remember it being and there were grey streaks in his hair — he was fifty now, only a couple of years older than her, but he didn't have the benefit of immortality.

'I'm coming with you,' he said. It wasn't a suggestion.

'Of course you are. I just need to get you out of here.'

Sean looked up at the ceiling, as if hoping that the goddess of fire would immediately descend and steal him away.

Grace shook her head, amused. 'Give me a minute and we'll do this the right way. We have twelve hours to come up with a decent plan. And I don't want to partner up with a fugitive.'

A slip of a smile stole onto his face. 'You interfering again, Boss?'

'Always,' Grace said.

***

'You can't kill her,' Zareth said. 'The queen is protected under the laws of her planet and we cannot circumvent those.'

The Head General stood with his arms linked behind his back, dwarfed by the large plexiglass window in his office. He had just logged Queen Jewel's missives into his archives; they had been heavily modified by Fei so that nothing relating to Grace or Finara remained in them.

Zareth wet his lips. 'Given that you are highly likely to break Enocian laws in the next few hours, I will be unable to provide you with any agents and, to be frank, I am stretched thin as it is.'

'We don't need your help or your permission,' Grace reminded him.

384

Sean hovered near the door, despite the fact that they wouldn't be using it to leave the room.

'What do you expect us to do with the queen then?' he demanded, shifting from foot to foot. He had a reason to be anxious. They'd already burned through one precious hour. 'I want to choke the air right out of those royal lungs. And if she's hurt my wife in any way...'

'If you kill her, I must hunt you,' Zareth said flatly.

Sean's fierce expression didn't alter. 'Then you'll have to hunt me.'

But Zareth wasn't looking at him. 'Grace, I will be held accountable if I release Mr Akiyama only for him to commit murder. I can't protect you if I lose my position. I can't protect *her*.'

Fei's name lay unspoken between them.

'Zareth.' Grace moved forward and rested her hand on his shoulder. He didn't jerk away, but she felt the tension in his muscles. 'You have my word. Queen Jewel will not be killed.'

'But you will be asking for She of the Fire's aid in this matter.' It wasn't a question. 'She is not known for her patience.'

Grace gave him her sincere promise. 'I'll make sure she knows to leave the queen unharmed.'

'Still...no cost is too great, for the right woman,' Zareth murmured.

Grace squeezed his shoulder and turned back towards Sean. But before she could even take a step towards him, twin pools of flames roared up from beneath their feet and swept them across the galaxy.

CHAPTER FOUR

The golden walls of the Enocian palace were reflecting a lilac dusk when Grace and Sean walked out of a swirl of fire and into the discreet alleyway that Finara had found for them. They made their way across the grand plaza, their feet passing over billions of tiny mosaic tiles, and began to climb the slightly too-large steps that were designed to dissuade any commoners from approaching the behemoth that served as Queen Jewel's home and political headquarters. Failing that, the armed guards surrounding the perimeter looked ready and willing to use more forceful persuasion.

The whole palace is rigged with vidcams to catch you out, Grace, Finara said as both e-paper reporters advanced, arms held out either side of them to reveal their lack of weaponry. *Sure, your face is frequently scrubbed off the Web, but it's still going to be pretty starking obvious that a goddess is present if I start throwing my powers around.*

Grace kept her eyes on the palace looming above her. *It shouldn't come to that. But if it does, destroy the vidcams before doing anything.*

I might miss some, Finara warned her.

I don't care at this point.

'I don't care either,' Sean added out loud. Clearly Finara had relayed Grace's words to him.

Grace nodded at Sean. 'I will make sure that Fei uses the

same face-scrubbing program on you and Numeni after this. I regret not doing it sooner.'

'Thanks, Boss,' he said tersely.

Grace's heart ached for him. In the unlikely event that Finara went missing, she wouldn't know how to take it. She'd tear apart the galaxy — and destroy herself in the process.

I'm glad I'm here for him, she thought.

Sean's cheek twitched. 'I'm glad too. I'd appreciate it, if we survive this, that I get kicked off this telepathy loop or whatever you've got going, She of the Fire.'

I definitely have no intention of letting you eavesdrop past today, Finara promised him.

A gauntlet of guards formed in front of Sean and Grace as they approached the palace entrance. To Grace's surprise, the guards carried spike-studded spears in place of lasguns and were covered in gleaming gold armour instead of the orange glow of personal shields.

'What is your purpose here?' one guard demanded after he diverged from the pack.

'We are here to see the queen,' Grace said with a pleasant smile.

He raised his spear. 'Turn back now!'

Grace held his eyes and straightened her spine. She was taller than most of the guards and they definitely noticed it. 'Tell your queen that Grace Pendergast and Sean Akiyama request an audience with her. There isn't much time, so I suggest you do it quickly.'

Their names sparked an instant response. The guard barked into the communicator on his collar, announcing their arrival, then jerked his chin up and threw harried orders at his underlings.

The two lines of the gauntlet stepped back from each other, spear tips aimed at the ground.

'She's expecting you,' the guard said. 'Don't keep her waiting.'

Taking their cue, Grace and Sean marched across the covered walkway and into the shining palace.

***

The grand foyer was dark and silent, its vast space strangely devoid of staff or visitors.

Grace paused between the gilt columns towering over the entrance and allowed her eyes to adjust. Flickering flames formed a pool of firelight on the floor in a side passage, the only indication of life in the entire building. When she and Sean moved towards it, they found the source — a torch on the wall, handmade, an oil-saturated cloth wrapped around the tip of a wooden staff. The stones above the flames were barely marred with soot, a recent stain and certainly not from years of use. The torch must have been purely decorative until today.

Now it was an invitation for a certain fire goddess.

How many of these does she have in here? Grace asked Finara.

Sixty-five. There's one every ten metres and only in this corridor. The mental equivalent of a snort. *You're supposed to follow the torches, apparently. They all lead to her royal chambers, where she's got an intense blaze going in her fireplace. She's waiting there for you. And sweating. A lot.*

Grace let her gaze roam down the corridor. She counted two vidcams, their mounts newly chiselled into the walls, but there had to be more of them. *Have you found all the vidcams?*

Highly unlikely, Finara replied. *She's got the coin-chips to buy those invisible hovering ones and I can see in her head that she deliberately didn't learn all of their locations, so no help there.*

Is my wife with the queen? Sean asked, his words hesitant as he used the unusual method of communication.

Yes. Tied to a chair.

Tied? With rope? Sean sounded bemused.

Yeah, the queen's gone old-fashioned for this one, Finara confirmed. *I wouldn't get my hopes up, though. Even a static blade can do a lot of damage and she's wielding one right now.*

Sean's jaw tightened and his pace noticeably quickened. Grace lengthened her strides to catch up to him, but didn't stop looking at the artworks lining the walls, all of them painted by hand and all of them meant to represent She of the Fire. One piece in particular featured the goddess' birth in the molten core of long-destroyed Old Earth.

The Desine wasn't even born then. Finara's derision filled the connection binding the three of them. *And I'm younger than him.*

Were you around for the bot uprisings? Sean piped up. *And the clones?*

Yes and yes, Finara answered, sounding smug.

Sean sighed out loud. *I imagine you'll only speak to one person about those times.*

There's only one person who'd do my story justice, Finara agreed.

Grace felt heat sweep from her toes to her crown and back down again. She wasn't sure if it was due to her wife's powers or because of the mixture of pride and pleasure that rose inside her. There was no time to decide which. Sean was now taking three steps for every one of hers and, according to Finara, his mind was filled with images of his wife being torn apart — or worse, alive until the very moment he reached her.

Sean stopped so abruptly that Grace nearly ran into the back of him.

He spun around, eyes wide. *Diana has the Magic. Can that help us, if she uses it?*

How strong is she? Finara asked carefully. *I know my brother, the Desine, gave his people some power over the deserts, but usually it's only on the level of conjuring sand to throw into someone's eyes...*

But that might be all we need, Sean said, gnawing on his lip.

Finara mulled this over for a few seconds. *Alright. I'll contact her, but I'll need to do it at just the right moment.*

She'll look surprised when we enter, Grace supplied. *Do it then. It will be less suspicious.*

I don't know why Diana hasn't used her powers yet, Sean pondered, looking concerned.

Finara's voice shimmered with tension and anger. *Queen Jewel threatened to kill you if your wife attempted to escape.*

Sean's face lost all colour.

'We need to get in there *now*,' he said.

Both Sean and Grace accelerated into a dead run. When they reached the queen's chambers, where the last of the torches burned, they took a moment to nod at each other and then entered, a united front backed by an invisible force.

Grace didn't dare look at Diana Numeni. Or the silver blade that was pressed to her throat. Or the ten very visible vidcams hovering nearby.

She kept her eyes on the woman holding the weapon.

Queen Jewel would have commanded the attention of everyone in the room even under normal circumstances. Fist-sized gems dotted the single piece of blood-red silksein that had been wound around her lithe body, again and again, until it completely encased her from her chest to her knees. Her skin was smooth and hairless from the neck down, and what was left on her scalp had been starched into the shape of a flame and dyed a vibrant orange. It wasn't just a hairstyle. It was a masterpiece.

Grace was gobsmacked by the effort the queen had gone to. How long had she sat still for her stylist? Had she expected her hair to remain this perfect until her deadline?

Or maybe she knew that the fire goddess would arrive much, much sooner.

It's done, Finara announced and for a moment Grace wasn't sure what she meant. Then she heard a sharp intake of breath, one that forced Diana Numeni's neck closer to the dagger. A bead of blood slid lazily down the blade.

Sean moaned in distress.

'But you're older!' Queen Jewel exclaimed, boggling at Grace. 'Why did you get older?'

The next sound that escaped Sean was a bitten-off laugh. He could be forgiven for this response, however, considering how highly strung he was. It was true that Grace had stopped ageing eight years ago, but she definitely looked older than she had during the events on Utalia. Expensive cosmetic work could easily account for the difference.

Grace shrugged. 'That's what tends to happen to us mortals.'

The queen scowled prettily. 'You do not need to pretend anymore. I know what you are. And you have been brought here at *my* bidding, She of the Fire. Admit it! A mortal has bested you!'

'I haven't been bested yet,' Grace remarked. 'But I haven't tried to best a sub-level god, something no mortal should ever try to do. None can survive their wrath. On a similar subject, I believe this woman is under the protection of the Desine and it's said his vengeance is truly something to be feared.'

Jewel's eyes darted down to Diana's grim expression, then shot back up again. 'You're lying. Stop lying! Just admit it.'

'Boss...' Sean rasped. 'Stop antagonising her...'

'Listen to him!' Jewel shouted and ripped the blade away from Diana's neck, thrusting it in Sean's direction. 'Will you be the reason that your devout follower loses his wife?'

Now! came Finara's voice.

Diana hurled a fistful of sand that had appeared out of nowhere right into the queen's face. Queen Jewel staggered, blinking wildly, and didn't see Sean when he bolted forward and threw himself bodily at her. The queen went down hard, the dagger clattering out of her hand. Sean roared in fury and smacked her with his knuckles, again and again and again.

Jewel laughed, blood spraying over her lips. 'Go ahead, pathetic mortal! Kill me! Kill me and you shall never know peace! The Chippers will hunt you across the galaxy!'

Sean rocked back on his heels, breathing heavily as he centred himself. When he'd finally managed it, he gave her a peaceful smile. 'I don't fucking care if they do.'

Jewel's eyes widened.

'Now,' Sean went on, 'I'm going to untie my wife. Then you're going to sit down in her place. I won't even tie you up like you deserve, but make a false move and I'll happily kill you.'

'But why?' Jewel whispered in confusion. 'Why not just kill me now?'

Sean's voice dropped to a growl. 'Don't tempt me. But if

you're dying to know, it's because there is nothing that could induce me to take a life. Even my desire for revenge.'

'Or my desire to protect my professional image,' Grace added, quickly burying the pride she felt for her former colleague.

Jewel stared at them. 'You're both mad. Mad!'

'Says the woman who thought she was goading a goddess,' Grace noted. 'If I really was her, you wouldn't have survived this encounter. Sean, will you do the honours?'

Sean cut his wife free in seconds. They shared a brief, intense kiss that made Grace think with longing of the last time she and Finara had made love — barely three days ago, actually. But it was a lot harder to schedule these private times now that they had a daughter to raise.

Sean gave the dagger to his wife and guided the stunned and shivering queen into the same chair with surprising tenderness. Grace saw his eyes dart around the room, to the vidcams that could condemn him. He was putting on a show, a good one — this kind of footage would mark him out as the hero, not the villain. Sean stepped back from Jewel, an arm protectively looped around his wife, and somehow managed to keep his murderous feelings from appearing on his face.

Grace crossed her arms much tighter than usual. 'Queen Jewel, you have managed to escape consequences for your entire life, since royalty cannot be prosecuted for breaking most laws on this planet, including kidnapping and murder. I wonder what your subjects think of that.'

'They're too rich to care,' the queen gloated, regaining enough of her composure to sit ramrod straight in her chair. 'So long as I offer them a tax haven, they'll think whatever I want them to.'

Grace nodded slowly. 'Yes, undoubtedly there are some who do not care. But there is a law that *should* concern you — it allows the deposing of an unfit monarch in favour of another member of the royal bloodline. And I believe some of your wealthiest subjects are related to you, however distantly. Do you suppose they would pass up that opportunity? To replace a queen who decided to make Enoc a galactic embarrassment by spreading such a ridiculous story? No one will believe that Grace Pendergast is a goddess. I'm too well-known and trusted. All I have to do is write a report that details just how unfit you are...'

'I am not unfit!' Jewel snarled.

'I see a lot of proof to the contrary,' Grace said, tipping her chin towards Sean and Diana, who were still clinging tightly to each other.

Sean nodded swiftly. 'There's quite a few vidcams in here, including the ones we can't see. That's a lot of proof.'

'And I can give my testimony to any of the two e-paper reporters present,' Diana Numeni added, grinning at Sean when he gave her a squeeze and a wink.

Grace held her breath, hoping Jewel hadn't recognised Numeni.

She hasn't. Finara sounded amused. *She still thinks she kidnapped Janiche Jones, a nobody.*

Queen Jewel lifted her chin, her eyes narrowing. 'My cams are not linked to the Web. You would have to hack them directly to get the footage you need. And theft is illegal here for you commoners. Just try to steal them. Go on. I'd love to set my guards on you.'

One of the nearby vidcams abruptly burst into flames and vanished.

Naturally, it hadn't been watched by any of the other vidcams, since all of them were focused on the four humans in the room.

'Oh dear, one of your vidcams just disintegrated,' Sean said cheerfully. 'I'd check to see if it's still under warranty, especially since you can't prove what happened to it.'

Horror filled Jewel's features. She frantically looked from the empty spot where the vidcam had been to Grace, who merely lifted an eyebrow. The vidcam was now in the hands of Feiscina Rforine. And better hands in the galaxy there weren't.

'You — you would need a good hacker, the cams are protected,' the queen said with a sneer.

'You think someone like me wouldn't have a hacker on standby?' Grace mused.

Jewel's eyes ballooned. 'The program...the program on the Web that erases your face...'

Grace let her smile speak for her. She hadn't given herself away to the vidcams. And Jewel had to know that.

The queen cried out in frustration and slumped in her chair, defeated.

'What do you want?' she asked sullenly.

'Not kidnapping my wife is a start!' Sean exclaimed. He drew several deep breaths before continuing, 'Look, you've lost. If you ever come after Grace, myself or anyone close to us again, you'll run the very high risk of losing your throne. And by "come after", I mean anything from a physical attack to an attempt to undermine our careers.'

Grace cleared her throat. 'Bear in mind, Your Majesty, that we don't care about certain consequences. Losing your throne is nothing. We could do far worse to you.' She let the threat hang for several long moments. 'Sean will not mention you in his memoir. He was never going to.'

Queen Jewel made a high, keening noise.

'Wanna get out of here?' Sean asked his wife, smirking.

'We should ensure that the queen gives us safe passage to the plaza,' Grace said.

'You'll have it!' Queen Jewel snapped. 'Just get out of my sight!'

Two famous e-paper reporters and a dead woman left the palace on Enoc without being accosted, sauntered into a nearby alleyway and then took two steps through a flaming vortex to an unremarkable planet called Dustball.

Well, unremarkable to someone who wasn't a member of the Numeni tribe.

CHAPTER FIVE

We shouldn't stay long, Finara cautioned Grace. *Diana used my brother's powers in an emergency situation so he might want to check up on her. And he's not going to like us being here.*

Grace had been among the Numeni tribe for several hours already, enjoying their hospitality and exploring the cave system that formed their sprawling home, something she would never have expected to find buried beneath the sandy surface of the planet. The tribe wasn't what she'd expected either; they weren't ignorant of the galaxy and they all seemed to have a good sense of humour. Most surprising, however, was the change that had come over Sean Akiyama.

He smiled easily, lost several years from his features and went about without a single piece of tech on his person. His communicator and techpad remained disconnected from the Web and were hidden somewhere in the separate cave he shared with his family. Here he contributed, just like everyone else, to the cooking, the cleaning, the childminding — but he'd told Grace that his main duty was to spin stories for his adopted tribe by the campfire at night (these gatherings occurred on the surface of the planet, because the Numeni preferred to commune with the Desine in the open air).

'Not bad, eh, Boss?' Sean said as he and Grace walked through one of the many tunnels chiselled into the sandstone bedrock.

'I can certainly see the attraction in basing yourself here,' Grace commented.

'Met the kids yet?'

'Yes, they're wonderful.' Grace smiled. 'It was good to see Selben again; she tells me she is home from her travels for another two weeks. I really shouldn't be surprised that you adopted her. And I'm pleased that Grace, my namesake, seems to be interested in following your footsteps as an e-paper reporter.'

Sean laughed heartily. 'Well, she said she was following in *your* footsteps because I'm a dag compared to you, but it's nice to pretend that I'm still her hero.'

Grace, we need to go, Finara said sharply. *He's starting to fight me.*

The Desine? Grace queried. Why? You just helped one of his followers.

Finara's voice grew frantic. *As if that will make him forgive me! I attacked his family and I sure as stark wouldn't forgive someone who did that. Grace, please — wrap this up. He feels really pissed off. And I think he wants to hurt you to get back at me.*

Grace forced herself to keep smiling. 'Sean, you'll be happy to hear that Fei has mocked up some IDs and DNA maskers for your children, including Selben if she ever wants to take advantage of that. The program Fei runs for me will now also remove any images of your wife that appear on the Web. We won't be doing the same for your face, as requested. Are you sure you won't change your mind?'

'Nah, Boss, I kind of need my face on the cover of my book.' Sean primped his hair with exaggerated gestures. 'My consultants say that'll help sales. And if anyone comes after me, I've got an unstoppable force to call on for backup — not to mention her wife, the fire goddess.' He threw Grace a wink.

Grace, hurry up and say your goodbyes! Finara ordered. *I can't protect you from my brother. He's too strong!*

'I look forward to reading your memoirs,' Grace told Sean and took several steps back, hoping the distance would spare him the Desine's wrath. 'But right now, I need to touch base with Zareth Sins and make sure this really has blown over. Take care of yourself, Sean.'

'You too, Grace.'

The sand lining the floor of the tunnel gave an almighty heave, dislodging Grace and causing her to stagger, her arms windmilling as she tried to steady herself. Sean looked about, startled —

— and an instant later, Grace found herself standing in Zareth Sins' office.

Zareth's distant gaze snapped onto her. 'Ah, Grace. I have some bad news.'

'What is it?' Grace asked, thinking frantically of Sean and his family.

'Relax,' Zareth said and waved a hand at the chair opposite him, which Grace immediately took. 'It's nothing to do with your friend. He's in the clear. Our lab lost the initial test results, but the newer DNA samples we took say the blood is his. Perhaps he was involved in a bar brawl and went to bed without bandaging himself — I will confirm that was he was indeed injured to anyone who asks. It must have been a glitch, the Diana Numeni result. She has, after all, been dead for over a decade.'

'Something's wrong,' Grace said. 'You don't usually stall this much, Zareth. It's making me nervous.'

'I have to keep sending agents to Enoc when the queen requests our help,' he said bluntly.

Grace stowed the grimace. 'I thought that might be the case. Enoc has many temples dedicated to the Creator God and Queen Jewel's subjects donate generously to your organisation, mostly in the hopes that you won't look too closely at their ledgers. And we didn't exactly expose Jewel's wrongdoing.'

Zareth coughed awkwardly into his hand. 'A lot of my agents go to Enoc to unwind. They get discounts at the Enocian Harem.'

'You don't approve?'

'Oh, letting off steam — that's perfectly acceptable,' Zareth said, his voice strained. 'But they should marry and give the Agency new blood, as intended by the Creator God. It is much better for them to find partners among their fellow agents, so that undue influences don't affect the next generation.'

Grace leaned forward, studying him closely. His tightened jaw and the vein flickering around the chip in his temple said a lot about how he really felt. He didn't believe the words he'd just given her. She knew that there were a growing number of Chippers who insisted that 'outsiders' were harming their organisation, but never had she thought that Zareth would bend to their wishes. He had been an outsider himself, only joining the Agency when he was in his late twenties.

'Zareth...' Grace hesitated. 'Please tell me it isn't true, what I've heard.'

'What have you heard?' he asked flatly.

'That Chippers who marry each other and produce offspring rise through the ranks much quicker than their single colleagues.' Grace paused for several long moments, inviting him to fill the silence. When he didn't, she added, 'As I recall, Zareth, you reached your rank completely single.'

He sighed heavily. 'Times change. And things...things have to change with them.'

'You can't let a loud minority of your agents force your hand like this.'

'It's not a minority anymore, Grace! If I don't comply with their demands, I'll lose my position. What good can I do then?'

'What good are you doing now?' Grace demanded. 'You're disparaging the outsiders who can bring new ideas into the Agency and build it into something better. The way you did! Outsiders have their uses, Zareth. And you're going to lose so many agents if you penalise them for following their hearts. What do you think Fei will say about this? Or maybe you've given up on trying to be worthy of her. Just like you gave up on any shred of integrity you had left.'

That was the moment she lost him.

He pointed at the door, his dark eyes burning. 'Get out, Ms Pendergast. Get out and don't come back unless She of the Fire needs my help. Get out!'

Grace complied, furious with herself. She should never have said that, should never brought Fei into the argument. It was uncalled for. It was amateurish. And it had cost her a friend. That door was now closed to her.

She started walking. The corridors were teeming with Chippers, many of them on their way to lunch in the mess hall. There were too many witnesses. Grace had no wish to anger Zareth further by returning to his office to teleport away discreetly, and she couldn't see a nearby storage closet that would afford her the privacy she needed.

Distracted, she clipped the shoulder of a passing agent.

'Sorry!' he said, as if he was the one at fault.

Grace looked down into his painfully blue eyes and her heart stopped. This wasn't attraction — Grace had never been into men — but something had made her vision tunnel down to just him, as though he was the only being worth noticing in the entire galaxy.

'C'mon, Krendasta!' a nearby woman in a similar purple jumpsuit hollered. 'Those thieves on Fintaz aren't gonna abandon their life of crime without our help!'

He strode off before Grace could regain her senses, let alone say something.

Krendasta, Grace noted. The name meant nothing to her.

This is your purpose, an unfamiliar voice told her, though who it belonged to was undeniable. His was a deep, commanding presence, one that had created and outlasted the aeons.

Grace froze, her breaths sharp and shallow.

This is your purpose, the Creator God repeated. *I chose you, Grace Pendergast, to record the history of the Galactic Pantheon, as you are the only one who will wield that information correctly. Consider this the biggest scoop in the galaxy. Now, go. You need no more than a name to begin your research.*

Then he was gone. Grace sagged against the wall.

Grace! Finara cried. *What happened!? I felt my father, he blocked me —*

I'm...I'm alright, Grace managed. *So he did have a plan for me. All this time.*

That bastard, Finara growled, fear shimmering beneath her words. *He can't have you!*

Grace thought of all she had done for the greater good, for causes much bigger than herself. This felt...this felt huge.

Whoever this Krendasta was, she wouldn't rest until she knew everything about him, until she knew what *his* purpose was.

'I have to do this,' Grace said out loud, not caring who heard her. 'And I want to.'

Finara sighed. *I can't stop you, can I.*

Not a chance, love.

SEAN AKIYAMA'S GREATEST ADVENTURE

Sean Akiyama, frustrated by his apparently impossible task, took a moment to admire the desert-born woman who was standing patiently out of range as he tried to erect a techtent — *tried* being the operative word. It should have been simple. A press of the button on the tiny device was all that was required of its operator. The instructions had assured him of this. And yet here he was, still waiting for the tent to burst out onto the ground in front of them.

Stark, the nights on Dustball were cold.

'Well, this is awkward,' Sean said, tapping the techtent pod against his thigh. 'Um. I don't suppose you have one, since your company makes these — wait, is it still your company if your clones are running it? Huh. I guess I should just stop talking now.'

Diana Numeni, now a galactic fugitive, watched him impassively for a moment. Then her lips slowly curled, untouched by the dark lipstick that she'd always worn in the Webcasts featuring her when she had been the president of Numeni Corp.

It wasn't that she looked any better or worse without the lipstick. It just...didn't matter, because somehow he knew who she was. No amount of surface alterations could change what lay beneath. Sean couldn't describe this feeling, this knowingness, and that made him uncomfortable. It was confusing as well. And he could also hear his boss' voice in his head, reminding him that an e-paper reporter *always* had to know how to describe things — that's what they did for a living, after all.

Not that Sean had made much of a living since deciding to work for Grace Pendergast, but she did cover his expenses (this was a step up for him).

'Are you always this nervous before you sleep with one of your sources?' Numeni asked him.

'You're gorgeous,' Sean blurted.

He expected a coquettish smile, a casual brush-off, not the grief that filled her eyes with shadows.

Sean tossed the malfunctioning techtent away and swept over to wrap his arms around Numeni's waist. She dropped her head onto his shoulder, seemingly content to be held. Which was a huge relief, given how forward he'd just been with her.

'Hey, no pressure,' Sean said, stroking her back. 'We don't need to sleep together just because I'm the last not-related-to-you guy you'll see for years. And I was just going to use the intimacy to get more information out of you anyway. You deserve better. Shit, I just said all that.'

He grimaced. She started shaking against him.

Sean's first instinct was to tell her not to cry. But he didn't see the point; he knew that in her position he wouldn't draw any comfort from such empty words. This amazingly beautiful and smart woman, who had been brave enough to leave behind the life of a sheltered tribeswoman to take on a galaxy, had just lost everything. She needed to cry. She needed to mourn.

'Yeah, this whole situation sucks,' he said, a little more hoarsely than he intended. 'And you're stuck with me for six more hours. I wouldn't want to be in your position.'

But when she lifted her obsidian eyes, he saw that they were clear and dry.

And she was *laughing*.

'No one!' she gasped. 'No one, in all my years out among the stars, was ever this honest with me. Not a one of them dared to speak their minds. It was exhausting. And here you are.'

'Here I am,' Sean echoed.

Numeni's palm was now seated against his chest, the warmth of her skin bleeding through his shirt. He couldn't look away from her beseeching gaze, didn't want to, not until he knew what she needed from him. She'd already captured his heart — what more could he give her?

'Why couldn't you have found me sooner, Mr Akiyama?' she asked softly. 'I waited for so long. Did I have to lose everything before you would come to me?'

Sean wet his lips. 'You — you feel it too?'

Her kiss answered him.

To stark with the tent, he thought and yanked off his jacket.

'Sean — stop,' she pleaded.

He froze, then took in her stricken expression, the distance she had put between them, the hands she held up to shield herself with.

'Diana?' he prompted, not even sure how they had ended up on first-name terms and, frankly, not caring. It felt right, it felt destined, and he had the unshakeable confidence that she was his.

'I might not be Diana,' she said, her eyes focused on some distant point over his shoulder.

'What do you mean?' Sean asked. He stayed right where he was, but had to fight the desperate urge to gather her back into his arms. 'Are you saying you're a clone? No way. My boss did the test. You don't have the telltale marker in your blood.'

Her voice was flat, toneless. 'They found a way to remove the marker. I don't know if I am Diana Numeni, the real one. I have no idea what shelf life I would be looking at as a clone. I cannot deceive you. And I won't. You should turn and walk away right now. Sean...just go.'

'Marry me,' someone said and Sean jolted when he realised it was him.

She stared. 'What?'

It was absurd. He shouldn't have thought it, let alone said it, but somehow he couldn't stop himself saying it again. 'Marry me. Marry me, Diana Numeni.'

'Why would you want to marry me?' she demanded. 'When I could die within months? When I might only be a cheap copy?'

Sean slid open the buttons of his shirt and flung the constricting item away, then hurriedly dropped his pants and stood unashamed before her, firelit shadows the only thing clothing him. He could no longer hide his desire for her; it was obvious now.

'I don't fucking care,' he said. 'Because you're the one I'm drawn to, copy or not. And if you only have a few months left, I want them to make sure they're *fantastic*.'

A frown twisted her lips. 'And if I have decades remaining?'

'Then they will be the best decades of our lives,' Sean decided.

But still she hesitated. And so did he.

The silence grew and grew until he abruptly became self-conscious. Sean dropped his hands over his crotch. 'Um, you know, this is weird. A bit too weird, actually. So maybe we should just, uh, forget this happened.'

Diana nodded, determinedly not looking at him.

She doesn't want to forget — don't let her! a voice commanded.

Sean started and looked around, hoping that his thoughts would be heard. *Fire goddess? She of the Fire?*

Good guess. I'm Grace Pendergast's patron. And I can be yours too.

'Uh...' he said out loud.

Shut up and listen, She of the Fire told him. *I can see into the minds of mortals and let me tell you, she wants this. She really wants this. She would have gone to you, accepted your proposal, if you hadn't hesitated. So don't hesitate this time.*

Why...why are you helping me? Sean asked.

This time her words were soft, less acerbic. *Because you protect the woman I love when I cannot. I have to go now. There is someone who requires my full attention.*

Diana was already turning to leave. He couldn't let her.

'Marry me,' Sean said again.

She looked over her shoulder at him, confusion creasing her forehead.

There was no stopping him now. Willpower was hammered into his spine and his veins were abuzz with love, something he'd never expected to feel, something that would only continue to multiply inside him. Sean advanced slowly, trying not to spook Diana. He no longer cared about what he was or wasn't wearing.

'Diana Numeni,' he said, his voice husky. 'I want you. Not just in this life, but in all my lives. Each time I am reborn, I will search for you and I will find you. And I swear by She of the Fire, my patron, that I will never take this long again.'

'You better not,' Diana said and came to him.

Skin met skin and it was electric. She pulled him down to the sand, kissed his lips, ran her hands over his chest and then claimed him, body and soul. The campfire burned down to embers and grew cold, but it was ignored by the lovers as they became one, reunited after a lifetime of searching. Sean had heard the stories, how one could choose between oblivion and reincarnation after they died, but he hadn't considered them important or in any way true. Now, now he did. Because he had finally found her.

Some time later, they lay together beneath several layers of shiny survival blankets, his body spooning hers and his fingers trailing over her thigh.

'I just realised,' Sean said, nibbling her shoulder, 'you never actually agreed to marry me.'

He waited, heart hammering in his chest, until Diana turned a smile up at him. 'Of course I will marry you, Sean Akiyama. But I must warn you — we will not be able to verify our marriage on the Galactic Database. I must fall off the grid, so to speak.'

'Grace will clear your name, I know she will,' Sean said confidently.

But Diana was already shaking her head. 'No, I don't want to go back to that life. A most grievous crime was carried out in my name and I will never allow myself to be put in that position ever again. Let me be dead to the galaxy.'

Sean fidgeted. 'I would like some sort of acknowledgement of our union.'

'We will have a binding ceremony,' Diana said, taking his hand and tracing a diagonal line down his palm.

'Oh, I've heard about those.' Sean wound his fingers through hers and pulled her into a sweet, slow kiss. He drew back, grinning. 'Can we do it now?'

She laughed. 'I know you are impatient, Sean. Please hear me out. Yes, I have Magic strong enough to accomplish the binding on my own, but I'd rather the ceremony was conducted in the presence of my tribe. *Your* tribe.'

'Magic...tribe...' He swallowed. 'Uh, what am I getting myself into here?'

'You ought to have asked me this earlier, husband-to-be,' Diana teased. 'You have agreed to marry one of the Desine's followers, and he gave me powers at birth — without these powers I would not have escaped my company's facility on Hoffa.'

'Powers,' Sean repeated nervously.

'Powers,' she agreed, smiling. 'Our children will likewise be gifted with them after they are born. And as for the tribe, it is like one large family. The Numeni, my people, travelled here from Ilbb to have a planet to themselves. They are fiercely loyal and look after their own. But all must contribute.'

Sean tensed. 'I...I don't have many coin-chips. Will they still like me if I'm dirt-poor?'

'I don't mean money, Sean,' she told him, nuzzling his neck and sapping some of his anxiety away. 'There are tasks that need to be done, like hunting, cooking and maintaining our home. Do you have a skill? One that doesn't involve luring sources into your bed?' A playful wink.

'Your family is going to *hate* me,' moaned Sean.

'I'm not worried about them. I'm more worried about you — you'll be heading into danger on Hoffa.'

He shrugged. 'It's what I do. But I've got Grace and the goddess of fire looking out for me.'

'She of the Fire?' Diana sounded sceptical. 'She is not known for playing favourites.'

Sean considered what to say. Finally, he said, 'That's because I haven't written the report on it yet — and never will. Oh, how I wish I could tell you more, but I can't.'

Diana briefly pressed her smile against his. 'It's alright. Just come back to me in one piece.'

'Hey now, I still have a few hours left on Dustball,' Sean

defended. Her eyes slid down his form, evoking a nervous cough from him. 'I'm not up for that. I, um, I've never been able to finish more than once in a single day. Hence why I'm so good at being generous to my, uh, partners.'

She laughed and it was familiar music to him.

They spent those hours simply holding each other.

***

The Desine's invisible presence filled countless planets, including Dustball. The desert was his body, each grain of sand a piece of him, an eye that saw everything. These two mortals, this man and this woman, were the only reason he hadn't attacked his sister or her girlfriend the moment they had entered his domain. His fury at being denied what Finara had been given simmered away inside him like poison, but for now he could ignore it in favour of the warm feelings emanating from Sean and Diana.

He had done nothing, knowing he should not interfere with their fate. Finara didn't realise it, didn't understand the mortals' connection, but he did. They had been lovers in many lifetimes and always chose to reincarnate upon their deaths to find each other again.

The Desine could see the destinies of most people in the galaxy. It was part of his foretelling gift, one that he alone had inherited from the father of all the sub-level gods. But the future was a murky place and anything the Creator God let him see was not to be wholly trusted. The desert god could not divine his own destiny, nor that of his estranged wife — or their child. This uncertainty tormented him daily. Every time he saw love in one of

416

his siblings' futures, he was consumed by a darkness that stirred lethal storms into being on multiple words.

But he never let the storms endanger his mortals, his beloved followers.

It amazed him still that once he had not cared for them at all. *Until Callista...*

The Desine brushed off this thought and assumed human form on a nearby dune, standing watch over the couple as they fell into a doze. A smile tweaked his lips. He tried to fight it, but even his heart was not so cold. *They will be very happy together. And I will smile on their binding, just as I have smiled on so many others.*

I should never have smiled on my own.

Knowing that the arrival of the ship the e-paper reporter had chartered was imminent, the Desine sent a gust of wind to wake Sean and Diana so that they would be decent by the time the ship's captain lowered the ramp of his vessel.

The two mortals kissed farewell and then parted, their fingers now clutching only air.

He will be back, the Desine told the woman when she began tremble. *And though he worships another, he will always be welcome here.*

She bowed and thanked him.

Her gratitude was unnecessary. He had made it his personal duty to ensure the happiness of his people. At least they could experience lasting love and all its joys.

***

Sean Akiyama hit the ground running. The starship took off behind him with a strangled howl, on orders to return in one

Old Earth week. It had been easy enough to convince Grace he needed a holiday — he hadn't taken a single one during his time at *The Pendergast e-Post*. Mostly because he hadn't been able afford it. Now he could. Cashed-up sponsors were now flooding in after their recent success, but he had no interest in resorts. Because his heart was here. On Dustball, of all places.

She was waiting for him.

Sean stopped dead in front of Diana Numeni and admired her. She was the real Diana, not that it would matter to him.

'Stop staring and kiss me,' she ordered.

He pulled her into his arms and did just that, drinking her in, marvelling that she could taste even better than he remembered. All too soon, she broke the kiss, then took his hand and led him away, across the barren plains to what looked like a tiny speck on the horizon. After a couple of hours, it still failed to grow very much.

'It's just a rock,' Sean said, bemused.

'It's a *doorway*,' Diana corrected. 'Come on, I'll show you the way in. This rock is hiding a complex labyrinth and only a Numeni tribesperson knows the safest path through it. My sisters are the guards currently on duty. I've told them not to shoot you, but whether they listened...' Her eyes sparkled.

Sean laughed, some of his tension easing.

A narrow slit in the rock admitted them into the maze and the air cooled considerably as they descended through one of the many snaking tunnels. The passageway was comfortably wide at first, but quickly narrowed into a defensible gap that was filled by two women. They were identical, right down to their matching denim pants and jackets.

'So that's him?' one of Diana's sisters asked, arching an

eyebrow. 'He's not much to look at. Oh well, I guess it's all down to personal preference, isn't it?'

'I hope you told the poor bugger that twins run in the family,' the other added.

Diana threw a grin over at Sean. 'He knows now. Wait, what are you two wearing? I thought you couldn't stand to be seen in the same thing.'

'We wanted to confuse him,' both sisters answered, cackling in unison.

'Are you confused?' Diana asked Sean wryly.

He shook his head, trying hard not to smile. 'No. Juno is carrying a fraction more weight than her twin and has done so since birth. And of course the other one is Luna.'

'You told him!' Juno accused.

'Forewarned is forearmed,' Sean told the twins. 'And I do have to impress you. Otherwise you might decide to shoot me.'

'Never!' Luna gasped. 'Diana is the only one of us three who wants children! We shouldn't discourage any potential DNA donors.'

'What would our parents say if they never had grandchildren?' bemoaned Juno.

Diana impatiently waved her hand. 'They will have enough great-nephews and great-nieces to entertain themselves with. You've had your fun, now get out of the way.'

'Do you have another good reason for us not to shoot you?' Luna asked Sean, patting her hip with her lasgun. Clearly, even out here on Dustball they'd found a way to equip themselves.

Sean looped an arm around Diana. 'There's no point. I've already been shot through the heart.'

'Ugghhh!' the twins cried in disgust.

They were nineteen years old to Diana's twenty-eight, a surprise to the would-be grandparents apparently, but Sean couldn't help being reminded of girls much younger than that.

'They've yet to see the galaxy,' Diana said in an undertone. 'They'll grow up fast when they do.'

'Not a starking chance!' Juno exclaimed.

Sean nodded in agreement. 'Yeah, I've been out there for years and I still haven't grown up.'

'Ooh, I like him,' Luna said, beaming.

***

Diana promised Sean that he'd remember the layout of the Numeni catacombs in no time. Sean seriously doubted that. It was an intricate network that ran in countless directions beneath the planet's sandy surface, many of the tunnels emptying out into rooms larger than most buildings Sean had seen during his travels. One such room actually contained a two-person starship and a retractable roof; Sean had scratched his head over this because he hadn't seen anything to indicate its presence topside.

Solar-charged lights glowed everywhere Sean looked and he was impressed by the complicated hydroponic systems that Diana showed him. The Numeni even received a Web signal out here, though it was unsurprisingly slow.

Sean didn't meet Diana's parents until she took him to the vast common hall. He judged them to be somewhere in their sixties, though it was hard to tell with humans who lived in such a harsh climate. But Sean had to admit that the Numeni seemed to be weathering it better than some tribes.

'My da, Naxan, is from Yabul, a tribe on Ilbb,' Diana told

Sean, a hand on her father's arm. 'My mother went there for a month to trade and he followed her home. So it's not unusual in our family to meet and marry very quickly.'

'These Numeni women, we've no real say in the matter,' Naxan Yabul stage-whispered.

'*Da*,' Diana scolded. 'Sean was the one who did the asking. In fact, he didn't ask. He just commanded that I marry him. Several times.'

'Uh, it isn't how it sounds,' Sean said hastily when Tyche Numeni, Diana's mother, gave him a stern look.

Diana's fingers coiled around his, but this didn't help him relax.

Tyche's frown kept on growing. 'You took him to bed already, I know that look, you are too comfortable with each other. This is not proper. In the Desine's eyes, we must only bed those we are bound to.'

Diana and Sean exchanged amused glances. They hadn't exactly gone over their sexual histories together, but they were well aware that the lists were extensive on both sides. This probably wouldn't make Tyche more inclined to like him, so Sean kept silent and let Diana handle it.

'The Desine has never made his views on premarital sex clear, Ma,' Diana said calmly. 'And not that it matters, but we were betrothed beforehand.'

Naxan broke into a laugh. 'Betrothed for a whole minute, the way I hear it.'

'They barely knew each other for an hour before that!' Tyche exclaimed. 'How can we trust that this outsider is truly in love with Diana?'

Sean's mind went blank. He didn't know how to explain that his love for Diana just *was*.

'Um,' he began.

'Because he's willing to have you for a mother-in-law!' Naxan said, slapping Sean on the back. 'Stop testing the poor man — you might chase him off. This tribe needs fresh blood.'

The common hall filled with a chorus of laughter as other tribespeople filtered in. Sean caught what he thought was a flash of amusement on Tyche's face, but she buried it fast. She made a *hmpf* sound, muttered something in a strange dialect and retreated a few paces.

'She welcomed you into the family,' Diana translated in a low voice.

Sean nodded vaguely. She had explained that the Numeni used their own language and were all comfortable with speaking the most common dialect in the galaxy. Thanks to learning the Yabul tongue from her father, Diana was multilingual and was also proficient at using a hand-signing system called All Tribes, one that every tribe in the galaxy used when trading.

'It won't take long for you to learn our language,' Diana told Sean. It sounded more like a command than an attempt at reassurance.

Sean kissed her forehead. 'I'll have to if I'm spending all my free time here.'

She melted against him and he held her close, aware of the whistling going on around them but not particularly caring.

'Enough, you two!' an old woman said, striding forward and swinging a cane as she did so. She had an aura of power about her so Sean assumed that she was Chief Minerva Numeni, Diana's grandmother. 'Get topside! Need to bind you two together before the Desine discovers and punishes you for your premarital pleasures.'

'He already knows,' Diana said offhandedly. Sean shot her a startled look and she smiled at him. 'He said you would always be welcome here, despite your patron.'

Chief Minerva harrumphed. 'Was a time the Desine didn't speak to any of us. Now we can't get him to shut up.'

'He's listening, Mama,' Tyche said in a strained voice.

'He'd have smote me already if he was as easy to offend as you are,' Chief Minerva chortled.

The entire tribe wasted no time in gathering on the windswept surface of the planet. There, beneath the stars and above the sand, was where they felt the closest to their god — or so Naxan had explained under his breath to Sean. Countless bonfires were lit, making Sean wonder if his new patron was around somewhere.

The Numeni fell silent. He forced himself to pay attention.

Diana had coached Sean on the steps involved in a binding earlier and now he watched her movements closely to make sure he didn't do it wrong and insult her tribe. He knelt when she knelt, only two seconds behind her. The sand around them began to stir.

Sean tensed.

'You're safe here,' Diana said softly.

Above them, Chief Minerva spoke in the galaxy's common dialect, most likely for Sean's benefit. Her voice was raw, ancient and underscored by the powers she was drawing upon. 'Tonight we witness the binding of Diana Numeni and Sean Akiyama.'

Sean offered his hands to Diana, who took them and pressed their palms together. Her smile grew as light began to emanate from between their linked fingers. He prepared himself for the pain she had warned him about, but it was so sudden and sharp that it caused him to gasp.

'You have her blood as she has yours,' Diana's grandmother continued, her weathered face solemn. 'You are bound and that cannot be easily broken.'

Sean pried his hands away from Diana's and studied them, surprised to see that the fresh, bloody cuts that he was expecting were actually two identical scars on his palms, so old and faded that he could have had them his entire life.

'May the Desine smile on your binding,' Chief Minerva finished.

'He smiles!' chorused the Numeni tribe.

That was his cue, Sean remembered. He swooped in and kissed his wife.

Their audience cheered, food appeared and the music began. Diana helped Sean off the sand and danced with him into the night, surrounded by the members of their tribe. Later, they sneaked out past the nearest dunes and made love just as they had the first time — skin on skin on sand — then spoke of how they soon hoped to add more members to the Numeni.

Neither of them was aware of the Desine in the sand beneath them, watching with equal parts envy and delight. He saw their future unfold before him. Sean and Diana would have five children, each as bright and glorious as a star to their parents.

How would it feel to witness a child's first steps, to help that child grow into an adult?

I wouldn't know, the Desine despaired. *And I never will.*

***

Sean stood before Diana, torn, not knowing which desire was greater — to stay among the Numeni with his wife, or to chase the career that took him to the stars and back. He said as much to Diana, fearing that she would be upset with him. But she touched one of her binding scars to his cheek and whispered, 'Go. Both of these desires are part of you. Don't deny either one of them.'

'I only just found you,' he agonised.

'You know where to find me again,' she said and kissed him.

He watched her walk into the horizon until the ship returned, exactly on time. The captain welcomed him aboard, seemingly amused that his customer had wanted to spend time alone on an uninhabited rock. Thankfully, the captain thought that Sean Akiyama was a survival nut and wasn't interested in talking about Dustball. He did want to hear about Sean's connection to the explosively popular Grace Pendergast, however. Had Mr Akiyama really been there on Hoffa only a week ago?

Sean kept asking himself the same question. It felt like a lifetime had passed since then.

He looked down at his hands, now encased in black leather gloves. If he'd gone back to Grace with the binding scars bared, she'd have known what he'd done. Sean had a feeling that his boss would consider cutting him from her e-paper if she discovered he'd married a fugitive. He couldn't allow that. She needed someone to watch her back when her goddess was busy elsewhere.

'I bought these just before I left Ilbb,' Naxan had told Sean hours ago, handing the gloves over with a proud smile. 'Figured they may as well serve the next man unfortunate enough to fall in with the Numeni. And Diana tells me you'll be needing them.'

Tyche hadn't appreciated Sean's decision to accept the gloves.

'He wants to hide the fact that he's bound to our daughter!' she'd hissed.

'Don't worry, I'll remember what's beneath them,' Sean had said. 'I always will.'

Gods, I miss Diana, Sean would often think during the many months without his wife, especially after he received that heart-stopping missive on his techpad — the one which announced that she had gone into labour much earlier than expected and he was now a *father*. He was lucky that Grace had allowed him to take leave without asking too many questions.

Sean quickly became an expert at wrangling days or hours (and on one occasion, just because he could, five minutes) out of his schedule to visit Dustball. He adored his growing family, even looked forward to returning to the quiet life that demanded he learn so much, including how to grow his own plants. But he was being ceaselessly shattered. His secret made it impossible to ask Grace for more time off.

The visits dwindled. And his unhappiness grew.

Finara had given him her true name, warning him that he must only use it in emergencies. And so one dark night, on some world he couldn't even remember the name of, he called out, 'Finara, I need to speak to you. I'm desperate.'

He took a hasty step back when a vortex of fire burst up from the ground. The flames roared and twisted into the shape of a human, announcing She of the Fire's arrival. Sean fell to his knees, not knowing where to look — not just because she was a goddess, but also because she wore very little and he was acutely aware that she was his boss' girlfriend.

'I'm sorry,' he said quietly. 'I know you need someone to look after Grace. But I can't. I can't do it anymore. I have two children and another two on the way...I just can't.'

Finara crouched in front of him, smiling. 'You've been with *The Pendergast e-Post* for six years. Don't you think it's time you stepped out of Grace's shadow and made your own e-paper? Hired your own employees to do the legwork while you spend more time with your wife?'

Sean stared at her. 'I have dreamed of doing this. But I *can't*.'

'Oh yes you can,' she told him, her voice so gentle, so unlike the roaring wildfire that she could become. 'Don't worry about Grace. She has a whole family to look after her now.'

Then she lifted her palms and showed him her binding scars.

'Grace is fretting about whether or not she should buy gloves,' the goddess remarked.

'She still hasn't guessed why I wear mine?'

'Nope,' Finara said cheerfully.

He kept laughing long after she had vanished.

'I've been waiting for this,' Grace Pendergast said a week later, when Sean's resignation appeared on her techpad. She noticeably kept her palms turned away from him. 'I need some decent competition and you're the only contender.'

Sean grinned. 'I'm more than decent, Boss, and you know it.'

And he went on to prove it to her.

***

Both husband and wife waited for the planet's next sunrise, nestled against the outside of the rock that hid their home. Diana was close to dozing off in his arms; Sean had half a mind to let her.

They had spent so many of his visits awake and wired, desperate not to waste a single moment, but now they could take their time, sleep in, let the galaxy pass them by just a little.

'There it is,' he murmured, watching as the star nearest Dustball raced into the sky in under a minute and threw its radiance down upon them.

'Sean?' Diana asked sleepily.

He pressed his lips to her forehead. 'I'm here, Diana.'

'Good. Keep it that way.'

Sean Akiyama would go on to have many adventures without Grace, but none so great and rewarding as the one he had in secret.

www.ingramcontent.com/pod-product-compliance
Lightning Source LLC
Chambersburg PA
CBHW020540120726
47903CB00001B/59